THE
SAND-RECKONER

Also by Gillian Bradshaw from Tom Doherty Associates

Island of Ghosts

THE
SAND-RECKONER

~~~

Gillian Bradshaw

A TOM DOHERTY ASSOCIATES BOOK
NEW YORK

THE SAND-RECKONER

Copyright © 2000 by Gillian Bradshaw

Book design by Jane Adele Regina

A Forge Book
Published by Tom Doherty Associates, LLC
175 Fifth Avenue
New York, NY 10010

www.tor.com

Forge® is a registered trademark of Tom Doherty Associates, LLC.

Library of Congress Cataloging-in-Publication Data

Bradshaw, Gillian.
    The sand-reckoner / Gillian Bradshaw—1st ed.
        p.   cm.
    "A Tom Doherty Associates book."
    ISBN 0-312-87340-9
     1. Archimedes—Fiction.   2. Engineers—Greece—Fiction.
  3. Mathematicians—Greece—Fiction.   4. Greece—History—
To 146 B.C.—Fiction.   I. Title.

PS3552.R235 S26 2000
813'.54—dc21

                                        99-089827

ISBN 0-312-87340-9

First Edition: April 2000

Printed in the United States of America

0 9 8 7 6 5 4 3 2 1

THE
SAND-RECKONER

1

The box was full of sand. It was fine, glassy sand, almost white; it was moist, and had been flattened, then scraped smooth to produce a surface as level and firm as the finest parchment. But the sunlight, falling obliquely with the afternoon, glinted here and there on the edges of individual grains, catching on facets too small for the eye to distinguish. Innumerable facets, one would say—only each made a distinct point of brightness, and the young man looking at them suddenly found himself wondering if he could number them.

It was an old box. The olive-wood frame was scarred and battered, the dull bronze which bound the corners scratched here and there into new brightness. The young man set his hand against one of those scratched corners, calculating: the box was four finger-breadths high, but there was a groove for the lid, and the sand only filled it halfway. He did not need to measure the length and width: he had long before marked the rim with notches a finger-breadth apart, twenty-four down one side and sixteen down the other. He crouched over the box, which he had carefully placed in the quietest part of the ship's stern deck, out of the way of the sailors. Using one leg of the set of compasses he was holding, he began to scratch calculations in the sand. Say that ten grains of sand could fit in a poppy seed, and twenty-five poppy seeds could sit upon the breadth of a finger. There would then be six thousand by four thousand by five hundred grains of sand in the box. Six thousand by four thousand was two thousand four hundred myriads; multiply that by five hundred . . .

He blinked, frowning. His hands slipped nervelessly down his sides, and the point of the compasses scratched his shin. Absentmindedly, he rubbed at the scratch, then raised the compasses to his mouth and sucked their hinge while he continued to stare. This was an *interesting* problem: the number of grains of sand in the box was a bigger number than he could express. A myriad—ten thousand—was the largest number his language had a name for, and his system of writing contained no symbol for the indefinitely extendable *zero*. There was no way to write down a number greater than a myriad myriads. What term could he find for the inexpressible?

Start with what he knew. The largest expressible number was a myriad myriads. Very well, let that be a new unit. Myriad was written M, so this could be M with a line under it: $\underline{M}$. How many of them did he need?

The blank white surface before him was suddenly covered in shadow, and behind him a voice said wearily, "Archimedes?"

The young man took his compasses out of his mouth and turned, beaming. He was thin, long-limbed, and angular, and the general effect as he twisted about was of a grasshopper preparing to jump. "It's a hundred and twenty myriads-of-myriads!" he exclaimed in triumph, brushing back a tangle of brown hair and regarding his interrupter with a pair of bright brown eyes.

The man behind him—a somewhat older, burly, black-haired man with a broken nose—gave an exasperated sigh. "Sir," he said, "we're coming into the harbor."

Archimedes didn't hear him; he had already turned back to the box of sand. There was no such thing as an inexpressibly large number! If a myriad-of-myriads could be a unit, why stop there? Once you reached a myriad-of-myriads myriads-of-myriads you could call *that* your new unit, and go on again! His mind soared over the exhilarating reaches of infinity. He put his compasses back into his mouth and bit them excitedly. "Marcus," he said eagerly, "what's the biggest number you can imagine?

The number of grains of sand in Egypt—no, in the world! No! How many grains of sand would it take to fill the universe?"

"Can't say," replied Marcus shortly. "Sir, we're in Syracuse. In the Great Harbor. Where we disembark—remember? I need to pack the abacus."

Archimedes put his hands protectively over the tray of sand—called by the same name as the more familiar reckoning machine—and looked around with dismay. He had come up to the ship's stern deck when the vessel had sighted the point of Plemmyrion and Marcus had started packing. Syracuse then had been only a patch of red and gold against green slopes; now a whole stretch of time seemed to have vanished into the sand, and Syracuse lay all around him. Here, in its harbor, the city—richest and mightiest of all the Greek cities of Sicily—appeared as nothing but walls. To his right loomed the citadel of Ortygia, a rocky promontory enclosed by massive battlements, and before him the seawall swept around in a long curve of gray to end in the tower-studded walls of the fort which commanded the approach from the marshes to the south. Two quinqueremes sat at the naval quays ready for sea, their sides feathered white with the triple banks of their shipped oars.

Archimedes shot a longing glance at the clear water of the harbor entrance behind the ship. There the Mediterranean stretched open and unbounded as far as the coast of Africa, brilliantly blue and hazy in the bright June afternoon. "Why the Great Harbor?" he asked unhappily. He was Syracusan-born, and the city's customs were as natural to him as its dialect. Merchant ships like the one on which he and Marcus were passengers usually put into Syracuse's Small Harbor, on the other side of the promontory of Ortygia. The Great Harbor belonged to the navy.

"There's a war on, sir," said Marcus patiently. He squatted down beside Archimedes and put out his hands for the box of sand.

Archimedes looked down sadly at the twelve billion grains of gleaming sand and his own scratched calculations. Of course. Syracuse was at war, and the Small Harbor was sealed off. All the traffic was forced into the Great Harbor, where the navy could keep an eye on it. He knew about the war: it was one of the reasons he had come home. The small farm his family owned lay to the north of the city, well beyond any possible zone of defense, and it was unlikely that there would be any income from it this year. His father was ill and could not practice his usual occupation as a teacher. Archimedes was the only son of the house, and supporting the family and protecting it through what was likely to be a very bad war was now his responsibility. It was time to give up mathematical games and find some real work. Walls, he thought miserably; unbreachable walls, closing in.

Slowly, he took his hands off the notched rim of the abacus. Marcus picked it up, found the lid, and closed the reckoning box away. He slid it into its canvas sack and walked off with it. Archimedes sighed and sat back, hands dangling over his knees. The compasses slipped from his limp fingers and impaled themselves in the deck. He stared at them blankly for a moment, then pulled up one side of the instrument and swept it around, scratching a circle in the rough wood. Let the area of the circle be K— No. He folded the compasses and pressed the cool double bar against his forehead. No more games.

In the cabin below, Marcus slipped the abacus swiftly into the space in the traveling chest he'd reserved for it, then forced the lid shut. A hundred and twenty myriads-of-myriads, he thought, expertly knotting a rope round the chest. Was that a real number?

It was certainly not a sensible one. He paused, however, and contemplated it a moment, as though it were a dubious bargain offered him by some unreliable shopkeeper. A hundred and twenty myriads-of-myriads! Was that the answer to that other new impossible question, "How many grains of sand would it take to fill the universe?"

Nobody but Archimedes would ask such an insane question. Nobody else would come up with such an incomprehensible answer. He had been a slave in the man's household since the young master was nine years old, and he still wasn't sure whether a calculation like that deserved admiration or contempt: both, probably. Just as well that the young lunatic was going to have to give up such questions and turn his mind to more practical matters. . . .

Marcus stopped himself and turned his attention back to the chest, jerking at a knot to ease the sudden apprehension that tightened his throat. Practical matters like the war. For three years he and Archimedes had been away from Syracuse, and for two of those years he had been urging his master to go home. Now they were in the harbor, and he wished that they were anywhere else. Syracuse was at war with the Republic of Rome, and Marcus saw no way that the future could hold for him anything but grief.

~ THERE WAS NOT MUCH SIGN OF THE WAR AT THE DOCKS, except that everything was quieter than usual. Destruction was still remote, a matter of armies maneuvering far away, a ruinous storm whose approach could be watched, with dread, from a distance. In a concession to its threat, however, the customs official usual to peacetime had been joined at the quayside by two soldiers. The pattern of crimson letter sigmas on the round shields slung over their left shoulders declared them to be Syracusan, but Archimedes recognized neither of them. Syracuse was a big enough city that he couldn't know more than a fraction of his fellow citizens, but he still watched the men apprehensively. They might be foreign mercenaries, and mercenaries, as every citizen knew, had to be handled more cautiously than live scorpions. Under the previous government they would have given a beating to any citizen whose expression offended them. Things were much better under the present ruler, but only a fool would assume that the breed's basic character had altered. At least these men appeared to be Greeks rather than any unpredictable type of barbarian: the body armor they both wore was of the standard Greek type—a cuirass made from layers of linen glued together to form a stiff carapace with a fringe of plates about the hips— and the helmets pushed back on their heads were of the popular

Attic Greek design, with hinged cheekpieces and no noseguard. It was impossible to tell more about their origin from their speech, however, for they said nothing, merely stood leaning on their spears, watching with bored expressions while the elderly customs official went about his business.

The customs official spoke first to the ship's captain, while the dozen passengers waited in a knot beside the gangplank. "You've come from Alexandria?" the official asked, and there was no doubt about *his* origin: he spoke in the broad Doric dialect of the city. Archimedes found himself smiling at the sound. The one thing he'd disliked about Alexandria was the way everyone had made fun of the way he talked. There were, after all, some good things about being home—and the best of them would be to see his family again. He wrapped his arms around himself in an effort to contain his impatience. He hadn't been able to tell his family what ship he would sail on or when it might arrive, and he was eager to surprise them.

The captain agreed that yes, the ship had come from Alexandria by way of Cyrene, and that the cargo was linen and glass and some spices. He produced the bill of lading, and the customs official began to go over it. Archimedes' attention wandered. A dead fish was floating in the water beside the ship. It lay on its side, its tail slightly raised. Live fish swam belly-down: why did dead ones always float on their sides? He imagined a piece of wood of approximately the same length and breadth as the fish. It would float on its side, too. What about a wider piece of wood, a box-shaped one? Would it float with one of its flat sides down, or with a long edge down?

The customs official had started to gossip with the captain. There was obviously going to be a long wait before the joyful re-union. Archimedes rubbed the dirty stone of the quay with a sandal, then squatted and pulled the set of compasses out of his belt. It was lucky he'd forgotten to give them to Marcus to be packed.

He was deep in the equilibrium of cuboids when a hand tapped him on the shoulder and a voice demanded, "Well?" He looked up from his sketches and realized that the customs official was talking to him. The two soldiers were staring and grinning and the sun was noticeably lower. Marcus was sitting patiently on the luggage chest at the foot of the gangplank, but all the other passengers had gone.

Archimedes sprang to his feet, his face hot with embarrassment. "What did you say?" he asked, still struggling to force floating cuboids from his mind.

"I asked you your name!" repeated the customs official in annoyance.

"Sorry. Archimedes, son of Phidias. I'm a citizen of Syracuse." He waved vaguely at Marcus. "That's my slave and my things."

The official softened at the discovery that he was dealing with a fellow citizen. Archimedes: an unusual name, particularly in a city where half the male population was named Hieron, Gelon, or Dionysios, after great leaders of the past. The name Phidias was vaguely familiar, though, linked with a couple of stories the official had heard of intellectual eccentricity. "Your father's the astronomer, isn't he?" he asked. "I've heard of him." He glanced at the geometrical figures scratched over the quay and snorted. "Got a son of his own breed, it seems. What were you doing in Alexandria?"

"Studying," said Archimedes, and swallowed a knot of irritation. It was no insult to be told that he was a true son of his father. "Studying mathematics."

One of the soldiers nudged the other and whispered something; the second man laughed. But the official ignored them. "You've come home because of the war?" he said approvingly, and when Archimedes nodded, he went on, still more approvingly, "That's the brave young fellow, to come back to fight for your city!"

Archimedes gave him a false smile. He was loyal to his city, as any man ought to be, but he had no intention of enlisting in the army if he could possibly avoid it. He was certain that he'd be far more use to Syracuse building war machines—and besides, he'd had the usual military training at school, and had comprehensively detested it. Drilling and hurling the javelin, wrestling and races in armor: exhaustion and blistered hands; humiliation by glamorous champions on the field and even more humiliating sexual advances in the bathhouse afterward. When his year with the state-issue javelin was finally over, he'd chopped the miserable weapon into sections and used the the bits to make a surveying instrument. He had no plans to buy a new spear now. But he knew better than to disagree with a customs official.

The customs official smiled back obliviously and walked over to inspect Marcus and the luggage. "The slave's your own man?" he asked, calling the question over his shoulder. Marcus politely slid off the chest.

"Yes," Archimedes called back, relaxing. "My father bought him here in the city, years ago, and gave him to me when I left for Alexandria."

"There's no duty to pay on him, then. And the goods are your own, for your private use? Nothing you plan to sell?" The official looked them over with a practiced eye: a large, coffin-shaped chest of wood and leather, very battered, and a new wicker basket lashed to it with rope. The chest had undoubtedly carried all the owner's luggage out to Egypt, and the basket had been purchased for the inevitable surplus which had been discovered when it was time to come back. "What's in the basket?"

"A, um, machine," Archimedes said awkwardly.

The official glanced at him with a lift of the eybrows, and for the first time the two soldiers showed some interest. "Machine" in those days meant, first and foremost, "war machine."

"What sort of machine?" asked the official.

"It's for lifting water," said Archimedes, and the soldiers lost interest.

The nudger whispered again, and this time Archimedes overheard his comment: "What non-mathematicians would call a bucket!" His face went hot.

"You planning to sell it?"

"Well, um, not *that* one. That one's the prototype. It's just a model. I brought it back so I could show people how it works. If somebody wants one, I'll build a bigger one." He spread his arms in a vague indication of the real machine's unbucketlike size.

The customs official considered the concept of a prototype. He could not recollect ever having encountered one before. "It's not dutiable," he decided. "No need to trouble you, then. You're free to go." He nodded toward the nearest gate.

Marcus went to the foot of the luggage chest and picked it up. Archimedes looked round for a porter, saw none, and went to pick up the other end himself—just as Marcus got tired of waiting and set his end down. The soldiers once again nudged each other and laughed. Archimedes' face flushed once more. "Marcus!" he called irritably, bracing the heavy chest against his knee.

But at the name, the soldiers suddenly stopped laughing. "Marcus?" one repeated sharply. Archimedes thought he was the laugher, not the whisperer. He strode forward and stared across the luggage chest at the slave.

Marcus stared back impassively, his hands at his side. "It's what I'm what called," he said evenly.

"That's a Roman name," said the soldier, and it was an accusation.

Archimedes set his own end of the chest down, frowning with a mixture of alarm and disgust. It was clear that a Roman—even an enslaved one—could not be allowed to wander about the city as he pleased. On the other hand, no sensible person would seriously expect to find a Roman as a slave: slavery was the fate that the Romans were accustomed to impose upon others. "Marcus isn't Roman," he declared. "He's some other sort of Italian, from somewhere up north."

"Why does he have a Roman name?" returned the soldier, and Archimedes' alarm and disgust grew as he recognized the accent. Doric, but not Sicilian Doric: that way of swallowing the ends of words was distinct to Tarentum, the city which had once been Taras and the proudest of the Greek cities of southern Italy. A Tarentine in the service of Syracuse had probably fled his own city when the Romans conquered it, and could be relied upon to hate all things Roman. This particular soldier was obviously longing for Marcus to be Roman so that he could punish him.

"Can't help my name," said Marcus mildly. "Lots of Italians with Latin names these days. Comes of being conquered by Romans."

The soldier regarded him with narrowed eyes. "If you're not Roman, what are you?"

"Samnite," replied Marcus promptly. The Samnites had fought three wars with Rome, and rumor had it that despite three crushing defeats and complete subjugation they still hoped for an opportunity to fight a fourth. Not even a Tarentine could object to a Samnite.

This Tarentine, however, proved to be not merely vindictive but well informed. "If you were a Samnite, you'd call yourself Mamertus," he pointed out. "Why the Latin form of the name, if you speak Oscan?"

Archimedes had in fact noticed a Protean quality to Marcus' nationality in the past. The slaver who sold him had called him a Latin, but Marcus himself had sometimes claimed to be a Sabine and sometimes a Marsian. Archimedes had no idea what the truth was—but he knew Latins, Sabines, and Marsians were all part of the Roman alliance. Disgust was swallowed entirely by alarm: Marcus might well be sent to the state quarries for the duration of the war. Given the conditions under which quarry slaves were kept, he'd be lucky to leave them alive. "Marcus is a Samnite," he declared firmly. "And he's been in the family for years. My father bought him when I was nine years old. Do you think I'd smuggle an enemy into my own city? If you want to accuse me of something, do it in front of a magistrate."

The Tarentine gave Archimedes a hard look before turning his assessing stare back on Marcus; Marcus stared back with the same unruffled impassivity he had adopted from the first. The soldier shifted his grip on his spear and commanded, "Say, 'May the gods destroy Rome!' "

Marcus hesitated, then raised both hands to heaven and said

loudly, "May the gods destroy Carthage, and grant victory to lovely Syracuse!"

The soldier whipped his spear up and around in a whistling blur; the shaft caught Marcus under his raised arm and knocked him sideways into Archimedes. Archimedes gave a yelp, nearly fell off the quay, and dropped to all fours, skinning his knee on the stones. Marcus fell on top of him with a grunt.

Archimedes was aware of a thick silence as he struggled to get back to his feet. He could feel Marcus on top of him shaking— whether with rage or with fear he couldn't guess. Then the slave's weight shifted and slid off, and Archimedes scrambled up. Marcus remained kneeling on the quay, right hand pressed against his left side where the spear shaft had caught him. Archimedes could feel blood trickling down his own shin. For a moment he was so angry he wanted to hit the soldier: what right did this *foreigner* have to knock him down on the docks of his own city? He took a deep breath and reminded himself that the soldier *was* a foreign mercenary, to be treated with great caution; that the soldier was armed and he wasn't; and that he did not want Marcus in trouble. "Why did you do that?" he demanded, struggling to swallow his rage. "He may not have said what you told him to, but he prayed for victory for the city!"

"He prayed for the destruction of Carthage," said the Tarentine. He was flushed now, and a bit breathless: he'd gone further than he'd meant to. Hitting slaves was one thing; knocking over freeborn citizens quite a different one. His comrade and the customs official were staring at him with distaste.

"Don't we all?" said Archimedes. Carthage had been the enemy of Syracuse since the city's founding nearly five centuries before.

"Carthage is our ally," said the soldier.

Archimedes was too astonished even to remember the caution needed with mercenaries. He looked from the Tarentine to the other soldier, then to the customs official. "*Carthage?*" he repeated disbelievingly.

The other soldier and the official looked embarrassed. "You hadn't heard?" said the official.

Archimedes shook his head numbly. He supposed that, in a way, it was a natural development. Carthage and Syracuse had long fought for the possession of Sicily, and the Carthaginians were undoubtedly as dismayed as the Syracusans by the intrusion onto the island of the rising power of Rome. Perhaps it was right that two old enemies should unite against a new common threat. But—*Carthage!* Carthage, which had tortured to death the entire male population of the city of Himera; Carthage, which worshiped gods that required her to burn her own children alive; Carthage, the crucifier, the deceiver, the enemy of the Greeks! "Has *our* tyrant really sworn a treaty with *Carthage?*" he asked.

"Our *king*," the Tarentine corrected him quickly. "He calls himself king now."

Archimedes just blinked. "Tyrant" to a Syracusan was the natural title for an absolute ruler: it implied no condemnation. If Syracuse's present tyrant wanted to call himself a king, that was his right, but it seemed a bit pointless.

"King Hieron hasn't sworn anything," the official said defensively.

"He's no fool," added the second soldier, for the first time speaking above a whisper and revealing his own accent—to Archimedes' relief—as the inimitable growl of the back streets of Syracuse. "If Carthage wants to help our shining city against Rome, she's welcome to, but King Hieron won't trust that sack-arsed lot, and I say, well done! He's agreed to a joint military operation against the Romans, nothing more." He gave the Tarentine a disgusted look: it was quite clear that he thought that a prayer for the destruction of Carthage in no way deserved a blow.

Marcus grunted, and Archimedes remembered what he was supposed to be doing. "We hadn't heard anything about this alliance in Egypt," he said stiffly. "I'm sorry if Marcus offended you, but he thought he was praying for a Syracusan victory."

The official and the Syracusan soldier both nodded, accepting the explanation, relieved that Archimedes had tacitly agreed to forget the blow. The Tarentine, however, only scowled. Marcus might have prayed for a Syracusan victory, but he had not prayed for the destruction of Rome. The man's dark eyes returned to the slave, who was still kneeling on the quay, head bowed, rubbing his bruise. Something flickered behind the scowl: the desire to hurt and humiliate.

Archimedes too was keenly aware of his slave's evasion. He cleared his throat. "If you really believe that Marcus is a Roman—though why you should expect a Roman to be a slave I don't know—we can go see whoever is responsible for deciding about such things," he offered. "On the other hand . . ." He dug into his purse and pulled out two silver staters—two-drachma pieces, each one worth more than a day's wage for a mercenary. "It's getting late, and I want to go home to my family, not hang about the magistrates' courts." He held out the coins toward the Tarentine: they gleamed in his palm, fresh-minted silver stamped with the head of King Ptolemy of Egypt.

The Tarentine just stared at them. The Syracusan soldier, however, hurried over and took the coins with a grin. The customs official also hurried over, sucking his teeth. He looked a question at the Syracusan. The Syracusan grinned again and declared easily, "We'll split it three ways."

The Tarentine gave Archimedes a black glare. But the other two were happy to take the money and forget about Marcus, and he didn't quite dare override them. "You can't split two staters three ways!" he snapped instead.

Archimedes forced himself to smile, though the effort nearly choked him. "Of course you can," he said. "It makes eight obols each if you do. But here." He pulled out another coin, identical to the first two. "Good luck to the defenders of the city!"

The Tarentine snatched the coin with a look of pure hatred and strode off toward the nearest gate. His comrade shrugged, gave Archimedes a look of apology, and turned to the customs official with the other two staters. Archimedes limped over to Marcus.

"Are you hurt?" he asked.

Marcus rubbed his bruise once more, then shook his head. He got slowly to his feet, scowling. "May the gods destroy that Tarentine filth in the worst way!" he muttered. "Three staters tipped into the sewer!"

Archimedes slapped him across the face, anger and relief adding force to the blow. "You worthless lump!" he exclaimed in a vehement whisper. "You might have been sent to the quarries! Why didn't you say what he told you to?"

Marcus looked away, now rubbing the slap. "I'm not his slave," he declared.

"Sometimes I wish you weren't mine, either!"

"Sometimes I do too!" replied Marcus, looking back and meeting his master's eyes.

Archimedes let out his breath in a hiss. "Well, you nearly got away from me there, didn't you? That fellow wanted you chained up cutting stone till the war ended, *whatever* your god-hated nation is, and you certainly did everything you could to encourage him. Herakles! I should have let him take you! Why couldn't you have called him 'sir' and lowered your eyes when he talked to you, like a good slave?"

"I'm freeborn," said Marcus sullenly. "I've never crawled to you and your father, so why should I crawl to some Tarentine without a house or half acre to his name?"

"You and your free birth!" exclaimed Archimedes in disgust. "I'm freeborn *and* a citizen, and *I* don't quarrel with mercenaries." He was on the point of adding, "Anyway, I don't know why I should believe in your free birth, when you can't decide whether it's free Sabine or free Samnite!" when he noticed that the customs official was walking off while the remaining soldier stood listening. He swallowed the words. They were pointless, anyway. No one born to slavery could ever have been as obstinate, awkward, and proud as Marcus.

"There wouldn't have been any trouble if we'd been seen first," growled Marcus, still defending himself. "They wouldn't've had time for it. And we would have been first, if you hadn't been too busy drawing circles to pay attention." He glanced at the scuffed and scratched quayside and corrected himself: "Drawing cubes."

"Cuboids," said Archimedes wearily. He gazed at the half-eradicated drawings, then started, grabbed at his belt, and exclaimed, "I've lost my compasses!"

Marcus glanced around and quickly retrieved the compasses from the ground beside the luggage. Archimedes seized them gratefully and began checking them for damage.

"That thing looks sharp," said the Syracusan soldier, coming over. "Lucky you dropped it. If it'd been in your belt when Philonides knocked you down, it would've speared you. That leg all right?"

Archimedes blinked, then glanced at his grazed knee. It had stopped bleeding. "Yes," he said. He put the compasses through his belt.

The soldier snorted at this piece of folly, but offered to help with the luggage. The guardsman was, Archimedes noticed, about his own age, a wide-shouldered man with a close-clipped curly beard and a pleasant, shrewd-eyed face. For all his whispered jokes to his comrade earlier, he seemed genuinely to want to be friendly now. Archimedes accepted the offer.

With Marcus carrying one end of the chest, the soldier the other, and Archimedes trying rather ineffectually to help in the middle, they started toward the gate. "Thanks for the money," said the soldier. "My name's Straton, by the way, son of Metrodoros. When you come to enlist, mention me and I'll see that you're looked after."

Archimedes blinked again, then remembered the customs official's assumption that he'd returned to fight for his city. He was silent for a moment. He had no plans to enlist; on the other hand, some advice from a friendly source in the city garrison would be very welcome. "I, uh, wasn't planning to enlist, exactly," he said hesitantly. "I, uh, thought the king would want engineers. Do you know how I should go about asking for a job as one?"

Straton glanced at the wicker basket strapped to the chest—the big bucket!—and smiled to himself. "You know anything about catapults and siege engines?" he asked.

"Um, well," said Archimedes, "I never actually *made* one. But I know how they work."

Straton smiled again. "Well, you can talk to the king about it, of course," he said. "He might want people. I don't know."

Marcus laughed. The soldier's smile vanished, but he said nothing.

"Is King Hieron in the city now?" asked Archimedes earnestly.

King Hieron, Straton informed him, was off with the army, besieging the city of Messana. The man in charge in Syracuse was the king's father-in-law, Leptines. Straton wasn't sure whether Archimedes should approach Leptines or whether he'd do better to go north to Messana and speak to the king himself. He'd ask around. Would Archimedes like to meet him the following evening, for a drink? He'd be posted to the docks again all day, but his shift finished at dusk, and they could meet at the gate. Archimedes thanked him and accepted the invitation.

They had passed the gate by this time, and they set the heavy chest down in the narrow dirt street on the other side. "Where are you going?" Straton asked.

"Other side of the Achradina," Archimedes supplied at once. "Near the Lion Fountain."

"You don't want to carry this all that way," said Straton authoritatively. "Gelon the Baker down the road has a donkey he'd loan you for a few coppers."

Archimedes thanked him and went off to see about the donkey. Marcus started to sit down on the chest; Straton caught his arm. "Just a minute!" he said sharply.

The slave's face went blank, and he stood perfectly still, making no effort to retrieve his arm from the other's grip. The two men were much of a height, and they looked directly into each other's eyes. It was beginning to get dark, and behind them the new guard shift was closing the sea gate of Syracuse.

"I'm not Philonides," said the soldier quietly, "and I don't beat other men's slaves, but you deserve a thrashing. I don't care what sort of Italian you are, but just at the moment the city doesn't like any of your nation, and if we'd gone to a magistrate, you wouldn't have escaped without a beating at the least. Your master got you out of a nasty hole there—and in return you were insolent to him. I don't like to see a slave laugh at his master. Plenty of other people feel the same way, and some *are* like Philonides."

Marcus had relaxed as he realized that he was in trouble for his conduct rather than his nationality. "When did I laugh at my master?" he asked mildly.

Straton's hand tightened on the slave's arm. "When he said he wanted to be an army engineer."

"Oh, then!" replied Marcus calmly. "It was you I was laughing at—sir."

Straton stared in offended surprise, and the corner of the slave's mouth twitched. He was beginning to enjoy this.

"*You* were laughing at him from the moment you set eyes on him," he said. "And when he said he'd never made a catapult, you made up your mind he doesn't know a thing about them, didn't you? Let me tell you this: if Archimedes makes catapults, and if King Hieron's half as clever as he's supposed to be, then whoever the king has making catapults at the moment is out of a job. Do you gamble?"

"Some," said Straton, puzzled now.

"Then I'll lay you a bet on it. Ten drachmae to the stater he gave you—no, make that twenty! I bet you that if my master becomes an engineer for the king, then whoever's in charge of whatever he's set to do will be demoted or unemployed within six months, and Archimedes will be offered his place."

"You have twenty drachmae?"

"I do. Before you decide about the bet, you want to hear how I got it?"

Straton stared suspiciously a moment, then gave a snort of concession. "All right." He let go of the slave's arm.

Marcus leaned back against the chest. "We went out to Alex-

andria three years ago. My master's father, Phidias, sold a vineyard to pay for the trip: he'd been to Alexandria himself as a
young man, and he wanted his son to enjoy the same opportunity.
Archimedes did enjoy it, too—Herakles, he did! They have this
big temple to the Muses in Alexandria, with a library—"

"I've heard of the Museum," said Straton with interest. "Myself, all I know is how to read, and that badly, but I've heard that
the scholars of the Museum of Alexandria are the most learned
men on earth."

"It's a lunatic asylum," said Marcus disgustedly. "Full of a lot
of Greeks drunk on logic. My master raced in to join them like
a lost lamb that's finally found its flock. Made a lot of friends,
did geometry all day, sat up drinking and talk, talk, talking all
night; didn't ever want to go home to Syracuse. You saw fit to
tell me I deserve a thrashing for the way I talk to my master: let
me tell you, I've earned the right to talk to him anyway I like! I
could've stolen every copper he had and run off with it, anytime,
and he wouldn't even have *noticed* until three days later. Instead,
I looked after him and tried to make one drachma do the work
of two. Phidias had given us money to last us a year—though
with the prices they charge in Alexandria, it wouldn't have. First
we spent that, and then we spent our return fare, and then we
bartered and borrowed and sold bits and pieces, and then, after
two years in the city, we were flat out of cash and in debt. I kept
pointing this out to Archimedes until he finally paid attention
and agreed to do some machine-making."

Marcus paused. "That's a common story, isn't it, apart from
the geometry? Young man away from home for the first time,
running wild in a big foreign city, faithful slave wringing his
hands and saying, 'Oh, sir, remember your poor old father and
come home!' All right, but here's where it gets uncommon. My
master builds machines. Not ordinary machines, but machines so
cunning and ingenious you could travel the world from one end
to the other and never see anything like them. That's how we
lasted two years in Alexandria: whenever we were short, he'd put
something together and I'd go sell it. He'd been playing around

with *that* for a while"—Marcus jerked his head at the wicker basket behind him—"but he'd never got around to seeing if anyone wanted a full-size one. Now he took it to a rich man we knew who'd recently acquired an estate in the Nile Delta and was looking for ways to improve his land. Zenodotos looked at the water-snail and fell in love—and that shows sense, because the water-snail is the most amazing machine Archimedes ever built, the most amazing machine I've ever seen in my life. Zenodotos instantly ordered eight of the things at thirty drachmae apiece. He agreed to supply us with all the equipment and the labor we needed to make them, as well as our keep while we were working and the traveling expenses to and from his estate.

"So we went up to his estate and set to work. When we got the first water-snail finished, people started coming around to have a look at it. Now in Egypt they've been irrigating since the creation of the world. They thought they knew everything there is to know about raising water—but nobody had ever seen anything like a water-snail. And everybody—I tell you, *everybody*—who had a bit of land in the Delta wanted one. I put the price up to forty drachmae, then to sixty, then to eighty: it made no difference. People still queued up to buy. And then, of course, the rich men in the queue didn't want to wait. They started coming up to me and slipping me a drachma and saying, 'See that your master does my order first.' *That* is where I got my money: selling the shavings of Archimedes' ingenuity."

"If it was so profitable, why aren't you still building water-snails?" asked Straton skeptically.

"Archimedes got bored with them," Marcus replied at once. "He always loses interest in his machines once he's got them working. He'd rather spend his time drawing circles—or, excuse me, cuboids. Of course, other people started making water-snails too, copying them from ours as well as they could. But still, everyone knew it was Archimedes' invention, and we were everyone's first choice of builder. We could have made a fortune, we could have! Instead, as soon as my master could afford to do geometry again, he found an enterprising fellow who was willing to pay a hundred drachmae for the design, handed our order book over to him, and went back to Alexandria to draw circles. I tell you, I could weep when I think of it. But listen! That's what happened the last time Archimedes applied himself to making machines. Now he's going to do it again. I'll bet on him against any engineer King Hieron ever heard of. You taking the bet?"

"Can I see this water-snail?"

Marcus grinned. "Certainly." Then, as the soldier moved toward the wicker basket, he added, "But I charge two obols for a demonstration."

Straton stopped in annoyance, one hand on the basket's lashings. "Your master lets you do that?"

"He lets me look after the money," said Marcus coolly. "Weren't you listening?"

Straton studied the slave a moment, then laughed. "All right!" he exclaimed. "I'm sorry I laughed at your master and insulted your loyalty. You're a good slave."

"I am not!" declared Marcus fiercely. "I'm freeborn, and not slave enough to forget it. But I'm honest. You taking that bet or not?"

"Twenty drachmae to a stater? Your master to be offered his predecessor's job within six months?"

"That's right."

Straton considered. It was an interesting bet. And despite what the slave had said, he thought he'd win. The slave was, after all, loyal to his master, and the master hadn't looked all that impressive to Straton. Ten to one was good odds. "All right," he agreed. "I'll take it."

Archimedes himself appeared as they were shaking hands on it. He was holding a torch, which flickered brightly in the growing dark, and a small boy followed him leading a donkey. Straton gave his new acquaintance the look of appraisal normally reserved for racehorses, and was reassured. No, this tall and gangling young man in a dirty linen tunic and shabby cloak did not look like a formidable genius. He was much in need of a haircut, a shave, and a bath, one knee was covered with blood while the other was dirty, and his face had a vague and vacant expression. The Egyptian stater, thought Straton, was pretty safe.

They loaded the chest on the donkey—the donkey was unhappy about it—and confirmed that they would meet next day. Archimedes handed the torch to Marcus, and the little party clip-clopped off down the road.

"What were you shaking hands about?" Archimedes asked his slave as they turned to climb the hill to the other side of the Achradina.

Marcus gave a self-satisfied smile. "I made a bet with that soldier. Going to get back that stater you gave him."

Archimedes looked at him with concern. "I hope you don't lose your money."

"Don't worry," said Marcus, "I won't."

2

The Achradina was an old quarter. The first Greeks to colonize Syracuse had settled on the promontory of Ortygia, and Ortygia—a grand region of temples and public buildings prudently fortified and garrisoned—was still the seat of the government. The Achradina had formed early, though, when the houses and shops of the growing city overflowed the crowded citadel and sprawled messily along the shore. When the city grew again, in wealth and power, the New Town had been laid out inland for the rich, while the Tyche quarter, a straggle of buildings along the road north, had become the place of settlement for the poor. The Achradina belonged to the old middle class. Narrow-streeted and dirty, bordered by the walls which guarded the city from attack by sea, it was the heart of Syracuse—dark, crooked, and full of secret delights.

Archimedes crossed it joyfully. A city-state customarily inspired in her citizens the most intense and passionate sense of patriotism and civic pride, and though Archimedes had always been something of a misfit in his own city, still every dusty crossroads seemed to him to be shining with the glory of Syracuse. Each step, too, took him closer to home. Eagerly he marked off each familiar landmark: the small park with its bedraggled plane trees; the baker's shop around the corner where the family had bought its bread; the public fountain with its statue of a lion, which had supplied water for the household. A scent of herbs and roast meat wafted from the cookshop down the road, where he'd often run to fetch an evening meal if for some reason one hadn't been prepared at home. Nikomachos' house; Euphanes the Butcher's shop, with his house on top of it . . . and finally, there it was. Archimedes stopped in the street and gazed in silence at the front of featureless mud brick and the weathered wood of the single door. His chest began to hurt and his eyes stung. At one time this house had defined what was meant by a house. It had been the only house that mattered, the center of the universe, that container for everything that was important in his small world. And it was still true that all the people he loved most were behind that door.

He wished they lived in Alexandria.

Marcus raised the torch and likewise gazed at the house, remembering the first time he'd seen it, when Phidias had led him back from the slave market in chains. *Not home*, he reminded himself fiercely, though uncertain why he was denying the joy that hovered at the edge of his awareness. *Just the house where I am a slave.* For a moment he remembered his own home in the hills of central Italy, his own parents. He shoved them quickly from his mind: probably dead now, anyway. Some of the bricks on Phidias' house were crumbling, he noted, and the roof needed retiling. Not surprising. He himself had been the only man in the household, unless you counted the masters, and you couldn't count them, not when it came to retiling roofs. The place must have been running down. He had work ahead of him.

Gelon the Baker's son, who'd come to look after his father's donkey, shuffled his feet and asked, "Is this it?"

They unloaded the donkey, set the chest down, and sent the baker's son home with his father's beast, handing the child the torch to light his way. In the soft summer darkness Archimedes took a deep breath and knocked upon the door.

There was a long silence. Archimedes knocked again, and at last the door cracked open and a woman peered anxiously out, the lines in her worn face deeply shadowed in the light of the lamp she held. "Sosibia!" cried Archimedes, breaking into an enormous smile, and the housekeeper gaped, then screamed, "Medion!"—the diminutive ending of his proper name, his family nickname, which he hadn't heard for three years.

The reunion was as noisy and as joyful as anything Archimedes had pictured to himself. His mother, Arata, came running and flung her arms around him. His sister, Philyra, seized him as soon as his mother let go. "You've grown up!" he told her, and held her at arms length to admire her. She had been thirteen when he left: now sixteen and a young woman, she had not, in fact, changed much. Still straight and thin, gawky and bright-eyed, with her unruly brown hair pulled into a knot behind her head. She knocked his hands away so she could hug him.

"You haven't!" she replied. "You're as much a mess as ever!" Sosibia and Sosibia's two children hovered grinning and exclaiming in the background. But there was an absence. "Where's Papa?" asked Archimedes, and the noise died.

"He's too ill to stand," Philyra said, into the sudden quiet. "He hasn't been able to get out of bed for months." Her voice was heavy with reproach. For months she had tended their father and watched him waste away, while Archimedes, the darling and only son, lingered in Alexandria.

Archimedes stared at her, stricken. He had known that his father was ill. For a couple of months that awareness had lurked in the back of his mind, putting a wash of anxiety over all his preparations for coming home. But despite that, he had expected to find his father much as he had left him. He would have reckoned illness to be a persistent cough, a bad back, chronic indigestion. He had not expected a deforming monster to have moved into the house and pinned his father to his bed.

"I'm sorry, my darling," said his mother gently. She had always been the family peacemaker, the voice of calm practicality. She was shorter than her children, wide-hipped, broad-browed; there was more gray in her brown hair than her son remembered. "I'm afraid it will be a great shock for you to see him. You can't have realized how ill he is. But I thank the gods you're safely home at last."

"Where is he?" asked Archimedes in a hoarse whisper.

Phidias's sickbed had been placed in the room Archimedes remembered as his mother's workroom. It was at the opposite end of the small courtyard which opened onto the street and formed the center of the house. The stairways to the bedrooms on the upper floors were steep and narrow, and a ground-floor room was much more convenient for an invalid. When Archimedes crossed to the old workroom, he found a lamp lit and his father sitting up and looking eagerly toward the door: he had heard the commotion, and was impatiently awaiting his son's appearance. Archimedes faltered on the threshold. Phidias had always been tall and thin; now he was skeletal. The whites of his eyes had turned yellow, and they stared out of deep hollows; his skin, too, was yellowish, and crumpled and dry. Most of his hair had fallen out, and what remained was white. When he stretched out his arms toward his son, his hands trembled.

Archimedes went through the door in a rush, dropped to his knees beside the bed, and threw his arms about his father's emaciated frame. "I'm sorry!" he choked "I didn't . . . if I'd known . . ."

"Archimedion mine!" exclaimed Phidias, and folded his stick-like arms about his son. "Thank the gods you're home!"

"Oh, Papa!" cried Archimedes, and burst into tears.

~ IN THE COURTYARD, MARCUS DRAGGED THE LUGGAGE IN out of the street and shut the door. When he turned back to the house, Sosibia caught his shoulders and kissed him lightly on the cheek. "You're welcome back, too!" she said softly. "I wish it were to a happier house."

He looked at her in surprise, touched despite himself. He and Sosibia had never been friends. When they first met, her chief concern had been to make it clear that though he might have been purchased to replace the household's previous manservant, she had no intention of allowing him to take the dead man's place in her bed. Marcus had not at first understood her (he had been eighteen at the time, fresh from Italy and almost Greekless), but when at last he did, he in turn had made it clear that the very idea of sleeping with a plain, fortyish household slave disgusted him. This unanimity about sleeping arrangements had not, obviously, led to any feelings of goodwill, and for years they feuded, Sosibia sneering at Marcus as a crude barbarian, and Marcus disdaining Sosibia as a servile old woman. Now she was welcoming him back. "Well," he said gruffly, "it's good to be here."

There was a silence, and then he nodded to the two children, who stood behind their mother, watching—Chrestos, a boy of fifteen, and thirteen-year-old Agatha. "You two have grown," he commented. Another reason not to be welcome, he thought privately. Four adult slaves was too many for one middle-class household: now that Marcus was back, it was quite likely that Chrestos would be sold. But Sosibia had not acknowledged this uncomfortable prospect, so he ignored it as well. "When we came up to the house, I thought to myself that there'd be a lot of work waiting for me," he said instead. "I'd forgotten we have another man about the place now."

Chrestos grinned. "Welcome home, Marcus," he said. "You're welcome to do my work if you want to!"

His little sister laughed, slipped forward suddenly, and gave Marcus a shy kiss on the cheek. "Welcome home!" she whispered.

Not home, Marcus reminded himself, but some part of him was still glad. The first year of his slavery had been a nightmare he still sweated to remember, but that nightmare had ended in this house, and he had waked again to a world governed by sane rules. "It's good to be back," he repeated gruffly.

There was another silence, and then Marcus jerked his head at the doorway on the other side of the small courtyard and asked, "Is the old man dying?"

Sosibia hesitated, then made a gesture against evil and nodded. "Jaundice," she said resignedly. "He can't eat now, poor man: he lives on barley broth and a little honeyed wine. It won't be much longer."

Marcus reflected on Phidias. A kind man; an honest, hardwo:king citizen; a loving husband and father. A good master. He might resent the man for that last, but it was not Phidias' fault that he himself was a slave. "I'm sorry," he said sincerely; then added, in a harsh voice, "The gods made us mortal. It will come to us all."

"He has lived well," said Sosibia. "I pray the earth receives him kindly."

ARCHIMEDES STAYED WITH HIS FATHER FOR HALF AN hour, retreating when the dying man fell asleep. He himself had no interest in anything more that night. Sosibia and his mother made up the bed in his old room, and he lay down and sought oblivion in sleep.

He woke early next morning, and lay for a while looking at the patterns the rising sun made upon the wall beside his bed. The window shutter was of wickerwork woven in a crisscross pattern and covered the whitewashed plaster with bars and triangles of orange light. As the sun rose higher, the light grew paler and the triangles shifted and widened. They slid from the wall onto his bed, where they lay in bright profusion over the sheet, like tiles of fresh ivory.

His eyes stung. In Alexandria he had purchased a game for his father, a set of ivory tiles cut into squares and triangles. They could be fitted together to form a square, or arranged to make a ship, a sword, a tree, or any of a hundred other figures. The puzzle was a geometer's delight. He'd liked it, so he'd been sure his father would too. Gifts given to his father now were destined for the grave. That fact was an enormity so devastating that it left him feeling as if half his soul had been removed.

When Archimedes was growing up, Phidias had been the one person who really *understood*. It had often seemed to Archimedes that everyone else had a blind spot in the middle of the head. They could look at a triangle, a circle, a cube—but they couldn't *see* it. Explain it to them, and they couldn't understand. Explain the explanation, and they stared and wondered aloud why you thought *that* was so wonderful. Yet it was, *un-*

speakably wonderful. There was a world there, a world without material existence but luminous with pure reason, and they couldn't see it! Only Phidias had seen it. He had shown it to Archimedes, taught him its ways and its rules, and joined in with all his exclamations of amazement. As Archimedes grew older, they had gone on to explore the other world together. They had been co-conspirators, laughing together over an abacus, arguing together about axioms and proofs. They had walked together into the hills on clear nights, to observe the rising and setting of the stars and take sightings of the altitude of the moon. Only the two of them, out of all Syracuse, were at home in the invisible world. Others—even the closest and best loved of others—were forever outsiders.

It had been Phidias who suggested that Archimedes go to Alexandria. "I went when I was your age," he said, "and I heard Euclid himself lecture. You *must* go." He had sold a vineyard he could not afford the loss of, parted with a slave he could not easily do without, so that his son could study mathematics at the world's greatest center of learning. And Alexandria had been everything Phidias had promised—but it had been more, as well. For the first time, Archimedes had found *others* who understood, and some of them were young men of about his own age. It was the first time in his life he hadn't felt like a freak; the first time he'd been free to open up his mind outside his own house. So he had tossed it open to embrace the sky, and the ideas came in—thronging, pushing for attention, scattering, battling, seething, dancing together. He had felt like a fish raised in a garden pond, suddenly discovering the vastness of the sea. It was a liberation more intoxicating than anything he had ever imagined.

At the end of the first year, Phidias had started to write letters asking, "When are you coming home?" and Archimedes had not known how to answer them. Instead he had written to tell his father about Aristarchos' hypothesis that the earth went around the sun, about Conon's work on eclipses, about the Delian problem, and the attempts made by various geometers to square the circle. And Phidias had replied in kind—amazed and enthusiastic, full of arguments and proofs—but somewhere in his every letter, there the question would be again: "When are you coming home?" Archimedes had known—oh, with perfect clarity!—that his father missed him terribly; that Phidias now had no one to share his ideas with, no one to understand *him*. But he had not wanted to go home.

Then, early in the spring, Phidias' last letter: "A war has started with Rome, and I am not well. I have had to stop teaching. Archimedion dearest, you must come home. Your mother and your sister need you." *Your mother and your sister*. Phidias himself had needed Archimedes long before, but for himself he had made no demands—only asked that one pleading question, persistently ignored.

This time the question was a command, and could not be ignored. Archimedes had slowly and reluctantly gone about the business of selling the furniture he'd bought in Alexandria, finding another tenant for the rooms he rented, disposing of a few machines he'd built and some of the tools he'd bought to make them. He had welcomed every delay. When his ship finally set sail for Syracuse, he had wept to see Alexandria dwindle behind him. Those tears seemed shallow now: the grief that lay before him would be much deeper.

The door to his room opened, and Philyra looked around it. She saw that he was awake, and came in.

Philyra was almost seven years younger than her brother, but tended to behave as though she were seven years older. She was a confident, outspoken, no-nonsense sort of girl; she'd been popular at her school and was well thought of in the neighborhood. She was very fond of her brother, but found him hopelessly vague and dreamy, much in need of firm management. She now advanced on him purposefully with a length of yellow cloth folded over her arm—towel or blanket or clothes, he wasn't sure. He sat up in bed, drawing up his long legs to make space for her, and she sat down and regarded him critically. He became uncomfortably aware that he was naked under the sheet, that his bare skin was blotched with fleabites, that his jaw and neck were scruffy with unshaved beard and his hair was dull with dirt. In daylight, too, he could see more clearly how she'd changed since he saw her last, how her body had filled out and rounded. Here in the house she was wearing only a light linen tunic, and it clung to her breasts revealingly. He felt abruptly embarrassed in front of her.

"When did you last have a bath?" asked Philyra, wrinkling her nose.

"You can't bathe on ships," he replied defensively.

Philyra sighed. "Well, you'll have to go to the bathhouse in the New Town as soon as you've had breakfast. You look perfectly disreputable! Do you have any clean clothes?"

He cleared his throat unhappily and didn't answer. "I didn't realize Papa was so ill," he said instead. "How long . . ."

"Since October," she said coolly. "He wrote to you then, but I guess you didn't get the letter until after the winter."

Ships did not sail on the Mediterranean between October and April; even if Archimedes had received his father's letter in late autumn, there would have been no way for him to come home until the sea-lanes opened again. But the thought of Phidias lying ill *all winter* while Archimedes enjoyed himself in Alexandria appalled him.

"I didn't get it until the end of April," he said miserably. "And even then I thought I had time to tie up all my business in Alexandria. All he said in it was 'A war's started and I'm not well.' I thought it just meant he wanted me home to help teach his students until he was better."

"He thought he would recover," said Philyra, and suddenly her eyes filled with tears. "He had a fever with jaundice, but Mama had it too, and she got better. We thought he was getting better, too. Only he wasn't, and this spring . . ."

Archimedes reached out and touched her shoulder, and she lost her no-nonsense composure, dropped her bundle, flung herself into his arms, and wept. "It's been *horrible!*" she cried passionately. "He gets worse and worse, and there's nothing we can do!"

"I'm sorry," he said helplessly. "I wish I'd been here."

"He wanted you," sobbed Philyra. "He kept sending Chrestos down to the harbor to see if there were any ships from Alexandria, and sometimes there would be, but you were never on them. And sometimes he'd say you must be dead, that your ship had sunk or that you'd died in Alexandria, and he'd weep for you and tell us all to go into mourning. That was the worst of all. Why didn't you come back last year?"

"I'm sorry!" he said again wretchedly, tears rising to his own eyes. "Philyra, I swear I would have if I'd known."

"I know," she said, swallowing her sobs. "I know." She patted him on the back, as though he were the one who had broken down, then drew away, wiping her eyes. Nothing could be done about death, and she was determined to bear the grief with all the dignity she could command. She picked up her bundle again and spread it out on the bed: it turned out to be a new cloak, woven of fine yellow wool, and a linen tunic with a yellow spiral pattern down the sides. "I made these for you last year," said Philyra. "You *don't* have any clean clothes, do you?"

"I don't think so," he admitted, tracing the pattern with one slow finger. It was a series of double spirals, all centered on a line from shoulder to knee; from each central point a line circled outward one turn, then twisted about and ran into the center of the succeeding spiral. An *interesting* pattern. A line constructed tangent to both spiral A and spiral B would . . .

Philyra firmly removed his hand from the pattern; he looked up and blinked at her in surprise. "It's to *wear*," she told him. "Not to do geometry on."

"Oh," he said. "Yes." After a moment, he remembered that the clothes were a present and added, "Thank you. I like them very much."

She shook her head in mock despair. "Ai, Medion! You haven't changed at all!"

He wasn't sure what to make of that, and she smiled again at his bewilderment and brushed back a stray lock of his dirty hair. "Now," she went on, businesslike and hopeful, "do you have any money? We've been running out. We had to sell some blankets and pots to pay the doctor."

Archimedes shrugged. Most of the water-snail's earnings had vanished in Alexandria. But there was a little left, and a little more from the odds and ends he'd sold on leaving the city. "I have a bit," he said. "About a hundred drachmae, I think— Marcus knows exactly."

"A hundred drachmae!" she exclaimed eagerly. "That's good! I was afraid we'd have to go around to Papa's old pupils at once, and beg them to take up mathematics again. But a hundred drachmae will buy us a couple of months' grace."

Archimedes cleared his throat and shifted nervously. "I'm not going to teach," he declared.

She stared at him in exasperation. "Medion, you can't make a living from geometry!"

"I *know* that!" he protested. "I'm going to get a job as an army engineer." He launched into the arguments he had carefully prepared beforehand. "With a war on, the city must need catapults, and the tyrant must be willing to pay for them. There's more money in machines than in teaching. And I'm good with machines, you know I am. That irrigation device I built last summer earned more in two months than Papa ever earned in a year. Besides, shouldn't I help defend the city if I can? I'm going to see somebody about it this evening."

At this she smiled, encouragingly rather than with conviction. She had heard about the water-snail from his letters home, but she rather doubted that it was as successful as he claimed, and as for catapults—well, the king already had engineers who could build them, so why would he want somebody new and completely untried? Even if he did, it seemed unlikely that anyone would get rich from it. Her brother had made lots of machines as they grew up together, and many of them hadn't worked at all. Machine-making didn't seem to her as reliable a source of income as teaching mathematics. Still, she liked his machines. As a small girl she had sat quietly watching as he built them, and listened to his explanations with solemn attention. As far as she

was concerned, her brother's constructions were the most wonderful of toys, whether they worked or not. She would be very
pleased if he could make a living from them. It was worth a try,
anyway—and the household now had a hundred drachmae and
a couple of months before the money ran out.

Archimedes saw that she had accepted his plan, and felt a
twinge of dread, as though another gate had closed in the walls
which surrounded him. He had decided in a rare moment of
practical planning that there were three things he was good at—
pure mathematics, mechanics, and playing the flute. To earn a
living he must put one or another of those skills to use. Music
was something personal, something he did for himself and his
friends; it seemed profane to play to order. As for pure mathematics, as Philyra had pointed out, he couldn't make a living
simply from *doing* geometry, and as for teaching it, he'd occasionally been called in to help his father in the past, and he was
uncomfortably aware that he was bad at it. The students never
understood things which seemed to him glaringly obvious, and
his impatient explanations only confused them. So machine-
making it would have to be.

He was dreading it. Building a *new* machine was fun—he liked
seeing the need set out as neatly as a geometrical proposition,
and devising an apparatus that would satisfy it; enjoyed the complete absorption in the task, the complex coordination between
his hands and his mind, and the unarguable solid reality of the
finished solution. But once a machine had been built, to make
another of the same type, and then another and another and
another—it was boring. No, worse: it was a stifling prison where
the soul's wings atrophied and died. Pure mathematics was light
and air and delicious freedom, and he loved it more than anything on earth. But he was not a nobleman, and couldn't afford
to devote himself to pure mathematics without a thought for
sordid considerations of gain. He had a family to support. The
invisible world could no longer be his homeland, but only a place
he visited when he had the time.

He would have no company on his visits to it, either; none.

He would be alone—as his father had been, these three years past. With a spasm of fresh pain, he supposed that Fate was just.

Then he remembered the war. In Alexandria it had been hard to believe in it; here in Syracuse it loomed larger, far more threatening. Lines from an old song wandered through his mind:

> Let none of humankind ever once say
> what chance tomorrow will bring,
> nor, seeing a happy man, that contentment will stay
> for, swift as a dragonfly's wing
> swifter again comes change.

"You get dressed," ordered Philyra, patting his hand. "I'll go talk to Marcus about getting your other things washed."

~ MARCUS WAS TAKING A BATH WHEN PHILYRA FOUND HIM. Private houses did not generally have bathrooms, and bathhouses in that age were for citizens only: Marcus was washing in the courtyard with a sponge and a bucket. It was not uncommon for even the free men of a household to walk about naked indoors, and a slave's nudity was nothing to worry about, but Philyra hung back awkwardly, waiting at the foot of the stairs until Marcus had finished. She felt uncomfortable about him. She too was aware that one of the household slaves would probably be sold, and she was hoping that one would be Marcus. She had always sided with Sosibia in the household feud, and regarded Marcus as an awkward barbarian. Besides, after a three-year absence he felt like a stranger. She could contemplate selling him; she couldn't bear the thought of inflicting that fate on any of the others. She noticed now that though Marcus had a shocking bruise on his left side, and though he was just as flea-bitten as her brother, he looked sleek and fit. That would mean a good price, but still her lips narrowed with disapproval. Marcus had been sent to Alexandria to look after Archimedes, but had returned glowing with health, while his master's ribs were like a washboard.

An inconvenient fair-mindedness, however, reminded her that

Archimedes had always been thin, and Marcus sturdy. And when Archimedes was doing geometry he would forget to eat unless you set his food on top of the abacus—and sometimes even then he'd simply move it out of the way and carry on calculating. It was probably unfair to blame Marcus too much for the state his master had come home in.

Marcus poured the remains of the bucket of water over his head, shook himself, and picked up his tunic. Philyra pushed herself out of the doorway into the sunny courtyard. "Marcus!" she said sharply. "Where's my brother's luggage?"

Marcus jumped and pulled his tunic hastily over his head before replying. He felt as awkward with Philyra as she with him. She'd been a schoolgirl when he'd left the house; now she was a young woman. "There," he said, indicating the chest in the corner of the yard. "But I wouldn't open it, mistress."

"Why not?" she demanded. "I can't believe the things in it are clean! It's going to be a good drying day." Indeed, the air was already hot: anything washed now would be dry well before the evening.

He shrugged. "It has presents in it," he said. "One of them is for you." His eyes lingered momentarily on the front of her tunic. She became aware of how it was clinging, and hitched it up, reddening.

"But I just told him I was going to see to his things!" she protested. "And he didn't say anything about presents."

Marcus snorted. "Would you expect *him* to think of a thing like that?"

No, she wouldn't. Archimedes probably remembered the presents, and must know that they were in the same chest as the clothes. But he would not put the two things together, and know that it would spoil her surprise if she opened the chest. She made an exasperated noise, Marcus grinned, and something swung into balance between them: they were both members of the same household, both aware of the tastes and foibles of the same small collection of people.

"There's no hurry, is there?" he asked.

There was not, not really. She just wanted everything to be *settled*: her brother indisputably home, in his own room as he should be, with the chest reduced from traveling chest to clothes chest. She walked over to the luggage and glared at it resentfully. "What's in the basket?" she asked.

"The famous water-snail," replied Marcus, grinning again. "We can unpack that, if you like." He went over to the chest and began to untie the rope.

"Won't he want to show it to me himself?" she asked doubtfully.

"No," replied Marcus, undoing another knot. Suddenly he wanted very much to show her the water-snail, to impress her. "We made thirty-two of the things in Egypt, and he's sick of the sight of them. But it's an amazing machine. Here, let me show you!" He drew the rope off the basket, hauling the coils under the chest. Philyra leaned against the courtyard wall with her arms crossed, trying to look uninterested, though in fact she was acutely curious. Marcus was sharply aware of the way her stance cast one thin hip into linen-hung relief. Too thin, he told himself—like her father and her brother—but somehow prettier than such an angular girl should be. Perhaps it was the brightness of her eyes. Not that it had any bearing on him: he was as much her brother's property as the machine he was unpacking. Still, where was the harm in showing a pretty girl a machine?

He untied the knot that secured the basket's lid, opened the basket, and lifted out from a nest of straw a wooden cylinder. It was about a cubit long—the distance from a man's elbow to his fingertips—and the outside was made of planks bound, barrel-like, with iron hoops. The interior held a complicated structure smeared with pitch. A stand was fixed to the cylinder's core with a pin, so that the whole thing could turn like a wheel.

"The Egyptians usually lift water with a machine called a water-drum," said Marcus, turning the cylinder in his hands. "A sort of wheel with eight buckets around the rim. A full-sized one moves a lot of water, but it's heavy to turn—it needs a couple of men to shift it. Your brother started off with one of them, and finished up with this. The real machines we built were bigger, of course—they stood about as tall as a man—but otherwise they were exactly like this. As you can see, this still has eight inlets"— he showed her the eight openings in the cylinder's base—"but they're not buckets. They're tubes." He stuck a finger into one, and she saw that it was indeed a kind of tube, and that it ran up around the core at an angle. "They coil right around the cylinder several times and come out here, at the top." He slapped the top edge of the cylinder, which was identical to the bottom. "Each one is a bit like a snail shell, which is why it's called a snail. They're made of strips of willow, stuck onto the core with pitch and closed over with planks. I don't know how he fixed on the angle they spiral at, but it's very important: a lot of the people who tried to copy it got it wrong, and then it didn't work. Now, what you do to work it . . ." Marcus glanced about, fixed on a large amphora of water sitting in the corner of the courtyard, and hurried over to it, holding the water-snail. He set the machine down, fetched the bucket he'd used for his bath, and poured some water from the amphora into the bucket. Then he set the bucket in a dip in the courtyard, balancing it with some loose stones so that it stood at an angle on its side, and placed a laundry footboard before it to make a platform. "It has to sit at an angle," he explained to Philyra. "The exact angle is important, too—that's another thing people who copied it used to get wrong. This one is right if the stand's straight." He set the foot of the water-snail in the water of the bucket and the head on the platform. "Now all you have to do is turn it." He gestured for her to oblige.

Philyra hitched the hem of her tunic away from her feet and crouched down beside him. She put one hand on the wooden cylinder and began to turn it slowly; it revolved easily on its stand. Water ran into the tubes at the foot of the snail. She kept turning, and presently water ran out of snail's head. She kept turning the machine gently, watching it: water ran in, ran down the tubes, and . . .

"It's running uphill!" she exclaimed, shocked. She took her hand off the machine as though it had burned her.

Marcus grinned. "Quick!" he said. "It takes most people a bit longer to realize that. Some need to have it pointed out to them. But it doesn't—not exactly. Watch more closely."

Philyra turned the machine again. Water ran into a tube; as the tube went up, the water ran down, into the spiral, and then along it as it turned on. She laughed delightedly.

Marcus grinned back at her. "It runs downhill all the way up," he said.

"Sometimes," said Philyra, "I think my brother is a mistake of Nature. He shouldn't have been born a human being at all; he should have been an attendant spirit in the workshops of the gods. I suppose a full-sized one of these is very much easier to turn than a water-drum?"

" 'Course it is," agreed Marcus. "You don't need two men; you don't even need one. A child can operate it—because all you have to turn is the snail itself: the water just runs downhill." He sat back on his heels and gazed lovingly at the machine. "We had people queueing up to buy it," he told her. "We could have made a fortune!"

"I thought you did!" Philyra said in surprise. "More in two months than my father earns in a year, my brother said."

Marcus shook his head sadly. "Eighteen hundred eighty drachmae. Enough to pay our debts and live well in Alexandria for a year. But we had orders for another thirty of the machines—at eighty drachmae apiece!—and every expectation of more again. He preferred to do geometry."

Philyra stared at the water-snail and swallowed. She could not imagine eighteen hundred and eighty drachmae all together in one lump; still less could she imagine spending such a sum. The rent from the family's small farm was three hundred drachmae a year—less, now that the vineyard had been sold—and Phidias' teaching had brought in perhaps as much again. The water-snail had earned not just more than her father's salary but three times the household's entire annual income—and Archimedes had spent it all, except for a hundred drachmae.

Marcus understood her sudden silence and wished he'd kept

his mouth shut. He shifted uncomfortably. "Alexandria's expensive," he said defensively. "And there was the debt, and the fare back." There'd been a woman, too, who had accounted for quite a lot of the money, but he had no intention of mentioning *her* to Archimedes' sister. "Your brother wasn't as extravagant as it seems," he finished instead—which was certainly true, given Alexandrian prices, to say nothing of the woman's. "Besides, there's a hundred and sixty drachmae left."

"A hundred and sixty?" asked Philyra suspiciously. "He told me a hundred."

Marcus shrugged and grinned again. "You expect *him* to keep track of money?"

This time she did not smile. Instead, she gave him a cool, assessing stare. "You were keeping track of it for him, were you?"

For a moment, he didn't understand. Then his face darkened. "I haven't taken a copper of it!" he declared indignantly. "You can ask him."

"If he wasn't keeping track of it, what good would that do?"

Philyra, watching his face, saw the anger in it suddenly dwindle into sullen impassivity. It was as though something else drained out with it—a sense of freedom, an identity. She suddenly regretted her suspicion. And yet—eighteen hundred and eighty drachmae! She didn't see how such a huge sum of money could have just vanished. Her vague, dreamy brother was easy prey for any cheat.

"I never took a copper of his money," Marcus repeated sourly. "You can ask him."

Bitterly, he remembered how he and his master had returned to Alexandria from making water-snails in the Delta. When the riverboat docked, Archimedes had leaped off and gone straight to the Museum, leaving Marcus to take the luggage back to their lodgings. The luggage—and the box containing eighteen hundred and eighty drachmae. A lot of money. Enough to buy Marcus passage on a ship back to Italy, and to pay for a pair of oxen, some sheep, and a year's rent on a little farm once he got there. He'd been painfully aware, as he trudged along with the heavy chest, how easy it would be to get away. It wouldn't even have been as though he were leaving his master stranded: Archimedes could always have gone back and made a few more water-snails. In the end what held him back was not the honesty on which he had always prided himself, but despair. The events that had enslaved him—the lost battle, the dead men—were still there, ineradicable and absolute. He could not go home, and there seemed little point in going anywhere else. His slavery, which until then he had always thought of as something imposed upon him contrary to his true nature, suddenly revealed itself as the inescapable condition on which he held his life.

He recognized now that he was putting off the girl with a slave's defense—*My master hasn't complained, so you have no right to*—and he stood up angrily, swept up the water-snail, and carried it back to its basket. Philyra followed him, her expression still a mixture of suspicion and apology. "Maybe I will ask him," she said.

"You do that," growled Marcus, tipping the last of the water out of the snail onto the dirt of the yard.

"In the meantime," said Philyra, drawing herself up, "take all the dirty things out of the chest and put them ready for washing. Just leave the other things in it, for my brother to sort out."

"Yes, mistress," said Marcus bitterly. He turned his back on her and ostentatiously began to put the snail away. But he sensed it when she left, and turned to watch her. She walked with a straight, stiff step, back straight and head with its knot of untidy hair held high, and she went directly to the room at the end of the courtyard where her father was dying. His resentment vanished, leaving only sadness. Her father was ill, her mother undoubtedly distracted by caring for him. She was trying hard to be a prudent and sensible guardian of the house and not a burden upon it: if he'd been free he would have applauded her for it. She was young and ignorant. It was not her fault he was a slave.

~ ARCHIMEDES STUMBLED DOWNSTAIRS A FEW MINUTES later. He was dressed in the new tunic, which, unbelted and crooked, he contrived to make almost as disreputable as the one he'd taken off the day before. He blinked at the heap of dirty laundry beside the chest as though it were the fragments of something that had broken and he were trying to work out what.

"I told your sister not to unpack the chest herself, because it had presents in it," said Marcus quickly. "The presents are still there."

"Oh," said Archimedes, but as though the words hadn't registered.

He looked, Marcus thought, even vaguer and more preoccupied than usual. "Do you want to take the presents out and give them to your family?" he suggested pointedly. "Your sister's in a hurry to shift the chest."

"Oh," said Archimedes again. He came over and stared into the chest. Marcus had already sorted the presents into one corner: a jar of myrrh for Arata, a lute for Philyra, and a box full of ivory tiles for Phidias.

Archimedes bent over and picked up the box. Like its contents, it was of ivory, and it had been decorated with a picture of the god Apollo and the nine Muses, sketched with a fine red line. He remembered looking at it in the shop, assembling the pieces of the puzzle, and smiling as he imagined his father's delight in doing the same. Phidias would not play with the puzzle now. He was too tired, too ill, too busy dying. One more puzzle abandoned—and there had been many, many other puzzles Phidias had been too busy and too tired to solve during the course of his life. He had needed to earn money for the household, bread for the children. He had needed to be a citizen, a husband, a father before he could be a mathematician and astronomer. Archimedes had profited from it. Now he numbly regarded the empty half of himself, an unpayable debt passed on.

Marcus saw his face fall slack and empty, like the face of an idiot, and was concerned. He touched his master's elbow. "You can still give it to him, sir," he said. "It's a good present for an invalid."

Archimedes began to cry soundlessly. He raised his head and stared blindly at Marcus. "He's dying."

"So I was told," replied Marcus evenly.

"I should have come back last year."

That was what Marcus had said at the time. Now he shrugged and said only, "You're back now. Sir, he dies after a good life, with all his family about him. No man can ask the gods for more."

"He lived on scraps all his life!" Archimedes replied fiercely. "Bits and pieces, hours snatched here and there, nothing! Oh, Apollo! Pegasus, hitched to a plow! Why should the soul have wings, if it's never allowed to fly?"

This made no sense whatever to Marcus. "Sir!" he said sharply. "Bear it like a man!"

Archimedes gave him a look of astonished incomprehension, as though Marcus had addressed him in some unidentifiable foreign tongue. But he stopped crying and wiped his face on his bare arm. He glanced at the door at the far end of the courtyard, then sighed and walked toward it, the box in his hand. Marcus picked up the jar of perfume and the lute and followed him.

Arata and Philyra were both in the sickroom, finishing the work of preparing the invalid for the day. When Philyra saw the lute in Marcus' hands her face went utterly still, but her eyes awoke into a sudden intense life. Archimedes glanced back at his slave and jerked his head, and Marcus bowed and handed the jar of myrrh to Arata, then bowed again and offered the lute to Philyra. Her face flushed as she took it, and her hands curved over the sounding board with a fiercely possessive tenderness. She looked at her brother and breathed, "Medion!"—half in protest, half in adoration. But Archimedes was not looking at her.

Phidias had slowly levered himself to a sitting position to accept his own present. He took the ivory box in his trembling hands and studied the picture on the lid. "Apollo and the sweet Muses," he observed softly. "Which one is Urania?"

Archimedes indicated her silently. Urania, Muse of Astronomy, stood at Apollo's elbow, pointing at something which lay on the low table in front of the god—the puzzle, probably. Her diaphanous draperies were identical to those of her eight sisters, but she was distinguishable from them by her crown of stars.

Phidias smiled. "Next to the god," he said quietly. "Just where she should be." He looked up at his son, his yellowed eyes still full of his smile—looked in the luxurious confidence that here at last he would be understood. "She's beautiful, isn't she?" he asked.

"Yes," whispered Archimedes, the expected understanding going through him in a warm flood. "Yes, she is."

3

Archimedes kept to his agreement to meet the guardsman Straton by the naval quay that evening.

The rest of the family had accepted his decision not to follow his father's career as calmly as Philyra had. Arata, in fact, was relieved to find him searching for any work: she'd worried that he might not appreciate the necessity of earning money. She fussed about to ensure that he looked an aspiring royal engineer, and sent him off bathed and barbered and dressed in his new tunic and cloak. He tried to avoid the cloak—too hot for June!— but his mother draped it firmly about his shoulders. "It looks distinguished," she told him, "and you need to impress this man."

"He's only a soldier!" Archimedes protested. "He's just going to tell me who I should really talk to!"

"Even so!" Arata declared. "If he's impressed, he'll pass that on to his superior."

She wanted to send Marcus with him, too: a gentleman ought to have a slave in attendance. Archimedes was nervous, though, that they might meet the Tarentine mercenary Philonides again. He explained to his mother and sister what had happened at the docks.

Philyra listened to the account with indignant astonishment. She glanced at Marcus' impassive face, remembering the bruise on his side. "That's outrageous!" she exclaimed angrily. "We have a right to keep our own slave! You *should* have taken that stupid mercenary to a magistrate, and complained."

Archimedes just shrugged. "I wouldn't threaten a mercenary!" he said with feeling. "And courts are chancy places, especially with a war on. I don't know what sort of Italian Marcus is—do you?"

Philyra glanced at Marcus again, startled this time. She had never connected him in her mind with the great new power to the north. Yes, she'd known he was Italian, but there had always been wars in Italy, and in each war some prisoners always ended up in the Syracusan slave market. It had always been enough to call them simply "Italian" and assume that slavery had absorbed all the differences between them.

"Well, what sort of Italian *are* you?" she demanded bluntly.

Marcus' face was carefully blank. "I'm not a Roman," he muttered. "Roman citizens are never slaves." Then he added, in embarrassment, "Mistress."

"It doesn't matter what sort he is," said Arata resignedly. "If the question were raised in a court, we'd have endless trouble trying to prove anything at all. Better to avoid courts if we can." She clapped her hands and jerked her head at Marcus. He retreated back into the house, relieved.

Archimedes started for the door, but Arata caught his arm and drew him aside before he reached it. In a voice too low for the slaves to overhear she said, "My dear, have you given any thought as to whether we should sell Marcus?"

"No, of course not!" said Archimedes, surprised. "We don't have to sell him just because he's Italian!"

"Not that," whispered Arata, gesturing for him to keep his voice down. "We don't need four slaves, especially since your father sold the vineyard, and we can't afford to feed them. If we don't sell Marcus, it will have to be Chrestos. We couldn't sell Sosibia, not after so many years, and little Agatha—it wouldn't be right, my dear."

Archimedes hunched his shoulders unhappily. He understood

now. His mother wanted him to start looking for a good buyer for one of the slaves right away. The decision about who to sell and where was his to make—because it would not be right to throw this sort of decision onto his father, not now, and the women lacked any authority in law.

He did not want to sell anybody. Marcus would hate to be sold, he thought absently. He would really *hate* it, no matter who the buyer. He liked Marcus, relied on Marcus: he could not possibly inflict such a humiliation upon him. But Chrestos—he could remember holding Chrestos as a newborn baby. How could he take money for a member of his family? Money wasn't worth it. He hated to think about money at the best of times.

"There's no hurry!" he protested at last. "The money I brought back from Alexandria will last us for a month or two, and after that, anything could happen. There's a lot of money in engineering. We could all become rich! It would be stupid to sell people if we don't need to."

Arata sighed. Some people might get rich from engineering, but she did not believe her son ever would. He was too unworldly, too softhearted. Like his father. She couldn't even complain at it: it was a quality she loved in them. She did not like postponing hard decisions, though, especially in such uncertain times. "If we wait until we're hungry," she pointed out quietly, "we'll have to take the first buyer that comes along. If we sell now we can choose a good home for him."

Archimedes squirmed uncomfortably. "Can't we at least wait to see if I get this job?" he pleaded.

His mother sighed again, resignedly this time. She did not want to sell any of the household slaves, either, and it was true they had a month or so of grace. She nodded, and her son gave a sigh of relief.

Philyra, who had hung in the doorway listening to this, went back into the courtyard of the house. Marcus was there, taking down his master's laundry. Philyra studied him for a minute, wondering, for the first time, what he had been before he was a slave. She had no clear memories of the time before he came to the household: he had always been there.

Earlier in the day she had indeed mentioned her suspicions of him to her brother. Archimedes had dismissed them at once. "Marcus?" he'd said. "Oh no! He thinks slaves who steal deserve the whip, not the stick, and he prides himself on his honesty. No, no, I'd trust Marcus with a fortune." Now he had backed that confidence with a refusal even to contemplate selling the slave.

But the problem was, he *had* trusted Marcus with a fortune, and she still couldn't imagine how that fortune could have disappeared in a year without dishonesty from *someone*. Archimedes' confidence merely made her feel guilty about her own suspicions.

The slave felt her eyes on him and turned toward her, his arms full of laundry, his face mild and inquiring. She noticed, as though for the first time, the crooked identation where his nose had been broken, and she wondered how that had happened, and when. "What sort of Italian are you?" she asked him again.

He let out a long slow breath, looking away from her. "Mistress . . ." he began, then gave a helpless jerk of one hand, flapping linen. "Mistress, I'm a slave, your brother's. You *know* that's true. Anything else I said might be a lie."

She gazed at him soberly. "When did you break your nose?"

He set his armful of laundry carefully down on an overturned washtub and turned back to the line for the last item. "Long time ago, mistress. Before I came to Sicily."

A soldier had broken it, during the first year of his slavery. He'd resisted the man's attempt to bugger him, and had been beaten senseless because of it. When he woke up, it was to find himself lying at the feet of the Campanian slave merchant who'd sold him to the soldier, and the soldier and slaver arguing about whether the soldier was due his money back. "Look what you've done to his face!" the slaver had complained. "Who's going to want him now?" Marcus had lain there, mouth full of blood, aching in every muscle, and hoped that nobody was going to want him now, because he didn't think he'd be able to resist so fiercely again; he'd give in, and make a whore of himself. He had been seventeen.

"Was it in battle?" asked Philyra.

Marcus shook his head. He folded the last tunic, set it down on top of the others, then picked the pile up. "Just a fight."

"But you were in a battle. You were enslaved after a battle."

"Yes," he agreed, meeting her eyes. "I was in a battle. We lost."

Philyra was silent a moment, thinking of the war to the north, and of the precariousness of the freedom of Syracuse. She shook her head, and Marcus took the gesture as dismissal. He gave a nod and set off upstairs with his pile of clean dry clothes.

〜 IT WAS DUSK WHEN ARCHIMEDES ARRIVED AT THE SEA gate. If the Tarentine had indeed shared Straton's shift, he'd taken himself elsewhere, and Straton was alone, leaning against the inside of the city wall, shield forced half over his chest, one leg resting on his slanted spear. He unfolded himself when he saw Archimedes and tipped his shield onto his back again. "There you are!" he said with relief. "When I asked around about your question, my captain got interested. He says they do need more engineers, for the army and the city both. He wants to talk to you. He's waiting for us at the Arethusa. That all right?"

Archimedes blinked and mentally thanked his mother for her fussing over the cloak. "F-fine!" he stammered hastily. Straton's captain was presumably the man in charge of the garrison of Syracuse while the rest of the army was away. He could, if he wanted, ensure that Archimedes was offered a job.

The Arethusa proved to be an inn on the promontory of Ortygia, near the freshwater spring of that name. Archimedes was not familiar with it—he had rarely ventured onto the citadel—but he noticed as they approached that it was a good inn. The building was large, faced with stone, and had probably been con-

verted from an upper-class mansion. Its sign, which had some
artistic pretensions, depicted the nymph Arethusa, spirit of the
spring and patroness of the city, reclining among the reeds with
the citadel of Ortygia in the background. Archimedes eyed her
shapely nudity, and decided that yes, the inn probably did rent
female company as well as sell food. He fingered the coins in his
purse resignedly. The evening was clearly not going to be cheap,
and he knew that he would be paying. He could not complain:
treating Straton's captain to an evening's entertainment would
oblige the man to be helpful.

Straton clumped into the inn's main room, spear over his
shoulder, and gave his name to an obsequious waiter. Archimedes glanced warily at the painting of carousing centaurs on the
wall and the silver-chased hanging lamps, and added another
three obols to the likely bill. The waiter smirked and bobbed and
led them to one of the inn's small private dining rooms. A short
wiry man in his early thirties was already seated on the single
couch, nibbling at a dish of olives; he rose politely when Archimedes and Straton appeared. Straton saluted; Archimedes extended his hand.

The captain smiled and shook hands. "You're the engineer?"
he asked. "I'm Dionysios son of Chairephon, captain of the garrison of the Ortygia. I've already ordered—I hope that's all
right?"

Dionysios was not wearing armor, though a red officer's cloak
hung over the back of his couch and a sheathed sword over the
arm. When Straton hesitated awkwardly in the doorway, his superior grinned at him. "We're both off duty, man," he said.
"Make yourself comfortable."

Straton gave a sigh of relief, set his spear and shield against
the wall beside the door, then dropped onto the free end of the
couch and began to unfasten his baldric. Dionysios grinned again,
this time with knowing sympathy for long hours standing guard,
for sore feet, a stiff back, and boredom.

Archimedes, feeling much the odd one out, took the least

comfortable place, in the middle of the couch between the two soldiers. The obsequious waiter bobbed about taking orders, then retreated.

"Straton tells me you've just come back from Alexandria and are looking to be of service to the city in the war," said Dionysios.

Archimedes nodded. "But," he added awkwardly, "I've found that I can't go up to Messana to join the army. When I got home—That is, my father's dying. I can't leave Syracuse until— You understand what I mean. If there's something I can do here in the city . . ." He trailed off with an uncertainty he did not feel. He had left his father to endure illness alone: he would stay with him now, until the end.

"Ah," said Dionysios. "I am sorry."

"Bad thing to come home to," said Straton sympathetically. "That, and the war."

Archimedes made an inarticulate noise of agreement.

There was a decent silence, and then the captain asked about Alexandria.

They talked about the city through the first course of the meal—the Museum, the scholars, the temples; the beauty of the courtesans. Straton was silent at first, nervous in his commanding officer's presence, but Dionysios was cheerful and relaxed, there was plenty of wine, and before long they were all three talking freely. Dionysios swirled the fragrant red in his wide-bowled cup and praised Egypt. "The House of Aphrodite," he said. "That's what they call Alexandria, isn't it? Everything that exists anywhere in the world is there, they say—everything anyone could desire. Money, power, tranquility, fame, learning, philosophy, temples, a good king, and women as beautiful as the goddesses who once came to Priam's son Paris to be judged. I'd love to go there!"

"It's the House of the Muses," agreed Archimedes warmly. "It draws the finest minds in the world as the Heraclean stone draws iron. I didn't want to leave it."

"But you've come back to Syracuse, because of the war?"

He nodded. "And because my father was ill."

Again there was a moment's silence, and this time Archimedes realized that it was more because of the mention of the war than from tact over his father's illness. The war was a subject that weighed heavy on the minds of the two soldiers, but one they did not want to discuss. Twelve years before, the Roman Republic had defeated an alliance consisting of all the Greek cities of Italy, half a dozen rebellious Italian tribes, and the army of the kingdom of Epirus across the Adriatic. The forces had been commanded by the brilliant and adventurous Epirot king, Pyrrhus, who was said to have been the finest general of the age. How could Syracuse alone succeed where such an alliance had failed? Her only hope of victory lay in the alliance with Carthage—and Carthage had always longed for her destruction. How could anyone discuss this war? What was there to say about a conflict where one's enemies were preferable to one's allies?

The waiter returned with a dish of broiled eel in beetroot sauce—the main course—then filled up the wine cups and departed again. Dionysios helped himself to some fish. "Do you know anything about catapults?" he asked, finally getting down to the business that had brought them there.

Archimedes' earlier discomfort had melted: the company and talk had been almost easy enough to be Alexandrian, and the food was better. Sicilian cooking had always been famous as the finest in the Greek world. He scraped some fish onto his piece of bread, took a bite, and gave the answer that came most naturally to him. "The really interesting thing about them," he announced around his mouthful, "is how you make them bigger. The critical feature is the diameter of the bore in the peritrete. To increase the power of the throw you have to increase the other dimensions in proportion to the increase in the diameter of the bore. So it's the Delian problem in another form!"

Captain and guardsman stared confounded, and he realized that the company wasn't very Alexandrian after all. "The problem of how to construct a solid a given amount larger than a similar solid," he explained apologetically. "You, um, have to calculate the mean proportionals."

"What's Delian about that?" asked Straton.

"People started trying to do it when the priests of Apollo on Delos wanted to double the size of an altar."

"Don't you just double all the measurements?"

Archimedes gave him a look of astonishment. "No, of course not! Say you have a cube measuring two by two by two; that gives a volume of eight. Doubling the measurements to four will give you a volume of sixty-four—eight times as big. What you need—"

"What I meant," interrupted Dionysios pointedly, "was, do you know how to build catapults?"

"What's the peritrete, anyway?" asked Straton.

Archimedes looked from one of them to the other. "Do *you* know anything about catapults?" he asked.

"Not me!" declared Straton cheerfully.

"A little," said Dionysios. "The peritrete's the frame, Straton."

"The part the arms stick into?"

Archimedes dipped his finger in his wine and traced on the table the peritrete of a torsion catapult: two parallel boards separated by struts. He added the two pairs of boreholes, one at each end of the frame, with a column of twisted strings running from the top bore to the bottom. Each mass of strings gripped one arm, which extended from the frame so that the catapult looked rather like an immense bow, lying on its side and with a gap in the center to allow passage for the missile. A bowstring ran from the tip of one arm to the tip of the other, and a beam with a slide was fixed beneath the frame's center to hold the missile.

The two soldiers leaned over the table and examined the sketch. The waiter came back to refill the cups, regarded the blotted table with displeasure, but, at a glance from Dionysios, refrained from wiping it.

"So *which* is the critical feature?" asked Dionysios.

Archimedes tapped the boreholes. "All the force of the catapult comes from the strings," he said. "The twist in them is what makes the arms of the catapult spring forward after being drawn back. The thicker the column of strings, the more force they exert and the heavier the missile you can throw. The greater the diameter of the bore that holds the strings, the more powerful the catapult."

"And how powerful a catapult could you, personally, build?"

Archimedes hesitated, blinking. Dionysios' question seemed to have missed the point of his own explanation. "There's no theoretical limit!" he protested. "The most powerful catapult I've ever examined was a one-talenter in Egypt, but—"

"A one-talenter?" interrupted Dionysios eagerly. "You could build a one-talenter?" Stone-hurling catapults were classified by the weight of the missile they could throw. A talent—about sixty pounds—was officially a man's load, and the one-talenter was generally the most powerful catapult in a city arsenal. A few larger machines had been made from time to time, by exceptional engineers for great kings, but ordinarily even one-talenters were rare. Many cities had nothing heavier than a thirty-pounder.

"Of course!" agreed Archimedes. "Or one bigger than that— but you'd need special equipment to load and draw it."

Straton had been looking more and more uncomfortable; now he cleared his throat and said anxiously, "Sir—yesterday he said he'd never actually built any war machine."

Dionysios looked at Archimedes with surprise and indignation.

"You don't need to have actually built one to know how it's done!" Archimedes declared, defending himself against the unspoken charge of deception. "You just need to understand the mechanical principles. I do. It will take me a little bit longer than it would take a more experienced engineer, but I can produce a catapult that works."

Dionysios regarded him a moment longer, unconvinced.

"Look," said Archimedes, "you don't need to pay me anything until I've produced a working catapult."

Dionysios' eyebrows shot up. "A one-talent working catapult?" he asked.

"If that's what you want. If you have the wood and the strings for it. You know it will be big, don't you?"

"Obviously," agreed Dionysios. "The king has one at Messana, and it's nineteen feet across." He studied Archimedes a moment longer, very thoughtfully now: he was not sure whether he had found a treasure or a self-deluding fool. But there was no need to decide, if no money needed to change hands until a catapult was completed. He turned back to his food. "When the army went off to besiege Messana," he said, "King Hieron left one of his engineers—Eudaimon son of Kallikles—here in the city with orders to make sure that all the watchtowers in the city wall were equipped with their full complement of catapults. Mostly that's just meant renewing the strings, but there are quite a few new machines to be built as well. Some of the old ones are completely worn out, and some of the watchtowers were never supplied to begin with. Now, Eudaimon has had no trouble building the arrow-shooting catapults, but he's not so good with the stone-hurlers. Unfortunately, stone-hurlers—particularly *big* stone-hurlers—are what the king wants most. So if you can do some, you've got a job."

"I can build stone-hurlers," said Archimedes happily. "When do you want me to start?"

"Come to the King's house in the citadel tomorrow morning," replied Dionysios. "I'll introduce you to Leptines the Regent, and he'll approve your conditions of employment. I warn you, though: I am going to take you up on your offer, and recommend that you not be paid until the first catapult you build has been seen to work."

Archimedes smiled. "Thank you!" he exclaimed. He glanced down at his sketch on the tabletop, and felt a sudden thrill of excitement. A one-talent stone-hurler would need careful planning if it was not to be unwieldy. This was something new, something interesting. He wiped up the drawing with his napkin, dipped his finger in his wine cup again, and began to calculate.

The other two watched him a moment. Then Dionysios looked at Straton and raised his eyebrows.

Straton's answering look was glum.

"What's the matter?" asked the captain.

"I think I may have lost a bet," replied the soldier.

Dionysios looked at him, looked at the now deeply absorbed Archimedes, guessed the general nature of the bet—and laughed. "Never mind!" he said consolingly. "Your loss will be the city's gain—and they have flute girls in this place who could make you forget far worse griefs than that." He clapped his hands, and the waiter, who had been standing impatiently outside the door, entered to carry out the dishes and usher the flute girls in.

⁓ IN THE HOUSE NEAR THE LION FOUNTAIN, PHILYRA WAS waiting up for her brother. Phidias in his sickroom fell early into a restless slumber; Arata settled on a mattress on the floor beside her husband, where she would wake easily if he needed her during the night. The slaves went to the hot upper room they shared at the back of the house. But Philyra went into the courtyard with the wide-necked lute her brother had given her, sat down on the bench beside the door, and began tentatively to pluck the strings.

Lutes were comparatively new instruments to the Greeks, unknown before the conquests of Alexander the Great. Philyra had seen them before, but never held one: one of her own was the best present she'd ever been given. This one was marvelously beautiful, with a round body of polished rosewood and a neck inlaid with shell. It had a deep, sweet tone, too.

Philyra plucked each of the eight strings in turn, then, with a breathless thrill, stopped them near the top of the neck and plucked them again. She was an accomplished player on the kithara, and knew how to raise the pitch of a string by stopping it on the crossboard with her finger—but for kitharists, such fingering was a virtuoso exercise and its use was limited. The lute promised a whole new dimension to music.

The whole family had always been musical. For as long as Philyra could remember, Arata and Phidias had played together almost every evening, he on the kithara, she on the lyre. Archimedes, as he grew older, had usually joined them on the auloi— the soft-voiced woodwind flutes that were played in pairs—and when Philyra in turn learned an instrument, she too had joined in the concerts. Sometimes the family had played for hours, late into the night, one offering a melody which the others would take up, alter, and pass back. It had often seemed to Philyra that music was an ideal world, that all the best things in the real world were there, but clearer, stronger, more poignant. There was her mother's steadiness, maintaining the balance and rhythm of their common life; there were her father's dreamy gentleness and his sudden tumultuous excitements. And there was her brother, not vague, as he so often was when you spoke to him, but fearfully, ruthlessly precise, and so deep and complicated that she had often struggled to follow him—though in the end he had always resolved his musical knots into an affectionate simplicity. When he left for Alexandria she had tried to play the auloi for a bit, because the strings had sounded so bereft without the flutes' voice to wind among them. But in the end she had gone back to her lyre and kithara. There was something disreputable about a girl playing the flute—and anyway, nobody could play like Medion.

She had missed him. She'd been angry that he hadn't come home when he was supposed to, and bitterly angry when their father fell ill—but now that he was back, the anger was already melting away. She hoped that he would soon return from his drink with the soldier, so that they could play some music together.

She experimented with the lute for perhaps an hour, then, tired by the intense concentration, put it away in her room and came back with her old kithara instead. Easily she plucked out a slow, soft tune with her left hand, while her right struck an occasional ripple of accompaniment with the plectrum.

"Remember once," sang Philyra, her low voice blending with the strings,

> "Remember when,
> I told you this holy word?
> 'The hour is fair, but fleet is the hour,

The hour outraces the swiftest bird.'
Look! It's scattered to earth, your flower."

She was very good, thought Marcus, standing at his window
and listening to her. But that was no surprise. She'd played well
before he left, and she'd had three years to get better.

Behind him, Chrestos was curled up on the pallet they shared,
while Sosibia and her daughter shared another bed behind a cur-
tain. But he could not sleep, so he stood there, gazing into the
darkness of the courtyard below, and listening to the music.

When he had first entered the household, he had found the
nightly concerts disturbing. In his own home there had not been
much music. His mother had sung sometimes while she worked,
and he and his brother had sung in the fields, but apart from
that, music had been something one paid others to perform. He
had bought some whenever he had money, because he loved it;
now he could not afford it, and had it all the time, for nothing.
At first he had resented his own pleasure in it: surely it degraded
him that he enjoyed any aspect of his slavery? But he'd got
used to music, accustomed to having it around, sensitive to its
patterns and undertones. He'd almost forgotten what life was like
without it.

Philyra sang on, her voice rising clear and sweet into the dark,
old songs from the countryside, new songs from the royal courts,
love songs and hymns to the gods. Marcus stood silently at the
window, listening and watching the stars above the rooftops of
Syracuse. After a while she stopped singing and simply played,
passing the tune from right hand to left and back again, and he
sat down against the bedroom wall, but kept listening, wondering
why this ripple of notes should say so many things more than any
human tongue.

At last Philyra stopped, yawned, and sat silent, her kithara
upon her lap. Marcus stood up hurriedly, so that he could watch
her go—but she did not. He understood then that the music had
simply been to amuse herself while she waited for her brother
to come home. He hesitated, nervous of approaching her. But

what harm would it do for a household slave to advise her to go to bed? He turned from the window, crept out of the room—silently, so as not to disturb Sosibia—and down the stairs.

"Mistress?" he called, stepping out into the courtyard, and even in the dark he saw how she jumped.

"What do you want?" she called, guilt from her suspicions of him adding sharpness to her tone.

Marcus stopped a few feet away, faceless in the dark. "Mistress, don't wait up all night," he said gently. "Your brother may not be back for hours yet."

She made an exasperated noise. "He's bound to be back soon! He's been gone *hours* already."

"Probably he's treating this man to an evening's entertainment. That means he may not be back until after midnight. There's no reason for you to wait up. I'll open the door for him when he comes."

Night hid Philyra's frown, but not the suspicion in her voice when she said, "He never *used* to go out drinking until after midnight!"

Innocent! thought Marcus affectionately. To *expect* that he'd keep the same hours after three years on his own in a famously luxurious city! "He was often out late in Alexandria," he told her. "And tonight he'll have to go along with whatever the other fellow wants, to be sure of his help. It's probably a good sign that he's late: means there's something on offer."

For a moment, Philyra said nothing. She told herself that Marcus was implying that her brother had picked up expensive habits in Alexandria, and that this was exactly what Marcus would say, to account for the missing money. "What was he doing out late in Alexandria?" she asked at last, in a brittle voice. Truth or lies, she didn't really want to know, but it was unfair to go on suspecting Marcus without knowing what he had to say.

But Marcus answered at once, and mildly, "Nothing you need to worry about, mistress. He had a pack of friends, and they'd sit about drinking and talking and . . . making music, half the night. When there wasn't a lecture on next day, they'd see the sun up."

It still didn't sound like her brother. He'd never been inclined to either drinking or talking, and he'd never had any close friends. She tried to think of a question that would catch Marcus in a lie, but at that moment there was a quick rap on the house door.

Marcus opened it, and Archimedes stumbled in, smelling of wine.

He had not stayed at the Arethusa for the inevitable conclusion of the evening. His father's impending death had shriveled up desire, and whatever their other talents, the Arethusa's flute girls hadn't played the flute very well. It had set his teeth on edge to listen to them. In another situation, he might have offered to play himself and let them just dance, but to have made the offer then would have invited the lewdest of ribaldry. So he had done calculations until his companions were provided for, then excused himself with apologies, paid the reckoning, and come home.

"Can you fetch me a light?" he asked Marcus breathlessly, pushing the flute girls' wreath of wilted parsley farther back onto his head. "I need to write something down."

Philyra jumped up and hugged him, but he shook her off hastily. "Careful!" he exclaimed. "You'll smear it!"

Marcus gave a snort and hurried off.

"Smear what?" she demanded.

"Some calculations I was doing. Marcus! Is there anything to write with?"

"You were doing calculations?" Philyra asked in bewilderment.

He nodded; the gesture was revealed by the sudden glow of the lamp Marcus had just returned with. Archimedes held his left arm toward the light: it was covered with figures sketched in lampblack.

"Medion!" exclaimed Philyra in horror. "It's gone all over your new cloak!"

"Don't worry," he said reassuringly, "I can still read it."

Since Marcus had not brought anything to write with, Archimedes picked up the laundry board, found a lump of chalk, and began to copy the figures from his arm. "I'm going to have to correct most of these when I can look at a smaller catapult," he told the other two, busily writing. "I couldn't remember most of the dimensions to scale them up. But this should be close enough to let me order the wood, which will speed things up."

"You got the job," observed Marcus with satisfaction, and Archimedes nodded absently, frowning at his chalked calculations.

"I thought the man you were seeing tonight was just a soldier!" exclaimed Philyra.

"Oh," said her brother vaguely, "yes. But he asked about who I should talk to and his captain wanted to see me. They really *do* want engineers. I'm to build stone-hurlers, starting with a one-talent machine."

"What's the pay?" demanded Marcus.

"Uh? To be arranged. Nothing, until the first catapult is complete. But there doesn't seem to be anyone else in the city at the minute who can build big stone-hurlers, and the captain said that they're what the tyrant wants most, so I think it will be good. I'm seeing Leptines the Regent about it tomorrow morning."

"Oh, Medion!" cried Philyra, torn between delight and exasperation. "You must give me your cloak at once. You can't go see the regent all covered in lampblack!"

"*You* can't start doing laundry at this time of night!" protested Marcus.

Archimedes glanced up, finally realized that his sister had been waiting for him, and blinked. "Philyrion darling," he said firmly, "you should be in bed." Then he noticed the kithara she was clutching and added, "It's too late for music, too. But tomorrow night we can have a concert."

"To celebrate your new job!" said Philyra, happily dismissing the state of his cloak. "Mama and Papa will be so pleased!"

~ THE FOLLOWING MORNING ARCHIMEDES REPORTED HIS success to his parents; they were, as his sister had expected, pleased. After the first unanswerable questions about pay, however, Phidias asked wistfully, "And will it leave you much time for study?"

"I don't know," replied Archimedes awkwardly. He did not want to admit to his father that he foresaw scholarship squeezed to the edges of his life. "I think—I think not right at the moment, Papa. Because of the war. I will do everything I can to make sure I still have time to talk with you."

"*Oi moi*, the war!" sighed Phidias. "I pray that our king finds some way to get us out of it soon. It will be a bad war, my Archimedion, a very bad war. Our lovely city is like a dove in the pit with two fighting cocks. I am glad that I at least won't have to see what happens to her. My dear boy, you must look after your mother and your sister for me!"

Archimedes took his father's trembling hand. "I will," he promised solemnly. "But I hope, Papa, that King Hieron does find some way out of the war. They say he's a wise man: he may yet bring peace."

"He's ruled well," Phidias conceded—reluctantly, for he had always supported the city's turbulent longings for democracy. Even Hieron's enemies, however, had to admit that he had ruled well. He had come to power eleven years before in a bloodless military coup, and had since governed with moderation, humanity, and a strict regard for the law—much to the surprise of the citizens, who did not expect such behavior from a tyrant.

"Yes, I pray you're right," Phidias went on, then smiled at his son. "I am glad you're back," he said tenderly. "I was afraid to think what would happen to the house, left headless while the city was at war. You go devise some weapon to destroy our enemies, child. And make sure you get a good price for it!"

"Yes, Papa." Archimedes kissed his father's cheek, kissed his mother, who was attending the sick man, then went out into the courtyard.

Philyra was there, trying to clean his cloak. She had brushed it, beaten it, and poured boiling water on it, and had succeeded only in spreading the oily lampblack more widely. She rolled her eyes at her brother distractedly. "You're going to have to wear something else," she told him.

"It's too hot for a cloak anyway," he replied.

Marcus appeared at the foot of the stairs, carrying an old cloak of plain Egyptian linen. "That has wine stains on it!" snapped Philyra impatiently.

"But you can fold the edge over so they don't show," Marcus replied, suiting action to words.

Archimedes groaned, but spread out his arms and allowed his sister and his slave to drape the linen cloak around him, insisting only that the drape go under rather than over his right arm— "It's more dignified worn over both shoulders!" protested Philyra; "It's also hotter!" replied Archimedes. The other two stood back, assessing whether he looked fit to be presented to the king's father-in-law. Archimedes, however, looked at Marcus thoughtfully.

He had been debating whether to take Marcus along to help with the catapult-making. Marcus could undoubtedly be useful at it. He'd helped with the water-snails and with dozens of less successful machines: he knew how to follow technical instructions. He was strong, quick, and handy with a saw or a hammer. On the other hand—on the other hand, Marcus clearly still had some loyalties to the people the catapults were to be employed against. And the catapult-making would take him in and out of the military workshops and the arsenal—the most vulnerable and strategically important buildings in Syracuse. If someone lit a fire in them . . .

"Marcus," said Archimedes, "I want you to stay here and see if my mother wants anything done around the house."

The slave's face went blank. He had foreseen this problem, but he hadn't expected his master to have foreseen it as well. "You don't want me to come with you, sir?"

Archimedes shook his head. "You're not Samnite," he explained quietly.

Marcus stood for a moment frowning at him. He was not sure whether he felt relieved, because he was not required to construct devices that might injure his own people, or hurt, because his master thought him capable of treachery. He could feel Philyra's eyes on him, full of shocked accusation: did she really believe he'd be happy to see her city fall to Rome, her brother killed, and herself raped and enslaved? At last he said, "Sir, I swear that I would never do anything to injure this city or this house. May the gods destroy me in the worst way if I'm lying!"

"I believe you, since you swear it," said Archimedes. "But I think it would be better, all the same, if you stayed home."

Marcus hunched his shoulders. "Very well, sir."

Archimedes slapped him on the shoulder. The linen cloak, which was too short to hold its drape properly with the edge folded over, fell off. Archimedes redraped it again awkwardly and set off.

"He thinks you would betray the city!" exclaimed Philyra hotly, as soon as the door had closed behind him. "You have to tell me: what sort of an Italian are you?"

"What difference does it make?" growled Marcus. "I'm not a *citizen* anywhere. Anyway, what kind of claim does this city have on me to begin with? No one has ever pretended I came here of my own free will." He was a little surprised at his own honesty. "I've sworn I won't do anything to injure the city. Archimedes took my word for it. Isn't that good enough?"

"You know what sort of people the Romans have come to Sicily to help?" demanded Philyra.

Marcus again hunched his shoulders unhappily. The Romans had come to Sicily to help the city of Messana against Syracuse. Messana, however, was a robber state, the home of bandits. More than twenty years before, a group of Italian mercenaries, Campanians, had been posted to the city as a garrison by a previous tyrant of Syracuse; tempted by Messana's wealth, they had taken advantage of the chaos when the tyrant died to seize the city for themselves. They had murdered all the men and taken the women and children as their slaves. Calling themselves Mamertini—"the sons of Mars"—the Campanians had gone on to raid or exact protection money from the neighboring towns, all of which were under Syracusan protection. Syracuse had made war on the bandits sporadically, as Carthage and her own affairs allowed, but with little success—until Hieron rose to power. He had defeated the Mamertini in the field and laid siege to Messana itself. To save themselves, the Campanians had appealed to both the great powers of the West—to Carthage and to Rome.

Carthage had responded first. Always happy to frustrate Syracuse, she had sent a garrison to Messana. But the Carthaginian intervention had provoked a response from the new mistress of Italy. Rhegium, just across the straits from Messana, had fallen to Rome only six years before: Rome was unwilling to allow her African rival to control Messana. She sent her own expedition to the Mamertine city. The Mamertini preferred a Roman garrison to a Carthaginian one—they were Italians, too, after all—and expelled the Carthaginians. Syracuse, which had wanted nothing except to rid herself of a long-standing nuisance, suddenly found herself allied to Carthage and at war with Rome.

"I don't think the Romans should have come to Sicily," muttered Marcus. "It's a bad cause, a bad war. The Mamertini don't deserve any help." He looked back at Philyra's suspicious eyes and declared with sudden fervor, "Mistress, please believe me. I will never betray this house while I live."

Her suspicion changed to puzzled surprise, and he saw that he'd said the right thing, and smiled.

~ ALL THROUGH THE WALK TO THE CITADEL, THE LINEN cloak kept slipping. Like all cloaks, it had weights in its bottom corners to help it drape, but with the end folded over this was simply not enough. At the gates to the citadel Archimedes gave up, shook it out, and draped it around himself again, this time with the stains showing. He brushed ineffectually at the new dust patches collected on the walk, then strode through the gates, past the temple of Apollo, and on into the heart of the Ortygia.

King Hieron's house was not a palace. It was a large and elegant mansion, set in a leafy quarter of the citadel, near the Council House. It didn't even have any guards outside it, and

Archimedes hesitated in the columned porch, wondering whether to knock on the door or wait for Dionysios outside. He glanced up and down the wide street. It was empty in the quiet morning light, so he knocked.

A middle-aged man in a red tunic opened the door at once and looked at him disapprovingly. "Your business?" he demanded.

"I, um," faltered Archimedes, "I was to see the regent this morning. Dionysios son of Chairephon told me to speak to him about a job. I'm a, um, engineer."

"Catapults," said the middle-aged man dismissively. "Your name is Archimedes? Very well, you're expected. Captain Dionysios is with the regent now, but they're busy. You'll have to wait."

Archimedes was ushered into the house and conducted to a vaulted anteroom which opened onto a garden. There were benches about the marble walls, and he sat down on one. The middle-aged man vanished back the way they'd come, leaving Archimedes to wonder if he was a doorkeeper; if so, he was a very abrupt and exalted one. But perhaps that's what slaves were like in kings' houses. Archimedes sighed and looked down at the marble floor. He scuffed it with a sandal, then took from his purse the piece of papyrus on which he'd fair-copied his calculations from the previous night, plus a few interesting thoughts he'd had that morning and wouldn't mind working on further. He wished he'd remembered to bring a pen and ink. He was looking about for something to use instead when he heard the sound of a flute.

Tenor aulos, he decided at once, set to the Lydian mode, playing a variation on a theme from an aria by Euripides. He listened to it intently for a couple of minutes: the player was good. The tune came to an end; there was a pause; and then the music began again, this time with a peculiarly breathy sound, skirting about the verge of dissonance. He grinned to himself: he recognized that sound. An aulos had a metal slide inside it which allowed a player to cover some of the fingerholes, and thus to play several different modes upon one instrument. This player had opened the slide which separated the fingerings of the Lydian and Hypolydian modes and was trying to play the notes between them. Archimedes had once tried the same thing himself. It had required some very tricky part-fingering, and it still hadn't worked.

He got to his feet and slouched out of the antechamber into the garden, following the music. He knew another way of playing those intermediate notes; he owed it to a fellow aulist to share it.

A passage led through a colonnade from the first garden into a second one. A fountain decorated with carved nymphs stood under a grape arbor, and there were roses flowering. On the edge of the fountain sat the flute player: a girl a year or two older than Philyra. Her black hair was caught up in a silver net, and she was wearing a rose-colored tunic fastened with a silver belt. But her hairnet was disarranged by the leather strap most aulists wore to support their cheeks during a long session, and she was so intent on her playing that she didn't notice Archimedes' arrival: she was a real aulist, not a decorative one. He wondered who she was. By her dress she was rich, but she was too young to be the king's wife and too old to be his daughter. Somebody's concubine, he decided. He coughed to attract her attention.

She lowered the aulos and frowned at him, irritated by the interruption. Her eyes were very black. In a moment, he thought, she'd tell him to go back to the public part of the house.

"It doesn't work," said Archimedes quickly. "But if you take your baritone aulos and set it to the Dorian mode, you can get the right effect if you avoid the B-flat."

Interest replaced the irritation in her eyes. She picked up a second aulos from the rim of the fountain beside her: it was an alto. "My other one's this," she said.

"Then set that to the Lydian mode and the tenor to the Dorian! But Lydian doesn't mix with Hypolydian, part-finger it as you will. When I tried it, I sounded even worse than you did."

She grinned. "Thank you for the compliment! Dorian's better?"

"Try it!"

"I will!" The girl shifted the slide on her tenor aulos, setting the instrument to the Dorian mode. She set the alto to the Lydian, raised both, and began to play the Euripides variation again. Her eyebrows rose; she played on to the end of the piece, shifting from one aulos to the other, from one mode to its neighbor, scattering the notes, bittersweet and sad. When she finished she set the flutes down and looked at him in surprised triumph. "You're right!" she exclaimed, and they grinned at each other.

Then she wiped the mouthpieces and asked, "Are you a professional?"

"What? Oh, flute player. No. I'm a mathematician." Then he bit his lip and corrected himself. "Engineer. I'm to see the regent about building some catapults."

"Catapults!" she exclaimed. "I wouldn't have expected someone who makes machines to be musical."

He shrugged. "Actually, it's a help. You have to tune them by ear."

"Catapults?"

"Mm, the strings. If a catapult's two sets of strings are out of tune with each other, the machine will shoot crooked when you come to fire it."

She laughed. "What do you do to tune them? Pluck them and tighten the key, like a lyre?"

"Exactly! Except you twist the strings, not the key. You have to use a windlass and wedges."

"I like that! The stringed instruments: lyre, kithara, harp, lute—and catapult. I suppose big ones have a low pitch, and small ones a high pitch?" He nodded, and she laughed again. "Somebody should write a catapult chorus," she declared. "For scorpions, ten-pounders, and thirty-pounders." She raised the auloi to her mouth again and piped a mad dance on three widely separated notes.

Archimedes grinned. "A friend of mine is trying to build an air-powered catapult," he said. "It could play the flute part. But I'm afraid that all it does is go bang, very loudly, so maybe it should be percussion."

"Oh, no!" she exclaimed, lowering her auloi and putting a hand over her mouth. "An air-powered catapult? Where was this, Alexandria?"

He laughed in surprise. "Yes!"

"It would be! They'll do anything in Alexandria. Since you've been there, tell me: I heard somebody there has built a machine which allows you to play thirty auloi simultaneously. Do you know—"

But Archimedes had broken into delighted laughter. "That's Ktesibios!" he exclaimed. "The same friend who's making the air-powered catapult. He calls the instrument a water-aulos. I helped him with it!"

The girl pulled off her cheek strap and put her instrument down. Her hair, disturbed from its net, dropped black curls around her face. "Does it work?" she demanded. "The—the multiple aulos, I mean. I don't see how it possibly can!"

"It's not really thirty auloi," Archimedes told her. "It's thirty pipes, but they only play one note each. Each is a different length, see, like the reeds in a syrinx. To sound them, you press a key which opens a valve in the bottom of the pipe. Air is forced up into the pipe by the pressure of water in a tank underneath. That's why it's called a water-aulos. See, you have this inverted hemisphere submerged in the water, and two tubes which—"

"A water-aulos," repeated the girl, tasting the new word: *hydraulis*. "What does it sound like?"

"More like a syrinx than an aulos. Louder, though, and richer-toned—almost bell-like. It can be heard above a crowd. The Alexandrians put one in the theater. I told Ktesibios he ought to call it a water-syrinx, but he preferred his own name for it."

"You said you helped to make it?"

"Mostly I just helped Ktesibios tune the pipes. He never actually had any training in music, though he's the most astonishingly ingenious man. He's—"

"Could you build one?"

Archimedes blinked.

"Not now," said the girl quickly. "I know there's a war, and it's more important to build catapults. But afterward, if there is an afterward—could you build me a water-aulos?"

Archimedes blinked again. "I'd love to," he told her. "But they're complicated. They—"

"You couldn't?"

"I—not that. They take a long time to build. I couldn't afford to do one cheap. Ktesibios charged sixteen hundred drachmae for his."

The girl did not look at all disappointed. "My brother likes music," she said. "And he *loves* ingenious machines. I'm sure he'd be willing to pay sixteen hundred drachmae for a water-aulos if you could make one."

"Your brother?" asked Archimedes, with a sudden horrible feeling that he knew who this was.

"Ah," she said, and her straight black brows came down. "You didn't realize. King Hieron."

"No," he said, feeling numb, "I didn't realize." He studied her a moment: the silver belt, the fine tunic. But he could not concentrate on the expensive clothes. His eyes kept sliding back to her round face with its black curls and brilliant dark eyes, and her strong musician's hands. He added accusingly, "You don't look old enough."

"He's my half brother, actually," she said. All the animation had left her face and voice, and she sounded the bored aristocrat. "He was almost grown up when our father married my mother."

King Hieron was a bastard, the result of a wealthy Syracusan's youthful indiscretion: all Syracuse knew that. Archimedes guessed that this girl must be the rich man's legitimate daughter. She was not of his class at all. He shouldn't really be here, in the private part of the house, talking to her. Syracuse allowed women more freedom than many other Greek cities, but still, it was grossly improper for a young man to slip into any private house and chat with the owner's unmarried sister, unintroduced and unsupervised, and this girl was the daughter of a nobleman and sister of a king. But he pulled his stained cloak straight and told himself defiantly that he was a democrat. "I can build a water-aulos," he declared. "If your brother's willing to pay for it, I'd love to build you one. I prefer wind instruments to stringed ones anyway."

At this she smiled again, a long slow grin, and he knew he'd said the right thing, and grinned back. "What's your name?" she asked.

He had just opened his mouth to reply when the answer was shouted at him—"Archimedes son of Phidias!"—in a tone of shocked disapproval. He and the girl turned together, and found four men bearing down on them. One was Dionysios, one the exalted doorkeeper, one a middle-aged workman, and the fourth, from his purple cloak, had to be the regent Leptines.

4

Archimedes stood staring at the regent stupidly, his mouth still open. The girl, however, was unalarmed. "Good health, Father!" she exclaimed, smiling at Leptines. "This gentleman plays the aulos. He was telling me a way to play the intermediate notes."

The regent was not appeased. He was a tall man, grim-faced and gray-haired. He stopped beside the fountain and gave Archimedes a scathing look.

Archimedes went crimson. He realized afterward that he probably should have been frightened, but at the time he was just excruciatingly embarrassed. Of all the idiotic ways to lose a job! "I, uh, I didn't know who was playing," he stammered defensively. "I didn't even realize it was a woman. I just, uh, heard the music, and I thought I'd share a trick with a fellow aulist. I didn't mean any disrespect, sir."

The regent appeared somewhat mollified at this, but he still asked icily, "Do you normally wander about the private parts of other men's houses uninvited, young man?"

"We're not in a private part of the house, Father!" exclaimed the girl. "We're in the garden."

"Delia, that's enough!" said Leptines severely. "Go to your rooms!"

Delia, thought Archimedes, stupidly pleased, even in the middle of everything, to have learned her name. He could not have asked it: it was almost as improper to ask a young lady's name as it was to talk to her unsupervised. Delia. "The Delian" was one of the titles of Apollo, the god most closely associated with mathematics. It seemed a good omen that the girl was named for his own patron divinity.

Delia did not go to her rooms; instead she wriggled more firmly into her place on the rim of the fountain. "I will *not* go if you're going to pretend I was doing something improper!" she snapped.

Archimedes was somewhat taken aback by this defiance, and more surprised still when Leptines merely rolled his eyes in ex-asperation and turned away from her. Girls were supposed to be obedient, and the heads of household were supposed to punish them if they weren't. But, of course, Leptines was not the head of Delia's household. Though she was calling him "Father," that was only courtesy: the regent was in fact merely her half brother's father-in-law, and it was her half brother who held the real au-thority.

"I wasn't doing anything wrong!" Delia insisted. "I was just sitting in the garden trying something tricky on the flute, and this young man—Archimedes, was it?—came up and gave me a tip on how to do it better. Herakles! Where's the impropriety in that?"

The regent looked even more exasperated at this, so Archi-medes said, "I am sorry, sir. I, uh, I realize now it was improper of me to have intruded here uninvited, and I, uh, sincerely apol-ogize for doing so. But, as I said, I had no idea who was playing, and at the time it seemed natural to share a trick with a fellow aulist."

"Very well," said the regent stiffly. "I accept your apology."

And that, surprisingly, seemed to be the end of the matter. Dionysios caught Archimedes' eye and raised his eyebrows: Ar-chimedes was uncertain whether the look was congratulatory or sympathetic. But he decided that it could not have been the captain who had called his name in that disapproving fashion; it must have been the exalted doorkeeper. He glanced at the doorkeeper, who still looked deeply disapproving, then at the fourth member of the party. This was a man of perhaps fifty, of average height, with graying brown hair and a deeply seamed face. He was dressed in a dusty cloak worn over a workman's apron, and he was scowling at Archimedes more ferociously than any of the others.

"Archimedes son of Phidias," said Leptines, still very stiffly, "I understand that you came here this morning looking to serve the city as an engineer."

"Yes, sir," agreed Archimedes earnestly. "Captain Dionysios said you wanted someone to build some stone-hurlers. I'm sorry if—"

"And I understand," Leptines interrupted, "that you claim to be able to build a one-talent catapult, although you have never, in fact, built any war machine at all."

Delia looked surprised; Archimedes was aware of it, and shot an apologetic glance toward her before replying, "Uh, that's right. You, uh, don't have to have actually built one so long as you understand the mechanical principles."

"Conceited rubbish!" exclaimed the workman, scowling still harder. "Experience is the most valuable part of mechanics. You have to develop a sense of how to do things, a wisdom in your hands. That comes only from making machines."

Archimedes looked at the workman again, and the workman glared back. The others were now watching the two of them, the regent and his doorkeeper like judges, Dionysios with an air of expectancy, and Delia as though she were intently following a play.

"Sir," said Archimedes respectfully, wondering who the workman was—he hoped not Eudaimon, the man in charge of providing the city with catapults, though he rather feared just that. "Sir, it's true that you have to have made machines to be able to make machines. I wouldn't quarrel with you on that. But you can't possibly mean to say that before you can make a particular *type* of machine you have to have made it already!" Delia grinned, and he was encouraged to continue. "I've made lots of machines. I know what works and what doesn't. As for catapults, I've seen them and studied them and I'm perfectly sure I can make them. I wouldn't be here otherwise. Didn't Captain Dionysios say that you don't have to pay me until you've seen the first catapult work?"

"Waste of wood, strings, and workshop time!" snarled the workman. He turned to Leptines. "Sir, you should throw this arrogant young fool out!"

"I would throw him out," said Leptines impatiently, "if you could promise to produce the catapults the king wants. But since you have failed to, and since he says he can, I am bound to let him try."

The workman's jaw set with indignation. So, thought Archimedes unhappily, the man *was* Eudaimon—and he plainly viewed Archimedes' appointment as an insult and a threat. The new job wasn't looking very secure.

But the regent turned back to Archimedes and said, "I am willing to authorize you to use the royal workshop to build a one-talent catapult. However, in view of your lack of experience, I am going to insist that if your machine doesn't work, not only will you not be paid for it, but I will require you to reimburse the workshop for the materials you have used."

"That's not fair!" Delia broke in indignantly. "The materials could be reused by somebody else!"

"Delia, be quiet!" commanded the regent.

"No!" she said angrily. "You're being unfair to him because he talked to me. You can't expect me to sit quiet for that!"

She cast a concerned glance toward Archimedes. He did not know what to feel in response: it was pleasing that she was worried about him, but humiliating that she so clearly expected him to fail. He pulled himself up straight, tossed his stained cloak back, and declared boldly, "Please don't be concerned, lady! My machine will work, so I don't mind agreeing to pay for the materials if it doesn't."

Eudaimon laughed harshly. "I hope you have money!" he told

Archimedes. "Do you have any idea how much wood and string a one-talenter will need?"

"Yes, I do," said Archimedes triumphantly. He took his sheet of calculations from his purse again, unfolded it, and offered it to the regent. "Here are the estimates."

Leptines stared at the papyrus with surprise, not touching it. Eudaimon, however, glared harder than ever, then snatched the sheet. "What is this nonsense?" he demanded, scanning it. "There's no way you could know what the diameter of the bore of a one-talenter should be! There isn't such a machine in the city!"

"The Alexandrians have come up with a formula," said Archimedes with satisfaction. "You probably wouldn't know it, because it's still new, but they did a lot of trials on it and it works. You take the weight to be thrown, multiply it by a hundred, take the cube root, add a tenth, and you get the diameter of the bore in finger-breadths."

Eudaimon sneered. "And what in the name of all the gods is a cube root?" he asked.

Archimedes blinked, too astonished to speak. The solution to the Delian problem, he thought, the keystone of architecture, the secret of dimension, the plaything of the gods. How could someone who was supposed to build catapults not know what a cube root was?

Eudaimon gave him a look of stark contempt. Then, deliberately, he crumpled up the sheet of papyrus, pretended to wipe his backside with it, and dropped it on the ground.

Archimedes gave a cry of outrage and jumped to rescue his calculations, but Eudaimon set his foot on the papyrus, and he was left tugging at the edge which stuck out from under the imprisoning sandal. "You think that you can make catapults because you know mathematics?" the chief catapult engineer demanded.

Archimedes, kneeling at his feet, still tugging at the crushed sheet, glared up at him. "Yes, by Zeus!" he exclaimed hotly. "In fact, I'd say it's perfectly evident that a man who *doesn't* know mathematics *can't* make catapults. *You* don't, and can't, or I wouldn't be here!"

Eudaimon, infuriated, kicked at him. The gesture was meant more as a threat than with any real intention of hitting him—but as soon as the foot shifted Archimedes lunged for his calculations, and the kick caught him squarely in the right eye. There was an explosion of red and green which seemed to lance up into his brain, and he collapsed, stunned. He clasped at his face with both hands and rolled back and forth on the ground, gasping with pain. Then he became fuzzily aware of people clustering around him and someone trying to pull his hands away from his face.

He had the papyrus in one fist, and he resisted.

"Come on!" said a man's voice—Captain Dionysios, he realized. "Let me see your eye."

At that Archimedes lowered his hands—though he kept firm hold of the papyrus—and Dionysios examined the injury gently. "Try to open your eye," he said. "Can you see?"

Archimedes blinked at him: the captain's face swam, clear on one side, blurred and reddened on the other. He groaned and put a hand over the blur. "Not clearly," he said. "You look red."

Dionysios sat back on his heels. "You're lucky. You could have lost the eye. No permanent harm done, though." He slapped Archimedes' shoulder and stood up.

Archimedes pulled himself up to a sitting position against the side of the fountain and nursed his eye again; it *hurt*. "By Apollo!" he muttered. He found Eudaimon with his good eye, standing back and looking embarrassed, and gave him a glare.

Delia suddenly bent over him. Without a word she slipped the crumpled papyrus out of his fingers and gave him a wet lump of leather instead. The cool wetness against his burning face was indescribably comforting. "Thank you!" he told her gratefully.

She noticed, however, that his good eye followed her a moment, and returned to the others only when he saw that she was not doing anything with his calculations.

The men began upon the incident's aftermath—Leptines rebuking Eudaimon; Eudaimon protesting that it had been an accident; Dionysios suggesting that he take his protégé out, and the protégé himself trying to get back to the subject of making catapults. Delia stood back and allowed them to get on with it. She uncrumpled the cracked piece of papyrus and looked at it. It held a drawing of a catapult, labeled with measurements, done in a precise and careful hand. She turned the sheet over: on the other side, in the same careful hand, were less intelligible sketches—cylinders, curved lines cut by straight ones, pairs of letters joined by squiggles or arrows—and some of the same numbers that had adorned the catapult. She frowned, then looked back at the young man propped up against the side of the fountain. Until that moment she had not really noticed him. She had been interested in what he told her about the intermediate notes on the aulos and excited by the water-aulos; she'd been pleased because he'd continued to speak to her naturally even after he'd discovered who her brother was; she'd been concerned that she might have got him into trouble. But she hadn't had any interest in who he was. Now she felt as though she'd stubbed her toe on a rock, and looked down to find that it was part of a buried city. He had guarded these incomprehensible squiggles more jealously than his own eyes, and she wondered what kind of mind would order its priorities so strangely.

Dionysios helped Archimedes to his feet; Leptines asked him if he was all right; Archimedes swore that he was. There was more discussion of catapult-making, and finally a price was set for the finished catapult if it worked—fifty drachmae. When this point had been resolved, Delia stepped forward and handed Archimedes his sheet of calculations. Archimedes bowed unsteadily, still pressing the wad of wet leather to his eye, wished the company joy, and wobbled off toward the door. Captain Dionysios followed him, caught his arm, and helped him out.

Delia waited. Leptines turned to her—then gave a sigh of resigned exasperation and strode off without saying anything. She had never been obedient, and he had long before given up trying to discipline her. Eudaimon bowed and stalked off in the opposite direction. The exalted doorkeeper waited until regent and engineer were gone, then crossed his arms and looked at Delia with his usual disapproving expression. "You want something," he said.

Delia felt herself flushing. The doorkeeper's name was Agathon, and he was a shrewd, sour man who missed nothing. He was a slave, but he had served her brother, Hieron, long before Hieron was a king, and his loyalty had won him an influence free men could only envy. Delia disliked his habit of guessing that she was going to ask him something before she asked it, but, like Hieron himself, she tolerated it because Agathon always knew more about what was happening in the city than anyone else in the house, including the king.

"Yes," she admitted. "That young man who was here—I want to know more about him."

Agathon's disapproval grew heavy enough to press olives. "A fine thing to ask!" he exclaimed. "The king's sister wants to know more about some brash young flute player!"

Delia made an impatient gesture. "Herakles, Agathon, not like that!"

"You, mistress, have no business being interested in wine-stained engineers!"

Delia sighed. "If Hieron were here, *he'd* be interested," she said.

Agathon's disapproving look lightened a little, and his eyes narrowed. "Eh?"

"Two things," said Delia, picking up her auloi and resting her chin on them. "First: he's confidently offered to make a bigger catapult than any machine in the city, even though he's never made a catapult before. You don't think that would interest Hieron?"

"Mmm," said Agathon, and waggled the fingers of one hand a little to show doubt. "There's no shortage of ignorant and conceited young men."

"Maybe—but before you and Father came up, he was talking

about catapults as confidently as he talked about auloi—and he *knew* auloi, Agathon: even you have to admit I couldn't be fooled on that."

"Boasting," said Agathon shortly. "Like many another man faced with a pretty girl. Second interesting thing about Archimedes son of Phidias?"

"He loved those calculations better than his eyes."

Agathon gave a sudden snort of laughter. "True son of his father, there. Phidias is supposed to have claimed that Euclid's *Elements* is a greater book than Homer's *Iliad*, and to have sacrificed to the gods in gratitude for some mathematical observation of the stars."

"You know something about him?"

"Most of Syracuse has heard of Phidias the Astronomer. Bit of an eccentric, bit of a reputation, see? Teaches, too: only man in the city who teaches advanced mathematics. The master studied with him for a little, oh, must be fifteen, twenty years ago now."

Delia stared. To Agathon, "the master" was always and exclusively Hieron. "I didn't know that!" she exclaimed.

"Why should you?" asked Agathon. "Long time ago, before he bought me, even. But the master's said a couple of times he wished he'd had more time to study mathematics with Phidias. He only had a couple of months, see? Then your father stopped paying the fees, and the master went into the army. I doubt Phidias even remembers him."

Delia nodded: she'd long known the story of how her father had paid for his bastard's education, but only until the boy was seventeen. Hieron had then been a year too young to join the army, but he'd been thrust into it anyway, and left to make his own way in the world—with spectacular results. "So why does Hieron regret not having studied longer?" she asked. "Was Phidias a very good teacher?"

"Don't think so," said Agathon. "No, it's that mathematics is useful to kings. War engines, surveying, building, navigation . . ." Agathon trailed off, staring at Delia, then lost his disapproving look completely and uncrossed his arms. "Very well!" he exclaimed. "You're right: he'd be interested in Archimedes son of Phidias. If that fellow's confidence is well founded, he's valuable."

Delia nodded.

"I'll see what I can find out," said Agathon. Then he looked at Delia again and asked, "And?"

He'd done it again. Delia sighed. "How much would you trust Eudaimon?" she asked.

"Ah," said Agathon, face relaxing to something as close to geniality as it was ever likely to attain. "You mean, do I think he's going to try to sabotage your dusty musician's one-talent catapult?"

Delia didn't answer for a moment. To suggest that Eudaimon would deliberately disable a machine which was potentially of great value to the defense of the threatened city was to accuse him of treason. "I don't know him very well," she said at last, humbly. "Father's been cursing him ever since Hieron went away, he's obviously furious to have a rival, and I don't like him—that's all."

Agathon shrugged. "He's a man that's worked all his life and never been much good at what he works at. He's the worst of the master's engineers, which is why he's here and not at Messana. He's bitter and he's tired, he's getting old, and he's clinging to his position by his fingernails. He doesn't want some Alexandrian-educated mathematical flute player traipsing in and showing him up—that much is certain. And I think he'll convince himself that that catapult would fail anyway, but still want to make sure it does. Yes, I think if he gets the opportunity to sabotage that catapult, he'll take it. You want me to ensure he doesn't get that opportunity."

"Isn't that what Hieron would want you to do?" she asked innocently.

Agathon gave another snort of laughter. "You and the master!" he said affectionately. "I don't know where it comes from. Can't be from your mothers, because you don't share 'em, but it can't be from your father, because he was a fool."

Delia smiled and got to her feet. "Can you do it?" she asked eagerly. "Without actually accusing Eudaimon of anything, I mean."

"Oh, yes!" said Agathon comfortably. "Few words in the ear of the foreman at the workshop. He knows who I am. He'll keep an eye on the catapult and Eudaimon both, and report anything suspicious. You want me to have a word with the regent as well?"

Delia nodded. "But," she added nervously, "don't tell him I . . ."

". . . have any interest in wine-stained players of the aulos. No."

"It would be misunderstood," said Delia, blushing.

"I hope so," said Agathon, with a return of the disapproving look. "I certainly hope that what he understood would be mistaken."

DIONYSIOS SON OF CHAIREPHON HELPED ARCHIMEDES from the king's house as far as the temple of Athena on the main road. There he stopped. "I'm headed for the barracks," he said, gesturing to the left, "but I think you'd better go home and lie down for a bit," gesturing right, toward the Achradina. "Eudaimon caught you pretty hard."

"He's a bugger-arsed idiot!" said Archimedes, with deep feeling. "By Apollo! Builds catapults and doesn't even know what a cube root is! Who's the *real* engineer for Syracuse?"

"Kallippos," said Dionysios at once. "A gentleman of good family and better skill. But he's with the king at Messana. The king thought Eudaimon could manage what there was to do here in the city, but there was more to be done than we realized. Wait here—I'll call your friend Straton and tell him to help you home."

Archimedes shook his head—cautiously, because his eye hurt if he moved it suddenly—and began turning his lump of wet leather to find a cool spot in it. "I'd rather go to the workshop and order my wood," he said. The leather suddenly unfolded and revealed itself as a long wide strap. Archimedes blinked at it: it was a shape he knew well. "Oh," he said blankly. "She's spoiled her cheek strap." Then he realized that he now had an excuse to see her again—to give her a new cheek strap—and despite the ache in his eye, he beamed. He folded the leather carefully and set it tenderly back in place.

"Do you really play the aulos?" asked Dionysios curiously.

"Of course I do!" said Archimedes, surprised. "You don't think the king's sister would have spoken to me for two seconds otherwise, do you?"

"I hoped not," replied Dionysios, relieved that his new associate realized when a girl was out of reach. "And, my friend, you should not have spoken to her at all. When I saw you chatting with her there in the garden, I not only expected you to be sent off at once, but I thought I was likely to be in trouble myself for inviting you there in the first place. *Nai* by Zeus, you were lucky you confined yourself to flutes! Well, if you're really going to the workshop, I can show you the way: it's right next to the barracks."

The royal catapult workshop was a big dirt-floored barn near the tip of the Ortygia promontory, secured by the same enclosing wall as the barracks of the Ortygia garrison. It was full of beams and presses and saws, and a forge jutted from one wall. The sides were stacked high with timber and iron, bronze and copper, oily boxes of sinew and of women's hair—the last the most favored material for stringing a catapult, a source of sorrow to slave girls and useful income to poor women. About a dozen people were busily at work about the room, some clustered around an arrow-firing catapult which stood half assembled in the center of the building, others making catapult bolts and heel plates. There was a smell of sawdust, glue, charcoal, and hot metal. Archimedes stopped in the doorway and took a deep breath of the scent, then smiled: it was a good smell, the smell of making. He wished Dionysios joy and strode forward eagerly to find the foreman and place his own order for wood.

~

~ MARCUS SPENT MOST OF THAT DAY DIGGING OUT THE latrines—a job too heavy for young Chrestos to manage easily on his own, and thus one which had been postponed since the beginning of the summer. In the Sicilian heat the delay had made the job even fouler than it would have been ordinarily, but he set about it stoically, and carted the night soil off on a borrowed donkey.

At evening, when he returned from dumping the last load, he found his master in the sickroom, just arrived back, cloakless, with an aulist's cheek strap tied over one eye, but enormously cheerful. A knot of unease that had been situated somewhere between his shoulders unraveled. He was only too keenly aware of what would happen to the household slaves if the young master failed to get a job.

Archimedes was happily telling the assembled family about the royal catapult workshop when Marcus came silently to the door. "They weren't very helpful this morning. They just pointed me at the stores and left me to my own devices. I thought that was fine—you should see the stores! Top-quality Epirot oak in any thickness you like, and a dozen sorts of glue! But about noon the king's doorkeeper came in to check that I had everything I needed, and after that they realized I was official. After that they set about doing anything I asked. It's amazing how much it speeds things up. I thought it was going to take me a month to make this catapult, and I was cursing the pay. But with this sort of help I can do it in a week."

"But how much is the pay?" asked Philyra anxiously. Marcus looked at her approvingly: it was what he was very anxious to know himself, but hadn't quite dared to ask, in front of his owners and still stinking of latrines.

"Fifty drachmae," said her brother, with satisfaction.

"Fifty!" cried Philyra, her eyes lighting. "Medion, fifty in a *month* would be good pay; fifty in a week . . . !"

Archimedes nodded, grinning. He had not thought fifty a

month good pay, but he supposed he'd been spoiled by the water-snails.

"You don't have to pay for the supplies out of that?" asked Arata anxiously.

Her son nodded. "I don't need to pay for the supplies unless the machine doesn't work. And you don't need to worry about *that*, Mama: I know what I'm doing."

Marcus frowned, suddenly anxious again, and Philyra caught some restless movement he made and glanced over. Their eyes met, and each recognized in the other the same anxiety: how much did the supplies for a one-talenter *cost?* This worry, however, was almost immediately eclipsed. "What happened to your eye?" asked Arata, and Archimedes told them about Eudaimon, then, obedient to their urging, took off the cheek strap.

The area around the eye had by this time turned blue-purple and swollen up, and, even worse, the white of the eye itself had turned red, and a veil of blood hung across the light brown iris. "Medion!" cried Philyra in horror. "You ought to sue him for assault!"

Archimedes just shrugged. "I'm going to stay away from him as much as I can," he said.

"Absolutely right," said his mother approvingly. "He's senior to you, and you don't want trouble." She frowned, sniffed, and glanced around at Marcus. "Oh, it's you," she said. "Go and wash."

Marcus bobbed his head and retreated back into the courtyard. He was engaged in cleaning himself when Philyra came out of the old workroom, still frowning. She paused when she noticed him, then came over resolutely. Marcus at once pulled his dripping tunic back on, embarrassed to be naked in front of the young mistress.

"How much do the supplies for a one-talent catapult cost?" asked Philyra.

"I don't know," Marcus admitted. "The strings would be the worst of it. They sell prepared hair by the drachma weight, and for a one-talenter you must have to buy it by the pound."

Philyra was silent for a moment. "He *can* build it—can't he?" she asked at last.

"He's good," said Marcus flatly. "He can."

Philyra studied him a moment, then let out a long unsteady breath. "I don't know anyone else who makes machines."

He nodded; naturally she had no way of judging her brother's skill. "In Alexandria," he informed her, "the best engineer in the city offered him a partnership. He wouldn't take it, of course—it wasn't geometry—but he could have had it if he'd wanted. He's exceptional. This fellow Eudaimon's absolutely right to be worried. Mistress, the only worries *I* have are about what happens if something outside your brother's control goes wrong."

She let out another long breath, looking at him closely, trying to determine how far she would trust his word. Then she smiled, relaxing. "Medion left his cloak at the workshop."

"At least we know where he left it," said Marcus. "In Alexandria I was always having to run all over the Museum looking for it."

She giggled. The sweet soft sound seemed to bubble a moment in his heart. "Fifty drachmae a week!" she repeated reverently, smiling over it. "We could buy back the vineyard! And I . . ."

She stopped herself. The vineyard sold to pay for her brother's Alexandrian education should have been her dowry, but she had always tried very hard not to acknowledge that painful fact. Her father, she knew, had hoped to save a new dowry for her from his earnings, but his savings had all been eaten away during his illness. She was of an age to marry, she had school friends who were married already, but with no dowry she was unlikely to find a bridegroom. That was a humiliation she tried not to think about, and not the sort of thing a young lady should confide to a household slave. She scowled at Marcus, who was waiting, his face open and alive, for her to finish her sentence.

Marcus abruptly understood how that sentence would have ended, and busied himself by bending down for his bucket of dirty water. Of course. He had silently disapproved of the vine-

yard sale precisely because it had seemed to him to cheat the
daughter of the house of an essential in order to pay for a luxury
for the son. But now he found that he was in no hurry to see
Philyra dowried and married off. He would miss her. No need
to worry yet, though. It would take some time to amass a dowry
for her, even at the rate of fifty drachmae a week. And with the
war . . .

He was determined not to think about the war. "If you'll excuse me, mistress," he muttered, and went to tip the water over
the scraggle of pot herbs by the door. Philyra watched him a
moment in surprise, taken aback by the way he had pulled off a
sore subject unprompted. She had not thought he had either the
sensitivity or the wit.

~ THE FOLLOWING MORNING ARCHIMEDES SET OFF EARLY
for the catapult workshop. Philyra, setting out to do the shopping
about midmorning, found only Marcus in the courtyard: Agatha,
who normally accompanied her, was helping her mother in the
kitchen, and the boy Chrestos had exercised his talent at making
himself scarce when he was needed. She looked at Marcus a
moment, thoughtfully, then clapped her hands to summon him
over and handed him the basket.

Walking behind her along the narrow street in the morning
sun, looking at her straight back, respectably swathed in a white
woolen cloak, Marcus found his steps light with an unaccustomed
happiness. Philyra was starting to trust him a little. He prayed
silently that the gods would offer him the opportunity to prove
his honesty. He kept his eyes firmly shut to the reason he wanted
her good opinion: there was nothing to be had there, except pain.
Getting that good opinion, winning her trust and liking—that was
a pleasure no one could deny him.

They went first to the baker's, and then to the greengrocer's
shop around the corner. The groceress, a thin shrewish woman
named Praxinoa, looked at them warily. Philyra bought some
leeks and some olives, and paid for the goods with one of her

brother's Egyptian silver pieces. The groceress studied the money a moment before putting it in her box and taking out the change. "How's your brother settling in?" she asked Philyra, with an eagerness that surprised the girl.

"Very well," Philyra told her; then, eager for the neighbors to appreciate the family's improved status, went on, "He's found work already. He's building catapults for the king."

"Catapults, is it?" asked the groceress. "Huh." She glanced around, then leaned closer to her customer and said in a low voice, "Perhaps that explains it, then. I had a fellow in here just before you came, asking about your brother."

"What?" asked Philyra, startled and alarmed. "Who?"

"I don't know who," said Praxinoa, with relish. "Never seen him before. He wasn't anybody from the neighborhood. He was smartly dressed, though. Official, I thought. Must be because of those catapults. They're strategic, aren't they?" Her eyes glittered, hungry for scandal.

"Yes," said Philyra, trying to sound resolute, though her heart had speeded up. In Syracuse, official interest could be very, very dangerous. "They probably ask about everyone who works in the catapult workshop."

"They do in Alexandria," put in Marcus dismissively. "Saw it there, too."

Praxinoa subsided, disappointed. "Learned about catapults in Alexandria, did he?"

Outside the shop again, Philyra looked at Marcus angrily. "You think it really was somebody from the king, because of the catapults?"

"I can't think of anything else it would be," Marcus told her.

Anger gave way to anxiety—and embarrassment at asking advice from a household slave. "Did people come and ask about him in Alexandria too?"

Marcus shrugged. "No. But in Alexandria he wasn't allowed in the royal workshops. King Ptolemy thinks a lot of his catapults, and never allows foreigners anywhere near 'em. Archimedes looked at some machines on the wall with his engineer friend, that was all. But catapults *are* strategic. I don't think this is anything to worry about."

Philyra nodded, but she was still frowning as they walked on. Phidias had never attracted any disquieting official interest. Of course, Phidias had never earned fifty drachmae in a week, either. Things were changing. She wished she felt more confident that all the changes would be for the good.

ARCHIMEDES WAS OBLIVIOUSLY ENJOYING THE WORK-shop. In the past he had always made his machines himself, assisted frequently by Marcus and occasionally by an unskilled slave lent for a particular task: there had always been a great deal of sawing, hammering, and blistered hands in between the *interesting* parts of machine-making. Now he only needed to say "I want a beam *this* big to be joined to *that* beam with tenons," or "I need an iron heel plate *this* shape to fit *that* aperture," and within an hour, there it would be. It removed the drudgery from machine-making and left only the agreeable inventive side.

He wore a linen patch over his eye for his first few days in the workshop, tying it on with Delia's cheekstrap. He had already resolved to give the king's sister her new cheek strap when he went to the house to announce the catapult's completion; in the meantime, it gave him a secret thrill each time he tied on the old one. He did not tell his family where he'd acquired the little leather strap, however. He thought they would disapprove.

He followed his own advice and tried to stay out of Eudaimon's way. It was impossible to do this entirely, of course. They were sharing the same workshop and the services of the same carpenters. But Eudaimon seemed as happy to avoid speaking to Archimedes as Archimedes was to avoid speaking to him, and for some days all proceeded peacefully. Archimedes made a trip to the nearer forts on the city wall, looking for a catapult whose dimensions he could copy. He eventually fixed on a fifteen-pounder with a particularly vigorous and accurate throw, and corrected the estimated dimensions of his own machine accordingly. The fact that his original was much smaller than his copy raised a few problems, which he enjoyed solving. The one-talenter would have an eighteen-foot arm span and be nearly thirty feet long; it was too heavy and too powerful to aim or draw by conventional methods, and he had to devise systems of pulleys and winches for it. That was fun.

Eudaimon paid no attention to what his rival was doing until Archimedes had been working on the catapult for four days and was ready to balance the stock on the stand. Then the chief catapult engineer came up and watched in silence as the beam— thick enough for a ship's mainmast, and still only partially finished—was suspended above its tripodal stand by a system of ropes and lowered carefully. When Archimedes signaled the workmen to stop lowering and secure their ropes, however, Eudaimon stiffened. With the beam dangling just above the pin, Archimedes began to thread about it the first of his aiming devices.

"What's that?" asked Eudaimon harshly.

Archimedes glanced at him—a process that involved turning his whole body, since his eye was still bandaged—then went on threading his pulleys. "It's to help it pivot," he said.

"There's nothing like that on the fifty-pounders at the Euryalus fort!" snapped Eudaimon. He sounded affronted by it.

"Isn't there?" said Archimedes, mildly surprised. "How do they pivot, then?"

"Didn't you look?" said Eudaimon.

Archimedes shook his head. Biting his tongue with concentration, he threaded a rope around a pulley set into the stand, looped it through the attachment on the stock, and fixed it back on the stand, to a windlass. Only when he'd made it fast did he realize that Eudaimon hadn't answered his question, and look back.

Eudaimon was still standing behind him, staring at him with a mixture of shock and outrage. "What's the matter?" asked Archimedes.

"You didn't look at the fifty-pounders in the Euryalus?" asked the chief catapult engineer.

"No," said Archimedes. "It's a long walk out there, and I found a machine I liked much closer."

"But they're the closest in size to what you're trying to build!"

"Yes," said Archimedes, "but I'd still have to scale them up, and it's just as easy to scale up a fifteen-pounder. How do they pivot?"

There was a silence. Then the workshop foreman, Epimeles— a big, slow, soft-spoken man in his forties—said, "They don't. To aim them you have get a few strong lads to move the stand."

"Well, that's stupid!" observed Archimedes. He began threading his second pulley. There would be one on either side of the catapult. The operator would turn a windlass on the side required and use a third windlass to adjust the elevation.

He paid no attention when one of the workmen sniggered, but looked up sharply at the sound of a blow and a cry of pain. He was just in time to see Eudaimon striding off and one of the workman clutching his ear. Archimedes dropped his rope and dashed after the chief. Eudaimon stopped abruptly and spun about, his seamed face black with anger.

"You had no business hitting that man!" Archimedes told him furiously.

"I will not be laughed at in my own workshop by my own slaves!" Eudaimon shouted back.

"They're not your own slaves, they're the city's. You had no business hitting him! And anyway, what was it to you? It's not as though you'd made those fifty-pounders!"

"I'm in charge here!" declared Eudaimon. "I can have that fellow flogged if I like. Maybe I do like. Elymos! Come here!"

The man he had struck stepped back in alarm, and the other workmen stared at the chief in horror.

"You don't dare!" cried Archimedes in outrage. "I won't let you!" He turned to the foreman. "You run up the road and tell the regent about this!"

"Do you think Leptines wants to be bothered with a squabble in the workshop?" said Eudaimon.

"He will if he has any decency!" replied Archimedes. "He's in charge, and nobody should allow people to go about flogging people when they haven't done anything wrong!"

"I will tell the regent," said the foreman decisively, and turned to go.

The foreman was as much a slave as the rest of the workmen, but he was a valuable, experienced, and trusted slave, and his word carried some weight even in the king's house. Eudaimon started in alarm and ordered, "Stop!"

Epimeles turned back and looked at Eudaimon levelly. "Sir," he said, "you and . . . this gentleman are both authorized to use the workshop. If you say Elymos is to be punished, and he says he is not, surely it's for our master to tell us which one of you to obey?"

"I am in charge!" grated Eudaimon.

"In that case the regent will tell us to obey you and flog Elymos," said the foreman quietly.

There was another silence, and then Eudaimon said, "I never gave any such order." He glared at them all. "You all know that! I never gave any such order." He turned on his heel and walked off.

The foreman let out his breath slowly. Elymos gave a whistle of relief and sat down, and his friends thumped him on the shoulder. Archimedes thought of thumping the slave's shoulder too, but refrained: he was aware that the threat of flogging had been made only because of him.

"Are you all right?" he asked instead, coming over.

Elymos nodded and grinned up at him. "Thank you, sir," he said. "I'll remember how you stood up for me."

"You shouldn't have laughed," Epimeles told him sternly, coming over as well.

Elymos ducked his head appeasingly: Eudaimon might order floggings, but Epimeles was the person who was really in charge of the workshop. "Couldn't help it! It was funny!" protested Elymos.

"But it wasn't even his fault that those fifty-pounders can't pivot," said Archimedes. "He didn't build them."

At this Elymos laughed again, more loudly this time. "That makes it even funnier!"

Some of the other workmen laughed as well. Archimedes stared, perplexed, and they nudged one another and giggled among themselves. Archimedes realized that the laughter was directed at himself, and flushed. He went back to his catapult and began rethreading the ropes in hurt silence. People had always laughed, were always laughing, at him. He got lost in his geometry and didn't notice things, or he got excited about things they didn't understand, and they laughed. Even slaves he had defended were laughing at him.

Elymos leaped up and followed him. "Oh, sir, don't be offended!" he said. "It's just a workshop joke, that's all."

"Well, I don't get it!" said Archimedes angrily.

The slave sniggered again, then, at a sharp glance, looked solemn. "Sir, I couldn't explain it. Not to you. Jokes are never funny if you explain them. But please don't be offended, sir. It's just a . . . a slaves' joke, that's all." He hurriedly took the third rope and tried to thread it around a pulley.

"Not that one!" Archimedes told him hastily. "That goes on top. No—no, leave it! Go fetch me the chalk, if you want to be helpful!"

The foreman, Epimeles, watched for a little while as the massive beam was set down upon the joint pin in its stand. Archimedes had calculated the approximate area of equilibrium and ordered a series of holes drilled along it. The stock was found to balance best upon the middle one: Epimeles smiled. He watched for a minute longer as the huge machine pivoted left and right in response to the windlasses—then sighed and reluctantly left the building. He had a long walk before him.

~ IT WAS DUSK WHEN EPIMELES GOT BACK TO THE ORTYGIA, but he did not go directly to the barracks next to the workshops, where he and the other workmen lived. Instead he went to the king's house and knocked upon the door.

Agathon opened it—that was his job, after all—and regarded the workshop foreman with displeasure. "Your business?" he demanded.

"Came to show you something," replied Epimeles calmly.

Agathon snorted and invited him in.

The doorkeeper had a lodge beside the door, a small but comfortable room with a couch and a carpet and a stone water cooler against the interior wall. Epimeles sat down on the end of the couch with a sigh of relief and began rubbing his calves. "Walked up to the Euryalus and back this afternoon," he commented. "I could do with a cup of wine."

Agathon looked even more disapproving than usual, but took a jar from beside the wall, poured some into two cups, and added some water, fresh and chill from the stone. "Why should I be interested that you were up at the Euryalus?" he asked, sipping.

Epimeles drank most of his wine off at once, then set the cup down. "Because I went up there for that engineer you told us to look after," he said. "I found this." He opened the small sack he'd been carrying and brought out a coil of fine cord. It was divided into sections by a series of regular knots, which had been dyed red or black.

Agathon inspected it straight-faced, then said, "There's something peculiar about a fort having a measuring line, is there?"

Epimeles pulled a second measuring line out of the sack. It was seemingly identical to the first, but older, fraying a little and discolored. He stretched the two cords out side by side, and it was immediately apparent that they weren't identical after all: the new cord's divisions were shorter than the old one's. "This one's mine," said Epimeles, touching the old cord. "It's accurate."

Agathon looked at the two cords expressionlessly.

"You know that when you're building a catapult, the essential thing is to make all the parts stand in exactly the right proportion to the diameter of the bore?" coaxed Epimeles. "You get a catapult that works, and you measure it, and then you either reproduce it exactly or scale it up or down."

"I believe I'd heard that," said Agathon. He did not, in fact, know very much about catapults, but he had no intention of admitting it—and he understood enough to grasp the implication of the cord. "You're suggesting that Eudaimon left this"—he touched the new measuring cord—"at the Euryalus, so that anyone who took measurements of the machines there would get the wrong figures, and any catapult built in imitation wouldn't work?"

Epimeles nodded. "See," he said, "the two fifty-pounders up at the Euryalus are the biggest catapults in the city at the moment. Eudaimon assumed that Archimedes would measure them, then guess at the increases necessary to make them throw the extra ten pounds: it's the way he'd have gone about designing a one-talenter himself. This afternoon it came out that Archimedes couldn't be bothered to walk up to the Euryalus and took his measurements from some little fifteen-pounder close by. Eudaimon was . . ." The foreman hesitated, picking his words, then said, ". . . outraged, shocked, and *disappointed*. When I saw that, I thought I'd go up to the Euryalus and see what he'd been up to—and sure enough, I found this, in the storeroom where the gear's kept. The lads at the fort all agree that it was just where their old one was, but that it's new, and they don't know how it got there. But they remember Eudaimon coming up there in the afternoon four days ago."

"I see," said Agathon grimly.

It wasn't evidence to convict a man of treason: they both knew that. But it could be an underminer, a question mark, a stone in the shoe. It could hurt Eudaimon.

Epimeles shifted the cord toward the doorkeeper. "I thought you should look after it."

Agathon nodded thoughtfully and picked up the false measur-

ing cord. He began winding it about his hand. "I'm surprised you
went all the way up to the Euryalus to look for it," he said. The
fortress lay at the extreme point of the city wall, six miles from
the Ortygia.

At that Epimeles grinned. "I would have gone twice as far if
it'd help get your lad put in charge of catapults. It will, won't it?"

Agathon looked up in surprise.

"Well, you know he's good!" said Epimeles, surprised at the
question on his face. "You told us to look after him and make
sure nobody interfered with his one-talenter, and we realized why
pretty quickly. He's so good he doesn't even realize how good
he is. That one-talenter—you know what he's done with it? The
little fifteen-pounder he copied can be pivoted, of course, so he
thought up a system with windlasses so that his will pivot as well.
When I told him that the fifty-pounders at the Euryalus don't
pivot, he just looked surprised and said, 'Well, that's stupid!' "

Epimeles laughed. Agathon looked at him sourly and asked,
"Is it?"

"People will say so now, won't they? But nobody ever used to
expect anything bigger than a forty-pounder to pivot. Archimedes
has just invented an entirely new system for aiming big machines—and he doesn't even realize! It was easier for him to
design it than it was to walk up to the Euryalus and have a look
at how other people did it. Some of the lads laughed about that,
and he didn't even understand why. Zeus! I almost feel sorry for
Eudaimon. He's never built a catapult that wasn't copied piece
by piece from another catapult, and when he can't get definitive
measurements—and on the big machines, each one is a bit different—he guesses and he struggles and he runs all over the city
trying to find out what the right figure is. Archimedes sits down
and scribbles for half an hour and has the perfect number there
in his hand. Zeus!" he said again. "Eudaimon's like some little
local athletics teacher who trains hard every year and toils to
come third or fourth in the city games—and he's trying to race
against a fellow who could take the crown at Olympia and barely

raise a sweat. He's not good enough to compete in the same event. He's not even good enough to realize that!"

"So he cheats," said Agathon sourly.

" 'Course he does," agreed Epimeles. "Mind you, he would against any opponent, and I can't entirely blame him. When he loses this job, where will he go? He's got family, too, depending on him."

"You're *almost* sorry for him?"

The foreman looked down. "No," he said, quietly, "I *am* sorry for him. But I don't want him in charge. Nobody likes building catapults that are feeble, or kick over, or can't shoot straight. That one-talenter, now—that will be a real Zeus, a hurler of thunderbolts. You can feel it when you look at it. It sort of pulls the whole workshop in around it like a whirlpool and it makes my hair stand up to touch it." He paused, then added, "And don't worry. Nobody's going to hurt that machine now. The lads and I will see to that."

"Has Archimedes asked you to guard it?"

Epimeles looked offended. "You think we need him to ask us? A divine thing like that? That catapult is our work as well! But no, he hasn't asked us. I don't think he's even noticed that he's putting Eudaimon out of a job, and it's never occurred to him that Eudaimon would ruin the catapult to hurt him. He doesn't notice Eudaimon much. He doesn't notice people much anyway, and when it's a person he doesn't like he notices him even less. He's pleasant enough when he does notice, though, and he treats the lads decently. I'll have no trouble working with him." He grinned at the prospect, and finished his cup of wine. "Will you show *that*"—he gestured at the measuring cord—"to the regent?"

Agathon sucked his teeth thoughtfully for a minute, then shook his head. He had a low opinion of Leptines. "I'll wait for the master to come home," he said. "He'll be very interested."

5

The catapult was completed in the middle of the morning four days later. It crouched in the center of the workshop like a predatory insect: a long low stock like an abdomen perched upon the three-legged stand, and at the far end, the great bowlike arms stretched wide like a praying mantis striking. The single eye of the aperture between those arms had the unblinking stare of death. When Archimedes winched back the string—an arm-thick leather cable—it gave a groan like a giant waking; when he released it, the clap of the ironclad arms against the iron heel plates was like the shattering of mountains. The workmen cheered and stroked the beast's bronze-plated back and wooden sides.

Archimedes had expected the machine to be finished that morning, but still he stood back and contemplated it with delight: his first catapult. "It's a beauty," he told Epimeles.

"The finest I've ever seen," the foreman agreed. Archimedes looked at him in surprise: he knew that Epimeles had been in the workshops for over twenty years, and he hadn't thought the man was given to flattery. Then he looked back at the one-talenter and grinned: best in twenty years or not, it *was* a beauty.

"Well," he said, and picked up the cloak he had brought along that morning in the expectation of another visit to the king's house. "I'll go tell the regent it's done, shall I? And ask him where he wants it, and when he wants the trial. But . . ." He dug in his purse. "Why don't you and the lads buy yourselves a drink to celebrate?"

"Thank you, sir—not yet," said Epimeles at once. "After the trials, sir, would be better."

Disappointed, Archimedes put his money back in the purse: he suspected that for all the flattery, Epimeles wasn't certain the machine would work. He sighed and walked off a bit disconsolately.

"What was wrong with a drink to celebrate?" asked Elymos, who was fond of wine.

"The gods hate arrogance," replied Epimeles. "We haven't got it safely through its trial yet. You want somebody to tamper with it while we're busy drinking?" He patted the huge machine with loving awe.

~ ARCHIMEDES RECOVERED HIS GOOD HUMOR ON THE walk to the king's house. The week just past had been thoroughly enjoyable. It had been fun making the one-talenter, and things were well at home: his father actually seemed to have recovered a little. Perhaps it was just not having to worry about when his son would return, but Phidias was sitting up in bed, drinking barley broth three times a day, and taking an interest in things. He listened to the music the rest of the family played for him, he discussed Alexandria with his son, he even played a bit with the puzzle. Archimedes decided that it would help again when he himself got a salaried position as a royal engineer; it would take another burden off his father's mind. Well, that should now happen as soon as the catapult had proved itself.

And now—now he would see Delia again. Archimedes fingered the small package he'd stowed in a fold of his cloak, the new cheek strap and the old one, and walked faster.

He had no serious expectation that there could be anything between himself and the king's sister. But he had no expectations about anything: he was living in the present and trying not to think of the future, which held at best a life of drudgery and at worst the horrors of defeat in war. Delia was a pretty girl. She was clever, she had made him laugh, and she played the aulos very well. Today he would see her again and give her a gift: what more could he ask for? He began to whistle an old song as he walked, letting the words run through his mind:

> Aphrodite in your gown of brightly varied hues,
> Zeus's wile-weaving child, immortal lady:
> My soul with grief and cares subdued,
> Don't break me!
>
> But come to me now, if ever, much-desired,
> you heeded what I sang to you in prayer
> and left your father's house as I required
> to save me,
>
> Golden your chariot yoked, and you all fair,
> Swift sparrows drew about the black earth,
> Wingbeats thickly whirling through the air
> from heaven . . .
>
> . . . to ask what next my mad heart longs for,
> who now shall I bring to love you? . . .

He reached the house and stopped whistling as he walked the last steps through the porch and up to the door. He straightened his cloak—the new yellow one, finally clean of lampblack—took a deep breath, and knocked.

The doorkeeper opened it at once and surveyed him with the usual expression of disapproval. "Your business?" he snapped.

"I've come to tell the regent that the catapult is finished!" said Archimedes triumphantly.

"Huh!" snorted Agathon. "The regent's out. I'll give him your message when he comes home."

Archimedes stood on the doorstep, crimson with embarrassment. He saw that he'd expected to be received like a victorious general—and he saw how stupid that had been. The one-talenter was, after all, only one catapult among several hundred owned by the city, and all the catapults in Syracuse were only a portion of the regent's responsibilities. Stupid! Still, out of some confused loyalty to his machine and the workshop that had produced it, he stammered, "C-could you tell me where the regent is, or when he's likely to be home?"

Agathon raised his eyebrows. "No," he said flatly—then, relenting a little, he explained, "Last night he had a message from the king. We have won a victory over the Romans at Messana, and King Hieron is lifting the siege and returning to Syracuse. He should arrive home tomorrow. The regent is likely to be extremely busy until he does. I'll give him your message as soon as I can."

"Oh!" said Archimedes, blinking stupidly and trying to take it in. Syracuse had defeated the Romans at Messana—Syracuse was actually *winning* the war? Praise to all the gods! But if Syracuse had won, why lift the siege of Messana and come home? Surely, if you won, you pressed the siege and took the city?

He shook himself and looked back at Agathon; something about the doorkeeper's face prevented him from asking for an explanation. Instead he returned confusedly to the subject which had brought him there. "I, uh, hope you *can* tell the regent soon," he said earnestly. "You see, the one-talenter—it's in the middle of the workshop, and it takes up a lot of space. We need to put it somewhere else, and we need to know where. Also, I don't get paid and can't start any more until it's been seen to work."

"I will tell the regent as soon as I can," the doorkeeper said shortly, then leaned back against the doorpost, crossed his arms, and gave Archimedes a cynical look. "And?" he said expectantly.

Archimedes licked his lips, wondering how the doorkeeper had known he wanted something else, and how to tell him what without appearing to be disrespectful. He fingered the package in the fold of his cloak. "I, uh," he began nervously. "The, uh, last time I was here I hurt my eye. The, uh, king's sister was kind enough to give me her aulos cheek strap soaked in water to put on it. I wanted to return the strap to her, and to thank her for her kindness." He fumbled the package out—a neat little bundle wrapped in a sheet of papyrus—and showed it to Agathon.

Agathon looked at him expressionlessly, debating whether to take the package and promise to deliver it and the thanks: the prospect of watching this young hopeful's face fall was tempting. But he decided against it. He had been deeply impressed by what Epimeles had told him about Archimedes' abilities, though the admiration he felt was all for Delia, not for the man she'd spotted. Hieron, too, could always pick out men who'd be useful, and Agathon found the skill wonderful. Delia, he decided, deserved to hear how her discovery was getting on. "Very well," he said tolerantly. "This way."

He showed the visitor through the front part of the house, past the waiting room, and into the garden with the fountain, where he commanded him to wait. The garden actually adjoined the women's quarters of the house, and men from outside the household were not permitted beyond it. Agathon disappeared into the house.

Archimedes stood beside the fountain waiting. It was a hot day. The yellow cloak was itchy and uncomfortably heavy, even in the shade of the garden. He scratched surreptitiously, then went to the fountain and splashed some water over his face. Footsteps sounded softly in the colonnade beyond, and he looked up, face dripping, and saw Delia sweeping toward him, accompanied by two women and a child. One of the women was dressed with the plain respectability of a slave, but the other—a handsome woman of about thirty—wore a long tunic of purple and gold, and her auburn hair was tied back by the purple ribbon of a royal diadem.

He had worked out what to say when Delia appeared, but the sight of the woman in purple put the speech out of his head, and he stared stupidly. He had not been so naïve as to expect to be permitted to talk to the king's sister alone again, but equally he had not expected her to be chaperoned by a queen. Of course, he realized numbly, there could be nothing *unusual* about such a person being in Delia's company. After all, Delia was the queen's sister-in-law; they probably spent a lot of time together. But the sight of his flute player escorted by a diadem suddenly made him feel how stupid it was for him to think about her in the way he had been thinking about her.

Then Delia smiled, and he went on thinking about her that way.

"Archimedes son of Phidias, good health!" said Delia pleasantly. "Agathon said you wanted to thank me for something?"

He remembered his speech; she'd just delivered the gist of the first line herself. He tried to think how to rewrite it on the spot, then, flustered, abandoned it. "Uh, yes, I—that is, you spoiled your cheek strap when you gave it to me—I mean, when you got it wet. I, uh . . ." His throat seemed to have become stopped up, and he gave up completely and simply offered her the little papyrus-wrapped package.

The queen gave him an amused look. The child, a boy, gave him an unnerving five-year-old's stare. But Delia took the package with a lift of her eyebrows and unwrapped it, then held up the two cheek straps. The old one was slightly—but not, in fact, badly—discolored by the water; the new one was the best he could buy that was still comfortable to wear, strong and soft and painted on the outside surface with a key pattern in blue.

"How very kind of you," Delia said, with real pleasure. The old cheek strap had been her only plain one. She had plenty with embossing or embroidery, but embroidery always itched, and embossing dug into your cheeks when you blew hard, and distracted you. This was a strap chosen by an aulist: she could wear this. She gave Archimedes a warm look. He was distinctly less stained and shabby this morning, she thought to herself. In fact, he looked quite well; yellow suited him. He had nice eyes, light brown, and a nice face, long-boned and expressive.

"I couldn't permit you to lose anything on my account, lady," he said, recovering himself a little. "Thank you for the loan of it."

"Your eye's better?" She could see already that it was, though the bruise was still fading around the socket, and an angry red mark remained on the white of the eye itself.

"Quite better, thank you," he replied, then swallowed and lapsed into an awkward silence.

Delia sensed her sister-in-law preparing to make small talk. When Agathon had announced Archimedes, she'd told the queen that this was a catapult engineer who happened to play the aulos, and that they'd exchanged a few words about flute-playing when he last came. Now Philistis was getting ready to say a few words about flutes—it would certainly be flutes; she didn't like war machines.

The small boy forestalled her. "Delia said you make catapults," he told Archimedes in an accusing tone.

Archimedes blinked at him. The child had auburn curls and the queen's hazel eyes. Hieron was known to have a son, Gelon. This chubby boy was undoubtedly that son, and would be the next tyrant of Syracuse, if democracy or the Romans didn't intervene.

"Yes," he replied politely. "I've just finished one."

"I like catapults," said Gelon eagerly, and Archimedes realized that the accusing tone had been due to simple interest. "Is it a big one? Does it throw stones or shoot arrows? How far can it throw?"

"It's a one-talent stone-hurler," replied Archimedes. "That's bigger than any other catapult in the city now, though there's another as big with the army. I don't know exactly how far it will throw, because we haven't done the trials yet. I came here to ask the reg—your grandfather when and where he wanted me to test it."

"How heavy is one talent?" Gelon demanded.

"Heavier than you, Gelonion mine," said the queen. "And that's enough about catapults!"

"That's big!" said little Gelon delightedly, ignoring his mother. "If there was somewhere soft to land, maybe you could shoot me out of that catapult. I'd go flying up through the air like a bird!"

The slave woman—evidently his nurse—clicked her tongue in horror. "Perish the thought, baby!" she exclaimed. "My precious lamb, it would kill you!"

"I don't see how flying would kill me!" replied Gelon indignantly.

"Not the flying," Archimedes told him. "The catapult throw. You think about it. My one-talenter should hurl a sixty-pound weight four or five hundred feet, and the missile is supposed to land hard enough to knock over stone battlements and smash houses. Think what the stone must feel when the string hits it!"

Gelon's eyes widened as he thought. Then he grinned admiringly. "That's a good catapult!" he said.

Archimedes grinned back. He would have preferred those words to come from Delia, but they were perfectly acceptable from the child. "I think so. The foreman of the workshop thinks so, too—at least, he *said* it was the best he'd seen."

Delia was pleased. Agathon had passed on a little of what Epimeles had told him, but she was glad to hear it confirmed. She was relieved, though, that she had not had to ask about the catapult herself. Her interest in Archimedes might be abstract and innocent, a ruler's interest in a potentially valuable servant of the state—but the people around her would never believe that. They all assumed that girls her age thought about nothing but love.

"It will *smash* the Romans!" gloated Gelon. He smashed a small fist into a palm, *smack*!

Archimedes grinned again. "That's what I hope!"

" 'Course, my papa's already smashed the Romans," the boy added importantly. "Have you heard? But I expect they'll have to be smashed again before the war's over."

"Gelon, that's enough!" said the queen firmly. "Phew, what a hot day it is. Much too hot to talk about the war. Archimedes son of Phidias, my sister-in-law tells me that you play the aulos. Perhaps—if you're waiting for my father—you'd amuse us with a little music to help pass the time?"

Archimedes blinked again. If Syracuse's tyrant had won a victory, why didn't the tyrant's wife want to talk about it? But he bowed and said, "I'm happy to play for you, if you'd like, Lady Philistis." Respectable women's names were not usually mentioned, but Hieron had made dedications to the gods jointly with his wife, and when a name was inscribed in the temples it was hardly improper to repeat it. "But I didn't bring my flutes with me."

"I'd like," said Delia quickly. She'd rather make music than small talk. She snapped her fingers and said to the nurse, "Melaina, go and fetch two sets of auloi." She smiled at Archimedes. "We could have a duet."

Archimedes grinned slowly back at her. Gelon made a disgusted sound: he'd far prefer to hear more about catapults. Since the adults weren't going to oblige, he abandoned them. He had an interesting hole he was digging under the shrubbery in a corner of the garden; he hurried off to it while his nurse was busy, before she could tell him not to get himself dirty.

When the nurse returned with the two sets of auloi, Archimedes slipped the reeds into the mouthpieces of the pair he'd been given and tried the slides. He had been handed a baritone and bass, presumably because instruments with a lower range had been considered more suitable for a man; Delia had an alto and tenor. He actually preferred the mid-to high-range auloi, but the fingering was the same. He looked at Delia, and saw, with satisfaction, that she was tying on the cheek strap he had given her. He smiled; she smiled back, then tossed him her old cheek strap. "Here," she said. "You can borrow this a little longer."

He murmured his thanks as he put it on. He remembered playing the aulos for the woman in Alexandria. She had heard him play at a party one of his friends had thrown, and the next day she had sent him a perfumed invitation to her house. She had a right to invite whomever she liked, since she was a courtesan—one of the legendary courtesans of Alexandria, the women who rivaled the gods for beauty. He'd expected her to send him away again as soon as she realized that he wasn't wealthy. But she hadn't. Not for a while, anyway. And when she had finally sent him away, she had been so gentle—"My dearest, you are ruining yourself for me. I cannot permit that, you know." He had tried to dissuade her:"I can build some more water-snails!" But she had replied, "My dearest, no. There is only one Pegasus. I will not be the one to bind him to earth when he might have the sky."

Laîs had liked his playing. He would see if Delia did.

She set her flutes to her lips, caught his eye, then began the same Euripides variation she had been playing when they first met. He listened for a couple of beats, then joined in. At first he simply played the same melody in a deeper tone, but as they progressed he began embroidering it with grace notes and syncopation. Delia's eyes lit with pleasure. She switched the tune to her alto instrument and used the tenor for accompaniment. Archimedes instantly imitated her, playing the tune on his bass aulos and the accompaniment on the baritone. Delia added the syncopation on the alto; Archimedes countered it on the bass. They played the piece through to the end, taking a keen pleasure in the way the high and low phrases of the tune reverberated against the middle.

When the tune was finished, Delia played a few ornamental trills, then launched suddenly and without warning into a dramatic piece of chorus music with a complex pounding rhythm. Archimedes joined her within a phrase, then began toying with the rhythm, resolving all the long beats and running the short ones together. She gave him a startled look, and he took the flutes away from his lips long enough to grin, then played on. He dropped all the long beats and replaced them with complicated phrases of accompaniment. Delia's eyes widened. Archimedes rejoined her on the tune; after a few bars, she let him carry the melody and began resolving notes as he had done, hesitantly at first, then with a sudden flush of delight, riding the beats in a flurry of quavers. Archimedes suddenly dropped the melody again and for perhaps a minute they both played an accompaniment to a tune that had become only an idea in two minds, an unheard force holding together two wild improvisations. Then

Archimedes returned to the tune; in half a beat, Delia had joined him, and together they slowed the tempo and finished in a single drawn-out note.

They lowered their flutes at the same time, smiled at the same time, and cried, "You're *good!*" in the same breathless gasp. Then they both laughed.

Delia turned to her sister-in-law. "Have you ever heard anything like that?" she demanded excitedly.

Philistis was frowning, and she shook her head.

"Oh, we play improvisations a lot in my family," said Archimedes, wiping the flutes' mouthpieces on his cloak. "But not on the auloi. That is, I do, but the rest of my family play strings. Playing with another aulist—by Apollo, it's like—like squaring the circle!"

Philistis abruptly stood up, smoothing her tunic. "That was very . . . interesting," she said, with an air of having found it just about survivable. "Very . . . unusual. But you mustn't let us delay you any longer, my good fellow. I'm sure you have plenty of work waiting for you at the catapult workshops. I'm sorry that my father isn't back yet. I'll tell him you were here."

Archimedes almost responded that he had finished his business at the workshop for the time being. Then he realized that he was being dismissed. He opened his mouth—and closed it again. He should not be surprised that the queen did not want him loitering in the house like an old family friend. Reluctantly, he untied the cheek strap and stood up. He bowed to Delia, handed her the strip of leather and her borrowed auloi, and muttered his thanks for the loan. Then, pulling his cloak straight with a regretful sigh, he wished the ladies joy and departed, drooping.

As soon as he was out of sight, Delia turned toward the queen angrily. "Why did you tell him to go?" she demanded, "That wasn't *interesting*, it was *wonderful!*"

"I sent him off because I could see you thought that," said Philistis. "Sister, he's a . . . a *catapult maker!*"

"Oh, Zeus!" exclaimed Delia in disgust. "Does that mean he shouldn't play the flute? No, I forget, you were the one who suggested that he play; it was only my joining in you didn't like. I'm *allowed* to play music, Philistis!"

Philistis grimaced. She'd always felt that there was something improper about a girl playing the flute, and wished that Delia were not allowed. That was not, however, what this argument was about. "Not with amorous young men," she said firmly.

"Amorous men!" cried Delia furiously. "You never think about anything else. I'm not allowed to go anywhere, do anything, or speak to anyone, because that filthy creature Love might spot me at it! It was *wonderful* playing like that, I've never played like that before, it was pure music and not the least bit improper—but it's stopped, because I was enjoying it!"

Philistis gave a sigh of exasperation. Her husband's sister was such a difficult creature, always wanting to do the impossible and flying into a temper when she couldn't. "I'm not accusing you of anything improper, my dear," she said soothingly. "I *know* you were simply enjoying the music. But men—especially young men—*are* amorous creatures. If you so much as look them in the eyes they start thinking about going to bed. It's your duty to make sure they don't think about it with you. Having a wonderful time with a young man who's poor and insignificant is a good way to make both of you miserable."

"It was nothing like that!" said Delia indignantly. "Nothing at all!"

She picked up the auloi—all four of them—and began wiping them off.

She had known for many years that she would eventually marry for her brother's political advantage, cementing some alliance with a great Sicilian nobleman or a foreign kingdom. She did not look forward to it, but she'd always accepted it, and accepted too the necessary corollary, that she must never interfere with that destiny by falling in love. She owed her brother that, for all he had done for her.

Delia did not remember her mother, and her father had died when she was five. For a year after his death, she had lived with her father's sister and her husband, and that year was the worst of her life. She was her father's only legitimate child, and heiress to his estates. Her uncle had managed those estates, and hoped that she would die so that he could gain control of them forever. She had not understood that at the time, of course. She had known only that there was something wrong with her, that he and his wife hated her, that she was a wicked girl who could do nothing right, that she was clumsy and stupid and that even the slaves hated having to attend her. She had swung between cringing attempts to win approval and outbursts of passionate resentment: the former had been ignored and the latter savagely punished.

Then, one afternoon, she had been summoned into the dining room and presented to her half brother, Hieron.

She had been aware of his existence, though mention of him in the household had always been conducted in disapproving whispers—"the *bastard* who's done so well in the army," "the *bastard* who's in joint command of the mutiny," "the *bastard* who's married Leptines' daughter and made himself tyrant!" But she had never met him before, and did not know what to say to him. Her aunt had scolded her for her silence, and Hieron had shaken his head.

The next day, her outraged aunt and uncle informed her that her half brother had insisted that she live in his household in future. She had gone to the mansion in terror, certain that she had displeased a new master—and found herself welcomed warmly, and swept effortlessly into happiness. For the first few years she had tried to earn her brother's approval by being good, but eventually she understood that she didn't have to earn anything. Hieron gave, generously, with a tolerant good humor that left her free to be herself.

Or he had done. The one advantage she had expected to give him he had not used, and she had been growing increasingly dissatisfied with her life. In a world where girls were often married at fourteen, she was eighteen and still a virgin. Girls who'd shared dancing and music lessons with her were now mothers, but she still remained in her brother's house with nothing to do.

Her brother was reluctant to marry her to a foreigner—the Roman and Carthaginian aristocracies practically never married outside their own circles, and there was little profit to be gained by attaching her to a minor princeling of some great Greek royal house. But when it came to the nobility of Syracuse, the political advantages offered by her wedding had never been advantageous enough.

Still, she did not question her fate now, either: if she could win Hieron any political advantage, she was glad of it. She merely told herself angrily that playing the flute with a man didn't mean you were going to fall in love with him.

ARCHIMEDES WAS STILL DROOPING WHEN HE REACHED the street, but more from the heat than from any disappointment. Delia had liked his present, and he had been able to play a duet with her. The music had been exhilarating. If they could play together regularly, and learn each other's styles, they could do something *really* interesting!

Then he tried to imagine how a catapult maker would manage to play regular duets with the sister of a king, and drooped in earnest. He loosened his cloak irritably. It was too hot to wear wool.

When he turned into the main road, he saw the regent Leptines, marching smartly away down the thoroughfare in the middle of a troop of a dozen soldiers. He grabbed the edge of his cloak to stop it from falling off and ran after them. When the guards at the rear of the party noticed him flapping after them, they halted, and half a dozen spears were leveled at him. He stopped short, panting.

Leptines had glanced around to see what the matter was; he noticed Archimedes and gestured for the soldiers to shoulder their weapons again. "What do you want?" he asked irritably.

"Um," said Archimedes. "It's about the one-talent stone-hurler, lord. I've just been to your house to tell you that it's ready, but you weren't there. Where do you want us to put it?"

"At least *something* in this god-hated city is ready!" exclaimed Leptines. "Does it work?"

"Yes," said Archimedes, without thinking.

"Then put it in the Hexapylon," said the regent.

There were catapults of one size or another all the way along the fifteen miles of Syracuse's city wall, but the largest machines were concentrated in the batteries of the great forts. The Hexapylon was the fort which guarded the gate on the main road north. It was the first defense against any army coming from the north and Messana. Archimedes licked his lips. "Yes, lord. And the trials for it?"

Leptines had either forgotten the arrangement he'd made with Archimedes or forgotten everything about catapults. "You said it works!" he cried indignantly.

"Uh, sir, I'm sure it does!" Archimedes protested. "But we can't fire it in the workshop, so we need trials before it's proven and, uh, I'm paid."

Several of the soldiers grinned; one of them, Archimedes noticed, was Straton. He had not recognized the man before, among so many others identically armored and helmeted.

Leptines frowned a minute, then gave a sudden snort of amusement. "Well, put it in the Hexapylon," he said. "And when you have it set up there, send word, and I'll send someone to observe. If it does work, start building another immediately."

"Yes, sir!" said Archimedes.

"Lord!" said Straton smartly. "Shall I arrange transport for the catapult, sir?"

"Do that!" said the regent. He gestured to his guard, and he and they moved off down the street, leaving Straton with Archimedes.

"Thank you," said Archimedes gratefully. "I didn't know who to talk to about moving it. We'll need a big wagon."

Straton grinned. "Thank *you*!" he replied. "I'm glad to stop running up and down. We've been from the arsenal to the naval docks and back twice this morning." He tipped his helmet back and put his spear across his shoulders. "Besides, I want to have a look at this one-talenter."

They started along the main street toward the workshop, the opposite direction to Leptines. After a minute, Archimedes said uncertainly, "At the king's house they said that we had won a victory."

Straton nodded. "That's the news."

"I don't understand, then," Archimedes said. "Why is the king lifting the siege and coming home?"

Straton moved his shoulders uncomfortably under his armor. " 'The fox has many tricks,' " he said.

" 'The hedgehog only one—but it's a good one,' " said Archimedes, finishing the proverb, then went on, "Yes, but why come back to the city and play hedgehog when you've the strength to be a fox and snap up rats? I don't understand. Was it a victory?"

Straton shrugged again. "They say it was. It wasn't a defeat, anyway. But I know one thing: King Hieron's a clever fox, and if he thinks it's time to raise the siege and come home, he's got a good reason for it."

They walked on for a little while in silence. The question Archimedes really wanted to ask was "Are the Romans going to follow King Hieron back here to Syracuse and besiege us in turn?" But he did not quite dare. He could remember the last time Syracuse had been besieged; he had been not quite nine years old. There had been a blockade, and food had grown short. The family had shared one loaf of bread a day among four adults and four children, and eaten rats when they could get them, weeds and beetles when they couldn't. Marcus' predecessor had fallen ill and died; if there had been more food, he would probably have lived. Once Archimedes had gone up to the city walls with his father, and they had measured shadows to calculate the distance to the besieging army they could see clearly, camped just out of catapult range. "What would happen if they got in?" he had asked, and Phidias had shaken his head and refused to answer.

That had been the Carthaginians, of course. And they had not got in.

They reached the catapult workshop and went in to see the great beast crouched as before. To Archimedes it looked suddenly more beautiful than ever. The Romans, if they came, would not get in either.

"Herakles!" said Straton, staring. "That's a monster!"

Epimeles had begun hurrying over the moment he saw them; his step faltered at the exclamation, and he gave Straton an irritated look. "It's a beauty!" he corrected him; then, to Archimedes, "Sir?"

"It's to go to the Hexapylon," said Archimedes. "Straton son of Metrodoros here is going to help us arrange transport for it. They'll send an observer to see that it works as soon as we've got it in place, and then we can start on another."

"Good," said Epimeles, with satisfaction. "The Hexapylon. Good."

They all walked over to the catapult and gazed up at it. "The Hexapylon," the foreman said again, softly this time. "We can call it the Welcomer."

Moving a catapult the size of the Welcomer was a laborious business. The beast had to be taken apart—stock, stand, peritrete, arms—and loaded onto an enormous wagon fetched by Straton from the military supplies depot. By the time this had been done, it was too late to set off for the Hexapylon, which was more than four miles distant from the workshop. The loaded wagon was instead put back in the military supplies depot to wait for the morning.

Archimedes went home. By then news of the victory at Messana, and the army's impending return, was all over the city. Marcus had heard it that afternoon.

He had gone over to the nearest tile yard, on the seaward side of the Achradina, to order some new roof tiles for the house, and he had taken the boy Chrestos with him. They had found the tile workers in a huddle in the middle of the drying yard, animatedly discussing the victory. "Attacked the siege works," Marcus heard as they approached, and "chased them back to the walls!" He stopped, saying nothing, afraid that his Italian accent would attract comment. It was left to Chrestos to hurry forward and demand the whole story, and receive in response a glowing account of King Hieron's wisdom and Syracusan valor. Marcus listened to it intently, but made no comment. It was clear to him that some element of the tale had been left out, and a moment's thought gave him a chilling awareness of what that could be. He confined his speech, however, to the subject of roof tiles.

When they got back to the house near the Lion Fountain, Chrestos excitedly repeated the account of the victory to the rest of the family. It was received with intense relief—a terrible threat was lifted. Philyra, however, also became anxious. If the king was coming home, his other engineers would be with him, and her brother's services would become unnecessary. What was more, if the war was already ending, the catapult wouldn't be wanted and Archimedes wouldn't be paid. When Archimedes himself returned slightly later, she rushed to question him about the machine's fate.

"They want it," he told her grimly. "And they want me to start on another one as soon as they're sure it works." At that his sister became silent, realizing in her turn that something about the story of the victory didn't ring true.

The household ate supper, then played a little music in the sickroom. Phidias listened attentively, but seemed to tire quickly, and the concert was stopped. Philyra left him talking astronomy with Archimedes and went into the courtyard to practice her lute. After a time Marcus came in from an errand down the street. When she saw him she stopped playing and gave him an accusing look. He hurriedly wiped his hands and looked back at her questioningly.

"What sort of Italian are you?" she demanded.

At that his face dropped into its mask of impassivity. "Mistress, we've already said all this."

"But you were enslaved fighting in one of the Roman wars on the Roman side, weren't you?"

He was silent for a moment, then looked away, remembering the onslaught, the screams of the injured and dying, the stink of his own terror. "Yes," he admitted at last.

"You've seen the Romans fight. What do they do when they take a city?"

"Same as anybody else."

"I've heard," said Philyra tightly, "that sometimes they kill every living thing within the walls. Even the animals."

"Sometimes they do," said Marcus reluctantly. "If they've made a vow. But mostly they don't. Mostly they just plunder and then put in a garrison. Same as anybody else."

"Barbarians!" said Philyra. She looked at Marcus with hot eyes. "What you mean is, sometimes they're as savage, cruel, and bloodthirsty as anybody else, and sometimes they're worse. Did you ever help them take a city?"

Marcus shook his head in protest. "Mistress, when I joined the army I was no older than you are now! You're supposed to be eighteen, but I lied. And the first time I saw war, I . . . ended up here. I don't know anything more about sieges than you do."

Some of the heat went out of her eyes, and the fear beneath it began to show. "You'd be free, wouldn't you, if the Romans took Syracuse?"

He shook his head again, in denial this time. "I don't think they'd even ask what I was. A slave's a slave. I'd get a new master or be killed. But it's pointless for you to worry about it, mistress, because they won't take Syracuse. And anyway, the news is that the city has a victory."

It was her turn to shake her head. "Why is the king coming home, if it was a victory? Why do they want more catapults, if it was a victory?"

"Where were the Carthaginians during that victory?" he replied in a fierce voice. "They were supposed to be our allies. But I haven't heard any reports of them doing any fighting."

Then he regretted his words. He should have remembered: Philyra was too intelligent not to understand their implications. Now her eyes widened in fear. What if the Romans at Messana had come to terms with the Carthaginians? Rome and Carthage had been allies during the war against Pyrrhus of Epirus: it was entirely conceivable that they had now agreed to divide Sicily between them. If King Hieron suspected that his new allies were going to turn on him, it would certainly explain why he was taking his army home in a hurry. Syracuse could not face Rome without help from Carthage. If she faced Rome and Carthage together, she was doomed.

"Oh, gods, no!" whispered Philyra.

Marcus crossed the courtyard to her in a few swift steps, then stopped, helplessly wishing he dared touch her thin shoulders. "Nobody will take Syracuse," he told her. "The Carthaginians have tried often enough, and never managed it, and I can tell you, mistress, that the Romans won't crack a city like this. They're not as good at siege craft as you Greeks. Nobody's ever taken Syracuse by storm, and nobody will take her now." Then he smiled, with an effort, and added, "Not with your brother's catapults to defend her."

Philyra took a deep breath, told herself that she wasn't a little girl to be frightened by rumors, and managed to smile back. She looked down at the lute in her hands, then set it against her shoulder and began playing something complicated, something that needed all her attention and left her no time to think of anything else.

◆ IN THE SICKROOM, PHIDIAS GAZED AT THE LAMP FLAME with his yellowed eyes, then looked over to his son, smiling. "Tell me again about the hypothesis of Aristarchos," he said.

Archimedes shrugged: this theory had been exciting great controversy in Alexandria, and his father was fascinated by it. "He says that the earth revolves about the sun in the circumference of a circle."

"And all the planets as well?"

"That's right."

"What about the stars?" asked Phidias. "If the earth revolved about the sun, the fixed stars would appear to shift as we saw them from different angles at different points in the earth's orbit."

"No! That's the most interesting part," said Archimedes, warming to the subject. "Aristarchos says that the universe is much, much larger than anyone believes. He says that the whole circle described by the earth's orbit is only a point compared to the size of the sphere of the fixed stars."

"That's nonsense," said Phidias. "A point has no magnitude at all."

"Well, not a point, then! But incomparably small. So small that all the earth's revolving doesn't make the least difference to our view of the fixed stars."

"You believe it, don't you?" said Phidias.

"It's a hypothesis," said Archimedes, flushing a little. "There isn't enough evidence to decide either way. I suppose the people are right who say that where there isn't evidence, you should choose the explanation that fits appearances best—which is that the sun goes around the earth. But—I like it."

"*Oi moi!* You like to think of the earth whirling about like a dust mote in an unspeakable immensity of space? It makes me dizzy!"

Archimedes grinned, but said, "It makes sense to me that the universe is incomparably great. After all, the more I look at it, the more things I see that I can't understand."

The words "If you don't understand much, what hope is there for the rest of us?" hovered on the edge of Phidias' tongue, but he did not say them. He was wary of admitting how hard he worked to grasp ideas which seemed obvious to Archimedes. His son had always regarded him as an equal, and he was almost as proud of that as he was of the son himself—his son, the most gifted student he had ever taught, the most profound mind he had ever encountered. Phidias watched him now, tenderly: Archimedes' grin was fading, and his eyes, still bright, were abstracted, reckoning up the vastness of the universe. Phidias knew that they no longer saw him. He felt for a moment the ache that any parent feels at realizing the utter foreignness of the child: the body that came from you, that you have nourished, now contains a mind full of things you will never comprehend. He reached over and caught his son's hand. "Medion," he said, a bit breathlessly, "swear to me that you will never, ever give up mathematics."

Archimedes looked at him in surprise. "Papa, you know that giving up mathematics is the last thing in the world I want to do!"

"You think that," said Phidias, "but it isn't true. The last thing in the world you want is for your family to starve or suffer—and that's right, that should be the last thing you allow. But promise me that however you have to snatch at learning and struggle for it when the day's work is done, however tired you get, however little anyone understands you, you'll never give it up and devote your soul to the earth. Swear to me."

Archimedes hesitated, then went to the basin of water beside the bed and ceremoniously washed his hands and lifted them to heaven. "I swear by Delian Apollo and Pythian Apollo," he declared solemnly, "by Urania and all the Muses, by Zeus and the Earth and the Sun, by Aphrodite and Hephaistos and Dionysos, and by all the gods and goddesses, that I will never give up mathematics nor allow the spark the god has given me to go out. If I do not keep this my undertaking, may all the gods and goddesses by whom I swore be angry with me and may I die a most miserable death; but if I honor it, may they be favorable!"

"So be it," whispered Phidias.

Archimedes came back to the bed and took his father's hand, smiling now. "But I didn't need to swear, Papa," he said. "I try to give it up, I tell myself, 'No more games!'—and it never works. I *can't* give it up. You *know* that."

Phidias smiled back. "I know," he whispered, "but I don't want you to try. Not for catapults or for anything else."

6

To most of the city, the following day was the Day King
Hieron Returned—but to Archimedes, the king and his
army were merely an annoying interruption on the Day We
Moved the Welcomer.

Only one workman—Elymos—assisted him with the catapult;
Eudaimon insisted that the rest remain in the workshop to help
on another arrow-shooter. Straton was still in charge of trans-
porting the machine, however, and Archimedes was very glad of
his assistance before the day was done. It took the heavy ox-
drawn wagon more than two hours to reach the Hexapylon, and
when they arrived at the fort they found that there was no crane
to move the one-talenter to the enclosed platform on the tower
selected for it.

This platform was the first floor of one of the fort's outer
towers—large catapults were normally placed on the lower floors
of towers, leaving the upper stories to the lighter machines. A
stone stairway ran up past the platform, which stood open to the
fort's interior yard, but it was not possible for three men to maneuver a thirty-foot stock up the stairs. Straton cajoled the fort
garrison into lending some rope and pulleys, and Archimedes
rigged up hoists, but it was still the middle of the afternoon
before the pieces of catapult were all lying on their platform, and
then they needed to be fitted together. King Hieron and his army
appeared before the gates while this was being done. All the fort

garrison went off to cheer the king as he rode past, and Straton joined them—quite unnecessarily, thought Archimedes, as he struggled to rearrange his hoists so that the catapult stock could be refitted to its stand. Straton, he told himself angrily, should have remained to haul on ropes when he was told to.

But when the king had gone, Straton said he must return the wagon and oxen to the Ortygia, and departed as well, leaving Archimedes and Elymos to continue the struggle alone. It was dark before the catapult finally stood intact in its place. Archimedes was staggering with exhaustion by that time, and his hands were blistered from the rope to the point where he couldn't feel any one particular ache. When the job at last was done, he examined his blisters, then looked at Elymos, who was, if anything, even more blistered and exhausted than he was himself. "If you don't want to walk all the way back to the Ortygia," he told the slave, "you can sleep at my house tonight."

"That's very kind of you, sir," said Elymos gloomily, "but Epimeles told me to stay here tonight."

"Here?" asked Archimedes in surprise, glancing about the bare room. The catapult was under cover, but nobody would describe its location as comfortable. The yard side of the platform stood open and the floor was rough planking. In one corner stood a pile of forty-pound shot, left over from the platform's previous catapult.

"That's right," agreed the slave mournfully. Epimeles had ordered him not to let the catapult out of his sight, and to make his bed beneath it.

"But—why?" asked Archimedes, totally mystified.

Elymos just shrugged and spat out the artillery port. Epimeles had also told him not to worry Archimedes. "We don't want that lad's mind distracted," he'd said. "We don't want him spoiling his chances. He'll win the crown now if he just runs easy down to the finish line; if he starts thinking he has to put on a spurt, maybe he'll trip over his own feet."

"Maybe," added Elymos hopefully, "you could ask the captain of the fort to give me a mat and a blanket and a bit of supper?"

"Very well," said Archimedes, bewildered. "I'll see that you get some wine, too, if you like."

"Thank you, sir!" said Elymos, eyes gleaming.

Archimedes decided during the long walk home that it was actually very sensible of Elymos to stay at the Hexapylon overnight. The Achradina wasn't quite as far as the Ortygia, but it was still a long way, and by the time he arrived home it was very late. Marcus, yawning, let him in, but the rest of the family had been asleep for hours. No, Elymos was quite right to get some sleep at once, with the catapult.

But despite his exhaustion, Archimedes had trouble falling asleep. He tossed in the heat, blistered hands aching, mind running swiftly through things that could go wrong with his catapult. When he did at last slide into an uneasy sleep, it was to dream of an army attacking the Hexapylon, equipped with battering rams and siege towers. He knew that if the enemy reached the walls, they would get in and kill everyone; he knew that if he could fire the catapult he could keep them back—but the catapult kept coming apart in his hands. In desperation he slammed at it—and the impact of his blistered hand against the bed woke him again fully.

He groaned, rolled onto his back, and lay staring up at the darkness. His hands throbbed. After a minute he got up, went downstairs, and poured some water into a bucket so that he could soak his blisters. Above the courtyard, the Milky Way hung shimmering. The stars had wheeled far around toward morning. Archimedes sat against the wall, soaking his hands in the bucket, and watched the stars. Infinitely far away, eternally lovely. All the earth was incomparably small, and Syracuse a speckle upon a mote of dust. He closed his eyes, imagining the illimitable sphere of the universe, and the image of the catapult faded at last.

ARCHIMEDES WAS STILL ASLEEP THE NEXT MORNING WHEN there was a staccato knocking at the house door. Marcus, who was in the courtyard, opened the door and found two men in full armor. One was Straton, polished almost out of recognition; the other a wiry man in the crimson cloak and scarlet-crested helmet of an officer, wearing a beautiful bronze breastplate decorated with glittering silver medallions. "This is the house of Archimedes son of Phidias?" asked the officer.

Marcus nodded, his face dropping into its mask.

"I need a quick word with him," said the officer.

Philyra came down the stairs into the courtyard in her tunic with her hair loose, realized that there was a strange man at the door, and backed into the stairway with a squeak. The officer grinned at her in an appreciative way Marcus very much disliked. "The gentleman wants a word with your brother, mistress," he announced, stressing the title to make it plain that this was the daughter of the house, not a slave girl. Philyra nodded and shot back up the stairs.

She burst into her brother's room, shouting, "Medion! Medion, an *officer* has come for you!" Archimedes picked his head up, then groaned and pulled the sheet over his head.

Philyra hauled it off and threw him the first tunic that came to hand, and presently he stumbled down the stairs to the courtyard, barefoot and unshaven. Dionysios son of Chairephon had been admitted to the courtyard and was chatting to Arata, while Straton stood at attention by the street door. When Archimedes appeared, the captain raised his eyebrows.

"Get dressed," he commanded.

"I, uh," said Archimedes, running a hand through his tangles. He was never at his best first thing in the morning, and he'd been too tired for supper the night before—and, come to think of it, too busy for lunch before that. "I, uh—are we going to do the catapult trial this morning?"

"The king is reviewing the forts along the wall this morning," said Dionysios shortly. "He has specifically asked to witness the trials of your catapult. I don't know when exactly he'll reach the Hexapylon, but I'm off to join his escort *now*. So—get dressed. If he shows up and you're not there, you're out of a job." He gave the company a nod and set off. Straton shot Archimedes a grin, and followed at a smart march.

Archimedes scratched his head again, then sighed. Philyra once more vanished upstairs, then returned with his good cloak. "Let me at least *eat* first!" he protested, gazing at the garment with loathing and wishing that Philyra had thought to weave of it of linen.

"Medion!" exclaimed Philyra angrily. "That was the *captain of the Ortygia garrison*, telling you the *king* wants you to hurry!"

"I believe in the equality of all citizens in law!" said Archimedes proudly.

"I believe in this household having an income!" Philyra hurled back.

Arata clicked her tongue approvingly: support for democracy was fine in theory, but money was good in practice, and you needed to bow to authority for that. "You can take some food with you," she told her son soothingly. "I'll pack a basket, and Marcus can carry it."

Archimedes, trailing Marcus, reached the Hexapylon before the middle of the morning. The king was not there: he'd begun his tour of inspection at the south end of the city, and nobody knew when he'd reach the Hexapylon. The fort's garrison were still busy polishing and tidying. Morosely, Archimedes went to the catapult platform where he'd erected the Welcomer.

Elymos was still lying underneath the great machine, but he sat up when they came in. He was pale and queasy: he had been generously provided with wine the previous night, and was suffering the consequences. Archimedes nodded at him vaguely, and began checking that the catapult strings were correctly tuned.

Marcus set down the basket of food and gazed at the catapult. He had never seen one so large. After a moment, he ran his hand along the rough oak of the stock, then went to the end of the slide and sighted along it out the aperture, one hand on the lax trigger. He imagined sixty-pound shot flying, and shivered.

"It's a beauty, isn't it?" Elymos asked him.

Marcus said nothing. "Beauty" was not the word that leaped to his mind at the sight of the Welcomer. He glanced over at his master, who had now opened the shutter on the artillery port and was gazing out. It was hard to associate anyone so vague and soft-hearted with anything so powerful and deadly. He felt for a moment physically sick in the self-contradiction of his own desires. He had wanted this machine to be an outstanding success, for the sake of the household, for the sake of Syracuse. But he did not want it used on Romans.

Archimedes pulled off his new cloak and dropped it across the sill of the artillery port. "Marcus, where's the food?" he asked plaintively.

They sat together by the open artillery port and ate the bread and figs Arata had packed for them. Elymos sat with them, but did not want food.

The morning sun flooded the landscape below them. The view was stunning. The founders of Syracuse had enclosed the harbor area alone, but this had left them vulnerable to any invader who could command the heights of Epipolae, above them to the west, so as the city grew mighty she had rebuilt the walls to run along those heights, miles from the heart of the city, commanding the landscape from all sides. The fortifications had not only been kept in good repair, but had also been renovated almost continuously to keep up with developments in warfare. The initial open ramparts were covered over with a steeply pitched roof to protect the defenders from catapult fire, while bronze-shuttered artillery ports had been added to the guard towers and to the wall itself. From the tower of the Hexapylon Marcus and Archimedes could see the north road winding off across the fertile landscape through field and vineyard, while Mount Etna loomed, snow-capped and smoking, in the far distance. When he'd finished his meal, Archimedes gazed at the volcano, wondering what made it erupt and whether its fiery nature had anything to do with its shape, which was certainly an obtuse-angled cone. Sections of obtuse-angled cones did have some extremely interesting properties. He looked around for something to sketch with.

When King Hieron finally arrived at the tower of the Hexapylon and climbed the steps to the tower, it was to find a young man in a worn tunic scratching on the floorboards with a bread knife. Two slaves who had been seated on the end of the enormous catapult beyond him jumped to their feet and stood at attention as soon as the king's head appeared up the stairway, but the young man scratched on obliviously.

The king climbed the last few steps and emerged onto the catapult platform. His entourage followed him: four staff officers; his secretary; Dionysios; the captain of the Hexapylon; Eudaimon, the catapult maker; Kallippos, his chief engineer; and six guardsmen, including Straton. Archimedes took no notice of any of them. He sat back on his heels and chewed on the hilt of the bread knife, frowning at his sketches.

Marcus eyed the king nervously, then took a step forward and despairingly hissed, "Archimedes!"

"Unnh?" Archimedes asked around the bread knife.

The king stepped closer and gazed down at the scratches: twin curves sliced from a broad double cone. "Hyperbolae," he observed.

Archimedes gave a grunt of agreement and took the knife hilt out of his mouth. "I wish I had my compasses," he said. "And a ruler."

"Here's a ruler, anyway," said the king.

Archimedes glanced from the drawing to the feet before him—then, suddenly taking in the gold-studded purple-laced sandals, looked up, leaped up, and went crimson.

The king smiled. He was a plump man, a full head shorter than Archimedes, and he had a pleasant face, round and good-natured, with curly black hair and sharp eyes dark as his sister's. He looked more like the host of a country inn than a Sicilian tyrant, despite his purple cloak and tunic and the purple band of the diadem across his forehead. He was younger than Archimedes had expected, too; not much above thirty-five. "I presume you're Archimedes son of Phidias?" he said.

"Uh, yes," stammered Archimedes, trying to remember what he'd done with his cloak. "Uh—good health, O King!"

"Good health! I knew your father," said King Hieron. "Studied with him for a couple of months, in fact, when I was young. I was sorry to hear that he's ill. What's wrong with him?"

Still scarlet with embarrassment, Archimedes stammered out a brief account of his father's illness. Hieron listened attentively, then asked Archimedes to convey his hopes for the sick man's recovery. "And tell him I've always wished I could have studied with him longer," he added. "But that's not what we're supposed to be doing today. This is the one-talenter you made for me, is it?" Hieron strolled across to the catapult. "Herakles, what a huge machine! What's this wheel for?"

"That's to help it pivot, lord," said Archimedes, and demonstrated.

Hieron's chief engineer, Kallippos, a tall hawk-nosed man of about forty, at once bore down upon the catapult and elbowed his king out of the way. He examined the system of pulleys and windlasses closely. "Is this Alexandrian?" he demanded.

"Um, no," said Archimedes uncomfortably, "I, uh, just developed that myself. It works, though."

Kallippos made a noise through his teeth, half hiss and half whistle, and looked disbelieving. Hieron gently moved his engineer out of the way again and took over the windlasses himself. He sighted along the stock through the aperture, aimed the catapult at an empty field to the north of the road, then reached for the third windlass to elevate it.

"That doesn't work so well," Archimedes told him, embarrassed again. "I'm going to try something different on the next one."

Hieron raised his eyebrows, then turned the windlass. It was very stiff, and Kallippos had to help him, but between them they tilted the great catapult slowly back to its maximum elevation. "It works," said Hieron. "What were you going to do that was different?"

Archimedes explained an idea he'd had about a screw fixed to a wheel beneath the catapult. Kallippos made his hissing noise again and looked even more disbelieving. Screws had previously been used solely for holding things together.

Hieron's smile broadened. "I'll look forward to seeing that," he said. "But we'd better see how this one shoots before you start building the next one. I have to see it work before you can be paid, isn't that the arrangement?" He nodded to the fort captain, who nodded to the soldiers. One-talent ammunition had been brought up that morning, and now a sixty-pound stone was rolled over, and the catapult string was winched back with its fearsome groan, so that the missile could be set in its place.

Archimedes blinked: that groan had differed from the one the machine had made in the workshop—lower, more dissonant. "Wait!" he exclaimed. He went to one side of the catapult and struck the solid mass of twisted hair that formed its strings: they made a hollow sound. He ducked under the uptilted nose and struck the strings on the other side. Another hollow sound—but a deeper one.

"It's gone out of tune!" he cried in horrified disbelief. The strings had been fine that morning.

There was a displeased stir throughout the king's entourage. The catapult's drawstring was allowed to slip back so that the tension on the strings could be readjusted. Archimedes scrambled onto the stock, ran up the slide to the peritrete, and worked the bronze guard cap off the top of the set of strings which had produced the lower sound. Catapult strings were always twisted on a crosspiece which was then fixed into a bracket with wedges; the gear all looked fine, but when the two sets of strings were struck again, the difference in pitch was even more marked. Somebody handed up the heavy winding gear—windlass and crank—and Archimedes fitted it to the crosspiece without looking to see who. Hooking a leg around the frame to brace himself, he twisted the strings, secured them, then nodded to Elymos to strike the strings on the other side. Again, the deep note; he struck his own strings again—and they were *still* too low, and what was worse, the note slid downward as he listened to it: something was slipping. He frowned and checked the wedges: they were fine. He struck the strings again, and the note slipped even further.

He looked around for the king, and saw that Hieron was stand-

ing immediately beneath him: it had been he who had handed
up the winding gear. Archimedes went red again. It was bad
enough that his catapult should fail to work properly; worse that
it should fail in front of the king; worst of all that the king should
be a man who actually knew something about catapults. "I'm
sorry, lord," he said miserably. "I think something's gone wrong
with the lower fixture. The tension's slipping. I—I'm going to
have to take the strings off and look, and then restring it."

Somebody sniggered. Archimedes glanced around, and realized that it had been Eudaimon.

Hieron merely looked commiserating. "Very well," he said.
"Do that."

"I-it will t-take about an hour," stammered Archimedes, utterly mortified.

"No matter," said the king cheerfully. "I was planning to stop
for some lunch anyway. Restring it, and we'll have the trial after
I've eaten."

"Lord!" exclaimed Eudaimon, shocked and astonished. "The
catapult doesn't work. Surely you're not going to waste any more
time on it?"

Hieron fixed him with a bright smile. "Son of Kallikles, I'm
not so ignorant of catapults as that!" he exclaimed. "Any catapult
can go out of tune. We don't know yet whether this one works
or not. After all, it's not as though we'd fired it and seen it hurl
crooked, is it? Which, of course, it would have done if it had
been fired while it was out of tune. Isn't it lucky that young
Archimedes here has such a good ear for pitch? Most people
wouldn't have noticed that there was a problem until it was too
late. That would have been doubly unfortunate here, because he
would have been dismissed, wouldn't he? Oh, but perhaps that
event would have pleased you."

Eudaimon, for some reason Archimedes could not understand,
went very pale. Elymos had gone pale as well. Archimedes himself was still red, too ashamed and embarrassed to worry about
them. He began pulling out the wedges to get at the strings.

"I'll help," Eudaimon offered suddenly.

"No," said Hieron, still smiling. "I think not. Kallippos, you stay and help: tell me if you find anything. Eudaimon, you come with me, and explain to me why we have so many arrow-shooters and so few stone-hurlers on the walls." He snapped his fingers, and he and his entourage descended the stairs again, the fort captain hurrying ahead to arrange their meal.

Kallippos watched them go, rather grimly, then turned to Archimedes. "Tell him if I find anything!" he exclaimed. "What am I supposed to find?"

Archimedes was up to his elbows in catapult strings. "Mmpff?" he said.

Kallippos looked at him, saw that it was pointless to say anything, and set to work helping to unstring the catapult.

When the mass of brown and black hair was drawn out of the bore, a piece of metal about as long as a hand tumbled from the strands and clinked against the floorboards. Kallippos picked it up: it was a razor.

"Zeus!" muttered the chief engineer. He checked through the tangle of tresses and found the place where the razor had nestled. Some of the strings must have been cut as soon as the razor was thrust in among them, but most had started to go when the drawn bowstring pulled them against the razor's edge. It had been a subtle trap, meant to be undetectable until it was too late.

Archimedes stared at the razor for a moment—then looked at Marcus with a mixture of disbelief and accusation. He could think of no one else who would want to disable a Syracusan catapult. But Marcus was staring at the razor too, in outrage.

The stunned silence was broken by a wail. Elymos flung himself at Archimedes' feet. "Oh, sir!" he cried. "He must have done it last night! He must have just come in and shoved it in quick, while I was sleeping. It wouldn't have made no noise, and I was so tired I wouldn't wake."

Marcus' face suddenly darkened. "Tired! You were drunk, sack-arse! You wouldn't have noticed if someone had taken a god-hated ax to the machine!"

Elymos whimpered. "I was tired! We'd been working all day

to get it set up, and there wasn't no crane. Please, sir"—turning back to Archimedes—"you tell Epimeles I did what he said, I kept near it, I slept right under it all night—but you know how tired I was."

"I don't understand," said Archimedes helplessly. "Are you saying Epimeles *expected* someone to sabotage my catapult?"

"I don't know anything!" cried Elymos frantically, realizing he'd said too much. If there was a judicial investigation of the incident, he could expect to be tortured—the law rarely trusted the testimony of slaves without torturing them first. "I just did what Epimeles said, sir, that's all!"

Archimedes stared, stunned. He thought of what would have happened if the catapult had failed. The strings alone would have cost him thirty drachmae and the wood . . . Epirot oak, imported, three drachmae a yard . . . and then there was the bronze, and the iron. He imagined going home and having to tell his family not only that he was unemployed, but that all his savings had been wiped out, just when the city perhaps faced a siege. "Delian Apollo!" he exclaimed, and sat down heavily on the catapult stock.

"I will show this to the king," said Kallippos, hefting the razor. "And you, fellow"—to Elymos—"you come with me."

Elymos gave another wail, and crawled forward to clutch Archimedes' knees in supplication. "Please, sir!" he begged. "Don't let them beat me!"

Archimedes recovered himself a little with a jump. "Let him alone!" he said.

Kallippos glared at him. Archimedes blinked back, then took a deep breath and said, "We still don't know if this catapult works, and if it doesn't, there's no point in worrying about the razor, is there? And if we're to test the catapult, I need this man's help to restring it."

Kallippos glared a moment longer.

"It's up to the king to say if he wants to talk to Elymos," Archimedes insisted.

Kallippos snorted, but he nodded. He stalked off down the stairs, the razor held gingerly between thumb and middle finger.

Elymos gave a long shuddering sigh of relief. Before he could say anything, however, Marcus strode over and clouted him on the side of the head so hard he knocked him over.

"Among my people," said Marcus in a low fierce voice, "a sentry who falls asleep on watch is beaten to death by the men whose lives he put in danger. You deserve to be beaten senseless! We were going to have pay for this brute ourselves if it didn't work!"

"Marcus!" protested Archimedes. "Leave him alone! We need to string the catapult." He got to his feet and began checking through the oily hair to see how much of it was salvageable.

When the king and his entourage reappeared about half an hour later, they found the catapult restrung, and Archimedes tuning it.

King Hieron looked as bright and interested as he had before, but Eudaimon was not with him. No one made any comment on the catapultist's absence, and no one said anything about the razor. Archimedes finished winding the strings and checked that the two arms of the catapult were at the same tension, and then the great machine was once more aimed and elevated. The string was drawn back, and the missile heaved carefully into place. Everyone stood well clear of the immense arms, which had folded back until they were almost parallel to the slide. Hieron sighted once more along the stock, then eased loose the trigger.

The Welcomer gave a deep bay—a sound made up of the hollow cry of the strings, the roar as the stone rushed along the slide, and the overwhelming crack as the arms hit the heel plates. The missile was gone too fast to follow, but when the watchers ran to the artillery port, they saw the stone falling black and heavy, far out in the chosen field. Hieron laughed and punched his palm with a fist. "Zeus!" he cried. "It's got the range of a machine half its size!" He circled a hand in the air to the others, and the catapult was reloaded. "Closer this time!" the king commanded, and the catapult was depressed, then fired again.

"Beautiful!" said the king. "Now, left a bit—right a bit—fire! Oh, beautiful!"

When the catapult had been fired about a dozen times, the watchers all stood back and grinned at one another. The captain of the Hexapylon was grinning nearly as hard as Archimedes. "Welcomer, you called it?" he said, stroking the machine's trigger. "By all the gods, after a welcome from this hero, the enemy will turn around and run!"

"I think we can all agree that this catapult has been seen to work," said Hieron contentedly.

Archimedes licked his lips eagerly. Now the money—and what was more important to reassure his family, the offer of a salaried position as a royal engineer.

But Hieron's next words were: "Can you build one bigger than this?"

"Oh!" Archimedes was surprised, but pleasantly so. He'd enjoyed making the Welcomer, but duplicating it would be much less interesting, even with the addition of a screw elevator. "Yes, of course. Um—how big?"

Hieron gave him a benevolent smile. "How big a machine could you build?"

"Well, I, uh . . ." He glanced around the catapult platform. "I mean, it's really a case of where you want it to go. I don't, uh, think you could fit anything bigger than a hundred-pounder on a platform like this."

There was an abrupt silence. Then Kallippos made his disbelieving hiss.

"Of course, if you, uh, put it on the *ground*," Archimedes continued awkwardly, "you could make a bigger one. I don't think you'd, uh, run into problems with the limits of the materials until you were over three talents. A three-talenter, though, would be a very big machine. It would take up a lot of supplies and you'd need, well, cranes and things"—he waved a hand vaguely in the air—"to load it, and it would be very hard to move it once you'd set it up."

"Could it be aimed, like this one?" asked Hieron quietly.

Archimedes blinked. "Well—might need tackle blocks. But you can move anything, with enough rope."

Kallippos shook his head. "Lord!" he protested to the king. "Nobody has ever built anything bigger than a two-talenter. Not even for Demetrios the Besieger or Ptolemy of Egypt."

"Hush!" said Hieron, still smiling genially at Archimedes. "Let me be sure I understand you. Are you saying there's no limit to the size of catapult you can build?"

"There *are* no limits in ideal mechanics," said Archimedes. "If you build something correctly and it doesn't work, that will be because your materials are too weak, not because the principles are wrong. It's like levers and pulleys. It is theoretically possible to move any given weight, however large, with any given effort, however small."

"So you say!" exclaimed Kallippos, now openly angry and indignant. "But I've never seen anyone moving a house with levers and pulleys!"

"With a place to stand, *I* could move the earth!" declared Archimedes.

"This is Syracuse, not Alexandria!" snapped Kallippos. "Earth, not Cloudcuckooland!"

"I could move a house, anyway!" Archimedes told him defiantly. "Or—or a ship."

Hieron was beaming now. "Would you say that's impossible, too?" he asked his chief engineer.

Kallippos divided one glare equally between Archimedes and the king, and nodded.

Hieron turned to Archimedes. "But you say you could do it?"

"Yes," Archimedes replied without thinking. "With enough rope."

"Then do it," ordered the king. "I want to see it. Do me a demonstration of ideal mechanics. I authorize you to use any ship, any of the royal workshops you like, and all the rope you want. But—catapults." He slapped the Welcomer. "Get Eudaimon to copy this, if he can—by the way, he's under your orders now. He's taking the rest of today off, but he should be back in the workshop tomorrow. If he isn't, or if he gives you any trouble, inform me. Correct any mistakes he makes, but otherwise let him supervise the actual labor; I want *you* to concentrate on a hundred-pounder. Three hundred-pounders, in fact, but I hope that Eudaimon will be able to copy those as well, once you've built the first of them. When you've finished the first one, you can start thinking about that three-talenter. No, make it a two-talenter—we don't have time for cranes. Don't postpone your demonstration to work on it, though. I do want to see you move a ship single-handed."

Archimedes blinked stupidly. He felt flattened. He had no idea what to say.

"Oh," added the king, "and my sister tells me that you're a very fine aulist. Perhaps you'd care to come to dinner at my house tomorrow, and bring your instruments?"

Archimedes felt his face going hot again. He opened his mouth, closed it when no sound came out, then tried again. "Uh, yes," he gasped, "thank you, O King."

"Excellent!" said Hieron. "Well, then, you'd better go see about your demonstration and the catapults—and I must go re-view the other forts. Do give your father my best wishes. Does he have a good doctor?"

"I—I," stammered Archimedes, "I think so."

"If you like, I'll send my own doctor around to have a look at him." He snapped his fingers at his secretary. "Remind me to do that. Well, then, I wish you joy!"

King Hieron turned and began to descend the steps. Marcus hurried over to Archimedes. "Sir!" he hissed in his master's ear. "The money!"

"Lord!" shouted Archimedes, and Hieron turned back with a look of mild inquiry. "Uh, Lord, I . . . I was supposed to be paid when the catapult was seen to work, and there was . . . that is, I thought there would be a salaried job."

"Ah," said Hieron. "A job. Do you mind if we leave the question of your job aside for the time being? I'm not at all sure what would be appropriate."

"You said Eudaimon was under my orders," Archimedes said faintly. "Won't he—I mean, he has a salaried position—doesn't he?"

"Indeed he does," said the king. His dark eyes flicked momentarily to Elymos, and he added, "And you, slave, can tell your foreman that much as I appreciate his taste in catapults, it was very stupid of him to expect me to sack a catapult engineer when I'm expecting a siege. Eudaimon stays as long as he obeys orders from Archimedes—which I think you'll find he's now willing to do. I wish you joy!" He turned and went on down the steps without looking back. His entourage, with various looks of speculation, curiosity, and doubt, gathered itself up and followed him. Kallippos was the last to go; he hesitated for a long minute at the top of the stairs, looking at Archimedes with a strange expression. It was no longer a glare, but something quite indefinable: anger was still there, but also pity, and perhaps even admiration.

He said nothing, however, and when the others had descended, he at last looked away and followed them.

Archimedes sat down heavily on the floor beside his catapult. "Am I a royal engineer or not?" he asked no one in particular.

"He hasn't paid you a copper," said Marcus sourly. "I'd say you're not."

"But he ordered more catapults," said Archimedes wonderingly, "and a demonstration. And he asked me to dinner." To dinner, and a bit of music. Would Delia be at the dinner? No: respectable women didn't go to dinner parties with men. But perhaps he would see her? He might even get another chance to play music with her. Delicious thought!

He smiled up at the two slaves, and found that they were both staring at him as though he were a dangerous dog. He blinked.

"I'd like it better if he'd paid you," said Marcus bluntly. "You're owed fifty drachmae, and he hasn't agreed on a price for any of the rest. Sir, you—"

"Can you really move a ship single-handed?" interrupted Elymos.

Archimedes suddenly beamed. He had always wanted to see how much weight one man could shift with an unlimited supply of rope, but nobody had ever before offered him the rope. He jumped to his feet, consumed with eagerness. "Elymos," he ordered, "you go back to the workshop and tell them the Welcomer passed. Tell them to get out the wood for another one-talenter, in the same amounts as before, and tell them that I'll be ordering the wood for a hundred-pounder tomorrow. Marcus, you go home and give them the news."

"Where are you going?" Marcus demanded suspiciously.

"Down to the docks, to see about my demonstration!" And he ran off down the steps, bright-eyed and smiling.

Marcus groaned. "Demonstrations of ideal mechanics!" he said in disgust. "Dinners and music!" He kicked the catapult stand. "What am I supposed to tell them at home? He's agreed to work for nothing!"

"Epimeles isn't going to like this," moaned Elymos. "He thought that once they fired the Welcomer, Eudaimon would go. And Eudaimon must know that!"

"It was Eudaimon who put that razor in the strings?" asked Marcus.

Elymos nodded. There seemed no point in lying about it now, to another slave.

"So that my master wouldn't get his job?"

Elymos nodded again. He was not surprised that Marcus had guessed this. His own life centered on the workshop, and he tended to assume that everyone knew about things—like Eudaimon's incompetence—which were important there.

Marcus stood still a moment, thinking. It was clear to him now that the king had expected the attempt at sabotage: he had hinted as much, and Eudaimon at least had understood. When Eudaimon offered to help restring the catapult, Hieron had refused him any opportunity to conceal the evidence of his crime; instead, the king had posted Eudaimon's superior as a witness. But as soon as the razor reached Hieron, it and Eudaimon had both disappeared, and the only result of the incident seemed to be that the king now expected Eudaimon to obey Archimedes without argument.

The only conclusion was that the king had enough evidence to charge Eudaimon with treason, but was using it to blackmail him instead. Why? And why hadn't the king given a job to Archimedes? Marcus began to chew on his lip. Hieron had a reputation for cunning, for unexpected twists of policy and unforeseen alliances. He had risen to power through the army, and yet had never used violence to get his way. He had never needed to: Syracuse had given him everything he wanted, though afterward she had sometimes found herself confusedly wondering why. Marcus had a sudden suspicion that he had just witnessed two demonstrations of supreme ability that day: one of technical competence, by Archimedes, and the other of manipulation, by Hieron. He had no idea what Hieron's manipulations were supposed to achieve, but he felt uneasily certain that they weren't finished yet and that his master was in the middle of them. Why?

There was a sound of footsteps on the stairs, and Straton hurried up, holding a letter. He glanced round the catapult platform, then looked irritably at Marcus. "Where's your master?" he demanded.

"Gone into the city to see about arranging a demonstration of ideal mechanics," said Marcus bitterly.

"He should have waited for the authorization for it!" said Straton, flapping the letter. "Where's he off to? The naval docks? Herakles! Does he really think he can move a ship single-handed?"

"Yes," replied Marcus. "You want to bet he can't?"

Straton looked at him, tapping the letter uncertainly against his hand.

"You owe me a stater," said Marcus deliberately. "You want to try to win it back?"

Straton sucked his teeth. "I don't owe you anything! The bet was that your master would be offered the job of whoever was in charge of whatever he was set to do. Eudaimon still has his job."

Elymos gaped at them.

"You're quibbling," said Marcus. "Eudaimon was in charge of catapults. Now Archimedes is in charge of catapults—isn't he?"

Straton shrugged uneasily. "King Hieron hasn't said."

"No," agreed Marcus sourly. "King Hieron hasn't even said whether he's going to pay my master the fifty drachmae that are owing to him. But the whole sense of our bet was that my master's war machines would be better than anyone else's. Now you know that's true—so pay up!"

Straton cast an embarrassed glance at the Welcomer. For all his ignorance of catapults, he was aware that this one was exceptional. He sighed, and fumbled in his purse.

"Of course," said Marcus, with deceptive casualness, "if you like you can add another stater to your stake, and bet that Archimedes can't move a ship single-handed."

Straton frowned, hesitating, staring at Marcus. Then he shook his head. "I'm not betting against your master again," he declared. Then suddenly he grinned and flipped Marcus the Egyptian stater. "Here," he said. "Take it and good luck. I know how to get it back! I'm going to lay Philonides odds of three to one that your master shifts that ship, and I don't doubt for a minute *he'll* take 'em!" He slung his spear over his shoulder and hurried off with the letter, still grinning.

Marcus scowled as he put the stater in his own purse. He had expected to enjoy winning that bet, but the image of the of the king's bright smile hung in his mind and soured the pleasure. Jobs were one thing: you knew what you were expected to give and what you could expect to receive. What Hieron was offering was undefined, and who knew what he might want in return for it?

"You bet that soldier that your master would be offered the job of *any* engineer he was set under?" asked Elymos, into the heavy silence.

"That's right," said Marcus shortly.

"Kallippos is good," said Elymos doubtfully.

Marcus shot him a look of irritation. "As good as Archimedes?"

Elymos looked at the Welcomer. Then he shook his head. "I suppose not," he said wonderingly.

For some reason, Marcus was even more irritated, and suddenly eager to get home. He glanced around the catapult platform once more, and noticed Archimedes' cloak lying abandoned in a crumpled heap under the artillery port. He went to pick it up, then paused and gazed out at the road north.

The king expected a siege. "It was very stupid of him to expect me to sack a catapult engineer," he had said, "when I'm expecting a siege." Soon, perhaps, a Roman army would be encamped there, in that field before him where goats browsed now. Marcus shut his eyes and imagined the camp: the neat squares pitched within an entrenchment, the campfires smoking, the sound of voices speaking in Latin. There was a bitter surge in the back of his throat. He had heard no Latin spoken for thirteen years now. Soon the Romans and their allies would be here: his own people. They had come to Sicily in a bad cause, and they threatened the city which had become some kind of home to him, the people he had come to care about. If they conquered, he would probably die. But they were his people still. He glanced up unhappily at the menacing shape of the catapult beside him, and reflected that if he were really loyal to his own, he would cut Archimedes' throat.

7

That evening Delia was informed that her brother wished to speak to her in his library. She was somewhat taken aback at the choice of location. Hieron generally received the leaders of Syracuse's army and city council in his dining hall or study, and talked to members of his household wherever they happened to be. The library was his private retreat. She picked her way through the gardens and along the colonnade with a mixture of curiosity and foreboding.

The library was a small room—the book collection of a private individual, not of a city—and it faced onto the smallest of the house's three courtyards. Three of its walls were lined from floor to ceiling with book racks, a neat crisscross of lathes from which the parchment title tags of the scrolls hung down, making the whole room flutter; the fourth wall held the door and a window. The only furniture was a couch, a small side table, and a lamp-stand. When Delia entered she found her brother reclining on the couch, frowning over a book which lay scrolled open in the light of the three lamps burning on the stand.

"Hieron?" she said, and he looked up with a smile, then sat up, swinging his feet off the couch and gesturing for her to sit. As she did so, she glanced at the open book, then stared at it hard. It was full of geometrical diagrams.

Hieron grinned and offered the scroll to her. The title tag

informed her that it was Euclid's *Conics*, Book 3. She waved her
hand at it in refusal and mock terror.

"I don't understand it either," said Hieron. "I was just trying
to see if something I saw today was in it. It isn't."

At this Delia guessed the reason for the summons. "You've
seen Archimedes son of Phidias?" she asked eagerly. She had
told her brother about her discovery as soon as he returned from
Messana.

Hieron nodded. "And you're right about him," he said. He
rolled the scroll up carefully. "He is a very, very clever young
man, and could undoubtedly be of value to the city." The rollers
clicked together; he tapped them straight and slid the book into
its parchment case. "The question is," he went on in a low voice,
"*how* valuable is he, and how much am I willing to pay for him?"
And he rested the scroll against his chin, eyes fixed thoughtfully
on nothing.

"Did the catapult work?"

"Oh, the catapult!" said Hieron dismissively. "Yes, it works. As
far as your friend is concerned, it's a good medium-sized catapult,
and he hopes it will earn him fifty drachmae and a job alongside
Eudaimon."

"Oh," said Delia, disappointed. "Alongside."

Hieron lifted his eyebrows. "I'm keeping Eudaimon. I can't
afford to lose any engineers just now, and his work is acceptable
when he has a machine he can copy. Now he can copy Archimedes'. Once he understands what it is he's copying, I expect
he'll be downright enthusiastic about it. It will take him a while
to work it out, though, and unfortunately he's going to have to
be kept on a tight leash while he does. That's in hand." The king
tapped the scrolled book against his chin again. "The question is,
what am I to do with Archimedes?"

"Hire him, of course!" exclaimed Delia.

Hieron shook his head and sighed. "As what?"

"As an engineer—what else? And if you expect Eudaimon to
copy from him, you ought to make him Eudaimon's superior."

"Yes, but do I gave him a rank and salary equal to Eudaimon— or to Kallippos? Or do I make up my mind that I'm going to keep him in Syracuse whatever he costs, and plan accordingly? I was hoping, sister, that you, who know the man better than I do, could give me a bit of advice."

Delia stared. "I—" she began; then changed it to, "But you said it was just a good medium-sized catapult!"

Hieron shook his head. "I said, as far as *he's* concerned. It's a one-talenter with a range of five hundred feet and an accuracy equal to the best arrow-shooter, and it can be pivoted with one hand. Archimedes is too young and inexperienced to realize how exceptional it is, but Kallippos didn't know whether to go wild with admiration or with jealousy." There was a pause, and then the king added, with a smile, "Being Kallippos, of course he did neither. He just scowled at it and hissed. But I'd bet anything he's in the workshop right now trying to replicate the pivot."

"I don't think I can advise you at all," said Delia, in a small voice. "I didn't expect—I just thought it was a matter of him replacing Eudaimon. Is he really *that* good?"

Hieron nodded seriously. "He may be even better. I've asked him to give a demonstration of ideal mechanics. He offered to move a ship single-handed. I'll see how that turns out before I make up my mind what to do about him."

"I don't understand," said Delia after a moment. "Why do you have to make up your mind about him *now*? Why not just—well, give him a job and keep promoting him?"

Hieron shook his head. He hitched himself up on the couch and turned himself to face her squarely. "Imagine I'm him."

"You don't look a bit like him," she said, smiling.

"Now, what is *that* supposed to mean? You think I should lose some weight? No, imagine I'm the son of Phidias, a mathematical engineer raised by a mathematical astronomer, the sort of man who amuses himself during his idle moments by working out theorems too advanced for Euclid. I studied in Alexandria at the Museum. I liked it. I didn't want to come home. But there's a war starting, my father's ill, and my family depends on me. I am a dutiful and affectionate son. I come home, I look for work making war machines, I find it. Right so far?"

"I think so," agreed Delia, beginning to be intrigued. "You're certainly right that he liked Alexandria. He talked about it even to me."

"Everyone Agathon spoke to about him mentioned it! He was apparently supposed to come home two years before he did. Don't look so surprised—*you're* the one who set Agathon onto him. All right, my first catapult has passed its trial and I've happily agreed to work for what Leptines offered me. I make some very large, very advanced catapults; I also produce countermeasures to seige towers and mines. I'm good at that, of course—the key to siege machinery is the accurate calculation of size and distance, and the key to *that* is geometry, at which I am adept. At first I don't notice that I'm exceptional, because I haven't made war machines before and I don't have any standard of comparison. But before long it dawns on me that none of the other engineers in the city can do the things I'm doing. And eventually the fame of my machines spreads, and other cities and kingdoms try to hire me. Now: am I a loyal citizen?"

"I think so," said Delia. "After all, you did come home when you heard about the war, and you hurried to place your abilities at the disposal of the city."

"Ye-es—but on the other hand, making catapults is the easiest way for an engineer to earn money during a war, and with my father ill my family needs money. Still, we'll say I'm a loyal Syracusan as well as a dutiful son. I reject the offers of Carthaginian Akragas and Roman Tarentum; I scorn Cyrene and Epirus and Macedon—but I feel aggrieved. My family's not rich, my younger sister is of an age to marry and needs a dowry, and I know that I'm worth more than I'm getting. Besides, it's mathematics, not war machines, that is my soul's passion: the yoke frets me. When one of my old Alexandrian friends writes to tell me that King Ptolemy would give me a job in Egypt—five times the salary and half the work—I accept it, take my family, and go. Any comments?"

Delia frowned. "You wouldn't abandon your city in time of war!"

"Maybe we'll be out of the war by then: gods, let us be! But if we aren't, won't it mean that I'm eager to take my family out of danger? Particularly when it means returning to a place I love and never wanted to leave. Besides, Egypt is an ally: serving her isn't betraying Syracuse."

"Would Ptolemy really offer that much?"

"Oh, that's certain!" exclaimed Hieron in surprise. "Ptolemy's spent a fortune on investigating catapult design, and his advisers perpetually scan the horizon for improvements. And Egypt is rich."

"Well then," said Delia, smiling with satisfaction, "you should offer him more from the start, so that he's got no cause to feel aggrieved and discontented!"

Hieron took a deep breath. "Perhaps. But start again. My catapult has passed its trial, and I'm made the equal of Kallippos and paid two or three times as much as I expected. On the strength of this, I can arrange for my sister to marry a man of good family, and perhaps marry a woman of good family myself. I become a citizen of some standing. I have wealth, I have respect. I'm grateful to the city. Even when I realize that my reward is merited, I'm still grateful, because the city recognized me before I recognized myself. When the offer from Egypt comes, I reject it . . ." Hieron paused, then went on softly, "Or do I?" He stood up suddenly and crossed the room to the book rack. He ran one plump finger down the shelves, then put the scroll of Euclid's *Conics* back in its place. "The thing I don't know," he went on quietly, "is whether he's merely very good, or invaluable. If he's merely good, treating him generously should be enough to keep him. But if he's what I think he might be, he'll be off to Alexandria eventually however much I pay him— unless I take steps to prevent it. Ptolemy can offer him the Museum, and that's something for which I have no substitute. So perhaps I would do better to save my time and money, treat him as nothing out of the ordinary, and profit by what he's willing to do before he leaves. Or perhaps—perhaps I should decide to keep him whatever he costs, and start chaining him to Syracuse now, before he can realize his own value and assert his freedom." Hieron dropped back down on the couch and put one foot on the cushions beside Delia. "So, what do you think, sister? Is he merely a clever young man, or is he inspired by the Muses?"

"I don't know," said Delia, low-voiced in confusion. She had imagined herself drawing her brother's attention to merit, and watching proudly as the merit was rewarded. Hieron, however, was not talking about reward, but of use, even of exploitation. She remembered Archimedes laughing with excitement at the thought of what his friends in Alexandria were doing, and suddenly regretted that she had mentioned him to her brother at all.

"What's the matter?" asked the king.

"You talk about him as though he were a slave," said Delia uncomfortably.

Hieron shrugged. " 'One man is my master,' " he quoted softly,

" 'Custom, yours—and he masters a myriad others too.
Some are slaves to tyrants, tyrants to fear.
Men are slaves to kings, kings, to the gods,
and gods, to Necessity: for Necessity, you see,
endows all things with natures great or less
and so forever is master of us all.'

"Although," he added, in a more normal tone, "I didn't feel like a king's slave even before I was a king myself, and tyrant as I may be, I don't think I'm slave to fear. But I'll grant the poet Necessity and the gods." He smiled at his sister. "Don't worry," he added. "I'm not going to hurt your fellow aulist. In fact, I've invited him to dinner."

~ ARCHIMEDES WAS LATE FOR THE DINNER PARTY. HE HAD spent the day at the naval docks, preparing his demonstration of ideal mechanics; when he did not come home to change his clothes late in the afternoon, Marcus was sent to fetch him. The slave found his master covered in dirt and soot and smelling strongly of mutton-fat pulley grease, perched on the roof of a ship shed fixing a pulley to the main roof beam.

Marcus hauled him down and bore him off to the public baths, ignoring the enthusiastic attempts to explain the system of compound pulleys and wheels—"*toothed* wheels, Marcus, so they won't slip"—by which Archimedes expected to move a ship. He saw to it that his master was washed and barbered, then brought him home, where a frantic Philyra was waiting.

"You're going to be *late!*" she told him furiously. "You're going to be *late* for dinner with the *king!* Medion, how do you expect him to pay you if you're going to be rude to him?"

"But he's the one who ordered the demonstration!" protested Archimedes, blinking.

Philyra gave a shriek of frustration and hurled his good tunic at him. "You never care about anything except your stupid *ideas!*"

Arata, calmer by nature and more resigned, ignored her children's quarrel and drew Marcus aside. "You go with him tonight," she ordered quietly. "But be careful."

Marcus looked at her with narrow-eyed reserve. He'd guessed that he'd be ordered to accompany Archimedes to the king's house. A guest did not arrive at a dinner party carrying his own flutes, like a hired musician: a slave had to act as porter, and he was the most natural slave for the job. But—be careful? "Is there some special reason for caution, mistress?" he asked.

Arata sighed and brushed back a wisp of graying hair. "I don't know," she said slowly. "But—there have been these people asking questions about my Archimedion. I suppose it's just because of the catapults, and understandable—but I don't like it, Marcus. Who can tell what's in the mind of a tyrant? Watch what you say to them in the king's house."

"Yes, mistress," said Marcus grimly.

She smiled. "I know I can trust you," she said. "You've served us well, Marcus. Don't think I haven't noticed."

Marcus hefted his shoulders uncomfortably and looked away.

When they finally reached the king's house, Archimedes was ushered into the dining room, where the king was already reclining, along with his father-in-law, Leptines, and two army officers (one of them Dionysios), three Syracusan noblemen, and Kallippos—with Archimedes, a conventional total of nine diners. Archimedes was shown to the lowest place on the couch to the left of the table, the most junior place for the youngest guest.

Marcus was led to a workroom which adjoined the kitchen. Most of the other guests had been attended by their own slaves, and the narrow dirt-floored room was packed with a small crowd. Most were men of about Marcus' age, dressed plainly, though one pretty, long-haired boy in a fine tunic had taken the only stool and sat sniffing disdainfully at the others. Marcus returned the boy's look of contempt: there was no doubt why that one was wearing such fancy clothes.

"Sit down," said the king's doorkeeper genially; he had been the one who showed Marcus to his place. "What's that you're carrying?"

Marcus settled on the floor and placed the armful of flute cases on his lap—there were four of them. "My master's auloi," he said neutrally. "He was asked to bring them."

The pretty boy tittered. "He's the flute boy, is he?"

"That's enough!" ordered Agathon sternly. "Several of the other guests have brought instruments, too. If you give those to me, fellow, I'll see they're put safe with the others."

"I can look after them," replied Marcus.

The slaves had been provided with a plain meal of bean soup and bread, and someone helped Marcus to a bowl. He sat back and began to eat in silence, careful not to drip on the flutes.

The doorkeeper appeared in no hurry to get back to his lodge. He leaned against the storeroom wall, crossing his arms. "You usually look after his flutes?" he asked casually.

Marcus gave a grunt of assent.

"Been with your master long?"

"Been in the family about thirteen years," replied Marcus evenly.

"Heard he went out to Alexandria. You go with him?"

Marcus gave another grunt, noting to himself that Arata had been quite right: they were trying to probe him.

"I'd like to go to Alexandria," said one of the other slaves enviously. "What's it like?"

Marcus shrugged and concentrated on bean soup.

"This fellow's some kind of barbarian," remarked the boy, sneering. "He doesn't know enough Greek to describe it."

Marcus cast him an irritated glare, then returned to his soup.

"What sort of barbarian are you?" asked the doorkeeper.

"Samnite," said Marcus firmly. "And freeborn."

That was where everything began to go wrong. One of the other slaves gave an exclamation of delight and began speaking rapidly in Oscan. Marcus stared for a moment in horror. He understood Oscan, but to try to speak it would betray his complete lack of a Samnite accent—which this speaker definitely possessed. He interrupted the flood of words with a hasty explanation, in Greek, that it had been so many years since he spoke Oscan that he'd forgotten his native tongue.

"I thought you said you'd only been a slave for thirteen years!" protested the disappointed Samnite.

"No, no, longer than that!" said Marcus. "Much longer. I had a couple of other masters—soldiers—before I was sold to my present master's father." That was true, too, though he had not had them for long.

"You were enslaved by the Romans?" asked the Samnite.

"Yes," agreed Marcus.

"May the gods destroy them!" said the Samnite. "I, also." He offered Marcus his hand.

Marcus made a vague gesture toward it and spilled soup on the flute cases. He swore. The Samnite helped him mop up; the pretty boy giggled. The doorkeeper just stood there watching with cynical eyes.

"What's your name?" asked the Samnite; and, when Marcus told him, exclaimed, "You shouldn't use the name a Roman gave

you! Your father must have named you Mamertus—that is the
name you should keep."

"I was sold as Marcus," said Marcus. "I can't change that now."

The Samnite made a disparaging remark about Greeks—in
Oscan—then began questioning Marcus about where in Samnium he came from and when he had been enslaved. Marcus
sweated and lied, horribly aware of the doorkeeper smiling.
Luckily, the Samnite was soon wholly engaged in recounting his
own history and did not probe Marcus'. But he could not be got
rid of. Even after the other slaves settled to a discussion of the
war and prices instead, the Samnite clung to Marcus' side and
rambled on about the wonders of Samnium and the wickedness
of the Romans. Marcus ached to tell him to be quiet, but did
not care.

After what seemed an eternity, the king's butler came in with
a basin of surprisingly good strong wine for the slaves. He gave
Marcus a hard look. "You're the slave of that new engineer?" he
asked, and, when Marcus admitted that he was, the butler demanded furiously, "Does he *always* draw on the table?" which
sent the pretty boy into floods of giggles. No sooner had he settled than the Samnite started up again.

After another eternity, however, another of the king's waiters
appeared to announce that the guests were ready for some music.
Marcus picked up the flutes and headed for the dining room in
a relieved rush. He did not care where he spent the rest of the
evening, so long as it was away from the Samnite—and the doorkeeper.

ARCHIMEDES HAD NOT BEEN ENJOYING THE DINNER
much more than his slave. When he first arrived, Hieron had
asked him how the preparations for the demonstration were going. He'd made a mistake: he'd answered. The preparations were
going very well, the project was tremendously interesting, and he
was ready to jump and down with excitement. He told the company all about the compound pulleys and toothed wheels, and

went on to the principles of the lever and the mechanical advantages of the screw; he sketched diagrams on the table in wine, and flourished table knives and bread rolls to illustrate points. Hieron and the engineer Kallippos asked occasional informed and interested questions, so he did not at first notice that the rest of the company was regarding him as though he were a dead earwig that had turned up in their soup. When he finally did notice, it was halfway through the main course. Then he realized that he'd been speaking virtually without a pause for half an hour, that the other guests were watching him with expressions ranging from outrage to stark disbelief, and that the butler and slaves were glaring at the mess he had made on the table. He went crimson and fell silent.

He kept quiet for the rest of the meal, too embarrassed even to notice what food he was eating. Leptines the Regent and the city councillors discussed finance, with occasional interested comments from the king; the army officers and Kallippos discussed fortifications, again with occasional comments from the king. Archimedes felt ignorant, young, and extremely stupid.

Eventually, however, the slaves brought in the dessert course of apples and honeyed almonds, and Hieron sat up and poured out a few drops of unmixed wine, the offering to the gods which closed the meal. This was supposed to be the moment when the most pleasant part of the dinner party began, when the food was out of the way and the participants could sit about drinking and talking and listening to music.

"My dear friends," said Hieron, as the slaves hurried about refilling cups, "I thought that, given the tense and unhappy situation in which our lovely city finds herself, we might cheer ourselves with a bit of music. For those gifted by the Muses, making music is surely a greater pleasure even than listening to it, so, as several of you are accomplished musicians, I've invited you to bring your instruments. What do you say? Shall we brighten the night with song?"

The party naturally agreed, and presently a number of slaves, including Marcus, hurried in with boxes or canvas-wrapped bundles. Archimedes was surprised to see that Leptines the Regent was handed a kithara and Kallippos a lyre. One of the city councillors had a barbitos—a bass lyre—and one of the army officers a second kithara. Archimedes himself was the only aulist. He took his flute cases nervously, then shot Marcus a startled look: the cases were sticky, as though something had been spilled on them. But the slave was at his most impassive and didn't respond to the look by so much as a blink. Archimedes hesitated, then opened all four sticky cases, inserted reeds in all four auloi, and tied on his cheek strap.

"Captain Dionysios," said Hieron, smiling, "I know you have a very fine voice. Perhaps you could favor us with . . . what about the 'Swallow Song'? We all know that, don't we?"

Everyone did. Dionysios son of Chairephon, looking slightly less comfortable in the king's house than he had at the Arethusa, stood up, waited for the scuffle of the instrumentalists to abate, then raised his head and began the old folk song:

> "Come, come, swallow,
> Come bring back the Spring!
> Bring us the best season,
> White-belly, black-wing!"

Marcus had succeeded in slipping out the far door into a garden, and when the music started he sat down beneath a date palm to listen. The night air was pleasantly cool after the hot sweatiness of the workroom, and the singing carried out clearly from the lamplit dining room. Dionysios did indeed have a fine voice, a clear strong tenor. Leptines' accompaniment was a bit too formal for a folk song, but the other players caught the spirit of the music quickly, especially the barbitos player, who was very good. Archimedes, Marcus noted, had chosen the tenor and soprano auloi: tenor for the melody, soprano for an embroidery of swallowlike chirps which swirled and swooped above the melodic line. It went well, and when the song ended, there was a ripple of applause.

There was a rustling among the ornamental shrubs as the next song started, and someone else came through the dark garden; the care with which the figure eased its way through the undergrowth made Marcus certain that it was a woman even when she was no more than a shadow on the other side of the courtyard. She did not notice Marcus until she almost stumbled over him. Then she demanded in an angry whisper, "Who are you?"

Delia was in a temper. She had spent much of the afternoon resenting the convention that barred her from attending the dinner party. The whole world might agree that respectable girls did not recline at table for men's parties, still less come in after the meal was finished and offer to play the flute—but she differed with the world on this and many other points. Now she had come quietly to listen to the music, and here was somebody or other standing watch to prevent her!

But the lumpish shape under the date palm whispered back, "Excuse me. I'm the slave of one of the guests. I wanted to listen to the music."

"Oh," said Delia. Nothing to do with her, then—and she could hardly object to someone else doing what she had come to do herself. "You may stay," she conceded.

She retreated a few steps to a stone bench under a grape arbor, and for a time they both listened in silence. The folk song was followed by an aria from Euripides—Leptines' formality came into its own—then by a drinking song, then by a lament. There was a pause, and then suddenly a duet between the barbitos and the auloi sprang into the still air—a fiery cascade on the strings and a swirl of notes from the flute so thick and fast that the ear struggled to follow them. The barbitos lit up the night; the flutes danced around it, now following the melody, now countering it, and suddenly, in the final phrases, blending with it in a shocking and breathtaking harmony. There was a moment's silence, then a thunder of applause.

The slave gave a satisfied sigh. Delia felt a sudden sympathy for him: banned, like her, from the feast, but sitting outside in the dark to drink in the music. "Whose slave are you?" she asked, remembering to keep her voice low. The music had stopped for the moment, as the guests drank more wine, and she did not want to be overheard.

"Archimedes son of Phidias'," said Marcus. Ordinarily he would have added his own name, but at the moment he was wishing that he were called something nondescript and Greek.

"Oh!" exclaimed Delia.

Marcus caught the note of recognition in her voice and set his teeth angrily. The whole royal household must have been discussing Archimedes! He had no idea who this woman was, but the way she had granted him permission to stay had marked her out as free and important.

After a moment, Delia said warmly, "Your master's flute-playing is superb."

Marcus turned the remark this way and that in his mind and concluded that it was harmless. He gave a grunt of agreement. "The fellow on the barbitos is good, too," he added.

There was a long silence, broken only by the sound of voices talking in the dining room and the buzzing call of a scops owl from some corner of the garden. Delia gazed intently at the slave's hunched black shape, struggling with an urgent desire to speak to him, to tell him something of importance . . . but what? She could feel it there, an undefined tension within herself, crying that she should make use of this providential encounter to warn Archimedes that . . .

She told herself not to be ridiculous. *Warn* Archimedes, against her tolerant, generous, much-loved brother? The worst Hieron was going to do was pay Archimedes no more than the salary agreed! Perhaps that was the message she really wanted to send: *Don't sell yourself too cheap!*

But with that thought she understood suddenly that she did not want Archimedes to sell himself at all. Not even to Hieron and Syracuse.

"Your master . . ." she said finally, not knowing how or even whether to begin. "Is he a good master?"

Marcus had scrutinized this question, too, before he was aware of it, and discovered that it was difficult to answer. It was, in a way, the wrong question—he very rarely thought of Archimedes as his master at all; when he did, he resented him. But most of the time he thought of Archimedes simply as Archimedes: a phenomenon exasperating, astonishing, and unparalleled. "I don't know," he said, surprised into honesty. "I think most of the time he forgets that he is my master. Does that make him a good master or a bad one?"

Delia made a noise of impatience. "Do you like him?"

"Most of the time," he admitted cautiously.

"Listen, then," said Delia. "Tell him I wish him well. And tell him . . . tell him that my brother is waiting to see how this demonstration of his turns out to decide what offer to make him. If it goes well he needs to be more careful than he does if it goes badly."

Marcus stared at her. In the night shadows of the garden, he could make out nothing but the gleam of eyes in a pale face. *Her brother.* "I don't understand!" he said in bewilderment. Then, urgently, "Lady, if the king suspects my master of anything . . ."

"Nobody suspects him!" said Delia. She was Syracusan enough to understand that the first emotion inspired by a tyrant's interest was fear. "Don't think that! Hieron wouldn't. It's just that Hieron thinks he may become invaluable, and there may be something in the contract that . . . I don't know, that may bind him in a way he might later regret. Just—ask him to be careful." She stopped, biting her lip. Now that she had delivered it, the nature of her warning seemed to have altered. Night and the unexpected opportunity had tricked her into a betrayal, a breach of the loyalty she owed to her brother. Her face went hot and she felt all at once sick with shame. She jumped to her feet. "No!" she said, in a fervent whisper. "Don't say anything to him at all!" She turned and blundered off through the dark garden as though the slave might chase after her.

Marcus remained under the date palm, too stunned to move.

After many more songs, the party ended, and Marcus slunk back into the dining room to collect the flutes. He found Archimedes busy discussing modes with the barbitos player; the barbitos itself had been collected by the pretty boy, who amused himself by sneering at Marcus as they both stood waiting for their masters to finish talking. Marcus was intensely relieved when the discussion finally ended and they were able to leave the house.

Archimedes had largely forgotten his humiliation early in meal: his flute-playing had been a success. The barbitos player in particular had been very gracious, and said that they must play together again. Since the barbitos player was one of the richest and most important men in the city, well known for his patronage of the arts, this was gratifying. Not that it mattered, Archimedes told himself—he was a democrat, after all—but still, it was gratifying. He set off down the road at a good pace, swinging a corner of his cloak and humming.

Marcus hurried after him, clutching the flutes and looking grim. When they reached the main road, the slave ran up beside him and said in a low voice, "Sir, something happened up there that you should know about."

"Mmmm?" said Archimedes, without paying attention.

"I was listening to the music in the garden," went on Marcus, "and the king's sister came up to listen as well, and—"

"Delia?" asked Archimedes, stopping short and turning to Marcus. The moon had risen and shone full into the wide avenue, and it showed plainly his look of delight.

Delia? thought Marcus, in disbelief. "I don't know her name," he said in bewilderment. "But she was the king's sister. She said to tell you—"

"Delia gave you a message for me?" cried Archimedes, even more delighted.

Marcus stared at him. He remembered now the girl's hesitant speech, and the way she had run off after trying to deny her message. In retrospect it seemed very like a maiden's first shy steps toward love. *"Perii!"* he exclaimed, surprised into swearing in his own language. "No wonder the king's been sending people to spy on you!"

"What?" said Archimedes, surprised in turn. "On me? Don't

be ridiculous! There's nothing for anyone to find out."

"May the gods forbid that there should be anything between you and the king's sister!"

"I just met her twice in the king's house when I went there to see about the catapult," said Archimedes stiffly. "She plays the aulos too, and we talked about it. She's very good. What was the message? You said I should know about it."

Marcus rubbed his hands through his hair. Maybe it was that innocent, he thought—but the fact remained that the king's sister—the *king's sister!*—was sending Archimedes clandestine warnings about her brother's intentions. What did she see in him? He wasn't particularly good-looking, wasn't rich, and certainly possessed no polished seducer's charm. But in Alexandria he had won the favor of Laïs, and now there was this!

He could not even tell Arata about it—a thing he regretted, because he knew she was concerned about the king's spies and he had deep respect for her good sense. But he could not inform his master's *mother*, of all people, about his master's romantic follies!

"Well?" demanded Archimedes.

"She said to tell you that she wishes you well," he said at last, "and she warns you that if your demonstration goes well you must be careful, because her brother may try to get you into a contract that binds you to something you might later regret."

Archimedes beamed. "That's wonderful!" He began walking again, this time with something of a swagger.

"Wonderful? Didn't you hear what I said?" demanded Marcus furiously.

"Yes, of course. Delia wishes me well, and the king is going to offer me a contract if my demonstration goes well. I thank the gods!"

Marcus groaned.

"What's the matter now?"

Marcus regarded his bright-eyed assurance and groaned again. "Nothing," he said despairingly. "Nothing at all."

〜 IN THE KING'S HOUSE, HIERON WAS SITTING IN THE doorkeeper's lodge, feet up on the arm of the couch, sipping a cup of cold water and discussing the evening with Agathon, as was his custom after a dinner party. He listened to his guests, his doorkeeper listened to his guests' slaves, and afterward they compared notes; it was a technique that had often proved valuable. The doorkeeper had revealed that the slave of one of the officers was worried that his master had been drinking too much, while one of the councillors had been spending a great deal of money lately.

"And Archimedes' slave?" asked the king. "Anything useful from him?"

Agathon snorted. "I think somebody must have noticed that we were asking about his master. He arrived determined that he, at any rate, was not going to tell us anything. Once the music started he slunk off and hid in the garden so that he wouldn't have to talk to anyone. But he was claiming to be a Samnite, and he's quite plainly a Latin."

"You're sure of that?"

"Oh, yes. His name's Marcus, and when he found out that Aristodemos' slave is a real Samnite, he was horrified." Agathon gave a cackle of laughter. "He had to pretend he'd forgotten how to speak Oscan, and he was such a poor liar it was pitiable."

The king frowned. "Has he had access to the workshops?"

"I'll check it," said Agathon at once. "But he's been in Phidias' household for thirteen years, and my impression is that he's loyal to his master."

Hieron nodded thoughtfully and took a sip of water. "Probably no use," he said. "But one never knows. Keep an eye on him."

"Yes, sir," said Agathon. He watched his master for a moment, then said, "And you, sir? What did the guests think about the war?"

Hieron stretched and sat up. "We did not discuss it."

Agathon raised his eyebrows. "That must have been difficult."

Hieron grinned. "Not too much so. Archimedes discussed ideal mechanics from the eggs through to the turbot. After that the other guests were perfectly happy to talk about *anything* nonmechanical. It needed very little steering."

Agathon cleared his throat nervously. "Sir . . ." He stopped.

"What?" asked Hieron.

When Agathon did not answer, the king leaned forward smiling and said, "Do *you* want to talk about the war, Aristion?"

It was an old nickname—the diminutive of "best" for Agathon's proper name, which meant "good." The slave plucked courage from it, met his master's eyes, and said, "What's going to happen, sir?"

Hieron sighed. "Whatever is fated, my friend. But what I hope for is that once the Romans have blunted their teeth on our defenses they'll offer me better terms than they offered at Messana."

Agathon sat silent for a long moment. It was stark hope, and severely limited. "There's no hope from the alliance, then," he said at last. "No hope of victory."

"There is always hope," replied Hieron evenly, "but I don't expect anything, no. Carthage has not made terms with Rome and has not moved openly against us, and as long as that's true I will continue to speak in public as though she were our steadfast ally. But the Carthaginians had a fleet which was supposed to be guarding the straits, and it notably failed to stop the Romans from crossing to Sicily. And while we were besieging Messana, the Romans negotiated with me and with the Carthaginians—separately. When I suggested to my allied commander that I send someone to observe his negotiations and he send someone to observe mine, he turned me down. And when the Romans attacked us, the Carthaginians did nothing. The enemy had two legions, Agathon—ten thousand of the fiercest fighters in the world. They quick-marched out of the city and attacked our siege works. We threw them off and chased them halfway back to the walls. If the Carthaginians had attacked the Romans in the flank as they retreated, it would have been a real victory. But they did nothing—*nothing!* Drew up their troops to defend their own camp, and stood watching. Oh, afterward Hanno sent a messenger congratulating me on my victory and explaining that he had not had time to arrange his forces, but it was perfectly clear from that battle how Hanno intends to fight this war. He hopes to use us to weaken the Romans and the Romans to break us, and to claim Sicily for Carthage when all is done. So I disengaged under cover of darkness and came home—Don't repeat any of this, Agathon, my dear. I will call Carthage my ally as long as there is any chance of her remaining so. And there may be something to be done at Carthage. There are always factions: I have some friends there and Hanno has some enemies."

"What terms did the Romans offer at Messana?" asked Agathon bleakly. They both knew that without Carthaginian help, the best Syracuse could hope for was survival.

"The same that they offer their Italian 'allies,' " replied Hieron dismissively. "We accept a garrison and send troops to aid them in their war. Oh, and pay five hundred talents of silver, to compensate the Romans for their trouble and expense in making war upon us. Highly unpleasant man, Appius Claudius." He took another sip of water. "Any comments?"

Agathon sighed unhappily and rubbed his nose. "They're saying in the city that the Carthaginians have betrayed us."

Hieron gave a rueful snort. "Didn't take them long to work it out! They're not panicking though, I hope?"

"No, sir. They've seen you behaving as though there's nothing to worry about, and they still hope. I suppose you're right not to confirm their fears."

"I'm so glad you approve! Shall I tell you what my hopes for this city's survival rest upon?"

Agathon nodded silently. Hieron looked down into his half-empty cup of water and said softly, "Walls, Agathon. Walls and catapults. The Romans are almost unbeatable on an open field, but they don't have much experience in siege work. Let them lay siege to Syracuse and die before our walls. Let them understand how much it will cost them if they want to break us. Then let them give us some terms we can accept." He emptied the cup.

"So that's why you're so interested in Archimedes son of Phidias."

"I'd be interested in him under any circumstances," said Hieron, getting to his feet and setting the cup down. "If I weren't interested in having the best engineers available, I wouldn't deserve to be king. But I admit, at the moment it cheers me just to see the fellow. The Romans aren't used to big catapults, and even a one-talenter will frighten them—as much as they can be frightened by anything in war, which I suppose isn't much." He yawned, stretching, and added lightly, "He plays the flute well, too."

8

Phidias' illness had taken a turn for the worse again. He slept most of the time, and it was hard to rouse him; when he did wake, he was often confused and could not understand where he was or what was wanted of him. To Archimedes' grief, he did not seem to appreciate even that the catapult had passed its trial and that his son was in a position to provide for the family. Hieron's personal physician had indeed come to visit him, but apart from leaving a drug which Phidias could take if he was in any pain, had done nothing the family's own doctor hadn't done already. "There is no hope of a cure," he had said.

Archimedes could not stop himself from hoping anyway. Every morning and evening he would go into the sickroom to see his father. He would try to start a conversation, and when that failed he would simply sit, doing calculations or playing music while Phidias slept.

On the morning two days after the dinner party, the day of the demonstration, he went into the sickroom as usual and found his father asleep. He sat down on the couch, took the skeletal hand in his own, and brushed back the thin white hair. "Papa?" he said. Phidias woke and smiled up at him in silence.

"I'm going down to the docks now," he told his father. "I'm doing a demonstration of mechanics for the king."

The brittle hand clenched suddenly on his own. "Don't go away!" Phidias begged.

"It's only for an hour or two," said Archimedes.

"Don't go away to Alexandria, please, Medion!"

"Papa! I'm not, I won't. I'm just doing a demonstration at the docks. I'll come home and check on you afterward."

"Don't go away again, please!" whispered Phidias, as though he hadn't heard; then, more softly still, "Look after your mother and sister for me."

"I will, Papa," Archimedes said. "I promise."

He stayed where he was for a few more minutes, and eventually the tight grip on his hand relaxed, and his father went back to sleep. He stood up very gently so as not to wake him, then stood looking down at the yellow face soberly. Was it imagination, or was there a translucent quality to the skin, a gasp to the shallow breath, which had not been there before?

Arata came in. Archimedes had invited her to come watch the demonstration, and she had put on her best gown preparatory to going, but at the sight of her husband's face she pulled her chair out from the wall and sat down to keep watch over him. "I don't want to leave him this morning," she told her son. "You take Philyra."

Archimedes did not protest. He said only, "Send Chrestos to fetch me if . . . if he asks for me, or if anything happens. I don't care about the king: I'll come."

Arata nodded, and Archimedes bent to kiss her forehead, then went out into the courtyard.

Philyra was already waiting, bright-eyed and impatient in her best tunic and cloak. Archimedes thought she needn't have bothered with the tunic, since it was invisible apart from the border around the hem: Philyra was respectably swathed in cream-colored wool from head to foot, and her face was already pink with the heat—unless it was excitement. Marcus and young Agatha, waiting beside her, both looked considerably more comfortable in plain linen tunics. Agatha was going because it was genteel to have a lady's maid, and Marcus was carrying a basket with some refreshments.

"Medion!" exclaimed Philyra, "You're not wearing *that* cloak!" It was the linen one.

"I'm not going to be able to wear any cloak to do the demonstration," objected Archimedes. "You can't haul on a rope in a cloak. So I thought . . ."

Philyra shook her head firmly. Marcus, grinning, set down the basket, ran upstairs, and came back with the yellow cloak. Archimedes swore under his breath, but put the thing on, and the party set out.

When they were approaching the docks, the streets grew crowded, with large numbers of people jostling along in the same direction as themselves. Archimedes eyed them dubiously. "Is something happening?" he asked a plump waterseller.

"Haven't you heard?" replied the waterseller. "One of the king's engineers thinks he can move a ship single-handed."

"But . . ." said Archimedes, blinking. "Are all these people coming to see *that?*"

" 'Course," said the waterseller reprovingly. "Should be quite a sight."

"But—but how do they all *know?*" asked Archimedes.

"It was posted in the marketplace," replied the waterseller. "What's it to you?"

"I'm the engineer," said Archimedes bemusedly, wondering who had posted it.

"So *you're* Archimedes son of Phidias!" exclaimed the waterseller, looking him up and down disappointedly. "I thought you'd be older."

Philyra gave a laugh of delighted astonishment and took her brother's arm. "Medion, you're famous!"

The quayside, when they reached it, was crowded with people standing about talking, eating, and drinking and pointing out to one another the ship Archimedes had selected. This was by no means the largest ship in the king's fleet, but it was nonetheless indisputably a ship: a fat single-masted transport about seventy feet long. It had been drawn up out of the water and its sides curved upward from the stone slipway twice as high as a man. Philyra stopped when she saw it, stared a moment, then looked at her brother anxiously. So did Marcus. They had both accepted Archimedes' assurances that his system would work, but now they were faced with an object larger than their house, the project suddenly appeared totally impossible.

"Can you really move it?" asked Philyra.

But he was surprised that she could doubt it. "Oh yes!" he exclaimed. "It only weighs about twelve hundred talents unloaded, and I've given myself a mechanical advantage of fifteen hundred. I'll show you!"

The area about the ship was in the process of being roped off to protect it from the crowd, but the sailors doing the roping recognized Archimedes and allowed his party through. He had just begun explaining the system to Philyra when there was a blare of trumpets, and they looked up to see the king arriving. First came a file of guards, led by an officer on horseback. The shields slung over their backs gleamed with color, and their helmets and spear points shone in the sun. Behind them came the king, riding upon a magnificent white horse and robed in purple. He was accompanied by Kallippos, on a tall bay, then followed by trumpeters, and by a covered litter carried by eight slaves. The crowd cheered and applauded, and—eventually—made way for him. Philyra clutched Archimedes' arm with excitement as the royal procession drew to a halt before them.

The litter was set down, and the passengers climbed out: first the queen, purple-cloaked like her husband; then the little boy, Gelon, also in purple and looking hot. Lastly a dark-haired girl climbed out and stood a moment straightening a cloak of very fine crimson cotton worked with gold stars. Archimedes stood up straighter, grinning with pleasure. So Delia had come to see his demonstration! She was even prettier than he remembered. He tried to meet her eyes, wondering how he could thank her for her message. But when he finally caught her gaze, she returned his smile only with a cold flat stare.

Philyra had no real idea who the girl in red was, but she

thought she would float up in the air with pride when the whole royal party came over to shake hands with her brother. She was aware of the watching crowd talking about them, pointing Archimedes out to one another as the son of Phidias the Astronomer, the Alexandrian-educated engineer who had offered to do something impossible.

Kallippos shook hands with Archimedes very brusquely, then at once strode off to inspect the system of pulleys, leaving Archimedes glancing nervously after him.

Queen Philistis smiled graciously at Philyra when Archimedes introduced her. "I believe we've met before," she said. "You won prizes for music at your school, didn't you, child? Your whole family is much gifted by the Muses, it seems."

Philyra blushed. She had indeed won prizes for music, and the queen had handed them out, but she hadn't expected Philistis to remember.

Delia merely gave Philyra a look of black-eyed disdain. Under the disdain, she was troubled. When she had first noticed that Archimedes had a girl on his arm, she had suffered a perplexing moment of indignation—followed by relief as she noticed the strong family resemblance between the two, and remembered that he had a sister. Such feelings were, she knew, entirely inappropriate—no, lunatic! It didn't matter if Archimedes had a girl or a boy or half a dozen strumpets. He was nothing to her, and that was how she wanted it. She transferred the disdainful look to him, and he blinked in confusion.

"And that's the ship you're going to move, is it?" asked the king. "Herakles!"

As Philyra had, he surveyed the height and length of it, then looked at the gangling young man beside him. The disparity between the two seemed insurmountable. The king silently approved his decision to have the time of the demonstration posted in the marketplace. If the fellow failed, as seemed likely, the public nature of that failure would make his own forgiveness of it appear more magnanimous, and strengthen his hold on the man. Of course, it would also make the failure more humiliating—but that couldn't be helped, and failure had sharp teeth whether or not anyone else saw it bite.

The little boy, Gelon, also stared at the ship, then at Archimedes. He did not usually like going to public functions with his mother, but when his father had explained what this one involved, he'd been eager to come. "You're going to move that all by yourself?" he asked.

Archimedes grinned and tugged his cloak straight. "Certainly."

"You must be strong!" said Gelon admiringly.

"I don't need to be," said Archimedes happily. "That's the point. There are two ways to move something heavy. One is to be very strong, the other is to use a machine. Do you see those pulleys?"

A spiderweb of rope ran between the front of the nearest ship shed and the stone mooring posts on the quay: running through pulleys attached to pulleys, reversed around tackle blocks, attached to other pulleys, run about the axles of toothed wheels, reversed again, and attached to more pulleys. Kallippos was standing by the mooring posts, counting them.

"That's my machine," said Archimedes. "Do you know how a pulley works?"

"You pull on it," said Gelon authoritatively.

"That's right. You pull on a rope which travels twice as far as the load moves, so it takes you half as much effort. By using enough pulleys you can move *any* load with *any* effort. But maybe we should see first whether strength will move the ship. Lord King, since you've brought along so many of your guardsmen, perhaps they'd like to push?"

Hieron had brought some thirty guardsmen along with him, under the command of Dionysios. (Archimedes looked for Straton among them, but for once did not find him.) The men were perfectly happy to set down their spears, brace themselves against the ship's sides, and push. Faces crimson with effort, feet skidding on the slipway, they struggled for a while without success, then gave up. The watching crowd groaned in sympathy.

Archimedes' grin broadened. "Dionysios!" he called. "Can I give you and your men a ride?"

Dionysios looked starkly disbelieving, and the guardsmen shook their heads pityingly. But when Archimedes hurried over to the ship and pulled down the boarding ladder, they hauled themselves aboard. Dionysios went last. He looked at Archimedes, began to say something, then shook his head and climbed in after his men.

"Me too!" shouted little Gelon, running down onto the slipway. When Hieron nodded his consent, Archimedes helped the child onto the ladder. Dionysios caught the little boy's hand when he was halfway up and lifted him the rest of the way. Gelon ran at once to the ship's prow and climbed onto the figurehead to wave to his father and mother.

Archimedes took a deep breath, then went to the thick rope which emerged from the pulleys and fastened it to the ring he had fixed securely to the ship's keel. He gestured for Marcus to follow him and made his way to the place where the other, thinner end of the rope emerged from its long and convoluted passage. He could feel the crowd watching him; closer at hand, the engineer Kallippos was staring at him, face tight with the same indefinable expression it had worn when they last parted. He tried to ignore them all, and took off his cloak; the sweat evaporated from his bare arms and damp tunic with a sudden delicious coolness. He handed the heavy folds of the yellow wool to Marcus.

"Is this going to work?" whispered Marcus nervously.

Archimedes looked at the anxiety on his face, and for the first time felt a quiver of doubt. He looked at the ship, at the spiderweb of rope between it and himself, mentally reviewing his mechanical advantage. It was sound, it should work. It *should*—but what if a pulley jammed? What if a rope thread jammed a wheel, or a tooth on one broke? Things did break. Had he made enough allowance for the weight of the rope itself?

Everyone was watching him. Oh, Apollo, if he failed, with everyone watching him . . .

"It's going to work," he told Marcus, with all the resolution he could muster. It *should*. There was a stool he'd sat on while he was working the system out; he went over and pulled it out from the shade of the ship shed, into the bright sun where everyone could see it, and sat down. "Just coil the rope up when I hand it to you," he ordered Marcus, and took hold of the rope.

Sitting down was bravado, really; it would have been easier standing up. He had allowed for an effort of one talent, but as he started pulling he suspected that he had not made enough allowance for the weight of the rope itself. Still, he might have to dig his heels in, but he could do it. Hand over hand, he slowly but steadily drew the rope; back and forth the rope wove through the pulleys, reducing the load again and again by the distance it traveled until it was commensurate with his effort.

The ship shuddered on the slipway, then began to glide forward. It did not jerk or pitch, but moved so smoothly that at first the watching crowd just murmured, uncertain whether it really was moving at all. Then, unsteadily at first, from a few throats, but growing, came a roar of delighted wonder. Beside him, Archimedes heard Marcus laughing. Seven tons of ship and thirty men were drawn up by a single pair of hands and the power of one mind.

Archimedes drew the ship up as far as the ship shed, then dropped the rope and stood up. The crowd was still cheering. He turned toward them: a sea of faces, with a purple patch before them that was the king. His arms were trembling from the strain of pulling, and he felt suddenly dizzy. Nobody had ever cheered for him before. He had expected to feel triumph, but he was suddenly afraid. Under this acclaim he felt exposed, freakish. It was not really such an exceptional thing. The principles had always been there, unchangeable as stars. He had simply applied them. "O Apollo!" he whispered, as though he were genuinely begging the god for help.

Marcus caught his shoulder. "Wave to them!" he whispered, and Archimedes waved: the cheers redoubled. He shook his head angrily.

"Sir," said Marcus, "your cloak."

Archimedes shook his head again and began walking back toward the king without it.

As he drew closer, he noticed first his sister's face. Philyra's cloak had fallen off her head and one arm, her hair was tousled, and she was radiant. Then, next to her, he saw Delia, still applauding, her eyes glowing with pride. His irrational dread suddenly lifted, and he grinned back at both of them. Philyra gathered up her skirts and ran over to him, laughing. "Medion!" she exclaimed, flinging her arms around him. "It was *unbelievable!*"

He put an arm around her, but said nothing, and kept walking until he was facing the king.

Hieron's face too had lit with sheer delight, and as soon as Archimedes was within reach, he seized one surprised hand in both his own and shook it. "You really could move the earth, couldn't you?" he asked, grinning.

"With another world to stand on," replied Archimedes, "anyone could."

The king laughed, still shaking the hand. Then his eyes flicked to the system of pulleys and he let go. "Can I try it?" he asked.

Archimedes blinked and looked back at the ship, from which the guardsmen were now leaping. "It will have to be pushed down the slipway the hard way," he said apologetically. "And I'll have to, uh, move some of the wheels."

Hieron at once turned to the guardsmen: "Dionysios!" he shouted. "Get some volunteers and push it back down again! *I'm* going to pull it up this time!"

"*I* want to!" shouted little Gelon, running to his father.

"You can help me," conceded the king, scooping the boy up. "Come on, Archimechanic, you can tell us where to pull."

The ship was moved up and down the slipway so many times that eventually the foreman of the shipyard came up and begged the king not to wear out the keel of a perfectly good vessel. The king moved it; Dionysios moved it; people fought their way through the crowd to take turns hauling on the rope. Archimedes

explained the principle of the pulley so many times he lost count.
It wasn't until some time had passed that he realized that he had
not seen Kallippos since he first took hold of the rope. He
glanced around, looking for the engineer—and noticed Chrestos,
just arrived flushed and out of breath at the edge of the crowd.
Archimedes stared in consternation, then thrust his way through
the startled mob to where the slave was standing.

"What's happened?" he demanded. "Did my mother send
you?"

The boy was so out of breath from running that he couldn't
speak, but he nodded.

"This is your slave?" asked Hieron quietly.

Archimedes stared at him blankly: he had not noticed the king
following him. Then he nodded. "I asked my mother to send
him," he said, "if my father . . ."

"She says . . ." panted Chrestos, "come . . . as fast as you can."

The world went cold, even in the hot sun. Time seemed to
slow down.

"You may borrow my horse," said the king.

Archimedes met the king's eyes, and felt a spasm of wild gratitude at the way his situation had been understood without explanation. "I can't ride," he choked out through a tight throat.
"I'll run. Lord, my sister . . ." He wasn't even sure exactly where
she was; she'd been beside him, but he realized now that she'd
gone off some time before with Marcus and Agatha. Probably
she was sitting down in the shade somewhere, but where? She
could not run, not in that thick cloak and long tunic, but she
should come home now too, if their father was . . . She should
not be abandoned on the docks.

"I will see to it that your sister gets home as quickly as possible," Hieron said evenly.

"Thank you!" exclaimed Archimedes passionately. He turned
and began pushing his way through the crowd that had trailed
eddylike after the king. As soon as he had a space of clear cobbles
before him, he broke into a run.

～

~ PHILYRA WAS SITTING INSIDE ONE OF THE SHIP SHEDS ON a coil of rope, disconsolately eating the picnic she'd expected to share with her brother. Outside the noise of the crowd bubbled on, festive but with a wildness to it. She felt as though her life had suddenly become dislocated from everything it had been before. She told herself firmly that it was *good*, it was *wonderful* that Archimedes was really going to succeed in his new career, that there was no reason for the apprehension that had tightened her stomach and taken away her appetite for the food. But her first exhiliration and pride were irrevocably gone. Things were going to be different now, and she was realizing that she'd liked them as they were.

A soldier came into the ship shed, then stopped abruptly. Philyra grabbed the hot cloak she'd taken off when she sat down, relieved at the way Marcus at once jumped up and stood between her and the soldier.

"Is this lady the daughter of Phidias the Astronomer?" asked the soldier, speaking correctly to Marcus rather than addressing an unmarried girl directly.

Marcus nodded warily.

"Please come with me," said the soldier.

Philyra hurriedly draped the cloak around herself while the slaves heaped the food back into the basket, and they followed the soldier out onto the sunlit quay.

The ship was being eased back into the water and the crowd was beginning to disperse. The soldier led them over to a crimson-cloaked officer and saluted. "This is the lady, sir!" he said, and Philyra modestly held a corner of her cloak up before her face. The officer was the one who'd come to the house once, the captain of the Ortygia garrison—Dionysios, that was the name. "The king wishes to speak with you, lady," he told her, his tone respectful. "Please come with me."

Philyra glanced nervously about, looking for her brother. He was nowhere to be seen. Beside her, Marcus was scowling.

King Hieron was standing beside his white charger. His son was in the saddle, looking pleased with himself, while his wife and the lady in red—the king's sister, someone had said—waited by the litter. Hieron came forward when Philyra was led up and inclined his head graciously. "Lady," he said solemnly, "I am very sorry to be the bearer of bad news. Your brother has been summoned back to his house: it seems that your father's illness has taken a sudden turn for the worse."

Philyra dropped her veil, forgetting modesty, and stared at Hieron in shock.

"I have promised him that I would see to it that you were conveyed home as quickly as possible," the king went on. "And my inestimable wife has kindly offered to take you in her litter. If you and your slave girl would get in, she will drop you off at home on her way back to our own house."

Philyra swallowed, looking at the queen. Philistis came over and took her hands graciously. "I am so sorry that you should receive such terrible news in public," said the queen sincerely.

Philyra bobbed her head, remembered her manners, and vaguely murmured, "Thank you, O Queen." She went over to the litter and climbed in. Agatha followed her, trembling, and then the queen and the king's sister.

Marcus watched the slaves pick the litter up and set off. He felt sick with apprehension, whether for Phidias or Philyra he could not say. No one was paying any attention to him; the king mounted his horse behind his son, the soldiers fell into line, and the royal party set off for the Ortygia. Marcus settled the food basket on his arm and began to walk away. He went slowly at first, but as he left the docks his steps grew longer and longer, and when he reached the house in the Achradina he was running.

HIERON REACHED HIS OWN HOUSE BEFORE MARCUS could make the longer journey on foot. As soon as he did, the king turned to his doorkeeper. "Kallippos needs to speak to me," he said. "Find him for me, and tell him so."

Before the chief engineer could be found, however, Delia returned with the queen, and went at once to see her brother.

Hieron had retreated to the library, where Delia found him

reading. He looked up quickly when she came in, then put his scroll aside and moved his feet so that she could sit down. "Did they arrive in time?" he asked.

Delia nodded. "But he wasn't conscious," she added. "They had their own doctor there, and he said it might be hours, and might be any minute. The . . . wife of Phidias came out to thank us for bringing her daughter home. Philistis offered her any help they wanted, on your behalf, and she thanked us, but said they didn't need any help."

Hieron snorted. "Well," he said, after a minute, "I'm glad they were in time." He picked up his book again.

"What are you going to do about Archimedes?" demanded Delia in a low voice.

He set the book down again. "Keep him," he said fiercely. "Keep him if I possibly can, no matter how much he costs. Zeus! You saw it. It was a game to him, moving that ship: when he understood how the rest of the world regarded it, he was shocked. He's as good as an extra army to any city lucky enough to own him."

"But what are you going to do?"

He shook his head. "I don't know. I've always thought the legends make King Minos sound a most appalling fool, but at the moment I can find some sympathy for the man. He had the most ingenious mind in the world at his disposal, and he didn't want to lose it. So he locked up its owner in a tower. It didn't work, but I can understand why he was tempted to it!"

"You're not planning to lock Archimedes up!" cried Delia. It was more a command than a question.

"Herakles!" exclaimed Hieron, looking at his sister in surprise. "Not if you're going to strangle me if I do."

Delia flushed. Her protectiveness surprised her as well. But that morning she had watched Archimedes do the impossible, and she had forgotten all caution in the wave of delighted pride. Surely she was entitled to feel proud, since she had discovered him? And to feel responsible as well, if her brother's notice threatened him. "You're not, are you?" she asked more quietly.

"No, I am not," said Hieron. "Minos *was* a fool. You don't get people to work for you by locking them up in towers, particularly when they're a great deal cleverer than you are yourself. Daedalus, you remember, simply devised an impossible means of escape and flew away. I don't *think* Archimedes could fly, but after today I wouldn't like to bet that he couldn't if he really applied his mind to it."

Delia relaxed. "You worried me," she complained, and at last took the offered space on the couch.

Hieron was gazing at her thoughtfully. "You like him," he stated.

She blushed again. "I discovered him," she said. "I . . . feel responsible. I don't want him hurt."

Hieron nodded, as though this made perfect sense. "I promise you, I won't hurt him. To tell the truth, I think it would offend the gods if I did. It would be like smashing a priceless work of art. I've never seen anything like him."

"I will not take orders from him," said a voice in the doorway, and they both looked up to see Kallippos standing there. The royal engineer was disheveled and sweat-stained, and his feet were covered with dust: he had been walking. He glared angrily at Hieron. Delia jumped nervously to her feet.

Hieron simply smiled. "Kallippos, my friend," he said, "I'm glad you've come. Shall we go into the dining room and have a cup of chilled wine?"

"I won't take orders from him," repeated Kallippos, as though Hieron had not spoken. "I'm not Eudaimon, King. I don't just copy, I think. I won't let somebody else do my thinking for me. I'm too old and my family's too good to stand being that man's subordinate. I resign."

"I was afraid you were going to say that," said Hieron. "Now, my friend—"

"You arranged it!" shouted Kallippos furiously. "You *invited* him to do something impossible, and *asked* me to say he couldn't. Well, I said it: I don't deny it. And I was wrong. But I am not going to take orders from some flute boy from a mud house in the back streets of the Achradina!"

"I don't ask you to," said Hieron.

"Hah!" sneered the engineer. "You may make his position officially equal to mine, but we both know you intend him to be my superior."

"I have no intention of appointing Archimedes son of Phidias to the position of royal engineer," declared the king. "May the gods destroy me if I do."

Kallippos stared for a moment in astonishment, then shouted, "Then you're out of your mind! You saw what that boy did! Do you think I could have done that? I couldn't even have done the catapult!"

"My friend!" protested Hieron. "You are the finest engineer in the city's employ, and if you left, I could not replace you. For you to resign now, when we are threatened with all the terrors of siege, would be a disaster for the whole of Syracuse. How can you contemplate such a thing? Archimedes is young and inexperienced. I know your quality, and I never expected you to work under him. Before the demonstration I thought it might be possible to appoint him as engineer with a rank equal to yours. Now I see that this is quite impossible. I repeat, I am not going to appoint him to a salaried position at all."

Kallippos opened his mouth to speak, then shook himself. "King," he said, trying again. "Don't you understand that he's better than I am?"

"My friend," said Hieron, "I know perfectly well that he has Apollo and all the Muses taking turns to breathe into his ear. But his natural home is Alexandria, and any job I gave him he would eventually come to regard as a prison. So I am not going to give him a job. For what he makes for the city, he will be paid, and generously, but what he actually does will be up to him: that will please him far more than any position I could offer. He is not, and never was, your rival. *You* are an engineer, and a very good one: *he* is a mathematician who happens to make machines occasionally. All I want you to do is to join me in asking him to assist in constructions for the good of the city where we judge he has a contribution to make. Now, do you want to come into the dining room, wash your feet, and have a cup of chilled wine?"

Kallippos stared at Hieron for another long minute. Then he made a slow, snorting noise, half laugh, half sigh, wholly relief. Delia saw that he had not in the least wanted to resign, but had felt that he had no other option. "Yes," he said now, starting to smile. "Yes, O King. Thank you."

Delia watched the two men go out, then sat back down on the couch, heavily. She knew her brother well enough to understand that Hieron had not said quite what Kallippos thought he had. Hieron had known that Kallippos was too proud to agree to become another man's subordinate—especially when the other man was younger and of a less distinguished family. Now he had arranged matters so that Kallippos would be content to ask Archimedes to "assist" with particular problems—and, no doubt, take all the "advice" he was given. Eudaimon, too, had been brought "in hand." There remained only Archimedes himself to bring under the yoke—and that would not be done in the way she'd feared. She should have realized that her brother would never do anything so crude as bind a man to an iniquitous contract of employment. The kind of chains he preferred were both subtler and stronger, forged in a gray area between manipulation and beneficence, put on with gifts and received with gratitude. But what sort of chains he might find for Archimedes she could not guess.

~ PHIDIAS DIED AT ABOUT FOUR IN THE AFTERNOON, WITHout regaining consciousness. Arata had watched him all morning with growing concern, and at noon, when his breath seemed to be failing, sent for her children. All through the long hot afternoon the family sat together about the bedside, while Phidias' breath stopped, then started, then stopped again. When the end finally came, they did not at first recognize it, and waited for some time for the frail gasping to resume. Eventually it became clear that it would not. Archimedes covered his father's face, and the women of the household began to beat their breasts and raise the high-pitched ritual keening.

Archimedes went out into the courtyard, splashed his face with some water, and sat down against the wall, hands dangling limply from his upfolded knees. He was not sure what he believed about an afterlife. Like most educated Greeks, he found the stories his own people told about the gods and the Underworld totally incredible, but to replace those stories he had only contradictory reports from the teachings of the philosophers. The soul was the true Platonic Form, immortal and unchangeable, struggling through the shadow play of the world, reborn many times until it could find its way back to the God who had made it. The soul of the Wise was king, and by virtue might attain eternal union with the Good. The soul was a handful of atoms, born with the body, disintegrating with that body's death, and the gods lived apart from the world and had no interest in it. What was he to believe?

It hadn't mattered much, before.

After a while, he went upstairs and took out his abacus and compasses. He drew a circle in the sand: *that* was immortal and unchangeable. Its end was its beginning, and it defined the total of all angles. The ratio of its circumference to its diameter was forever the same number: three and a fraction. What that fraction was, though, was impossible to calculate. Less than a seventh. Try to define it further, and it slipped away from you, more precise than your measurement, infinitely extendable, infinitely variable. Like the soul. Like the soul, it could not be comprehended by reason.

That thought was comforting.

He inscribed a square in the circle, then an octagon, and began calculating in earnest.

When Arata came up about three hours later, she found her son crouched over the abacus, sucking the hinge of his compasses. Scratched into the sand was a multi-sided polygon, circumscribed by a circle and filled with a tangle of superimposed reckonings.

"Dearest," she said gently, "the neighbors have started to arrive."

It was traditional for friends and neighbors to pay their respects to the dead as soon as possible, and for the family to greet them dressed in black, with hair cut short in mourning. Arata's hair was freshly cropped, and she had draped about herself a black cloak bought many years before for her mother's funeral and worn infrequently since. Philyra, too, was dressed in mourning; even the slaves were prepared. But Archimedes still wore the good tunic he had put on that morning, and his hair hung in tangles over his forehead. Faced with his mother's summons, however, he merely took the compasses out of his mouth and said, "It's more than ten seventy-firsts and less than a seventh."

Even if the evening light hadn't shown clearly the dry trails of tears across his cheeks, Arata would have known better than to mistake his absorption for lack of feeling. She crouched down beside him as quietly as though he were a wild animal she was trying not to startle. "What is?" she asked.

He gestured with the compasses at a point on the diagram where the circle's circumference was cut by its diameter. The letter π had been written in the angle between them. "That." There was a silence, and then he said, "People often say it's three and a seventh, but it's not. It's not a rational number at all. If I could draw more sides to the polygon, I could approximate it more closely, but no one can ever calculate it absolutely. It goes on forever."

Arata regarded the circle and the scratched figures. Phidias would have understood them. That thought had just become painful. "Why does it matter?" she asked.

He stared blindly at the circle. "Some things do go on forever," he whispered. "If some part of us wasn't like them, would we be able to understand that?"

At that she saw the reason for his calculations, and, strangely, found comfort in them. Her husband too had loved and believed in these infinite things, and now he was with them. She put an arm about her son's shoulders, and for a moment they were both quite still. Then Arata sighed. "Dearest," she said resolutely, "you're the head of the family now. You must change and come down and greet the neighbors."

Archimedes dropped the compasses and put his hands over his face. He did not want to speak to anyone.

"You must," Arata insisted. "He was always so proud of you. Let everyone see that he left a son who honors him."

Archimedes nodded, pulled himself to his feet, and went with her. The black cloak she found for him had been his father's. Putting it on made him shudder.

Several of the neighbors, alerted by the commotion earlier in the day, were already gathered in the courtyard. Archimedes greeted them courteously, and they responded with condolences, then went to pay their respects to the body. Phidias, washed, dressed in his best clothing, and garlanded with herbs and flowers, lay on the sickroom couch facing the door, eyes closed, one thin hand clutching a honey cake as an offering to the guardian of the realms of the dead. Archimedes gazed at the corpse with a curious sense of indifference. This formal object had nothing to do with the astronomer, the solver of puzzles, the musician who had brought him up.

Philyra had already seated herself at the head of the couch and begun playing a dirge upon the kithara; as the women of the neighborhood arrived they sat down next to her and joined in, either singing or simply keening, so that the room filled with the thin moaning of grief. Arata sat down on a chair next to the couch, but made no sound, and covered her head.

Archimedes wondered if there were more people he should inform of the death. Phidias had been an only child, but Arata had a brother, and there were friends. Should he ask his mother about it? It seemed better not to disturb her. What about the funeral? In this hot weather it would have to take place next day. He supposed he should be arranging wood and incense for the pyre, and seeing about a funeral feast. Did he have money for it all? Presumably the shopkeepers would give him credit.

It seemed unbelievably strange to be worrying about such things, with his father lying there dead.

He went back into the courtyard, and was relieved to see Marcus returning from the public fountain with a heavy amphora of the water the visitors would need to ritually purify themselves from the contact with death. "Marcus," he whispered, hurrying over to him, "who should we send to about this?"

"Your mother's already informed everyone," said Marcus. Archimedes blushed, ashamed that Arata should have had to worry.

The visitors kept arriving all evening. When it began to grow dark, the slaves found torches and set them up in the courtyard and by the door. They had just been lit when Archimedes became aware of a commotion in the street outside—and then Hieron came through the open door, followed by his secretary. The unexpected appearance of the lord of the city caused an alarmed ruffle in the now-crowded courtyard, but Hieron ignored the stir and walked straight to Archimedes. "My condolences," he said, shaking hands. "You have lost a father who was one of the best men in the city, and your grief must be great."

Archimedes blinked, fiercely pleased by such a public declaration from such a source. The neighborhood had always liked Phidias—but it had always laughed at him, too. "Thank you," he replied. "I do grieve for him, very much."

"It would be your shame if you did not," said Hieron.

Like any other mourner, he went on to the sickroom to view the body; when he entered, the women were so startled that they stopped keening, and there was a sudden, profound, reverberating silence. Once again, Hieron ignored the effect he produced, and he bowed his head respectfully to the dead. "Phidias, farewell!" he said. "I always regretted that I could not study with you longer. May the earth be light upon you!" Then he went up to Arata, who was was still sitting veiled beside her husband's body. "Good lady," he said, "your loss is great. But I trust that the outstanding promise shown by your son is some comfort to you."

Arata was utterly speechless. She clutched her cloak tightly against her breast and nodded wordlessly. Hieron nodded back, in farewell, and withdrew.

Back in the courtyard, he turned again to Archimedes. "Please," he said, "allow me to show the esteem in which I held your father, and the respect I have for you, and permit me to provide for the funeral. If you agree, my slaves and the resources of my house are at your disposal."

"I, uh," stammered Archimedes, almost as speechless as his mother. "I, uh—thank you."

Hieron smiled. "Good. Just tell my secretary Nikostratos here what you want, and he'll see that it's arranged for you." He gently directed Archimedes toward the secretary with a pat on the arm, and turned to go. Then he turned back again. "Oh," he added, "it struck me that you haven't yet been paid for that astounding catapult you built. I'm ashamed that I can't possibly pay as much as such a fine machine is worth, but Nikostratos has something for it. I wish you joy!" With that he gave his hands a perfunctory ceremonial wash in the water which stood ready by the narrow door, then stepped out into the night.

Archimedes looked at the secretary. Nikostratos, a bland-faced, nondescript man in his thirties, burdened with a heavy satchel, looked back. "Do you wish to tell me what arrangements you want now, sir?" he asked.

"Uh—yes," said Archimedes, keenly aware of the astonished neighbors. "Um—I suppose we should go into the dining room."

Marcus fetched lamps for the dining room, then stood listening while the secretary jotted down the requirements for the funeral. He added up the bill in his own mind as they proceeded: wood, incense, wine and cakes for a hundred—Archimedes said sixty at first, but the secretary thought this too mean. It was not going to come to less than twenty-five drachmae, Marcus concluded, and would probably be considerably more. The king was not going to save money by paying for a funeral and skimping on a catapult. And Marcus doubted that Hieron meant to skimp on the catapult either, despite his words about not paying as much as it was worth. He just wished he knew *why* the king of

Syracuse was putting himself out to flatter and conciliate a catapult engineer.

When the funeral requirements had been fixed, the secretary took out an olive-wood box, which he set down before Archimedes. "The money for the catapult," he stated. "Can I ask you to sign for it?"

Archimedes looked at it vaguely and asked, "How much is it?"

"Two hundred and fifty drachmae," replied the secretary matter-of-factly. He pulled a ledger out of his satchel.

Archimedes stared, then lifted the lid from the box. New-minted silver which had been packed to the rim spilled out onto the dining table. He shook his head. "It was supposed to be fifty!" he protested. "And the king said that—"

"I was instructed to say that if the catapult were priced according to its value, it should be a thousand," said Nikostratos.

Archimedes stared at him for a long moment in silence. Then he looked down and picked up one of the coins which had fallen onto the table. Hieron's face, diademed and smiling, had been stamped in profile on the obverse. He studied it. A number of things he had seen and heard without really paying attention fell into place. He had always known that he was exceptional as a mathematician, but he'd thought that at mechanics, which were merely a hobby to him, he was only ordinarily good. But he realized now that Epimeles had not been flattering him: the Welcomer really was the best catapult built in Syracuse in twenty years. That pivot—that was something nobody had thought of before. The reason the workshop slaves had laughed was that he hadn't realized that. Eudaimon had been not merely short-tempered, but jealous. Kallippos had really believed that it was impossible to move a ship single-handed.

He was the best engineer in the city, and what his mind and hands could shape was so powerful that the king himself was now trying to cultivate him. This piece of silver, shining in his hand, was a tribute to his power. It was deeply satisfying, but at the same time frightening. The Roman army might soon be arriving to lay siege to Syracuse, and his own abilities would be in the first line of defense against it. The danger at once seemed much closer, and much more real.

He took fifty drachmae out of the box, then pushed the box itself back toward Nikostratos. "Tell the king I thank him for his generous offer," he said, "but I will take the price agreed, and no more."

Nikostratos was genuinely surprised—a strange sight, in such a dry man. He tried to push the box back. "This is the sum the king instructed me to pay you," he protested. "He won't want it back!"

Archimedes shook his head, "I am Syracusan; I don't need to be paid extra to defend Syracuse. I will take the agreed price for the catapult because my family needs it, but I will not profit from my city's urgent need by taking more."

The secretary stared. Archimedes took the ledger out of his hands and found the entry—"To Archimedes son of Phidias, for the one-talent catapult for the Hexapylon, 250 dr." He crossed out "250 dr" and wrote above it, "50 dr., as agreed," and signed his name.

Nikostratos suddenly smiled widely. "The gods have favored Syracuse," he said quietly. He took back his ledger and the olive-wood box, and put both away. Still smiling, he murmured his good nights and departed.

Archimedes looked at Marcus, who still stood watching by the door. "I suppose you disapprove of that?" he said challengingly.

But Marcus grinned widely and shook his head. "Not me," he said. "If a man isn't willing to fight for his own city, he deserves slavery."

And you, Marcus thought to himself, *have just refused to be bought.*

9

Four days later, Delia watched Agathon set out sour-faced and hurrying on some errand of the king's. Then she walked up to the great double door of the mansion on the Ortygia, opened it, and stepped through.

It was as easy as that: open the door and step out into the street. Nothing there, she told herself, to cause this pounding of the blood in her ears, this sense of vertigo that slowed her footsteps as she started down the road. There was nothing dangerous in what she was doing—it was just that she had never done it before.

Never before walked through that door without someone in attendance upon her. Never before set off, telling no one, for an appointment of which the household would not approve.

It was a shocking thing. She should not do it; of course she should not. But ever since the demonstration, her pretense that her interest in Archimedes was no more than that of a patroness in a potentially useful servant of the state had been vanishing like water into sand. She was chagrined at how completely she had been deluding herself. And yet, she was sure that at first she had not been pretending. When she first met the man she had simply been intrigued by him—but that had changed. It was ridiculous! She had seen him three times, spoken to him twice, played music with him once—and she felt that if she allowed him to slip away she would regret it all her life.

She had written him a note: *I must speak with you. Meet me at the fountain of Arethusa tomorrow at the tenth hour. I wish you well.* She had addressed it to "Archimedes, son of Phidias, at the catapult workshop," sealed it with one of Hieron's seals— he kept several about the house—and set it in a pile of the king's letters which were about to be distributed through the city. It had been fearfully easy. It was still easy: the end of a working day, the streets of the Ortygia as full as they ever were, and herself easing her way down the street, inconspicuous among the others, swathed in a voluminous cloak of linen with a fold pulled modestly over her head to conceal her face. Of course, nobody had been trying to prevent her leaving the house: nobody had ever imagined that she would do such a wanton, shameless, and disloyal thing as to arrange an assignation with a young man.

When the possibility of what she was doing had first occurred to her, she had striven to force it from her mind. It would be wickedly self-indulgent and disloyal to return all her brother's kindness to her with nothing but callous ingratitude and shame. *The king's own sister went whoring after an engineer*, the gossip would say. She promised herself that she would do no such thing. She did *not* love Archimedes—she barely knew him. She could certainly live without him!

And yet, and yet . . . in a way, not knowing him was the worst of it. It was as though she had been walking all her life along the same narrow streets and then, unexpectedly, at the top of a hill, glimpsed a unfamiliar and breathtaking vista. Perhaps the new prospect was as narrow and confined as the old streets when you were inside it—but if she never explored it, she would never know. That was the thing that gnawed at her: not to know, to marry some nobleman or king and have children and grow old, never knowing what she had missed.

In the end she told herself that if she *did* know him better, she would probably discover that she didn't much like him. Then she could go home and settle to her lot in life, not perhaps content, but at least untroubled by wild suppositions of how much better things could have been. This small, this easy, disobedience,

wasn't much to pay for peace of mind, was it? And she would
not *do* anything with the man. He wouldn't dare take liberties
with her. They would talk a bit, and then she would see how silly
she was being, and go home.

She had never been so frightened in her life. But she walked
on resolutely toward the fountain of Arethusa.

She had chosen the fountain for three reasons: it wasn't far
from her brother's house; it wasn't far from the catapult workshop; and it was enclosed by a small garden which could provide
some cover for a private conversation, while remaining public
enough to give her a sense of security. She did not at all believe
that as soon as she was alone in private with Archimedes he
would leap on her like a maddened satyr, but she had been
warned of the wickedness of men and the dangers of impropriety
so often that she wanted to feel that someone would hear her if
she shouted. So she walked into the garden with one eye on the
passersby she might have to call on: two guardsmen sharing a
drink under a date palm; a couple of girls sitting on the ground
by a myrtle bush; a pair of lovers kissing under a rose trellis. The
girls would all be whores: respectable girls didn't sit about in
public like that—like her. She tugged a fold of her cloak farther
over her head, to hide herself from curious eyes.

The fountain itself was a large oblong basin of dark water,
shaded by pines. The sweet water welled up silently from its
depths. Tall, feathery-topped papyrus reeds grew in the shallows,
a gift from Ptolemy of Egypt; in all Europe, the papyrus grew
only here. Above one side of the basin towered the city wall, and
at the far end, white and lovely, a statue of the nymph Arethusa
gazed upon her fountain. Flowers garlanded the base of the
statue, and coins gleamed in the water's depths: offerings to the
protectress of Syracuse.

There were people here, too, but she noticed only one of
them: a tall young man who crouched by the fountain's edge,
intently regarding a collection of sticks which floated upon the
surface. He was dressed in black, and his hair was cut short in
mourning. She guessed that his cloak was quite a good one, since

it looked heavy, but it was patched with dust and he was at that moment treading the hem into the mud. The water cast wavering reflections upon his long-boned face. He felt her gaze on him and looked up sharply. His eyes, she thought, catching her breath, were the color of honey.

Archimedes smiled delightedly and stood up. His cloak was at once pulled off by the trodden edge and collapsed about his feet, half in the water and half in the mud. "Oh, Zeus!" he exclaimed, and stood there gazing at it helplessly. His black tunic was even dustier than the cloak had been.

He had guessed that she was the one who sent that note, even though it was unsigned. *I wish you well:* she had sent the same message through Marcus. All through that day, working in the catapult workshop on the hundred-pounder, he had contemplated this meeting with a thrill of excitement. He had brought the cloak along that morning out of a desire to look dignified; he had been astonished to find it so shabby and dusty-looking after a day spent on the workshop floor. Now it was utterly disreputable, he looked a fool, and the king's beautiful sister was watching him from under a white linen veil, her dark eyes astonished.

Then Delia laughed. He did not like being laughed at, but for a laugh like that he would have put on a mask and gone into comic mimes. He grinned ruefully, picked up the cloak, and wrung out the damp end. "Excuse me," he said. He thought of adding, "I didn't mean to undress in front of you," but this was both so highly inappropriate and so close to what he would like to do that it threw him into confusion and made his face hot.

"Good health to you," she said politely.

"Good health!" he replied. He tried to brush the crumpled cloak straight, then gave up and simply folded it up and put it over his shoulders: his gesture toward dignity had gone wrong, so there seemed no point in persisting with it. Too hot for a cloak, anyway. "I, umm . . ." he began.

"Shh!" she said urgently, glancing at the miscellaneous citizens who were relaxing beside the fountain. "Can we go somewhere quieter?"

She walked rapidly away from the fountain, and he followed her. There were people everywhere, and they ended up making a complete circuit of the small garden before settling for a comparatively quiet spot under a grapevine in the shadow of the city wall. There were no benches, but Archimedes spread out his cloak on the ground and sat on the damp end himself. It could hardly get any muddier, after all. Delia sat down beside him nervously, pulling her own cloak forward again, and looking at her hands upon her doubled knees. She had worked out her excuse for the meeting. She had sent him a warning through his slave, and she was certain that the slave must have delivered it even after she told him not to. "I . . . wanted to speak to you," she said breathlessly. "I needed to explain." She swallowed, and risked a sideways glance at him.

He nodded: he had assumed that that was what she wanted. She had warned him to be careful of his contract. The king had not, in fact, offered him a contract—but it was only four days since his father's death, and it wouldn't have been appropriate to enter into business with him in the period of deepest mourning. Hieron had put in an appearance at Phidias' funeral, but he had made no reference either to engineering posts or to the money Archimedes had refused. So Delia had come to follow her warning with some advice. Archimedes was happy to think that she was his supporter in her brother's house. He had played with the delightful possibility that her feelings might be warmer than that, but he had dismissed the notion as wildly implausible.

"When I sent you that message, I was afraid Hieron meant to tie you to something in your contract," Delia went on. "I was wrong. I shouldn't have said anything to your slave. It was simply that he was there, and I had the opportunity. I hope it didn't alarm you." She shot him another sideways glance.

He was frowning. "King Hieron isn't going to tie me to anything in my contract?" he asked.

She took a deep breath. The least she could do to atone for her own disloyalty would be to reassure him about Hieron. "He's not going to give you a salaried position as a royal engineer at all. He thinks you'd like it better if he simply pays you well for what you do. He said that any job he gave you you'd come to regard as a prison. So, you see, I was quite wrong, and shouldn't have said anything. I should have known Hieron wouldn't do anything . . . *unjust*." Guilt at her own behavior added warmth to her tone.

"But I thought . . ." he began—then stopped. The frown was deepening. "I don't understand. What does the king want of me?"

"You must know you're exceptional," she said. "As an engineer, I mean."

The frown did not lighten. "I'm better at mathematics."

She thought of the ship gliding along the slipway, and laughed. "You must be *very* exceptional at that, then! The whole city is talking about your demonstration."

That was true: Agathon had reported it. The whole city was talking about the man who had moved a ship single-handed, and adding that the same man was now building astounding catapults for the defense of Syracuse. The threatened citizens comforted themselves with the thought of Archimedes' skill.

Archimedes made an impatient gesture with one hand. "There's nothing new about pulleys! But I've done some things in mathematics that nobody else has done before." He chewed on a thumb.

"What?" she asked.

He looked at her hopefully. "Do you know anything about geometry?"

She hesitated uncomfortably. "I can keep household accounts."

He shook his head. "That's arithmetic."

"Are they so different?"

He looked at her. She was already beginning to be annoyed when she realized that it was not a look of disgust at her stupidity, still less the condescending don't-trouble-your-pretty-head-about-that look that Leptines the Regent gave her far too often. It was a look that might have come from a stammerer confronted with an urgent need to speak: a passionate longing to be understood and the hopeless knowledge that he would not be. "Arithmetic is a natural system," he said. "But geometry is something the god of the philosophers invented to design the world. Rome, Carthage, Syracuse—we're all *that*"—he snapped his fingers—"to geometry. Oh gods, it's a divine and beautiful thing!"

She studied his face, the line of the cheekbones and the brightness of the eyes. She recognized remotely that it was this "divine thing" which had attracted her to him—or rather, its reflection in music. Utterly pure and inhumanly precise, it enlarged the world simply by existing. And she wanted, she had always wanted, more than her own world was willing to offer her.

"The gods have given you a great gift, then," she said, torn between admiration and envy.

"Yes," he replied, seriously and without hesitation. Then he went on, embarrassed, "You should get someone to teach it to you. I'd offer to, but I wouldn't be any good. I have tried teaching—my father used to get me to help with his students. But the students said I confused them." His hands tightened on his knees at the memory of his father's patience with those students, and the recollection of the previous day's prescribed offerings at his father's tomb. He did not want to think of his father; he had been immersing himself in catapults precisely so that he wouldn't have to think of his father, and now that the subject had come up, he leaped away from it. "I didn't mean to bore you, lady. But I'm sorry, I don't understand why you asked me here just to tell me that your brother intends to deal with me fairly. Did he send you?"

She looked at him wide-eyed, then blushed. "No," she said.

"Then I don't understand . . ." he began—then suddenly, looking at her, he did. She sat there, watching him, her eyes frightened and her cheeks ashamed, but the lift of her head a determined challenge. Hieron had not sent her; she had come, alone and heavily cloaked, to meet him in secret. He had not wondered at that, and he should have. The liking he'd felt for her, casual, expecting nothing, crystallized all at once into a shape with edges sharp enough to wound.

"I'm sorry," he said, awed by it, and afraid now. "I was stupid.
I . . ."

He could not think what to say, and they looked at each other,
both now blushing furiously. In the back of his mind echoed the
warnings: "*You were lucky you confined yourself to flutes!*" "*May
the gods forbid that there should be anything between you and
the king's sister!*" What would a tyrant do to a man who seduced
his sister?

What would the sister do if he refused her? Old stories swirled
about his mind: Bellerophon, Hippolytos, falsely accused of rape
by the queens they had rejected. Looking at Delia, he did not
believe a word of it—and yet, this whole situation was unbelievable, and the stories were *there*, whether he credited them or
not.

"You mustn't think I mean to betray my brother's trust," she
said, with a sudden fierce determination. "Hieron has never
treated me with anything except kindness, and I would never
dishonor . . ." She stopped, knowing that she had already betrayed her brother's trust, already taken the first step to dishon-
oring the house. Only a small step, so far, but this meeting had
done nothing to convince her heart of its folly: quite the reverse.
"It's only that I wanted to know you better," she went on, more
uncertainly—and suddenly saw that she was treating him even
more disgracefully than she was treating Hieron. Even as much
as she'd done already could injure him, devastate his career, and
blast his reputation.*The king treated him with great kindness, and
he responded by trying to seduce the king's sister!* Seduction was
a crime, and she was asking him to risk the penalties without
even a seducer's reward. Shameless, selfish, heartless! She turned
away, in an absolute misery of shame, shame on all sides, and
pulled her veil forward to hide the hot tears that were bursting
from her eyes.

He looked at her for a moment—the tears, the confusion—
and forgot, as he kept forgetting, that she was the sister of the
king. He caught one of her clenched hands, and she looked back
at him, her face wet and red and hopeless. The only natural thing

to do seemed to be to kiss her, so he did. It was like finding the ratio, solving the puzzle, or coming home. A flurry of notes fell perfectly upon the beat, and two pitches blended into harmony.

She broke away first, pushed him back with the heel of her hand, wrapped her arms around herself and tried to separate the chaos she was feeling into coherent emotions. "Oh, gods!" she cried frantically.

"I'm sorry," he lied awkwardly: he was not sorry at all. He was enormously pleased and flattered; he was frightened and wished himself out of this—and underneath it all, complicating everything, he was enchanted by Delia, clever, witty, proud, determined girl, with such beautiful black eyes and a wonderful neat warm body whose imprint still tingled against his own. He didn't just want to go to bed with her; he wanted to sit up in bed with her afterward, talking and laughing and playing the flute. Like a new theorem, the range of possibilities ramified away from her, a ladder of inevitable connections: *if* and *then* all the way down to the final conclusive *this is what was to be proved.*

Only most of those possibilities were bad. After a moment he added doubtfully, "Do you really think it's wise that we should know each other better?"

"No," she said, half laughing, half sobbing. "I think it would be very stupid."

Only, only, said something in her blood, only I want to. I want you to kiss me again, I want to touch your face and run my fingers through your hair, your eyes are like honey, did you know? Ruin to you, and shame to Hieron. No.

"I thought this would convince me I didn't want to," she admitted miserably, "but it hasn't."

He sighed. No, she was no Phaedra, and he was no Hippolytos. He remembered the song he had been humming when he went to her door after finishing the Welcomer, beseeching Aphrodite to bring him this girl's love. The goddess had heard him, it seemed. Laughter-loving, they called Aphrodite, but her sense of humor tended to the black. He wished his father were alive. Not that he could have told Phidias about this—gods, no!—but at least then he wouldn't be burdened with this aching loss in the heart, this urge to find comfort. "Then what do we do?" he asked, and recognized even as he spoke that leaving the choice to her was fatally weak. Only it was perfectly clear to him what they ought to do, and it wasn't what he wanted to do at all.

She had always prided herself on her strength of mind. She might not be gracious and regal, like her sister-in-law; she might not be modest and charming, like the girls who had shared her lessons. But she had strength of mind. "We should do what's wise," she said firmly—and instantly regretted it. She looked at him and saw that he regretted it, too. She reached over and touched the side of his face, and at once he kissed her again, which was what she wanted and was not wise.

When she left the garden shortly afterward, they had reso-lutely made no arrangements to meet again. And yet already her mind was reflecting on how easy it would be, and already she suspected that wisdom would not prevail.

~ THE ROMANS ARRIVED BEFORE THE GATES OF SYRACUSE only eight days later—twelve days after Phidias' funeral.

Archimedes had spent most of the intervening time making catapults. He had been in and out of the workshop even while he was preparing the demonstration; after the funeral he im-mersed himself in the work. He did not want to think about his father or his own future, still less about the net he was falling into with Delia. She'd sent him a note arranging a second meet-ing, and he'd told himself that he should not go, and had of course been there early. They had walked from the fountain of Arethusa to a quiet public square near the temple of Apollo, where they had sat down to play the flute—she'd brought her flutes. And they'd kissed, of course. It was innocent and very sweet, all of it, and he had no notion what was going to come of it, though he suspected nothing good. If he spent every waking moment thinking about catapults, he didn't have to worry.

The workshop hadn't been quiet before, but during those twelve days it was frantic. Extra workmen were drafted in from

the army to help hammer and saw, and the catapults were assembled almost as fast they could be designed—two of them
simultaneously, one by Archimedes and one by Eudaimon. The
old catapult engineer had been sullen and resentful since the
Welcomer passed its trial, but he gave way at every point of
conflict and devoted himself to copying what Archimedes had
designed: a one-talenter like the Welcomer and two hundred-
pounders. Archimedes periodically went and checked that the
dimensions of the copies were correct, and was rewarded with
ten drachmae for every copy completed.

Kallippos, as chief engineer, had overall responsibility for the
defenses of the city. This seemed to mean principally that he
ordered buttressing or parapets for the walls and directed where
catapults were to be sited. The copy of the Welcomer and two
of the hundred-pounders went to the Euryalus fort, and another
hundred-pounder to the south gate, overlooking the marshes.
When Archimedes started the two-talenter, Kallippos came to
see how big it really was, with a view to determining where he
could put it. In fact, the machine was not as large as its designer
had initially feared; the increase needed in the size of the bore
was only five finger-breadths, giving a proportional increase of a
quarter all round.

"We could put it almost anywhere," said Kallippos, scrutinizing
the thirty-six-foot stock, which lay in the center of the workshop
floor. "In the Hexapylon, for example, on the floor underneath
the Welcomer."

"We could call it 'Good Health,' " suggested the workman Elymos slyly. "As in 'Welcome to Syracuse!' " He punched a palm.
" 'Good health to you!' " Another resounding *smack!*

The other workmen laughed, and Kallippos smiled. "And the
three-talenter could be called 'Wish You Joy'?" he asked Archimedes.

Archimedes blinked: he'd been trying to picture whether the
catapult would fit on the floor beneath the Welcomer. "I suppose
so," he said. "But look, I, um, think it will need a bigger platform.
Not for the machine itself, but for the men operating it. The yard

there is low, and even though the platform's on ground level you still have to climb a few steps to reach it. The, um, ammunition will be heavy, and they'll have to have a hoist to raise it. They'll need a space to stand while they lift it, and then . . ." He hesitated, then glanced around, found a stick, and squatted down to sketch on the dirt floor the things the catapult operators would need.

Kallippos watched intently, then squatted down next to him and began saying things like "The main roof support's about *here*," and "You can't put the crane on the roof—too exposed under fire." After a little while, the workmen went back to work around the two engineers; the engineers issued a few furious orders about not stepping on the sketches, then gave up, retreated to a quieter part of the workshop, and began chalking their plans upon the wall. Hoists gave way to arcs of fire and outworks. When the chief engineer finally departed, he shook Archimedes' hand warmly and declared, "I'll see to it." And when Archimedes accompanied the completed two-talenter to the Hexapylon, he found most of his suggested modifications in place.

That was the day the Romans arrived. The wagon with the catapult drew up at the fort to find the garrison buzzing with excited apprehension: a messenger had just galloped up to announce that a large Roman army was only a few hours' march away.

There had been some news of the enemy since Hieron's return to the city. Shortly after the Syracusans had left Messana, the Romans had sallied out from the city to attack the remaining, Carthaginian, besiegers. The Carthaginians, like the Syracusans, had managed to beat off the attack—and, like the Syracusans, had decided to withdraw afterward, unwilling to continue the siege without support from their allies. For a little while the Romans had remained in Messana, apparently debating whether to go after the Carthaginians or the Syracusans. When they at last made up their minds, they marched due south toward Syracuse.

The Romans had two specially strengthened legions—ten

thousand men—plus the army of their allies the Mamertini, which alone nearly equaled the number of the Syracusan army. Outnumbered and facing enemies famed for their ferocity and discipline, the Syracusans had no intention of venturing into the field. Refugees from the outlying farms and villages came flooding into the city, laden with as many of their possessions as they could carry and lamenting the harvest they had been forced to abandon. As Hieron had said, the hope of Syracuse lay in her walls—and her catapults.

The captain of the Hexapylon was delighted to see Archimedes. "That's the two-talenter?" he asked, as soon as the wagon had rolled to a halt. "Good, good! See if you can get it up in time to wish the Romans good health when they arrive, hah!" And he gestured for his men to help move the catapult to its selected platform.

Between the throng of eager helpers and Kallippos' hoists, the bits of the catapult were soon in place, and Archimedes afterward realized with astonishment that he had not once had to pull on a rope himself. He was assembling the pieces when Hieron arrived with a troop of guardsmen. He came up to the catapult platform and watched silently while Archimedes threaded the pulleys. Archimedes concentrated furiously to avoid those bright interested eyes.

"Will it work as well as the others?" the king asked when the stock had been fixed upon its stand.

"Unnh?" said Archimedes, fiddling with the screw elevator. "Oh. Yes. Probably won't have the range of the Welcomer, though." He walked back along the stock to the trigger and sighted along the slide—then stood upright with a jerk. There was a vast shadow on the road north—a shadow that glittered as the bright noon sun caught upon the points of the thousands of spears. He looked at the king in shock.

Hieron met his eyes and nodded. "I imagine they'll want to set up camp before they test our teeth," he said. "You don't need to rush the tuning."

In fact, the Romans were impatient. The main body of the

army halted in the fields to the north of the Epipolae plateau
and began entrenching, but a smaller group could be seen assembling on the road. It was easy to make out two masses of
men falling into square formations, with an irregular line of other
men before them.

Hieron, who was watching out the artillery port, gave a snort
of dismay. "Two battalions?" he asked no one in particular.
"Two—what do they call them?—maniples? Only about four
hundred men. What do they think they're doing?"

As if in answer, the two squares began to march toward Syracuse, one to the left and one to the right of the road. "Anyone
with better eyes than me see a herald, or any tokens of a truce?"
asked the king, raising his voice.

Nobody saw any evidence that the Romans were coming to
talk.

Hieron sighed and stared at the two maniples a moment
longer with a look of loathing. Then he said, "Very well," and
snapped his fingers. "Get the men drawn up," he ordered his
staff. "There are a few things I want to tell them."

The Syracusan soldiers assembled in neat ranks in the fort
yard, facing the open-backed catapult platform where the king
stood. The Hexapylon had a regular garrison of a single infantry
file—thirty-six men—plus servants and errand boys and hangers-
on, and the king had brought four more files with him. But the
crowd that assembled now numbered well over three hundred,
and Archimedes realized that men from other units along the
wall must have been arriving while he was busy with the catapult.
Hieron had concentrated some strength here, where the first
attack was expected—but not too much. All up and down the
fifteen-mile circuit of the walls, Syracusans must be standing to
the alert, checking the tension on their catapults and arranging
supplies of ammunition. Who knew which way the Romans
would turn?

Hieron strode to the edge of the platform and looked out at
the rows of helmets before him, all with their cheek flaps turned
up so that they could listen. Archimedes glanced over the ranks,

then, feeling out of place, went back to Good Health and resumed work on the strings. Despite the king's advice, he had been rushing to get the catapult ready to fire, and now it only needed tuning. He climbed up onto the stock with the winding gear.

"Men," shouted the king, in a strong clear voice, "the Romans have decided to send some fellows up to see whether or not we have teeth. We're going to let them come as close they want to, and then we're going to bite so hard that their friends watching will shit for fear."

The soldiers gave a roar of understanding and struck the butts of their spears against the ground. Archimedes waited for the noise to die down, then struck the second set of catapult strings.

"Good!" said Hieron, drowning the note. "So don't do anything to scare them off early! No shouting, and absolutely no shooting, until I give the order. When they're nice and close, we're going to give them a warm greeting. You probably know we have a couple of new catapults here especially designed for greeting Romans. One says 'Welcome!' and the other says 'Good health!' When a two-talenter wishes you health, you'll never be ill again!"

Another roar, of laughter this time. Archimedes glanced around irritably, then tried striking the strings again.

"I want them *smashed!*" shouted the king, punching the air. "When the catapults have done that, the lads that came up here with me can go pick up the pieces, and carry the bits back. I want prisoners, if we can take them. But the main job today is to let the enemy know what he can expect if he attacks Syracuse. Understood?"

In answer, the men bellowed the war cry, the fierce ululation howled out just before the clash of arms: *alala!* Hieron lifted his arms above his head, his purple cloak flapping, and shouted, "Victory to Syracuse!" Archimedes set the winding gear down in exasperation. Hieron left the troop cheering and turned around to look at Archimedes. "I hope it is ready to fire?" he asked, in a normal tone of voice.

"It would be," said Archimedes disgustedly, "if you would just keep *quiet!*"

Hieron grinned and gave an apologetic go-ahead wave of the hand. One of the men who was to operate the catapult struck the fixed strings, and Archimedes hit his own strings. Too low.

He tightened them a turn and a half, struck them again, and nodded to the catapultist. The man rapped out a sharp hollow note while the first sound still reverberated, and the two notes blended low and deadly on the still air.

"It's ready!" Archimedes said breathlessly. The king smiled tightly, gave a nod, and departed to watch from the gate.

Archimedes patted Good Health nervously, then went to the open artillery port to watch. He was vaguely aware of the catapult shifting beside him as its new team of operators tried the wind-lasses and elevator to train it on the enemy's advance. In the fields beyond, the Romans were continuing their slow march up the hill toward the walls of Syracuse.

At the limit of catapult range the Romans were faced with a deep ditch and a bank; they hesitated a moment, then raised their shields above their heads and began tramping down the ditch and up the other side. The shields were painted red, and as the men descended into the ditch they looked like a swarm of brightly colored beetles.

Archimedes heard someone come up behind him, and he glanced around and recognized Straton. "Oh," he said vaguely, and looked back at the advancing Romans.

"I was sorry I missed your demonstration," said the guardsman, as casually as though they were meeting in the marketplace. "The fact is, the captain had me cleaning the latrines that day."

Archimedes glanced back at him, surprised, and Straton grinned. "I'd made some bets with the other fellows in my unit that you'd do it, and there was a bit of argument about it. The captain doesn't like arguments. But you earned me a month's pay when you moved that ship. I've come to say thanks."

Archimedes gave an embarrassed shrug. "I don't know why

people thought it was so impossible. Pulleys have been around for centuries." His eyes were drawn irresistibly back to the Romans. They were well within catapult range now, and were looking more like men and less like insects. "How close does King Hieron mean to let them come?" he asked.

"You heard him!" said Straton, surprised. "As close as they're willing to come! See, they've been sent up here to have a look at us, to find out what kind of defenses we've got. They've probably got orders to fall back as soon as we start shooting. The idiots have come too close for safety already—and in loose formation, too."

Archimedes chewed his thumbnail. There was a limit to how far a catapult could be depressed: if the Romans got too close, they'd be inside the arc of fire. "What if they run for the walls?" he asked.

"Shouldn't think they will," said Straton. "If those fellows knew anything about catapults, they wouldn't have come as close as they have—and it takes a lot of experience to convince your feet that you'll be safer running toward your enemy than away from him. But if they're stupid enough to try it, we've got enough men here to wipe them out."

They both stood for another endless minute gazing down at the advancing ranks of shields: two squares in an open formation, twelve men deep, with a double line before them. It was now possible to see that the men in front were light-armed skirmishers, equipped only with a few javelins, a helmet, and a shield; the men in the rank had breastplates and and heavier spears. At the front of each square gleamed the standards—gilded eagles, set upon tall poles, trailing crimson banners which juddered as the standard-bearers made their way cautiously over the uneven ground. "Idiots!" whispered Straton. "Don't they realize?"

The Romans might be idiots, but the silence of the walls was clearly making them nervous: they marched more and more slowly, and at last stopped altogether.

At his shoulder Archimedes felt the air stir as Good Health's nose dipped. He retreated from the artillery port and went back along the catapult stock to where the new team of operators stood. There were three of them: one to load, one to fire, and one to assist. All three grinned—and then the captain of the team, a tough-looking man twenty years senior to Archimedes, stood aside from the trigger. "You want to test your new catapult, Archimechanic?" he asked.

Archimedes blinked at the nickname, but nodded, then moved to the foot of the catapult to sight along the stock; the machine was already aimed and loaded, and he found himself staring through the aperture at the air above one of the Roman standard-bearers. The man was only a couple of hundred feet away. Archimedes could make out the sandy color of his beard under the wolfskin he had tied over his helmet. The standard-bearer had lowered his shield while he talked to a man in a red-crested helmet. As Archimedes watched, the light-armed troops began to move back past the two into the gaps left in the formation of the heavy infantry: clearly, the Romans had decided that they'd come far enough and should retreat. It seemed to be what Hieron was waiting for: from overhead and along the city wall came a barking order, and then the sudden crack of catapult arm against heel plate; the air darkened with bolts. The standard-bearer at once lifted his shield above his head again. From the floor directly above came the deep bay of the Welcomer—and then there were screams.

"Now, sir!" said the catapult captain impatiently. "Now!"

Archimedes fumbled at the trigger.

Good Health's voice was deeper than the Welcomer's, a fearsome bellow ending in a smash of iron. The stone was gone too fast to follow—and then the standard-bearer was down, and the missile was tearing through the Roman line behind him like a harpoon through water. Screams—they were close enough that he could hear the screams clearly, even over the whoops of glee that rose from the catapult team as they saw their target go down. Archimedes stumbled back, still staring along the stock through catapult aperture and artillery port. The standard-bearer's body sprawled backward on the ground, red-topped, helmetless—no, headless! The two-talent stone had knocked his head clean off his body and gone on to kill or maim everyone behind him in the line of fire.

"Quick!" yelled the catapultist, already winching back the string. "Reload!"

His two assistants already had the hoist ready; another stone was dropped into place. On the floor above them, the Welcomer cried out again, and Archimedes glanced along the line and found another trail of bodies traced through the Roman maniple, but not quite so far; the one-talent stone seemed to fail after claiming its four or fifth victim. As he lifted his eyes, he saw that the rear ranks were falling, too. From the parapet of the city wall the small, long-ranged arrow-shooting scorpions struck methodically at the rear of the Roman force. The Romans were still trying to protect themselves with their shields, but catapult bolts went through shields, piercing wood and leather and bronze as easily as flesh and bone. From the upper towers of the fort, the lighter stone-hurlers volleyed steadily, sending weights of ten or fifteen or thirty pounds flying with hideous force into the middle of the rank. Battered by forty catapults at once, the Romans fell like grass to a scythe.

His survey had taken only seconds; beside him, Good Health now bellowed again. Another bloody furrow tore through the Roman force from front to back; a new set of screams rose audibly above a steady background of howls and the endless percussion of arms on heel plates. "Reload!" screamed the catapult captain; and the string groaned as it was winched back again.

In the field beyond, the Romans were throwing away their shields and running away as fast as they could, but even as they fled, the storm of death followed and cut them down.

"Oh, gods!" whispered Archimedes. He had never in his life before seen anyone killed.

Straton too was staring out the artillery port, his face contorted in a grin that was more than half snarl, his fist rising and falling in sympathy with the baying of the big catapults. "*Welcome* to Syracuse, you bugger-arsed barbarians," he muttered. "*Good health!*" He straightened abruptly and flipped down the cheek-pieces of his helmet. "Almost time to pick up what's left," he said, and ran lightly down the steps to join his unit. As he went, Good Health's bellow arose again.

Archimedes retreated from the catapult platform and sat down on the steps. He thought he was going to be sick. If he closed his eyes, he could still see the standard-bearer's body lying there headless. What had happened to that sandy beard? It must be smeared all over the stone—oh, Apollo!—with the man's brains and blood . . . his catapult!

There was a blast of trumpets, and then the high sweet sound of a soprano aulos, piping the men out into battle. The stone-hurling catapults stopped baying, though the percussion of the arrow-firers continued, picking off the Romans as they fled. No war cry followed from the Syracusans, however. As Hieron had promised, the Romans had already been smashed: all the Syracusans needed to do was pick up the pieces. And at last even the stuttering of the scorpions ceased.

Of the four hundred–odd Romans who had advanced on the city, perhaps twenty-five men made it back to their camp. Another thirty or so who had dropped to the ground to avoid being shot surrendered to the Syracusans, and fifty-four other prisoners were carried into the city, too badly injured to walk. All the rest were dead.

Hieron went through the Hexapylon, congratulating his men. When he reached Good Health's platform, he found the new catapult's team busily loosening the strings. The machine could not be kept at full tension without strain, and it was clear that the Romans would not try another assault on the fort that day. Of the king's new engineer there was no trace.

"Where's Archimedes?" asked Hieron, glancing about with a frown.

"Gone home, lord," said the catapult captain, climbing down from the stock. "He was looking a bit green. I don't think he's seen one of these in action before—and he'd finished here, any-way."

"Ah," said the king. His frown deepened.

"He can't have been upset by that!" protested the assistant in surprise. "He built the machine—he must have known what it would do."

"There's knowing and knowing," observed Hieron quietly. "Everyone who rides, for example, *knows* that it's dangerous to gallop downhill. But there are plenty of cavalrymen who do it all the time, because it looks bold and dashing. Once a fellow I knew killed a horse and broke his arm in three places doing it, and after that he *understood* that it was dangerous."

"And never did it again?" asked the catapult assistant expectantly.

The king gave him a sharp look. "He could never again bring himself to gallop at all. He had to resign from the cavalry. There's knowing and knowing." His frown lifted as he looked at Good Health. "I noticed that this machine worked every bit as well as its brother."

The catapult captain gave a contented sigh and patted the new machine. "Lord," he said, "it's the best I've ever handled. I don't know what you're paying the fellow for it, but you should double it. We fired five times before they were out of range, and it was as easy as killing blackbirds with a sling. Three direct hits, one partial, one miss. The range is about four hundred feet. I reckon this darling must have given permanent good health to thirty or forty of the enemy. Lord, a machine like this—"

"I know," said Hieron. "Well done! We've shown the enemy a thing or two about Syracuse, eh?"

When he had finished speaking to his men and given orders for the watch on the Romans and the treatment of the prisoners, Hieron went back to the gate tower from which he had observed the assault and climbed up it to the highest floor. A single scorpion crouched there alone, its operator already gone and the tension on its strings relaxed for the evening. The king glanced out the artillery port at the Romans—now firmly entrenched for the night—then turned to stare in the opposite direction, out at the city of Syracuse.

From this angle most of the city was hidden, masked by the plateau of Epipolae. But the Ortygia thrust out into a brilliantly blue sea, and to the south he could make out the sea gates and the naval docks. The temple of Athena shone red and white, and the mansions of Ortygia made a patch of green, with the fountain of Arethusa a deeper, more vivid green by the harborside. The air shimmered with the afternoon heat, making the city look as insubstantial, and as beautiful, as a dream city in a sunset cloud.

Hieron gave a long sigh, feeling a hot sick tension ebb away. He sat down in the doorway, resting his chin on his crossed hands. His lovely city, Syracuse. Safe—for the time being.

He hated killing. He had been horrified when he saw the two Roman maniples advancing on the city, because he had known at once what he was going to do to them. He thought now of the self-satisfied face of Appius Claudius, the Roman in command, and swallowed down a lump of raw hatred. It had been an act of crass stupidity to send out those four hundred men. Claudius should have sent a few scouts under cover of darkness— or a couple of thousand men in close formation, with siege machines. But Romans didn't understand mechanics, and, being Romans, were reluctant to admit it. Claudius would probably blame his assault's failure on the men who had died in it. Not brave enough, not resolute enough, not sensible enough! Throw the survivors out of the camp and give them rations of barley instead of wheat! The general erred and the men suffered: that was the Roman way.

Claudius had probably ordered the assault at once because he was in a hurry for a victory. He was a consul, elected by the Roman people to supreme power—but only for one year, and that year was already more than half over. Hieron suspected that the decision to attack Syracuse rather than a Carthaginian city had been taken because Claudius had thought it would be quicker to take one city than to defeat a great African empire, and he wanted to return home triumphant. Appius Claudius, conqueror of Syracuse! He would be credited with a glorious victory, and have a parade given in his honor. There was no doubt a place reserved in that parade for Hieron, too: walking behind the triumphal chariot in chains.

It had been Appius Claudius and the rest of the Claudian family who had started the war in Sicily in the first place. Hieron had always made a habit of collecting gossip from Italy, and he knew that the Roman Senate had in fact opposed the Sicilian expedition. Rome had had a treaty of peace with Carthage, and the senators strongly disapproved of the Mamertini: a Roman garrison which had committed similar atrocities in Rhegium had been beaten to death by its outraged fellow countrymen. But a faction headed by the Claudii had favored the expansion of Roman power to the south and had played on Roman distrust of Carthage to persuade an assembly of the Roman people to countenance this act of brazen aggression.

"Greedy, ignorant, vainglorious fool!" Hieron said out loud— then set his teeth. It was no good hating Appius Claudius. He might yet have to humble himself before the man. Claudius must have seen now that Syracuse was not a city that could be crushed as an apéritif, before the main war began. He might now offer reasonable peace terms so as not to go home empty-handed. Hieron had to be prepared to accept any realistic offer, even if it allowed Claudius to claim a victory and get his parade. He was bound by the absolute and unalterable facts that Syracuse alone could not contend with Rome, and that she could not trust Carthage: he had to accept terms. It was no use hating. Even the gods were slaves to necessity.

Perhaps the Roman people would now regret their decision to go to war. Syracuse had humbled them once at Messana, and now had humbled them again. Those men camped out there would not forget seeing their comrades butchered before their eyes. It was too much to hope for that they would give up and go home—Rome had *never* abandoned a war after declaring it— but the next Roman commander might well be more flexible, even if Claudius proved stubborn.

Hieron thought again of the Romans dying under the catapult fire; remembered the two-talent stone smashing its bloody way through the rank. That must have frightened them, surely? It had frightened Hieron, and he was on the right side of it! Perhaps when the three-talenter was working he could arrange for some Romans to see it.

If he got that three-talenter in good time. The engineer had gone home looking green. Hieron could understand how he felt; he'd felt that way himself after killing his first man. It had taken him months to get over it—as much as he ever had: he still woke up sometimes at night remembering that mercenary's face and feeling the hot stickiness of blood on his hands. Any man could lose his nerve. The cavalryman who'd galloped downhill had never recovered it. Should he go after Archimedes and try to talk him through the crisis? No. If the man were pressed to create more engines of death, the revulsion he must feel against those engines now would spill over onto the king as well. Better to leave him alone. Archimedes understood the importance of his work: his answer to the money had proved that. He would work himself around to the task if he could.

Hieron sighed. There were plenty of tasks awaiting him, too, down those stairs. But he sat for a while longer, alone at the top of the tower, looking out over his shining city.

10

Archimedes had walked most of the way back to the Achradina before he even noticed that he'd left the Hexapylon. Then he stopped in the middle of the dusty road and looked up at the sky. Light. Because of what he had made, thirty or forty men who had seen the light that morning would never see it again. No—more than that. Thirty or forty were only what Good Health had killed; the Welcomer had accounted for some too. To say that they had been foreigners bent on conquest was surprisingly little comfort. They were dead, and he had shaped their death for them, devising it with great cunning from wood, stone, and the hair of women.

He had never believed that a man's head *could* be knocked off like that, and now something inside him had revolted. If he put the hand of his mind to catapults, it went numb and dead. Some part of him wanted nothing more to do with such things. Trying to force it there by loyalty and will was like trying to wrestle a donkey through a door. And yet the city still needed every defense he could contrive for her. Her enemies were camped before her gates, and if they got in everyone within her would suffer. What had happened that day would only make the rest of the Roman army angry.

He sat down in the dust of the roadside and covered his face. He thought of Apollo, who had "come like night" upon the

Greeks at Troy, and caused the funeral pyres to burn night and day. There was nothing to be gained by praying to such a god, so he did not pray. He thought instead of cylinders. They began as cylinders of catapult strings, but altered suddenly into abstract cylinders, ideal in form. A section cut through a cylinder at a right angle to its axis was a circle. He imagined that circle, then rotated it to form a sphere which his imaginary cylinder precisely enclosed. Diameters, centers, and axes whirled through his mind, forming a pattern that was fascinating, complex, bewitchingly beautiful.

He realized with a shock that he had not thought about any problem in geometry since his father died. He had sworn to Phidias that he would never give up mathematics for catapults, and yet he had been devoting himself absolutely to the engines of death. He took his hands off his face and stared at the dust beside him. Nice, even dust. He felt about at the roadside, discovered a twig, and began to sketch.

ARCHIMEDES WAS NOT HOME BY SUPPERTIME, SO THE women of the family—who disapproved of the hours he'd been working—sent Marcus to the Hexapylon with orders to fetch the master home whether the catapult was ready or not. Marcus set out in a hurry, hungry and impatient; he took a shortcut through the back streets and up the edge of the Epipolae plateau, missed his master, and arrived on the main road just as the Roman prisoners were marched past on their way into the city.

News of the assault had yet to penetrate the Achradina, and it was not at first clear to Marcus what this procession was. The people of the Tyche quarter, the poor inhabitants of the dirty shacks, had gathered along the road to watch, and Marcus made his way into the line to see what they were staring at. A double file of Syracusan soldiers, marching to the flute, enclosed an unsteady line of men in plain tunics who carried stretchers laden with wounded. Marcus surveyed them in surprise, then asked the man nearest him what was happening.

The man, an elderly goatherd, spat and replied, "Romans—and may the gods grant that we see the rest of them the same way!"

Marcus looked back at his countrymen in shocked silence. They had been disarmed, but they were not bound, and the injuries of the wounded had been tended; only the expression of bewildered shame on each face betrayed their status. The question "How?" formed in his throat, but he did not utter it, aware as never before of the accent that would mark him out.

The procession of stretchers passed, and was followed by a small group of walking wounded. Afterward it seemed utterly inevitable to Marcus that the third man among them should be his brother Gaius.

Gaius had his right arm in a sling, and his tunic, unpinned on the right shoulder, showed that his chest was bandaged as well. His face was white with pain, but he walked steadily—until his eyes, brushing blindly over the faces that watched him, snagged on Marcus'. Then he stumbled. The Syracusan soldier next to him caught his good arm to stop him falling, and Gaius gasped and stood still, sweating and shuddering with pain from some injury that had been jolted. His eyes, recovering before the rest of him, sought out Marcus again, in amazement and disbelief.

Marcus stared silently back. A part of him seemed to be standing somewhere beyond them both, observing the meeting; another part burned and froze with shame. Gaius had no doubt believed him dead. He should have been.

"Marcus?" whispered Gaius; Marcus could not hear his name, but recognized its shape on his brother's lips. He did not respond; instead he made himself glance over his shoulder as though to see who this stranger could be speaking to.

The Syracusan soldier beside Gaius asked him, in Greek, if he could walk. Gaius replied, "I not speak Greek," and began walking again. As he passed Marcus he glanced back, his expression stunned.

Marcus forced himself to watch the rest of the procession, though his legs were shaking. He was astonished that no one

turned to him and asked, "Why was that man staring at you?"
He realized later that that meeting of eyes, which for him had
burned like the sun, must to others have appeared as nothing
more than the blank stare of a wounded man encountering the
curious gaze of an onlooker.

When the noise of flute and marching feet had faded away
down the road, and the small crowd had dispersed, Marcus went
on toward the Hexapylon, then stopped and sat down on a stone
at the edge of the road. His mind was in such a chaos of shame
and astonishment and excitement that it was several minutes before he was aware of any one thought or feeling. Gaius, alive and
in Syracuse! Gaius had seen him, knew he was here. What was
he to do?

"Marcus?" said a voice just beside him. He looked up with a
guilty start and found the guardsman Straton standing over him.
He stared stupidly: it was not anyone he'd expected.

"I thought it was you," said Straton. "What's the matter? You
look ill."

Marcus forced himself to stand and struggled to collect his
wits. "I ran too fast for the heat," he said. "I'll be fine in a minute.
Are you coming from the Hexapylon?"

Straton nodded. "Taking a message back to the Ortygia," he
explained. "Did your master leave something at the fort?"

"Isn't he there?" asked Marcus, surprised.

Straton was equally surprised. "He left hours ago! Isn't he
home?"

When Marcus explained his own errand, the soldier blew out
his cheeks and rolled his eyes. "I hope nothing's happened to
him!" he exclaimed. "The king wouldn't trade him for a battalion,
and rightly so. Those catapults of his are worth one. You heard
the Romans assaulted the walls?"

"I saw the prisoners on the road," replied Marcus cautiously.

Straton grinned. "All that's left of two maniples," he said
proudly. "The catapults did that. You should have seen the two-
talenter!" He punched a palm with a fist. "Ten or more of them
down with every stone! What a test-firing! The rest of them are

camped out there, thinking about it. If they have any sense they'll leave Syracuse alone now."

"What will happen to the prisoners?" asked Marcus, still too shaken to wonder if such a blunt question was wise.

Straton, however, had forgotten all about Marcus's dubious nationality and was too preoccupied with triumph to be suspicious. "They'll be locked up in the Athenian quarry," he said. "The king gave orders that they're to be treated well; I'm sure he has plans for them. He wanted prisoners. —Do you suppose your master's all right?"

"He's probably stopped to draw circles," said Marcus. "He does that sometimes." He turned from the Hexapylon and began walking back along the road into the city.

Straton followed, spear slung across both shoulders. "Will he be able to make a three-talenter?"

"Yes."

"What about a four-talenter?"

"Probably."

"A five-talenter?"

Marcus glared. "You've heard him yourself! He can build them as big as wood and iron and strings will stand. That's probably a lot bigger than anybody wants. But iron will give out before Archimedes' ingenuity does."

Straton laughed. "I believe you! He earned me a month's pay when he moved that ship. I boast now about knowing him."

Marcus grunted. Archimedes' fame had been growing ever since the demonstration. All the shopkeepers and neighbors had become remarkably polite. Marcus didn't like it: they always asked about catapults. Marcus imagined a two-talent stone smashing into his brother's arm, and winced.

Straton kicked a loose stone in the road, then said, "There was a matter my captain asked me to sound you out about, if I could. Your master's sister: is she promised to anyone?"

Marcus' head lifted with a jerk and he stared at the soldier. Straton gave an embarrassed grin and hefted his shoulders. "See," he said, "the captain's not married. He noticed your young mistress, and thinks she's charming. He's a fine man, and the king thinks highly of him. It would be a good match."

"The house is in mourning," said Marcus.

"Well, yes," conceded Straton. "The captain really just wants to know if it's any good him talking to your master when the period of mourning is over."

Marcus imagined Philyra marrying Dionysios son of Chairephon. A good match. An officer with a responsible position and the king's favor, not too old, well liked by his subordinates . . . musical, too. He thought of Dionysios singing while Philyra's angular body folded about the lute—thought of her low voice that blended with the swift intricacies of the music, her hip outlined against the thin tunic, her hair, her smile, her bright eyes—gone? Out of the house, out of his life.

He had always known she would go one day. Stupid to have thought about her as he had; stupid to feel now this utter desolation. Stupid to worry about a future he might not live to see.

He realized on the last thought, with a chill of pure dread, that he did mean to do something about Gaius.

"She's not promised to anyone," he forced himself to admit—then, despite everything, found himself adding, "But in Alexandria Archimedes talked about marrying her to one of his friends. He wasn't head of the household then, and couldn't arrange it, but he may want to now. I don't know."

"A friend in *Alexandria?*" demanded Straton, startled.

Marcus nodded solemnly, disgusted but unable to stop himself. He was not exactly lying, but he wasn't telling the truth, either. "A Samian called Conon, a student at the Museum. He and Archimedes each thought the other the cleverest mathematician alive. Conon's of very good family, and rich, but he would have been happy to forgo a dowry in order to call Archimedes brother."

That was all true—but Conon's wealthy and distinguished father had been far less romantic. He had long before arranged for his son to marry a Samian girl of his own class as soon as she came of age. The talk of brotherhood had never been more than daydreams.

"Archimedes can't be planning to go back to Alexandria!" exclaimed Straton.

"He can go where he likes!" replied Marcus sharply.

"B-but—the war!" stammered Straton.

"It won't last forever."

Straton chewed his lip, and Marcus knew that he was thinking of catapults—of the biggest catapults in the world being built in Alexandria instead of in Syracuse. He realized suddenly that the king had thought of that from the first, and saw the purpose of those obscure manipulations.

"A loyal citizen . . ." began Straton, then stopped: he had just seen Archimedes.

They had followed the road down from the heights now and reached the edge of the Achradina. It was dusk, but there was still enough light to read by. Archimedes was sitting at the edge of a small public square, folded up like a grasshopper in the middle of a patch of dry ground, chewing the end of a stick and staring at the dust before him. His black mourning tunic was hitched up, exposing thin thighs, and he looked like a delinquent schoolboy.

An elderly woman who'd been drawing water at the fountain in the square noticed them staring and paused beside them. "He's been there for hours," she confided in an anxious whisper. "Drawing in the dust. We think he must be possessed by a god. I pray it's not a bad omen!"

"It's geometry," Marcus informed her. "It's true about the god." He walked over, stopped when he reached the diagrams scrawled across the ground, and called, "Archimedes!"

"Unnh?" replied his master absently.

"It's time to come home," said Marcus firmly. "Your mother and sister sent me to find you."

Archimedes raised one hand in a wait-a-minute gesture. "Jush let me work thish out," he said indistinctly around the stick.

Straton had followed the slave cautiously; now he gazed down at the thicket of endlessly repeated cylinders and spheres, letters and lines that were scraped into the dry ground. "What are you trying to do?" he asked wonderingly.

Archimedes took the stick out of his mouth, glanced up, then returned his eyes to the diagram before him as though this extraneous presence had not registered. "I'm trying to find the ratio between the volumes of a cylinder and an enclosed sphere," he said dreamily. "It isn't straightforward. If I could only . . ."

"Sir," said Marcus, "it's getting dark."

"Oh, leave me alone!" exclaimed Archimedes irritably. "I'm doing *this*!"

"You can do it at home."

Archimedes jumped suddenly and unexpectedly to his feet. "I told you to leave me alone!" he shouted, glaring into Marcus' surprised face. "If it were some god-hated *machine* I was working on, you would have obeyed me, wouldn't you? But this is only geometry, so you interrupt. *Slaves* can interrupt geometry, but kings keep quiet when it's catapults!" He lashed out furiously with the stick, and broke it with a crack against his slave's arm. "Catapults! They're lumps of god-hated wood and some strings. They're graceless and they kill people. This is wonderful and beautiful! You never understand that—any of you!" He turned the furious glare onto Straton as well. "Geometry is more perfect than anything ever seen with the eyes. That ratio was true before we were all born, will still be true when we're all dead, and would still be true if the earth had never been created—even if no one ever discovers what it is. It matters—we're the ones who don't!"

He stopped, breathing hard. The other two looked back at him in bewilderment; Marcus was rubbing his arm. Archimedes met their gaze for a moment, then looked down at the calculations at his feet, perfect and unsolved. His rage began to trickle away, and he shuddered. What he'd said was true—but they would never, could never, understand it. For a moment he felt fully the pain of his isolation, as he had not felt it for years—not since he was a little boy, and had first understood that all the things he found most wonderful were to the rest of the world mere confusion. He longed for his father, and then, wistfully, remembered Alexandria, house of Aphrodite where existed all things that anyone could desire, magnet of the mind.

"Even if that's true," said Marcus at last, "you can't calculate in the dark."

Archimedes gave a small groan of despair, dropped the end of his broken stick, and walked silently away.

Straton swallowed as he watched the tall black figure slouch off, shoulders hunched and head hanging. "Is he often like that?" he asked Marcus.

The slave shook his head. "No," he said dazedly. "I've never seen him like that before. I suppose it's the war, and his father dying."

The soldier nodded, relieved. "Enough to upset anyone. You'd better go look after him. We *need* his catapults, whether he thinks they're worthless or not."

~ THEY WALKED IN SILENCE AS FAR AS THE DOOR OF THE house in the Achradina. There Archimedes stopped, staring blankly at the worn wood. He didn't want to go in. Everything that had happened since he returned from Alexandria seemed to be falling into a kind of a shape inside him—his father's death, the king's favor, Delia—everything. He realized that he needed to see the king, now, while the force of what he felt still armored him against fear and respect.

"Sir?" said Marcus, and he shook his head.

"Tell them I'm going to speak to King Hieron," he commanded, and turned on his heel. Marcus called again, "Sir!" but he paid no attention and strode angrily on.

It was night, and when he reached the citadel the streets were quiet, with no sound but the crickets calling and, far off, the sound of the sea. He made his way rapidly to the king's house, knocked determinedly, and told the surprised doorkeeper, "I would like to speak to King Hieron."

Lamplight deepened the severe shadows of Agathon's face as he gave the visitor a look to crush stone. "It's late," he said.

"I know," replied Archimedes, "but see if he'll speak to me anyway."

The doorkeeper snorted angrily, but nodded. He shut the door; only the sound of his sandals clacking away across the marble floor provided any assurance that he was indeed going to check whether his master would speak to the visitor. Archimedes leaned wearily against a column in the porch and waited. Presently the door opened, and the doorkeeper looked out, more disapproving even than before. "He will see you," he admitted reluctantly, and beckoned Archimedes in.

Archimedes followed him into the mansion, past the marble antechamber and directly into the dining room. Two lampstands provided a strong soft light, and the remains of a late supper were spread over the table. Hieron was reclining on his couch, while his wife and sister sat either side of him in chairs, as was the custom for a private family meal. Archimedes stopped just inside the door, nodded to the king and his family in greeting, then crossed his arms and rubbed an elbow uncomfortably. He became aware that he was dressed only in the plain black tunic, and that it was covered with dust and oil and not fit at all for a king's house; that he was tired and overwrought and was probably going to say something stupid. Delia's eyes were wide with surprise. He tried not to think of her as he'd last seen her, flushed from kisses and flute-playing, laughing as she untied her cheek strap. She had warned him, then tried to retract her warning: who knew how far she could be trusted? Next to her the queen looked almost as disapproving as the doorkeeper.

"Good health!" said the king, smiling. "Won't you sit down and have a cup of wine?"

Archimedes sidled to the nearest couch and sat down on it; one of the slaves at once filled a cup with watered wine and set it before him.

"What was it you wanted to see me about?" asked Hieron.

Archimedes cleared his throat, his eyes on the king's. "What is it you want of me?" he asked quietly.

Hieron's bright pleasantness faltered. He sat up, swinging his legs off the couch, and regarded Archimedes assessingly. Then he said evenly, "You know that you are exceptional."

Just what Delia had said. Archimedes nodded once, quickly.

"What do you *think* a king wants of an exceptional engineer?" asked Hieron, lifting his eyebrows quizzically.

Archimedes gazed at him for a moment longer, baffled again. Then his eyes dropped to the table in front of him. "I have a . . . method of analysis," he said. "A way of thinking about geometrical problems mechanically. It doesn't provide proofs, but it helps me understand the properties of things. I think of plane figures as consisting of a set of lines, and then I see if they balance. This is a bit like that. The way a king treats an exceptional engineer—if I think of that as a triangle, then the way you've treated me is more like a parabola of equal base and height. The two don't balance."

"Don't they?" asked Hieron.

"No," said Archimedes. He dipped his finger in the cup of wine and carefully traced a parabola on the tabletop: a tall humped curve. Then he traced a triangle inside it, point touching the curve's peak, corners at its edges. It was instantly clear that the two would indeed not balance. Archimedes looked up, meeting the king's eyes again. "The area of the parabola is four-thirds that of the triangle," he said. "I worked it out myself."

Hieron craned his neck to see, and his quizzical look reappeared. "You don't like getting a third more than you expected?"

Archimedes made a small dismissive gesture with his hands. "I simply want to understand what I am dealing with. The properties of parabolae are different are from the properties of triangles."

"Are you accusing my husband of deceit?" interrupted the queen angrily. "After all his kindness to you? What . . ."

Hieron raised his hand, and she stopped. Husband and wife looked at each other a moment. Then Philistis sighed. She got to her feet, went to her husband, and brushed back his hair gently. "Don't let him upset you," she ordered.

Hieron smiled affectionately and nodded, and she kissed him and swished out of the room.

Delia scrunched herself deeper into her chair, telling herself fiercely that she had an interest here. Hieron didn't know how much of one, but she had a legitimate interest, too. Hieron showed her that he had noticed with an ironic glance, but made no comment. He looked back at Archimedes in silence and made a go-ahead gesture with one hand.

"You asked me to do that demonstration," said Archimedes. "And it was you who had it posted in the marketplace, wasn't it?"

Hieron nodded fractionally.

"They all cheered when it worked," Archimedes went on slowly, "and since then things have been different. I didn't notice at first, but they have been. I was warned"—he did not glance toward Delia—"that I should be more cautious if my demonstration went well than if it went badly, but I didn't understand. I thought it meant to watch the contract—only I haven't been given one. What has happened is that now people know who I am. If I start to do something, they run about to help. People I don't know call me by a nickname which you gave me. Everyone has heard what you said at my father's wake, and how you paid for his funeral—out of respect for me. Everyone has heard, too, that you thought that first catapult I made was worth a thousand drachmae, even though your man only said as much to me in private. You've *arranged* for me to be famous, haven't you? As an engineer, as an . . . *archimechanic.*"

"You would have been anyway," said Hieron, "in time."

"You arranged for it to happen at once," replied Archimedes. "And you arranged it so that Eudaimon does what I say and Kallippos follows my advice. Even though they have titles and contracts with the city and I don't, still somehow or other my standing is higher than theirs. You tried to give me money the same way, too—something extra for something undefined. Something that doesn't come from the city, but belongs to me—

because I am a great engineer. But I never *chose* to be a great engineer. That status, like the fame, is something you arranged."

"Very well," said Hieron, in an absolutely neutral voice, "you've noticed all this. What do you *think* I want of you?"

Archimedes blinked at him for a long minute, then said slowly, "I think you do want only what a king wants of an exceptional engineer. But for some reason you don't think I'll give it to you, so you're trying to . . . to maneuver me into a room to which only you have the key. And if I go in, you'll lock the door behind me, and I won't be able to get out again."

Hieron looked at him for another moment—then shook his head and gave a long sigh of acknowledgment and disgust. "Oh, Zeus!" he exclaimed. "I've botched it, haven't I? I should have remembered that you're more intelligent than I am." He hitched himself forward in his seat and slapped the table. "But look, I can't lock you into anything, because—unfortunately!—there *is* no room to which only I have the key. Your parabola has the same base and height as your nice straightforward triangle. I want only what a king wants of an engineer—that you should build things for me—and in return I can offer only what kings have to give—money and status."

Archimedes' cheeks had flushed with anger. "You were fixing that 'Archimechanic' name onto me as though you were title-tagging a book! In a year or so, if I tried to claim that I'm really a mathematician, everyone would laugh at me and tell me to get on with my real work. My own family would start hiding the abacus. I swore to my father on his deathbed that I would never give up mathematics, and you—"

"No!" cried Hieron urgently. "May the gods destroy me if that's what I intended! I know you only build machines to get the money to do mathematics, and the main reason I haven't offered you a contract is to leave you free to do just that."

"Then what *is* the point of all your arrangements?" demanded Archimedes.

"To keep you in Syracuse! When Ptolemy of Egypt offers you a position at the Museum, I wanted everyone you know—from

your own household through to the man who sells you vegeta-
bles—to tell you fervently that you must not accept, that for you
to leave Syracuse would be treachery to the city that gave you
birth. If I'd really succeeded, you wouldn't even have found a
Syracusan ship willing to carry you to Alexandria, and you would
have had to stay for very shame. I swear by all the gods, though,
that beyond that I intended nothing for you but wealth and
honor. Right now you're upset because you've seen what your
catapults can do to people, and I understand that—I do, I hate
killing, too! But if you think about it when you're calmer, you'll
see that nothing I have done is going to oblige you to abandon
mathematics. Nothing! With the enemy at our gates, no one can
think of anything but war, but I pray to all the gods that we will
have peace again, and then there will be space for better things."

Archimedes blinked at him stupidly for a long time. "Why are
you so certain that Ptolemy will offer me a job?" he asked at last.
"He has some very clever people in Alexandria already."

"He'll want you for exactly the same reasons I want you!" said
Hieron impatiently. "I don't think you appreciate yet how exceptional you are. You think that compound pulleys and screw ele-
vators are just things anybody else would have used to solve the
engineering problems you were faced with. And they are—now.
Now they seem obvious to everyone. But last month they
weren't, because they hadn't been invented."

"But—pulleys are used all the time!" protested Archimedes.
"And screws have been used to hold things *down* for ages."

"So it's perfectly natural to use one pulley to turn another, and
a screw to lift things up? Certainly. Only nobody ever did. Only
somebody who's happier with the theory of screws and pulleys
than with the objects themselves could have adapted them like
that. You approach engineering through mathematics—and
mathematics is probably the most powerful tool ever employed
by the human mind. I knew that before I met you, and when I
heard about you I suspected at once that you were going to prove
exceptional. Ptolemy had Euclid for a tutor, and he knows the
value of geometry even better than I do. Probably the only reason

he hasn't offered you a job already is that the problems you were working on in Egypt were so extremely advanced that only about half a dozen men in the world were capable of understanding them, and Ptolemy's head of Museum didn't happen to be one of that half-dozen. But even so, you would probably have been offered a post this summer, if you hadn't come here instead. You have planted your fame in Egypt now, though it's taken a little while to grow. A ship's captain I spoke to recently told me about an irrigation device invented by one Archimedes of Syracuse which obliges water to flow uphill."

"It doesn't, exactly," muttered Archimedes. "You have to turn it."

He sat for a moment, contemplating what Hieron had just told him, stunned by it. The unbreachable walls he had sensed closing about him had turned out to be low enough to vault over. The power he possessed could bring him not merely wealth and the favor of kings, but freedom as well. The sea lay before him, and it was his sole choice what course to set on it!

He looked back at Hieron and managed an unsteady smile. "Thank you for telling me this," he said.

"I wouldn't have," replied the king sourly, "if you weren't on the point of working it out for yourself. I still want to keep you. I can't offer the Museum, but anything else you might expect to find in Egypt is yours for the asking."

Archimedes grinned. He picked up his cup of wine and drank it off thirstily, then stood up. "I'll bear that in mind."

"Do!" said Hieron sharply. "And bear in mind, too, that when Alexandria takes the best minds from all over the world, the rest of the world is impoverished. Syracuse is your own city. She is a great and beautiful city, and fully deserves the love of all her children."

Archimedes hesitated, looking at the king with curiosity, then replied impulsively, "That calculation about the areas of a parabola and a triangle—it was the parabola I was interested in when I did it. Not the triangle."

For the first time Hieron was thoroughly taken aback. He

stared at Archimedes in honest and straightforward astonishment.

Archimedes grinned again, and for the first time since he'd come into the room his eyes flicked over to meet Delia's, with a look as though he were sharing a joke with her. "I wish you joy," he said to them both, and departed the room with a swagger.

~ THE FOLLOWING MORNING ARCHIMEDES SET OFF FOR the catapult workshop at the usual time, looking tired but determined. Marcus watched him go, then silently let himself out of the house and set off in the opposite direction, toward the Athenian quarry.

The quarries of Syracuse lay within the city wall. The plateau of Epipolae was composed largely of limestone, a great dry island lying upon the coastal shelf. Its southern, city side broke off in steep cliffs, and into these the Syracusans had cut a series of quarries for building stone. The Athenian quarry was the most famous of these. It took its name from its use nearly a hundred and fifty years before as a prison for the seven thousand Athenian prisoners of war taken at the conclusion of their city's disastrous attempt to subdue Sicily. Within its limestone walls the Athenians had suffered horrors, the living crowded in a narrow pit together with the dead. Many had died, and their bones lay still beneath the quarry floor.

There was nothing in the appearance of the place now to speak of its grim history. The morning sun was just rising above the overhanging cliffs, casting deep cool shadows, and at the quarry sides a thick tangle of cistus and juniper covered the rock spoil with a canopy of sweet-scented green. There was a stone wall across the quarry entrance, however, and the only gate was guarded. Marcus walked boldly up to the gate and wished the guards good health.

The guards—there were six of them—looked back at him suspiciously. "What do you want, fellow?" asked their leader.

"I'm the slave of Archimedes son of Phidias," replied Marcus—and noticed the sharpening of interest as the name was recognized. "He wanted me to check the quarries to find which has the best stone for catapult shot."

At this, suspicion was completely swept away. "Is he building a three-talenter?" asked the youngest man eagerly.

"He starts it this morning," said Marcus. "It'll probably be ready in six or seven days."

"Zeus! A three-talenter!" exclaimed the young guard happily. "More than a man's weight! Imagine that hitting you!"

Marcus forced himself to grin back. "They're going to call it 'Wish You Joy,' " he said.

All the guards laughed. They reminded one another of the names of the other new catapults at the Hexapylon, and punched the air as they recalled how well they had performed.

"But why does the archimechanic want you to check the quarries?" asked the man in charge—not suspiciously, but with genuine puzzlement.

"Think about it," said Marcus. "You can get stone for thirty-pound shot anywhere, but a three-talent boulder is a big piece of rock. If it's flawed or uneven it may not fly straight. So Archimedes told me to go out to all the quarries and check which one would be best for the size of ammunition he needs." He dug into the leather sack he carried and produced a hammer and chisel. "He told me to bring him back a couple of samples, too."

The guards' leader took the hammer and chisel and examined them thoughtfully. Marcus waited, trying to keep his face blank, trying not to think about what he was doing or what he was about to do. He was already in trouble if news of this visit got back to Archimedes—though not in as much trouble as he would be in if it continued.

"I can't let you take this in," said the guards' leader regretfully. "We have Roman prisoners in this quarry. I can't risk something like this falling into their hands."

"Romans?" asked Marcus, tension giving his voice a strained note that passed well as surprise. "Here? Well, bad luck to them!"

"You're an Italian, aren't you?" said the guards' leader.

"A Samnite," agreed Marcus. "And a slave because of Rome.

But a Syracusan for the last thirteen years. What's the king going to do with these Romans, then?"

The guards shrugged. "He wants them for something," said the leader. "They get the best of food and the king's own doctor is attending their wounded. He's in there now, in fact."

"With some guards?" asked Marcus.

"Of course!" exclaimed the young guardsman, shocked at the thought of the king's own doctor going unguarded among enemies. "There's a half-file of us here."

Marcus grunted. "Well, bad luck to the Romans anyway!" he said. "Can I go in and check the quarry, even if I can't take samples? I may be able to tell straight off that the stone's no good for my master's catapult."

"Of course," said the guards' leader, smiling. "Your master's welcome to any help we can give his catapult. Good health to him!" And he gestured to his men to unlock the gate.

The youngest guardsman accompanied Marcus into the quarry. The eastern part of the quarry floor was still in shadow, but the morning sun shone warmly on an empty expanse of stone. "Where are the Romans?" asked Marcus.

The guardsman gestured toward the north face of the cliff, where a collection of sheds nestled under an overhang. "In there," he said disgustedly. "Nice and comfortable, out of the sun."

Marcus scrutinized the sheds. There were three of them: long, low, windowless buildings which had probably been set up to house a slave workforce when the quarry was in use. He could make out guards on the doors. "You've only got two people on each shed!" he objected.

"All we need," replied the guardsman. "Most of the Romans are wounded, and we've put leg irons on the rest. All the men on the sheds have to do is let prisoners up to use the latrines. If you want to look round, I'll just tell them who you are, so they don't bother you." He crunched off across the quarry floor to explain Marcus's presence to the other guards.

Marcus made his way slowly about the perimeter of the

quarry, ostentatiously examining the spoil heaps and occasionally picking up a chunk of limestone and putting it in his sack. When he was finally approaching the sheds, he was relieved to see the king's doctor come out of the nearest, accompanied by three guards.

The doctor noticed him, recognized him, and came over to ask what he was doing; Marcus explained. The doctor sighed and shook his head sadly. "At times I wish catapults had never been invented!" he exclaimed. "The injuries they produce—but it's for the good of the city. I wish you joy!"

Marcus waited until the man was well on his way back to the gate, then walked slowly up to the shed. The guards were at the far end and were not watching him, but his stomach was so tight that he thought he would be sick. He reached the wooden wall and leaned against it, trembling. There was a gap in the rough planking; he set his eye to it and gazed in.

The only light inside was what shone through the many gaps in the uneven walls, and it took a little while for his eyes to adjust. The building had a dirt floor, and in winter would have been cold and drafty, but it was comfortable enough for the Syracusan summer. About thirty men were within it, some of them lying very still on straw mattresses on the ground, but some, in leg irons, gathered together in little knots, talking or playing dice. Marcus made his way silently along the space between the cliff and the back of the shed, shielding his eyes from the light to preserve their adjustment to the dimness and checking each prisoner in turn, but it was soon clear that none of them was Gaius.

He waited until both the guards at the shed door were facing into the building, watching the prisoners, then glided out from behind the wall of the first shed and crept on to the next. He found another gap in the planks and peered through it.

He spotted Gaius at once, about halfway along the shed and on his own side of it, lying on his back on a mattress with his injured arm across his chest. Marcus made his way noiselessly along the side of the shed toward his brother. He could hear the guards at the door beyond talking, and his skin prickled with tension. He told himself that even if they did notice him, he could explain himself by saying he was simply curious to see the prisoners. But his skin prickled anyway. It was not really the guards he was afraid of.

When he had reached Gaius he knelt in silence for several minutes, inches away behind the thin planking, watching through a crack. Gaius was awake, his eyes open and staring darkly at the ceiling. His tunic was loose about his waist, and his chest was wrapped in bandages.

Marcus tapped lightly on the wall. Gaius' head turned slowly, and their eyes met.

Gaius sat up, bracing himself against the wall, trying to see more of his brother than showed through the crack. "Marcus?" he whispered. "Is it really you?"

"Yes," whispered Marcus. He was trembling again. The Latin word, *sic,* tasted strange in his mouth. For a long time he had spoken Latin only in his dreams, and to use it now made him feel that he was dreaming still.

"Marcus!" repeated Gaius. "I thought you were dead. I thought you died at Asculum!" On his right, his neighbor looked around at the raised voice, though the man on his left was asleep.

"Softly!" hissed Marcus. "Don't look at me; the guards may notice. Just sit with your back to me and keep your voice down. Right. Now, I've got some things for you—"

"What are you doing here?" whispered Gaius, sitting stiffly against the wall with his back to his brother. "What are you doing *alive?*"

"Being a slave," replied Marcus flatly. The man to Gaius' right was still listening, he noticed. He was not looking any more than Gaius was, but the expression on his face showed that he was listening intently. He was a lean, thin, dark man with something dangerous-looking about him; his head was bandaged, but he didn't seem to be otherwise injured, and his feet were imprisoned in irons.

"How?" demanded Gaius in a furious whisper. "Nobody was enslaved at Asculum! King Pyrrhus returned all his prisoners without ransom."

"He returned all his *Roman* prisoners," Marcus corrected him. "The other Italians were offered for ransom, and if nobody ransomed them, they were sold. There were a couple thousand people enslaved, Gaius. Not 'nobody' by any . . ." He found he could not remember the Latin for "reckoning" and fumbled to a halt.

"No Romans!" Gaius pointed out angrily.

"One at least," said Marcus bitterly. "Gaius, don't be stupid. If nobody told you what happened, you must have guessed. I deserted my post in battle. I was frightened, and I ran."

Gaius gave a jerk of pain. Roman did not desert their posts. A Roman who did would be beaten to death by his comrades. Even at Asculum, where the legions had tasted defeat at the hands of King Pyrrhus of Epirus, most of the Roman troops had been so afraid of the punishment for flight that they resisted to the death, and made Pyrrhus' victory so expensive that it cost him his campaign.

"Our square broke," said Marcus bluntly, "and most of the men died. I knew that the survivors would list me as one of the ones who ran. So after the battle I said I was just an allied Latin, or a Sabine or a Marsian, or anything except a Roman. I wasn't returned, and of course nobody ransomed me. I was sold to a Campanian, a vulture who was following the war about picking up scraps, and he sold me to a private citizen here in Syracuse."

"Oh, gods and goddesses!" whispered Gaius.

"It's what I chose," said Marcus in a harsh voice. "I wanted to live."

There was a long, wretched silence, a silence fully as bad as anything Marcus had imagined beforehand. There was nothing either of them could say. He had preferred life as a slave to death as a Roman, and for that there was neither condolence nor excuse.

"How are things at home?" he asked at last.

"Mother died eight years ago," said Gaius. "Valeria married

Lucius Hortensius and has three daughters. The old man's still in charge at the farm, though his chest is bad." He hesitated, then added quietly, "I won't tell him you're alive."

There was another silence. Marcus thought of his mother dead, his sister married, his father . . . his father would not learn of his disgrace. Good, good, good; the thought of the old man's rage still made him cringe inside. He wished that it were his father who was dead, that he could have gone back to his mother—and was ashamed of the thought.

"Thank you," he said finally. "I've come to help you. I've brought you some things."

"Can you help me get out?"

It was exactly what Marcus had expected his brother to say, and he sighed. "You're better off where you are, Gaius! The king"—he used the Greek title—"wanted prisoners, and that means he wants an exchange for something. You'll be safest staying here until you're exchanged. And your arm's broken, isn't it?"

"My arm and my collarbone," said Gaius flatly. "And three of my ribs. Can you help me escape?"

"Was it a catapult?" asked Marcus unhappily. It seemed ridiculously important to know whether it was his own master's contrivance which had injured his brother.

"Yes, of course it was," replied Gaius impatiently. "May the gods destroy it!"

"What size?"

Gaius started to glance around, then remembered that he should not do this and leaned his head back against the wall. "Marcus, all I noticed was that it hit me! There were catapult stones everywhere, and some of them were enormous. Why does it matter?"

Marcus didn't reply. "I've brought you some money," he said instead. "If you put your left hand up against this crack I'll pass it through. Your guards will probably buy things for you, for a cut. It's twenty-three drachmae."

"Twenty-three!" exclaimed Gaius in a strangled voice. "How did you—Marcus, your master will notice it's missing!"

Marcus remembered suddenly how scarce silver coin was in Rome, remembered with a shock how his family had bartered for almost everything, and used the heavy bronze *as* for almost everything else. When he was sixteen, twenty-three drachmae would have seemed a fortune. It was plain that to Gaius it still did.

"It's my own money," said Marcus. "I've never stolen yet, though I will if I must to help you. This isn't as much as you think—a month's wages for a soldier. But it may be useful."

Gauis set his hand against the crack, and Marcus fed the coins through. "What are these?" whispered Gaius, watching the silver fall into his palm. "They're . . . strange."

"They're Egyptian," replied Marcus. "We spent a few years in Alexandria. Don't worry—they're the same weight as Syracusan, and people here will take them."

Gaius said nothing, only stared at the silver, and Marcus remembered a time when Alexandria had been remote as the moon. It had ceased to seem that even before he visited it. At Syracuse one met ships from all over the Greek-speaking world, and he had grown used to the idea of traveling even before he'd traveled himself. But in central Italy people hadn't traveled much. Gaius had never traveled—except, of course, with the army. He had enrolled in the legions for the Pyrrhic War, and had presumably gone home to the family farm afterward, enrolling again for the Sicilian campaign. Marcus was oppressed by confusion and disquiet. It was quite wrong that he, a slave and coward, should feel superior to his elder brother.

"I have a saw and a knife as well," Marcus said, the confusion adding to the harshness in his voice. "And a coil of rope, but I think they're better left out here. If you decide you want them, I'll hide them." He did not really want to help Gaius escape— he sincerely believed that his brother was safest where he was— and yet he could not refuse to help. Besides, he could be wrong. The prisoners might yet be executed, or murdered by a Syracusan mob furious at some Rome atrocity.

"How did you get in here?" asked Gaius. "How did you get

the guards to allow you to bring in saws and ropes?"

"They didn't know I had 'em," replied Marcus. "Though they did take my hammer and chisel. I told them I was on an errand for my master. They know my master, so they let me through. I told them I'm Samnite, too, so that they wouldn't suspect me of wanting to help. Now, listen. I can invent another errand and come again if you need me, but if I do it too much, someone will start to suspect. So it's better if I don't come again soon, and I need to know now: are you going to try to escape?"

"Can you pass the saw in?" interrupted the man on Gaius's right.

"Who are you?" demanded Marcus.

"Quintus Fabius," replied the other. "Friend and tentmate of your brother. He's not going to get out without someone to help him."

"You're safer staying where you are!" warned Marcus.

"We'll get out if we can," said Gaius. "I don't care to find out what the tyrant of Syracuse wants prisoners for."

"There's nothing wrong with King Hieron," said Marcus. "He's cleverer than a fox and more slippery than an eel, but he's not cruel."

"He's a Sicilian tyrant!" protested Gaius in astonishment. "He cooks his enemies alive in a bronze bull!"

Marcus gaped. "Don't be ridiculous!" he exclaimed, recovering a little. "He's never put a single citizen to death, let alone cooked one alive. It was Phalaris of Akragas who had the bull—a man who lived centuries ago and in another city."

There was a bewildered silence, and then Gaius said, "I heard that Hiero"—he used the Latin form of the name—"had a hundred of the wives and children of his enemies impaled on stakes."

Marcus realized that his brother had undoubtedly heard dozers of stories of Syracusan atrocities. The Mamertini would have told some when they asked for Roman help, and more would have sprung up among the legions as they prepared for war. The Senate must have known the tales were false, but had said nothing.

"You heard a brazen-faced liar," snapped Marcus in disgust. "A stinking bandit who wanted an excuse for his own crimes."

"How can you be so sure?"

"Gaius, I live here! I've met Hieron, been to his house! If anything remotely similar had happened, I'd know about it. King Hieron has never killed or injured any citizen—which is more than the people you've come to Sicily to help can say!"

"You've gone very Greek," said Fabius quietly.

"I don't have to have gone Greek to say that the Mamertini are a tribe of bandits!" replied Marcus heatedly. "We put our *own* people to death for doing what they did—but you've come to fight and die for that bunch of filthy Campanian murderers." He stopped himself, swallowed a lump of anger, and went on, more moderately, "But what I meant to say is, if you think you need to escape because King Hieron's likely to harm you, think again. You'll be well treated until he exchanges you. Things are likely to be much worse if you try to escape than if you stay where you are."

"I mean to escape anyway," said Gaius, "if I can."

Marcus sighed again: it was no more than he'd expected. "I can probably manage to get two out of the city," he said, "but no more."

"Can you pass us the saw?" asked Fabius.

Marcus passed in the saw, though he had to take the handle off to get it to fit through the crack. Fabius tucked it under his mattress.

"With this and your knife and rope we can get out," he said. "Hide them under a rock beside this plank. You wouldn't happen to have noticed how many guards there are, and where they're posted?"

"Half a file," said Marcus. "Six on the gate, two on each of the sheds. Presumably the other six are on the wall, though I didn't see them when I came in. Don't even think of going up the cliff: it overhangs. The spoil heap by the west edge of the wall is probably your best chance: it's high, and it's overgrown pretty thickly and can give you cover while you wait for a sentry to turn his back. If you get out, come to our house, and I'll get you out of the city. All I ask is that you wait at least three nights first. If you come at once, somebody's bound to remember that I was here, and know where to look for you: a few days will give them a chance to forget. And Gaius needs the time to recover his strength, anyway."

He gave careful instructions on how to find the house. "The brick on the left side of the doorframe about halfway up is crumbled," he finished. "You can't mistake it. I'll find an excuse to sleep down in the courtyard, starting in three nights' time, and if you come at night I'll let you in secretly. If you don't come—and I tell you again, I think you'd do better to stay where you are!—I'll come back in ten days with some more money."

"Whose house is it?" asked Fabius.

"You're not to ask for it!" said Marcus. "That would give everything away."

"I just want to know," said Fabius. "Who's this master of yours that all the guards know, who goes to visit the king?"

"His name's Archimedes," admitted Marcus. "He's an engineer."

"The catapult maker!" said Gaius, turning his head to stare through the crack.

"Don't look!" growled Marcus. "Yes, he makes catapults."

"They were telling us about him at the fort. They showed us one of the catapults and said he was building an even bigger one."

Marcus said nothing.

"They said that the next one would be the biggest catapult in the world. They said it was bound to work, because his catapults always work. They said it was no use hoping to take Syracuse by storm, because Syracuse has the greatest engineer in the world. He's your master?"

"If you come to his house," Marcus said suddenly, between his teeth, "you're not to harm him. You have to swear that to me."

Silence. "It would be better for Rome if a man like that were dead," said Fabius slowly.

"You're not coming into the house unless you swear not to harm him," said Marcus. "I'm not having anyone in that house hurt."

Again, silence. "He's treated you well?" asked Gaius at last, with a mixture of bewilderment and shame. Marcus should never have been in the position where it mattered how a master treated him.

"Oh, may I perish!" muttered Marcus. "He *trusts* me. And—and he ought to exist. Someone like that—there aren't any others like that, not even in Alexandria. He can do *anything*—make water flow uphill, move a ship single-handed, tell you how many grains of sand it would take to fill the universe. It's not better for *anybody* when a man like that is dead. It means that there are a lot of things which the human race could do once and suddenly can't anymore." He stopped, utterly sick with confusion. He felt suddenly that he must have died without noticing: the Marcus who had run away at Asculum would never have thought the sort of things that were in his mind now.

Again there was a silence. Then Gaius said resignedly, "I swear that I will not harm him. May all the gods and goddesses destroy me if I do."

"I also swear it," muttered Fabius.

"Then come when you will," said Marcus, "and I will help you as much as is in my power."

11

Archimedes found that it was, after all, possible to understand what a catapult was for and still build it. The trick was to take each step of the construction independently and concentrate on the technical problems, without looking beyond them to the finished machine.

Not that the technical problems were interesting. The increase in the diameter of the bore needed for a three-talenter was only three finger-breadths, giving a proportional increase of three twenty-fifths all around—a laborious figure to calculate with, but not a difficult one. He was aware that if he'd been feeling happier about the work, he would have devised a new pivoting system— but the old one was adequate, and it sufficed.

The most disconcerting thing about working on another, and yet larger, catapult was the way everyone else in the workshop kept *grinning* about it. Even Eudaimon. The old engineer came up while he was working out the dimensions, shuffled his feet and cleared his throat a few times to attract attention, then asked—very humbly'—for the plans for Good Health, "since the king wants me to copy it." Archimedes found him the notes he'd made and explained a few of them, and Eudaimon nodded and made notes of his own—and then *grinned*, and said, "I never thought I'd ever build a two-talenter, heh? Make the next one another beauty for me, Archimechanic!" He trotted off, clutching his notes, leaving Archimedes staring after him in consternation.

It seemed that merely recognizing what the king had done wasn't enough to stop it. Archimedes wasn't sure what to do about it; wasn't even sure what he *wanted* to do about it. His response to his growing reputation depended on whether he was going to Alexandria or staying in Syracuse, and on that question he had not yet made up his mind. There were things to be said on both sides—but the things were different in kind, and he couldn't balance them. He found Hieron interesting, much more so than King Ptolemy—but the Museum was in Alexandria. His family was *here*, his closest friends *there*. And the image of Delia kept intruding itself and confusing him. She had not sent him another of her notes arranging a meeting, and he wasn't sure whether to be crushed or relieved. He had even less idea what to do about her than he did about Alexandria. His instinct was to postpone everything. After all, there didn't seem to be any urgent need for him to make up his mind at once. Anything that happened or did not happen with Delia was in Delia's hands, and as for Alexandria, he was obviously not going to abandon Syracuse, his home city, while the enemy was at her gate. The question of Alexandria could safely be left until he had time and energy to spare for it.

The trouble was, other people didn't seem to agree. Two days after he started work on the new catapult, Philyra received an invitation to visit the king's house and play a little music with the king's sister. She went to the mansion in the Ortygia suspicious at this royal condescension—but when Archimedes returned home that evening, it was to find his sister in a rage, with his mother at her side looking quietly resolute.

"The king's sister really wanted to talk about *you!*" Philyra told him indignantly. "And the queen was there: she said the king promised to make you rich! Medion, what's going on and why haven't you said anything about it to *us?*"

Archimedes gaped and stammered excuses: he'd been busy, the house was still in mourning, it hadn't seemed the best time. He became aware even as he floundered that the real reason he'd kept the king's machinations to himself was that he knew that his mother and sister would not want to go to Alexandria. He might well decide not to go himself, so why quarrel with them about it? As for Delia—well, they wouldn't approve of *that*, would they?

"My dearest," said Arata, with a quiet firmness that was much harder to face than Philyra's anger, "you should not leave us to find out such things from others. Ever since you came home from Alexandria, the tyrant has been chasing you like a lover. He's sent people to ask about you; he's invited you to his house; he's offered you large amounts of money; he's dropped compliments about you where other people will be sure to hear them . . ."

"He might just as well have chalked 'Archimedes is beautiful' up on the walls!" put in Philyra hotly—then subsided at a warning glance from her mother.

"Do you expect us not to notice?" went on Arata. "And when you don't tell us anything, do you expect us not to worry?"

"I'm sorry!" exclaimed Archimedes helplessly. "You've never *needed* to worry, Mama. I would have told you, if there had been anything to worry *about*."

"What does the king want from you?" demanded Arata.

"Only that I make machines!" protested her son. "It's just that some of the things I've been doing—I thought they were obvious, and that other people must have done them before. But it turns out that they're new, and the king thinks—well, you see, nobody's ever built a three-talent catapult before, or a system of compound pulleys, or a screw elevator. So I suppose Hieron's right."

"It started before you'd built anything," said Arata suspiciously.

"Well," said Archimedes, "Hieron's a very clever man. He knows enough to realize how important mathematics is for machine-making, and he thought I'd be an exceptional engineer as soon as he heard about me. I suppose he asked for that demonstration mainly to see if he was right. He's a good king—he knows how important engineering works are to the security and prosperity of cities. So he wants me to work for him, and in return he's promised wealth and honor. See? Nothing to worry about."

Arata gazed at her son steadily. "That's not all," she concluded.

She had always known when he was trying to deceive her. Broken pots blamed on the wind, the kitchen mortar or the loom weights he'd borrowed for a machine and then claimed never to have touched—none of it had ever fooled her. He sighed and lifted his hands in a gesture of surrender. "He wants to keep me in Syracuse. The other night, Mama, I asked him exactly the question you just asked me, and he admitted that he has been deliberately inflating my reputation in order to make it difficult for me to leave. He thinks that before long Ptolemy will offer me wealth, honor, *and* a position at the Museum."

There was a long silence. Arata's face flushed slowly. "You're *that* good?" she asked at last, breathless from sheer pride. So good that kings vied for his services?

"Yes," agreed Archimedes. "At least, Hieron thinks so. It's not something I can judge. Compound pulleys *still* look obvious to me. I'm sure Ktesibios at least would have thought of them."

Philyra's face, too, was crimson, but in her case not with pride. "You wouldn't go back to Alexandria!" she exclaimed.

"I don't know," said Archimedes honestly. "I'm not going anywhere until the war's over, so why worry about it now?"

The attempt at evasion was doomed; Philyra began worrying about it at once. She did not want to go to Alexandria; what was more, she believed that if he was really as good as the king thought, he shouldn't go either. She said it would be treachery to Syracuse, and for Archimedes to tell her that this was exactly what Hieron had intended her to say made not the slightest difference. She loved her city and was furious that he could contemplate deserting it.

Arata was more restrained, willing to postpone an argument that might never be relevant—and yet, she too made it plain that she did not want to leave Syracuse. Archimedes' tentative suggestion, however, that if it ever came to such a point, Philyra could marry a Syracusan and Arata live with her, while he himself went to Egypt, did not appease anyone. Arata, like her daughter, though it would be wrong for her son to leave the city, though she was too much of a peacemaker to say so before the issue had come to the crisis.

The quarrel was eventually suppressed by Arata's diplomatic suggestion that they eat some supper, but it flared up again after the meal. In token of peace they tried to play some music together, but as Philyra tuned her lute she remarked to her brother, "The king's sister loves the way you play the flute," then stared to see him beam delightedly.

"Oh, Medion!" Philyra burst out, as something else became clear to her. "You're not going to tell me *she's* interested in engineering, too?"

"No," said Archimedes evasively. "In auloi. She's very good, isn't she?"

"When did you ever hear her play?"

"At the king's house. She was in the garden, and . . ."

Philyra jumped to her feet, holding the lute as though she meant to hit him with it. "You never said anything about *that,* either! You go and do things that change everything for all of us, and you don't seem to think we have any right even to *know* about it!"

"I haven't done anything!" Archimedes protested feebly. "I've only spoken to Delia a few times!"

"Delia! O Zeus! Why did she keep *asking* about you?"

Arata looked at Archimedes in startled concern. "Medion!" she exclaimed. "You don't mean that the king's sister . . ."

Archimedes fled upstairs and buried himself in calculations on the abacus.

He was relieved when Dionysios invited him out to supper the following evening: it was an escape from the questions at home. But it turned out that Dionysios, too, wanted to talk about Alexandria—and about Philyra.

"I'm sorry to bring this up at a time like this," the captain said apologetically, when they were reclining at the table in the Arethusa. "I know your house is still in mourning, and there's the war as well. But I heard that you were thinking of marrying your charming sister to an Alexandrian, and I thought I'd better put in my own offer before it's too late."

Archimedes choked on his mouthful of tunny-fish and had to be pounded on the back and fetched a cup of water. By the time he'd recovered his breath, the captain was telling him seriously that it was his duty to remain in Syracuse. "I would not presume to dictate to you who your sister should marry, of course," Dionysios went on. "But as a loyal citizen, I must urge you not to leave our lovely city. The king—"

"Who told you I was thinking of marrying my sister to an Alexandrian?" interrupted Archimedes.

Dionysios was taken aback. "I believe your slave said as much to one of my men," he admitted. "Isn't it true?"

"There was never any *Alexandrian*," said Archimedes doubtfully. "My friend Conon and I used to talk about becoming brothers-in-law. But he's a Samian. And we never . . . that is, I never said anything about it at home. Oh, by the gods, don't spread it around! I'm already in trouble with my sister because of some other things I didn't tell her about, and if she thinks I was trying to marry her to a foreigner without consulting her, she'll brain me with a kithara. Are you really saying you want to marry her?"

It seemed that Dionysios really was. He began listing his qualifications: his rank, his prospects, his property. He apologized for his lack of fine breeding: he had been born poor and worked his way up through the ranks, and he had not thought of marrying until his most recent promotion gave him the standing to make a good match. But he had acquired some land to the south and a third share in a merchant ship, and he had every hope that after the war he would do very well. He was well thought of by the king and respected in the army. He had noticed Philyra at Archimedes' house and again at the demonstration, and he thought her quite charming. He gathered, too, that she was musical: he had always loved music, and wanted to marry a girl who could share his enthusiasm. Naturally, if he was so fortunate as to acquire her, he would treat her with all the respect that was due to the sister of a man like Archimedes.

Archimedes listened in astonishment. It seemed incredible that Philyra should marry, and that he should be the one who decided whom. He supposed that she *was* of marriageable age, and that he *was* the head of the household—but still it seemed incredible. Daydreams with his friend Conon had not prepared him for this. And Dionysios! He quite liked the man—good company, intelligent, capable; a fine voice; he was sure that what the fellow was saying about his prospects was quite true. But did he want such a man for a brother? And suppose he got it wrong, and Dionysios made Philyra miserable? How could he possibly make such a decision?

"I can't give you an answer right now," he said, when the captain had ground to a halt and sat blinking at him anxiously. "As you said, the house is in mourning. It would be quite wrong for my sister marry with her hair still short from the funeral."

"Of course," said Dionysios hastily. "But—afterward?"

"I need to think about it." He sat still for a moment, trying to imagine how his mother and sister would react to this news. Arata would consider the captain of the Ortygia garrison a catch, though she'd want to meet him before making up her mind whether to say yes. Philyra would certainly be excited. Not at all eager to leave home, he thought, but thrilled that such a man had asked for her—and assessing. She would want to know more about Dionysios. He met the captain's anxious gaze and declared suddenly, "I don't know what you think about women, but I've always felt they're just as capable as men, at least in everyday matters. My sister's a very sensible girl. She and my mother are really much better at arranging practical matters than I am, so I'm going to consult them before I answer anything. I don't know what you think of that." He held Dionysios' eyes. Many men would find it deplorable that he allowed his women to dictate his decisions. He was aware that his admission had just confronted Dionysios with a test, and wondered what the other man would have to say to pass.

Dionysios, capable soldier and experienced officer, went red. "I thought your sister was probably that sort when I saw her at the demonstration," he muttered. "She looked so confident and happy. Tell her and your mother that . . . I send my respectful greetings."

Archimedes nodded. He realized that if Dionysios had in any way appeared to slight Philyra's opinion, he would have opposed the marriage even if Philyra herself had wanted it, but that now he would dwell on the captain's good points when he informed his sister of the offer. Dionysios was willing to listen to Philyra, and he liked her confident and happy: he passed.

"You're not set on this Alexandrian, or Samian or whatever he is, though?" asked the captain hopefully.

Archimedes shook his head. "Philyra's already said she doesn't want to leave Syracuse."

Wistfully, though, he pictured to himself the beaming moon face of Conon of Samos. In Alexandria he and Conon had spent hours together in cheap taverns, drawing calculations on the table or the walls; they had laughed over other people's mathematical mistakes, and told each other jokes which nobody else had been able to understand. Each had been the first person the other came to with a new discovery, and neither had ever been disappointed of the expected enthusiastic reception. Their differences had merely fueled their friendship. Conon was short and plump; he liked food and drink and dancing, but when it came to music, he always sang out of key. He was rich, and came from a distinguished family, so he had lent his friend money, slipping it into his purse unasked and often unnoticed; Archimedes had no idea how much it had come to in the end. He in turn had made Conon a dioptra, an astronomical sighting instrument, which Conon had thereafter treasured above every other possession. Conon was no good at making things; his pudgy hands were clumsy, though his mind skipped among the stars as nimbly as a lizard.

Conon's family would never have permitted him to marry Philyra, even if Philyra had been willing. He and Conon loved each other like brothers anyway—best to leave it at that.

Dionysios grinned. "Good luck to your loyal sister! I hope you're not planning to leave either."

Archimedes muttered something unintelligible, and concentrated on his food.

"Pardon?" said the captain, polite but relentless. "I didn't hear that."

Archimedes abandoned the food. "Look," he said, "how I can I make promises about what I'll do three or five years from now? We may all be dead by then! I'm not planning to leave while I'm needed to make catapults, so why can't everyone leave it at that?"

But Dionysios was no more able than Philyra to leave it at that. He was very cautious of offending a man he wanted as a brother-in-law, but "as a loyal citizen" he felt it his duty to persuade Archimedes to stay in Syracuse, and his tactful attempts to do this lasted the rest of the meal. Archimedes was heartily sick of him by the time the waiter came in to clear the dishes.

When the dishes had been cleared away, the Arethusa's flute girls were once more ushered in. Dionysios, however, immediately detached the pretty young thing who fastened herself to him. "I'm on duty tomorrow morning," he said gently, though a glance at Archimedes indicated that he was also embarrassed to settle with a whore in front of a man whose sister he had just offered to marry. "But perhaps my friend . . . ?" His glance became interrogative.

Archimedes suddenly wanted very much to get drunk and go to bed with the flute girl—to escape from the questions, to forget Delia, to drown and befuddle the faultless precision of his own too-active mind. "Yes!" he said, stretching out a hand to the girl.

She came at once and draped herself over his knee. "You're Archimedes, aren't you?" she asked throatily, stroking his cheek. "The one they call the archimechanic?"

"Don't call me that!" he told her despairingly. She was holding a set of flutes, and he took them away from her before she could start playing. "Here! I'll show you something much more worthwhile than catapults."

~

~ AT THE HOUSE NEAR THE LION FOUNTAIN MARCUS SPENT
the earlier part of the evening nervous. He suspected the reason
for Dionysios' invitation, and it sickened him. His attempt at
discouragement seemed only to have spurred the captain to im-
mediate action. He wondered how Archimedes would respond.

But after supper Arata and Philyra sat in the courtyard playing
music in the cool dusk, and the sweet clear ripple of the strings
soothed him. The desperation that had crushed him for the past
three days lifted a little. There had been no repercussions from
his visit to the quarry. The Roman army was still camped before
the north gate, and his brother and his brother's friend were
probably planning their escape, but life in the household went
on much as it had always done. He was aware of the family
quarrel, but aware too of its essential shallowness, the way it did
not even touch the deep ties of affection that bound the family
together. As he sat silent in the courtyard listening to the music,
the house seemed a richer and more tranquil place to live than
it ever had before.

But everything was changing. The family was growing wealthy
and important; Philyra would marry and move away—and he
would go, too. Somewhere.

When Arata had gone to bed, and Philyra was putting her lute
away, Marcus came silently to her side and picked up the kithara,
which she had already set in its case. "Thank you!" she said,
without looking at him.

He shrugged. "Mistress," he began unhappily—then stopped,
not knowing what it was he meant to say to her.

Something in his voice troubled her, and she lifted her head
and looked at him, peering to make out his face in the gathering
dark. "What?"

"You—don't still believe I took Archimedes' money in Alexandria, do you?" he asked.

She stared, surprised at his earnestness. She had almost forgotten her suspicions. There had been a lot of money coming in
since her father died, and Marcus had been very careful with it.

Messengers kept bringing bags of coin down from the king's house—a hundred and eighty drachmae for catapults, so far, plus all the funeral expenses. Archimedes barely even looked at it; it had been left to Marcus and herself to keep track of it all. She realized at the slave's question how many pains he had taken to account for every obol. "No," she said, slightly ashamed of herself. If anyone had cheated her brother in Alexandria, it had not been Marcus.

"I'm glad," he said in a low voice. "I don't want you to think ill of me. Whatever happens, please believe that I've never wanted any harm to this house."

"Whatever happens?" repeated Philyra in concern. "What do you mean?"

"I—just mean, with the war, mistress. I know that it's my own people out there. But they've come here because they've been told lies, and I don't—Philyra, if they got in, I would fight to defend you."

She was touched. She reached over and rested her hand for a moment on his. "Thank you, Marcus," she said. Then she straightened, picked up her lute, and declared fiercely, "But they won't get in! The gods will favor Syracuse!"

"I pray they do," he said.

He carried her kithara upstairs for her and watched her go into her room—a slim shadow, black-clad with mourning in the dark house. Then he went back down and sat in the courtyard. He pressed the hand she had touched against his stubbled cheek; his throat was swollen with what he felt. It was no good. He was only property. Still, he wished that he could indeed fight for her—rescue her from his countrymen, carry her to safety, reassure her while she clung to him and . . . It was no good. He wished her brother would come home and say what answer he'd given to Dionysios.

For hours he waited in the dark courtyard, watching the stars. At last the soft rap sounded on the door. Marcus pulled himself up and hurried to open it. "Sir . . ." he began.

"Marcus!" whispered his brother, and clasped him in a one-armed embrace. Beside him Quintus Fabius flowed smokelike through the door.

Marcus had almost forgotten that this was the first night he could have expected them. He stumbled backward, then hastily closed and bolted the door behind them. "Are you being followed?" he whispered—then had to repeat himself in Latin.

It was Fabius who answered. "No," he said. "But we had to kill a sentry. They'll certainly miss the fellow before morning, and start searching for us. You said you could help us get out of the city. I hope you can do it tonight!"

"Yes," said Marcus, dismayed. Which of the sentries had they killed? The young man, the leader, one of the others who'd laughed and punched the air when they named his master's catapults? Killed with his knife, undoubtedly. He had known when he left the knife that it was a possibility, but he had hoped . . . "Keep your voices down," he ordered. "You don't want to wake anyone. Gaius, how are you?"

"Sore," replied Gaius. "But I can manage. That Greek doctor knew what he was doing." He reached out again to seize his brother's arm, and squeezed it. "How are you planning to get us out?"

"Do you still have the rope I gave you?"

Two heads, dimly seen, shook together. "We left it hanging from the wall," whispered Fabius.

"I'll get another, then," said Marcus.

Another soft rap sounded suddenly on the house door.

"May I perish!" exclaimed Marcus. He pulled Gaius hurriedly to the door of the dining room and shoved him in. "Hide!" he ordered, as Fabius slipped past him.

A second knock, louder. Marcus closed the door to the dining room behind the two fugitives and went to open the one to the street, just as Archimedes called, "Marcus!" from outside.

"Sorry, sir," he said, opening the door. "I was asleep."

Archimedes wavered through unsteadily and slumped down on the bench against the wall. He smelled of wine and cheap perfume. Marcus closed the door again. "You'd better get to bed," he told his master.

"Not yet," said Archimedes. "There was a tune I thought of, and I want to get it memorized before I forget it. Fetch my flutes." His speech was slurred, but voluble. Marcus recognized the mood with dread: lively-drunk like this, his master would usually try to explain geometry all night.

"Sir?"

"My flutes! The soprano and the tenor."

"But sir, it's after midnight! The neighbors . . ."

"Oh, Zeus! If they wake up, it's only music!"

Marcus stood where he was. He was aware of Gaius and Fabius crouching in the dining room as though all the night were one block of stone and he carved into it with them, solid with their fear. He realized with horror that he did not trust them. He knew Gaius would not break an oath, but Fabius? There was something hard and lethal about the man. He had wanted to kill the catapult maker the city had boasted of. Archimedes sat there, drunk and at home, suspecting nothing. It would be easy for Fabius to slip out while he was unattended and—what had happened to the knife?

"Marcus!" said Archimedes impatiently. "Do I have to fetch them myself?"

Gods and goddesses, thought Marcus, are the flutes in the dining room? "No, sir!" he said hastily. "I'll get them."

In the dining room, he could just make out Gaius and Fabius crouched exactly where he had imagined them, next to the window. He groped for the flutes on the sideboard and couldn't find them.

"Marcus, did you tell one of Dionysios' men that I wanted Philyra to marry Conon?" Archimedes called from the courtyard.

"I may have," replied Marcus. It was no use: he was going to have to light a lamp. Sweating with horror, he felt for and found the one that normally sat on the table.

"Why'd you say that?" asked Archimedes. "You know Conon's father wouldn't have agreed."

"But you always used to talk about it," said Marcus, abstract-
edly feeling for the flint lamplighter. "I thought maybe now that
we're rich . . ."

"No," said Archimedes. "No, he has to marry that Samian girl
next year. You should have remembered that. And anyway, you
know Philyra doesn't want to leave Syracuse. You shouldn't have
said anything. If she finds out I even *thought* of marrying her to
someone in Alexandria, she'll be furious. And Dionysios was very
worked up about it. You know what he's done? He's offered for
Philyra himself!"

Marcus froze, then forced his shaking hands to strike a light.
The lamp wick caught at once, casting a warm yellow glow about
the room. It gleamed on the eyes of the two men crouched beneath the window; revealed the smear of blood on Fabius' cheek
and the knife in his hand. Marcus shook his head and frantically
gestured for the man to put the knife away, then glanced about
the room for the flutes: they were nowhere to be seen. "Sir,
where *are* your flutes?" he asked distractedly.

"I don't know," replied Archimedes, yawning. "Hurry up and
find them!"

Marcus went back into the courtyard, carrying the lamp.
"What answer did you give Dionysios?" he asked.

His master sat sprawled over the bench, cloakless in mourning
black, with another wreath of parsley pushed to the back of his
cropped head. Parsley was supposed to prevent drunkenness; it
hadn't worked. "I didn't," said Archimedes. "I'll let Philyra say
what she thinks. Though it might be a good match."

"But Philyra's just a girl!" urged Marcus, somehow still finding
time to worry that she might agree with her brother. "And you
can't expect any sixteen-year-old to make a sensible decision
about the future."

Archimedes laughed loudly. "Oh, by Apollo! Marcus, you know
perfectly well you don't expect *me* to make a sensible decision
about what to buy in the market! Why do you think I can pick
a husband for Philyra when I can't even buy olives?" He pulled
his knees up and looped his arms round them. "Philyra will make

a much more sensible decision than I ever could. Sensible Philyra. Marcus, you think geometry is completely and utterly senseless, don't you?"

"No."

"Don't you? You always used to. You used to watch the scholars going into the Museum with a look on your face like a . . . like a banker watching an heir squander his estate. So much intelligence to be spent on air! Deep down, Dionysios agrees with you. When we first met, he praised Alexandria and called it the house of Aphrodite, but tonight he did nothing but tell me what I owe Syracuse. —I think my flutes may be in my room."

"I'll fetch them," croaked Marcus helplessly. He set the lamp down beside his master, hoping that its light would be some protection, then ran up the stairs three at a time and burst into the bedroom. The clothes chest was a black oblong under the gray rectangle of the window. He felt along it and found first the notched rim of the abacus and then, like fresh air in a dust storm, a set of smooth wooden boxes heaped one on top of another: the flute cases. He grabbed all of them and ran downstairs again, heart pounding.

Archimedes was still sitting quietly on the bench, turning one hand back and forth in the light of the lamp, watching the shadows shift in his palm. Marcus closed his eyes a moment, weak with relief.

The auloi were seized upon at once, and Archimedes sorted eagerly through them for the soprano and the tenor. He slid the reeds in, adjusted the slides, and without another word launched into a complicated melody.

It was a dance at first: a rapid joyful trill on the soprano, with a quick steady beat supplied by the tenor. A ring dance, a line dance, a tune to dance to in the street. But it changed under his quick fingers. The rhythm shifted to the soprano, and the tenor took up the tune with sudden disquieting shifts of tempo, speeding up and slowing down again, almost out of synchrony, then suddenly resolving into it again. The mode shifted without warning, and the tone became plaintive, with an underlying coloration of darkness. The disquiet grew. What had been fast became faster still, a headlong rush of sound over a chaos of dissonance; the tenor and soprano fought each other, irresolvable notes clipping each other's heels, almost but not quite out of tune. And then, all at once, the notes did overlap, and they were in harmony: the true harmony that was rare in Greek music, two notes singing a chord that brought a shiver up the backbone, and the melody they sang was sad and slow. The dance theme returned, but it was a march now, a slow march of farewell. Harmony became unison, sang quietly to the night, then faded softly into stillness.

There was a long silence. Marcus realized that he had no idea how long the music had lasted, and that while it had lasted he had been aware of nothing else. Archimedes blinked at the flutes in his hands as though he'd forgotten what they were.

"My darling," came Arata's voice from an upstairs window, "that came from a god. But the neighbors may not appreciate it, and you ought to be in bed."

"Yes, Mama," Archimedes called back at once. He slid the reeds out of the auloi and set the instruments back in their cases, then stood up and ran his hands through his stiff hair.

"What was that?" asked Marcus, in a shaken voice.

Archimedes hesitated. "I think it was a farewell to Alexandria," he said bemusedly. "But there's no hurry to decide." He wavered across the courtyard, and Marcus heard the stairs creak as he went up to bed.

Marcus sat down on the bench and stayed there for a little while, trembling. Then he noticed that the lamp was guttering, and blew it out.

The door to the dining room opened soundlessly, and the two fugitives slipped through it. "Jupiter!" whispered Fabius. "I thought that young fool would never stop playing!"

"You be quiet!" Gaius whispered vehemently back. "Gods and goddesses, that boy can play the flute!"

"We don't have time for concerts!" replied Fabius. "If we're going to get out of the city, we need to go!"

"Sshhh!" said Marcus. "Let the household settle."

Gaius sat down on the bench; Marcus could feel the taut linen of the sling that supported his brother's splinted arm. They sat together in silence, feeling the heat of each other's body through the warm, soft dark. Marcus remembered a time when he was eight years old and his father had beaten him, and Gaius had sat beside him, like this—not touching because he was bruised raw and a touch was painful; merely giving him the comfort of his presence. The love he had always felt for his brother, which had lurked baffled under his own shame and confusion, now flooded him, and with it a blind, bewildered grief that they should meet again only like this.

The house was still, still. If the neighbors had been disturbed by the concert, they had chosen to say nothing about it and gone back to sleep. Marcus at last rose and went to the storeroom next to the kitchen. Archimedes had built machines at home when he was still a child, and the storeroom still contained all his equipment. There was plenty of rope—there had been a phase when every machine was a kind of crane. Marcus took all of it, setting it in a large wicker basket, which he slung over his shoulder, then added a windlass and little wooden anchor that had been part of a hoist. Fully equipped, he went back to the courtyard. "All right," he whispered. "We can go."

As he unbolted the door, he caught a faint gleam out of the corner of his eye, and he glanced around quickly to see Quintus Fabius checking the knife. He shivered, reminded himself that the man had, after all, kept his oath, and set out.

The back streets of the Achradina lay dark and deserted under the stars. A watchdog barked as they went past, then fell silent. Marcus led the others quickly through the maze, then up along a narrow path which zigzagged up the side of the Epipolae and emerged on the plateau opposite the temple of Fortune. He kissed his fingers to the goddess and trotted past her temple to the right. They quickly passed the last of the hovels of the Tyche quarter and struck off across the bare scrubland of the heights.

"Where are we going?" asked Fabius, moving up beside him

and taking advantage of the open country around them to talk.

"I'm going to let you down the sea wall just where the plateau turns inland," Marcus replied. "Since you don't have a fleet, there aren't many guards posted on it. The wall runs along the top of the cliff and the cliff's steep, but we've got plenty of rope. At the bottom there's a bit of broken rock to scramble along, and once you're over that you've only got to walk north and inland a bit to reach your camp."

"You keep saying 'you,' " observed Fabius. "It should be 'us,' shouldn't it?"

"No," replied Marcus evenly. "Not while you're besieging Syracuse."

"Marcus!" exclaimed Gaius, also moving forward to join him. "You're coming with us!"

"No."

"You are a Roman!" Fabius protested angrily. "You don't belong here!"

"I'm a slave," Marcus said harshly. "A Roman would have died at Asculum."

"Stop it!" cried Gaius. "Asculum was a long time ago. You panicked, but you were sixteen, and you'd had about three weeks' training. You should never have been in the legion to begin with. I was the one who brought you along—what happened was more my fault than yours."

"Liar," said Marcus wearily. "You know I'm the one who insisted on coming. I didn't want to stay home with Father. I'm the one who ran away, and I'm the one who chose to stay alive afterward."

"You were telling that flute player that a sixteen-year-old can't be expected to make a sensible decision about the future," said Fabius. "Why are you making an exception for yourself?"

"You speak Greek?" asked Marcus in surprise.

"A little."

"Asculum's over with," said Gaius, returning to the point. "You can come back now."

"To accept my punishment?" demanded Marcus.

"No!" said Gaius, catching his shoulder. "To come home. I'm sure you'll be pardoned. It was a long time ago, and you've redeemed yourself by helping us escape. You can go to the consul and tell him what you know about the defenses of Syracuse, and he'll give you a free pardon. I'm sure he will."

"Oh?" asked Marcus bitterly: he had thought of this. "But what if I *don't* tell him what I know about the defenses of Syracuse? What would happen then?"

"Why wouldn't you tell him?"

"Because I'm not going to help *anyone* take Syracuse," said Marcus firmly. "May the gods destroy me if I do!"

"B-but, Marcus!" stammered Gaius disbelievingly.

"*You're* the ones who have no business being here!" Marcus exclaimed, turning on him furiously. "Don't you see that? Rome and Carthage have both been expanding their power, neither trusts the other, they've been building up to war for a long time. Fine! All that makes sense. But now Rome makes an alliance with *Messana* and attacks *Syracuse!* Where's the sense in that?"

"It's what the Senate and People decided was best," said Fabius reprovingly. "You think you know better than they do?"

"Yes!" declared Marcus. "I know Syracuse, and you've proved to me yourselves that the Roman people don't. Some bandit spews out a brazen-throated lie about Syracuse, and the great Roman people lap it up like dogs! When Rome started this war I don't think she had any more idea what she was doing than your general did when he sent your maniple out against the catapults. Gaius, I'm sorry, but it's true."

"Marcus," said Gaius urgently, "Marcus, you *must* come with us. Those guards will remember you came to see us, and they'll guess that it was you who helped us. If you stay here, they'll crucify you!"

"You really don't know anything about Syracuse," Marcus told him in disgust. "It's the Carthaginians who crucify: Greeks behead or poison. But I don't think they'll do that, either. Nobody knows I saw you. As far as the guards are concerned, I was looking at the quarry. My master's well-known and trusted, and his reputation will protect me. And even if I'm caught—listen to me, Gaius!—even if I'm caught, I'm willing to pay the penalty. I deserted my post once, and I've had to live with it. I destroyed my own place in life, and crawled into slavery for a refuge. Now my place is here. I'm not deserting my post again."

"Oh, gods and goddesses!" exclaimed Gaius wildly. "Marcus, you can't do this! I thought you meant to come with us! If I'd known you planned to stay, I would never have tried to escape myself!"

"So?" replied Marcus. "I told you not to. I told you you'd be better off staying where you were. You didn't want to. But nobody forced me to help you: that was my own free choice. If I can live with the consequences, why can't you?"

"I've already had to live with having caused your death once! Don't force that on me again! You *must* come with us!"

"No."

"Jupiter!" exclaimed Fabius, after a silence. "All this for *Syracuse*. What was it your master's son said about the Alexandrians?" He repeated in heavily accented Greek, " 'So much to be spent upon air!' "

Marcus stopped walking and frowned at him. "My master's *son?*" he asked.

"Nephew, then," said Fabius. "Or lover, if that's what he is—I know these Greeks incline that way. The flute player."

"You didn't realize who he was!" exclaimed Marcus. He was instantly certain that his instinctive suspicion had not been wrong, after all: that if Fabius had known who was sitting there, Archimedes would have died.

"Well, who was he, then?" asked Fabius impatiently.

"My master," said Marcus with satisfaction, and began walking again.

"That *boy?*" said Gaius in astonishment.

"He's twenty-two," replied Marcus. "I was originally sold to his father."

"But you said—and they said at the fort—and I thought . . ."

Gaius stopped, then suddenly burst out laughing. "Oh, Jupiter! I'd pictured him as a stern old man with terrible eyes and a white beard! A fearful magician, I thought. I was wondering what that talkative young flute player could be doing in the same house!"

Marcus was suddenly swamped by another wave of love for his brother, and he joined in the laugh. "Fearful magician?"

Gaius flipped his good hand dismissively. "You said he could number the sands and make water flow uphill. That sounds like magic to me."

Marcus laughed again. "It practically is," he said, longing suddenly to tell his brother everything he had seen and done and thought since he was enslaved. "The water-snail still seems magical to me, and I've helped build them. That's the machine that makes water run uphill, Gaius, it's a sort of—no, you have to see it, really, to appreciate it. It's—"

Gauis's laugh suddenly stopped. "Marcus, come with us!" he repeated. "Please!"

"Gaius, if I come with you, I'll die," Marcus replied wretchedly. "You know I will."

"You won't! Not if you come back as a loyal Roman who helped us escape."

"I'd have to prove it by betraying Syracuse! And I won't. I owe her too much."

"What can you possibly owe to a city where you were a slave?"

Marcus shrugged. He thought of music: the family concerts, the public concerts he'd heard while he attended the family; the plays. And there were people—neighbors, the other household slaves, Arata, Archimedes. Philyra. More than that, there was the vastness of the world he had touched, the constant stream of ideas that had flowed past him, uncomprehended and bewildering, but, now that he looked back on it, enlarging. He had hated his slavery and he hated it still—but he could not regret the rest.

"More than I can explain," he said softly. "Trying to talk about it is like trying to weigh things with a pint measure: I can't do it. But believe me, Gaius, if I betrayed Syracuse, I'd destroy whatever honor and loyalty are left in me. Don't ask me to do that."

Gaius touched his shoulder gently. "I pray to all the gods, then," he whispered, "that you're right, and that they don't suspect you. If they kill you for helping me, Marcus, I . . . don't know what I'll do."

12

At dawn the following morning, Agathon woke the king with the news that Dionysios son of Chairephon had arrived at the house and was asking to see him.

"Dining room," commanded Hieron succinctly. "Tell him I'll join him in a minute."

A minute later the king appeared in the dining room, barefoot, belting his tunic, and found the captain of the Ortygia garrison standing to attention by the door. Dionysios had the crumpled, excessively awake look of a man who's spent most of the night on his feet and the expression of one who brings bad news.

"Sit down," said Hieron, taking his own place on the central couch and gesturing toward the place on his right. "What's the matter?"

Dionysios ignored the invitation to sit. "Two of the Roman prisoners escaped last night," he said bluntly. "My troops were guarding them. I accept full responsibility."

Hieron looked at him curiously, then sighed. "Was anyone hurt?"

Dionysios grimaced. "One of the guards was killed. Straton son of Metrodoros—a fine man, one of my best. I had my eye on him for promotion. I have informed his family."

Hieron was silent for a moment. "May the earth be light upon him!" he said at last. "Tell me exactly what happened, as far as you know it, and—Captain? *I* will decide who is responsible. Not you. Also, do sit down, or I'll get a crick in my neck."

Dionysios sat, stiffly. "About an hour after midnight," he said, "the guard on the middle section of the quarry wall noticed that Straton, the guard on the western section, wasn't in his place. He went to look for him, and found him lying on top of the wall with his throat cut. There was a rope hanging down the front of the wall beside him. The sentry raised the alarm at once, and the file leader in charge at the quarry—Hermokrates son of Dion—instantly doubled the watch on the walls and sent a messenger running to find me. He himself went to check on the prisoners. Most were sound asleep, and the guards on the sheds were awake and in their places, but two men from the middle shed were missing: Gaius Valerius and Quintus Fabius, both heavy infantrymen from the same maniple. Fabius was an officer of some kind—*tessararius*, I think the title was."

"Watch commander," translated Hieron. "A junior rank within a century."

"The two missing men had been next to each other," Dionysios went on. "Valerius was wounded—broken arm and ribs—and had not been shackled, but Fabius had been in leg irons. He'd got them off somehow, probably just by working his feet out through them—they'd been left in his place, weren't obviously damaged, and guards on the shed say they were old and he was built like a snake. Behind where the two had been, two planks in the shed wall had been sawn through, then propped back into place. Hermokrates had the shed searched, and found the saw tucked under a mattress." Dionysios removed it from a fold of his cloak and set it down on the king's dining table: an unremarkable strip of toothed iron, with a strip of cloth wound about one end in place of a handle. Hieron picked it up and examined it, then set it down again. The captain continued, "I arrived while Hermokrates was questioning the other prisoners—they claim not to have noticed the escape, though it's plain at least some of them must have. I'd brought two files of men with me. I sent my men out to search for the fugitives at once, but by then they'd had some time to make good their escape, and we found no trace of them. I wish to make it plain, however, that I entirely support Hermokrates' decision not to search the streets at once. He did not initially know the scale of the escape, and he did not have enough men to secure the quarry and search the streets as well."

"I agree," said Hieron. "Have you informed the captains of the forts on the wall?"

"I did that as soon as I arrived at the quarry. They should be on the watch for any attempt to leave the city."

"Good. It seems likely, then, that the two men are still in the city, presumably hiding with whoever it was that brought them the saw, the rope, and the weapon they used on that poor guardsman. Who has had contact with the prisoners?"

Dionysios shrugged his shoulders wearily. "You, me, their guards. Your doctor. Beyond that, I don't know. You know that they were originally in the charge of the garrison of the Hexapylon, and I and my men only took over yesterday. I doubt, though, that Captain Lysias has been lax. However, there is one thing . . ." He took a piece of knotted cloth out of his purse, set it down on the table, and unknotted it to reveal a silver coin. "One of the guards says that the prisoner Valerius gave him this yesterday and asked him to buy oil. The guard used some change to buy the oil, kept this, and last night passed it on to me."

Hieron picked the coin up and examined it. It bore a crown and thunderbolt on the reverse, and, on the obverse, the smiling, diademed profile of Ptolemy II. "Surprising," commented Hieron in a neutral voice, then, raising mild eyes to Dionysios, "And I take it your guard was surprised, since he passed it on to you?"

Dionysios nodded. "He says he made some comment when he was offered it, and the prisoner told him that it was the same weight as Sicilian ones."

"And so, of course, it is," said Hieron. "But unexpected in the hands of a Roman." He set the coin down. "It may be irrelevant," he added after a moment. "If a Roman did get such a coin, its rarity might induce him to keep it for good luck. Perhaps he kept it around his neck as a sort of talisman, and only spent it since his other money was taken when he was captured and he was desperate to buy some oil to help his friend slip off the shackles."

"Oh, Zeus!" exclaimed Dionysios, startled. He had seen nothing odd in the request for oil: it was used like soap, and it had seemed natural for even a prisoner to want to wash.

Hieron gave him a tight smile. "On the other hand, this *could* come from the same source as the rope. I take it you've checked whether any of your men have been to Egypt recently? Are any of them Italian mercenaries? Greeks from one of the cities of Italy?"

"A couple are Tarentines," admitted Dionysios. "But I wouldn't think—that is, I know that one of them at least is fanatically anti-Roman; it's always causing trouble."

"Check their backgrounds anyway," ordered the king. "See if they could have been blackmailed. And another thing: check if anyone has visited the quarry, but not the prisoners."

"What?" asked the captain, surprised.

"There's no handle on the saw," Hieron pointed out. "Would a man who was smuggling in a saw deliberately choose one with no handle? I'd say it's much more likely that the handle was taken off in order to fit the tool through a crack in the wall."

"Zeus!" exclaimed Dionysios again, staring. "I know already of one man who visited the quarry and not the prisoners, and though he's unlikely to be relevant, there may have been others claiming the same errand."

"What errand is that?"

"Stone for very large catapults," said the captain. "Lysias told me that Archimedes had his man around checking which quarry would be best for ammunition for the three-talenter."

Hieron's head jerked up, and he stared at Dionysios, wide-eyed in alarm. "Oh, gods!" he exclaimed.

"What's the matter?" asked Dionysios, surprised. "It *was* Archimedes' slave. Your doctor was there at the time and recognized the man, Lysias said."

Hieron shook his head. He clapped his hands, and Agathon appeared sour-faced in the doorway. "Take half a file of men from the guards' barracks," commanded the king, "and hurry to

Archimedes' house in the Achradina—I believe you know where it is. There are two escaped prisoners of war who may be hiding there. Get the household to safety, and then search the house for the prisoners. The citizens are to be treated with every courtesy. Ask Archimedes to come up here. If that Italian slave of his is about, send him as well, under guard. Hurry! *Run!*"

Agathon, astonished, bobbed his head and ran. Hieron got to his feet and stood biting the side of his thumb with anxiety. Dionysios stared at him in consternation.

"Lord!" he exclaimed. "You can't think that Archimedes . . ."

"That slave of his is a Latin," said Hieron. "What's more, he was in Egypt. And if Archimedes wanted special stone for his three-talenter—and I haven't heard any report that he did!—he would have used someone from the workshop to look for it. He's been quite careful to keep that particular slave away from anything strategic."

"How do you . . ." began Dionysios weakly.

"Because I had it checked!" snapped Hieron. "The slave claims to be a Samnite, but is obviously lying, and he's been in Syracuse for thirteen years—in other words, since the Pyrrhic War, when there were quite a number of Latins enslaved. Probably he saw some men he knew among the prisoners, and agreed to help them escape if they would help him back to home and freedom. Herakles, I hope I'm wrong! I hope we don't find Archimedes with his throat cut, like that poor guardsman!"

"He was with me last night," said Dionysios faintly. "I'd invited him to dinner at the Arethusa. I . . . wanted to ask if I could marry his sister. When I left he was playing the flute with a girl. That was an hour or so before midnight."

"I hope she kept him distracted until dawn!" said the king. He sat down again.

"Why would Archimedes have kept a slave he knew was disloyal?" asked Dionysios.

"Don't be stupid!" said Hieron impatiently. "The man had served his family for thirteen years and accompanied him to Alexandria—obviously he *didn't* think the fellow disloyal! But he just as obviously had some reason to suspect the slave's nationality, and so he confined him to domestic duties to avoid any patriotic crisis of conscience. What else was he supposed to do? You don't send a person who's been a member of your household ever since you were a child to the quarries without good cause!" The king rubbed his face wearily, then looked back at Dionysios. "I hope I'm wrong," he repeated grimly.

~ MARCUS HAD BEEN BACK AT THE HOUSE FOR ABOUT half an hour when the guardsmen knocked on the door.

He had arrived back at the house at dawn, slipped in through the door he had carefully left unbolted, put away his basket of equipment, and moved directly to his usual first duty of the day: cleaning the latrine. He was in the middle of this when he heard the knock, and then Sosibia's voice, shrill with alarm, answering a man. He froze in his place for a moment, listening, then got up, washed his hands carefully, and came out into the courtyard, where the rest of the household was assembling.

Archimedes was waked out of a deep sleep into a hangover. He stumbled down the stairs pale with headache, his black tunic crumpled from having been slept in, and regarded Agathon and the half-file leader from the Ortygia with queasy bewilderment. They explained that two Roman prisoners had escaped during the night and might be hiding somewhere in the house.

"Where?" he asked disgustedly. "It's not a very big house. I think we might notice two Romans."

"The king gave orders for us to search it, sir," said the half-file leader. "He was concerned for your safety."

"That's ridiculous! You can *see* there's nobody here but my own household!"

The half-file leader scanned the small group in the courtyard, who had been crowded into the doorways by his own men, then looked back to the disheveled master of the house. "I am still obliged to search," he said. "One of your slaves can remain to explain the arrangement of the house to us, but the rest of the household should go to a neighbor's, out of harm's way. Believe me, sir, we have strict orders not to disturb anything."

"Zeus!" exclaimed Archimedes in disgust.

"I'm sure Euphanes would be happy to have us," said Arata pacifically. She was standing in the workroom door, veiled with a hastily seized cloak, Philyra beside her.

Archimedes opened his mouth to make some reply, and Agathon said to him sharply, "The king wants *you* to come and speak with him at once."

Archimedes turned back and glared. "No," he declared flatly. "Delian Apollo, the *arrogance* of it! To turn my family out of our own house and expect me to come running the moment he claps his hands! If Hieron thinks he owns me, he'll soon learn otherwise!"

Arata gasped and dropped her veil. The king's doorkeeper went crimson with indignation and drew himself up to his— unimpressive—full height.

Before he could speak, Archimedes struck again angrily: "This is my house, and I didn't ask you in! Get out!"

The half-file leader looked to Agathon for guidance, but Agathon could only splutter. The half-file leader looked back at Archimedes, remembered the great respect showed to him by the king, and decided that conciliation was called for. "Sir," he said, "this is being done out of concern for your safety, not because—"

"The king also ordered your man Marcus brought to him *under guard*," declared Agathon, finding his voice again.

"That's . . ." began Archimedes—then looked at Marcus and stopped. The slave's face was impassive, inert as clay, but told him instantly that the implied accusation was true. Perhaps it was only that it contained neither confusion nor surprise. He stared for a long moment, appalled. The half-file leader went on about the king's concern for his safety.

Archimedes raised his hand for silence, and the half-file leader stopped. There was a sudden silence, which deepened like a stone plummeting as he and Marcus looked at each other. "Are they here?" he asked at last, the words dropping into that stillness.

"No," replied Marcus in a grating voice. "Let them search."

Archimedes looked at him for another moment. Marcus, meeting his eyes, felt that for the first time he had his master's full attention; that always before that gaze had been fixed on something beyond or to the side of him, and only now was the full power of the mind behind it bent on him where he stood in the silent courtyard. The aperture of a three-talenter, he thought, would have seemed less absolute.

"*Were* they here?" asked Archimedes quietly.

Marcus hesitated—then nodded. "Last night," he whispered. "They were here when you came back from your dinner. They hid in the dining room until it was quiet again. They're gone now." He pulled himself up, and went on, for the sake of all the household, but especially for the girl who was watching him in shocked amazement, "One of them is my brother. I helped him because I was bound to, but first I made him swear not to harm anyone in this house. He urged me to escape with him, but I refused. I wanted no part of the attack on Syracuse. I am prepared to accept the consequences of what I have done."

"Where are they?" demanded the half-file leader.

"Already out of the city," replied Marcus proudly. "They'll be back in their own camp by now. You can search as much as you like, but you won't find them."

"You'll come with us as the king ordered," said the half-file leader, and Marcus at once bowed his head in agreement.

"I'll—come as well," said Archimedes hoarsely.

He crossed the courtyard to his mother, took her by the arms, and kissed her cheek. "Don't worry," he told her. "Let the men search the house—though I don't think there's any point in bothering Euphanes at this time of morning. Stay and make sure they don't take anything. And don't let them be insolent." He looked from Arata to the half-file leader, and his next words were intended for the whole party. "We are not insignificant people."

⁓ THEY LEFT THE HALF-FILE LEADER DIRECTING THE search of the house and started off toward the Ortygia: Agathon,

Archimedes, and Marcus, walking between two guardsmen but, at Archimedes' insistence, not bound. Agathon said nothing, though every line of his rigid back and every glance of his sour face expressed the most absolute disapproval. Marcus, who walked silently with his head bowed, could feel those glances like a flick of the fingers against his face. Archimedes' looks of unhappy concern, however, were much more painful.

When they reached the king's house, they found Hieron and Dionysios still in the dining room. The king jumped to his feet when they entered and beamed at Archimedes. "Good health to you, and I thank the gods!" he exclaimed, coming over to shake hands. "Forgive me if I've disturbed you unnecessarily, but—"

"The slave has admitted it," interrupted Agathon harshly. "He says he smuggled the two prisoners out of the city last night."

Hieron turned to Marcus. The smile he had given Archimedes was still fading from his lips, but the expression in his eyes was already something quite different. "How?" he asked.

Marcus cleared his throat. "I lowered them down from the seawall just where it turns inland. There's only one guard on that stretch, and he didn't come downstairs to check the catapult platforms on the ground floor. There was no moon, and it was simply a matter of waiting until he was out of the way." He looked at Archimedes. "I borrowed that hoist you built when I last retiled the roof. You know, the one with the windlass that clamps onto things? We clamped it to the artillery port, and I lowered Gaius down in the tile basket—his arm's broken, and his ribs, and he couldn't have gone down a rope. Fabius just slid down after him. Then I pulled the basket up again, unclamped the windlass, and went home."

"Why?" asked the king softly. His clear dark eyes rested on Marcus' face, their expression impenetrable.

Marcus straightened his shoulders. "One of the escaped men is my brother. Gaius Valerius, son of Gaius, of the Valerian voting tribe."

"A Roman citizen," said the king.

"Yes," said Marcus. "I used to be a Roman as well." He

glanced at the expressions on the faces about him: the doorkeeper disapproving; Archimedes stunned and miserable;
Dionysios and the two guards angry and confused; the king—
unreadable. He might as well go on—there was no sense in keeping anything back. Even if he had not admitted it, they would
have known what he had done. They'd sent guards for him: someone must have remembered his visit to the quarry. "I happened
to see the prisoners when they were being marched into the city,
and I recognized Gaius. Gaius saw me, too. I couldn't leave him.
He was wounded and . . . I could not leave him to think I'd forgotten everything I was. I went to speak to him next day. You
know about that. The other man, Fabius, was next to Gaius and
overheard us talking, so I had to involve him as well."

"*I* don't know about it," said Archimedes numbly.

"You don't," agreed Marcus, and looked back at the king. "You
probably realize that already, lord, but I can confirm it: Archimedes didn't know anything about any of it. I never told him
even that I was a Roman." He turned back to his master. "Sir, I
told the guards at the quarry I was your slave and that you'd sent
me to check which quarry would provide the best stone for the
three-talenter. They let me in at once. I went up to the shed and
spoke to Gaius through the wall. He asked me to help him escape. I told him he was better off where he was, but he didn't
believe it. —They'd been told a lot of stupid stories about you,
lord," he added apologetically to Hieron.

"Really?" asked Hieron. "What stupid stories?"

Marcus hesitated, and the king said, "Please! I will not blame
you for repeating what they said, and I would very much like to
know."

"They had you confused with Phalaris of Akragas," said Marcus
uncomfortably. "They told me you cooked people alive in a
bronze bull. And they said you had people impaled on stakes."

"Tch-tch," said Hieron. "Is there anyone in particular I'm supposed to have had cooked or impaled, or did I choose my victims
at random?"

"You're supposed to have cooked your opponents, I think," said Marcus, even more embarrassed, "and impaled their wives and children. A hundred of them, I think they said. I told Gaius it was all lies, but, as I said, I don't think he really believed me. His friend told me I'd gone very Greek. They know nothing about Greeks and less about Syracuse."

"I impale children, do I?" said Hieron thoughtfully. "Gods! Very well, go on. You agreed to help your brother and his friend escape. You gave them money, a saw, some rope, and a weapon of some kind."

"A knife," said Marcus. "Yes. I hoped they wouldn't use it, but I've heard that they did. I'm sorry for the man, whoever he was."

"His name was Straton son of Metrodoros," said the king. "I believe you knew him."

Archimedes and Marcus both stared, appalled. "Straton?" asked Marcus in horror. "But—it wasn't the troops from the Ortygia who—"

"I was given charge of the prisoners yesterday," said Dionysios coldly. "Straton was watching the western end of the wall last night. They cut his throat."

"Oh, gods!" groaned Marcus. He covered his face: he could no longer meet the eyes that watched him. The whole of the long sleepless night, the anxious days before it, came crashing down on him, and he feared that he would burst into tears. Straton! Not a nameless guard, but a man he'd known, a good-natured gambler, a fellow who liked a joke, a man with the same real and urgent life as himself.

"You liked him," came the king's quiet voice.

Marcus nodded behind his hands. "I . . . yes, I liked him. He was a man who deserved a long life. Oh, gods! I should never have given them anything except the money! Gaius said he wouldn't have tried to escape if he'd realized I didn't mean to come."

"Why didn't you go with them?" asked the king. "Why are you here to begin with? One does not expect to find a Roman citizen as a slave. I'd assumed that you were merely a Roman ally who'd recognized someone who might help him, but it seems the situation is altogether more complicated than that."

Marcus lowered his hands. "It's not complicated," he declared bitterly. "I enrolled in the legions for the Pyrrhic War. At Asculum I panicked when the Epirots charged. I dropped my shield and ran. Afterward I claimed not to be a Roman so that I wouldn't be sent back."

"Ah," said Hieron, in a tone of revulsion.

"I don't understand!" exclaimed Archimedes. "Why . . ."

"The Romans kill men for deserting their posts," said the king. "They strip the unfortunate deserter naked and stand him in front of his comrades, who are then urged to beat him to death with sticks and stones. They consider this a great incitement to valor—which it undoubtedly is, if you think valor worth purchasing at such a price." Hieron moved closer to Marcus and peered quizzically into his face. He was close enough that Marcus could feel the heat of his breath, but with the guards boxing him in he could not move away. Trapped under that scrutiny, for the first time that morning he really felt himself to be a prisoner.

"They are not always as ferocious in inflicting such extreme penalties as they pretend, however," the king went on. "Men who merely flee out of panic are usually let off with a beating. And Asculum was a long time ago. I would have thought that after so many years in exile, you would have been able to return."

"They would have asked me for information about the defenses of Syracuse," said Marcus. His voice was flat; he felt beaten. Who was going to believe this? He had given a knife to the enemies of Syracuse, and they had used it to kill a citizen: how could he claim he was loyal, after that? But he went on anyway. "When I refused to give it to them, they would have killed me."

"And you would have refused?"

"Yes!" Marcus said, collecting the last limp remnants of his strength and glaring into those impenetrable eyes. "Disbelieve it if you like, but I would have refused. Syracuse has committed no offense against the Roman people, and Rome has no business attacking her. For my own part, this city allowed me life. If it was a life of slavery, that wasn't her fault, and she's given me things that I hadn't even known existed. I am in her debt, and I will never repay that debt with injury. May the gods destroy me if I do—and may the gods favor Syracuse, and crown her with victory!"

"That is not a prayer I ever expected to hear spoken by a Roman," observed Hieron dryly. "But you have done injury to the city already, in abetting the murder of one of her defenders." He went back to his couch at the table and sat down. "Let us return to what happened last night. Did you go to the quarry to help your brother and his friend over the wall?"

"He was at my house," put in Archimedes abruptly. "He would have been missed in the evening if he'd been away. And he let me in when I came home. That was a couple of hours after midnight."

"He said they were already there then," said Agathon. "Hiding."

Marcus nodded and numbly recited the facts. "They arrived just before Archimedes. I'd told them to come to the house when they could, beginning on the third night after I spoke to them. I made them swear not to hurt anyone in it." With a shudder he remembered again how Fabius had crouched under the dining-room window, knife in hand, blood on his cheek, eyes gleaming. But there was no reason to mention that to the king.

"Lord," said Archimedes urgently. "This man is mine."

"Questionable," replied Hieron. "He is, it seems, a Roman citizen, and should not be a slave at all. Marcus—*Valerius*, I suppose it is. Son of Gaius, of the Valerian voting tribe."

"My father purchased him legally," said Archimedes stubbornly. "He has been in my family for a long time, and he has always shown himself faithful, until now. He wouldn't have been disloyal now, either, if he hadn't been bound by an older loyalty to his brother. He refused to purchase his own safety at the cost of treachery to the city, and he remained here to suffer the consequences of his offense."

"Did he?" asked the king. "Or did he just hope that he wouldn't get caught?"

"I hoped that I would not get caught," said Marcus readily, "but I was prepared to suffer the consequences if I was. I am ready to suffer them now, O King." He wished they would get it over with.

"And just what do you think those consequences *are?*" inquired Hieron.

Marcus stared at him in silence. The round, bright-eyed face was still unreadable. "You will have me put to death," he said. He was proud of how calm he sounded.

"Ah, death!" exclaimed the king. He leaned back on the couch, put his legs up, and crossed them. "Phalaris of Akragas, am I? You know, Archimedes, I've always wondered about that bronze bull. Is it even technically possible? I don't mean casting a hollow statue, I mean the rest of it—that the screams of the victims were distorted into a lowing such as a bull might make."

Archimedes blinked. "It's technically possible to distort a sound, yes, of course. But . . ."

"So it might have existed? A shame. Don't worry, I'm *not* going to ask you to build me one! Marcus Valerius, what am I supposed to have you put to death *for?* A fine man died because of what you did—but you didn't kill him yourself, clearly didn't want him killed, and were not present at the murder. The most you can be said to have done is to have provided a murder weapon, and that is not generally reckoned a capital offense. Neither is it a capital offense to help a kinsman out of prison, and you are not, so far as I can tell, guilty of anything else. You have certainly abused the trust of your excellent master and put his household in danger, but he seems more inclined to plead for you than to accuse you. Since I am *not* Phalaris of Akragas, I am not going to put you to death for crimes to which a jury would assign a lesser penalty.

"Now, if your offenses are not capital, they remain serious, but what penalty you should receive for them depends on your status, which is, as I said just now, questionable. You say that you are a

Roman citizen; Archimedes says that you are his slave. As a slave who has deceived his master, betrayed the city, and abetted the murder of a citizen, you should be flogged and sent to work in the quarries. As a Roman, however, you are an enemy national, and your treatment depends entirely upon the military authorities of Syracuse—in other words, on me." He glanced about the room, as though inquiring whether anyone disputed this. When his eyes met Archimedes', they stopped for a moment.

"I withdraw my claim to this man," said Archimedes in a low, unsteady voice. "Or, if necessary, I will free him. He is in your hands, O King."

Hieron inclined his head in acknowledgment. "I think it's sufficient that you withdraw your claim. Do you want compensation for him? How much did he cost?"

"I don't want compensation."

Another nod. The king turned back to Marcus. "Marcus Valerius, son of Gaius, of the Valerian voting tribe of the city of Rome, you have assisted two of your countrymen to escape from the prison in which they were being held. It seems to me most fitting that you should take their place in that prison, and that you should be exchanged, ransomed, or released with those of your fellow citizens who were taken in arms. Should you think that I am by this means after all sentencing you to death, and making your own people your executioners, let me add that, as far as I am concerned, you are welcome to tell Appius Claudius about the defenses of Syracuse. Nothing you could say would injure this great city, and it might help her. I had in fact intended to show those very defenses to your fellow prisoners, as a remedy to the contempt in which the consul appears to hold us.

"As for Straton son of Metrodoros, he died at the hands of the enemies of Syracuse. I decree that he is to receive a state funeral, and that his family is to be provided for as though he had died in battle—for he fell guarding the city no less than those who die in defense of the walls."

Hieron stopped and again surveyed the room. Archimedes inclined his head at once. Dionysios hesitated, obviously consid-

ering a protest, but, after a glance at Archimedes, yielded. Then
Hieron nodded as well, satisfied. "Take the prisoner to the
quarry, and put him in his brother's place," he commanded the
two guards. "Captain Dionysios, I disagree entirely with your as-
sessment as to who was responsible for this incident, but, with
hindsight, there were not enough guards on the quarry. We relied
too heavily on the prisoners' wounds. Take another half-file, and
improve matters. Agathon, ask Nikostratos to come here and
write some letters: I need to double the watch on the seawall.
Archimedes . . ." The king hesitated. "Perhaps you'd care to stay
to breakfast?"

Archimedes shook his head.

"Then, please, use my house as your own if you wish to rest
a little and compose yourself before going home."

The guards escorted Marcus out. He went quietly, though his
expression was one of shame and bewilderment, not at all appropriate to a man who has just heard that he is to be freed from
slavery and returned to his own people. Dionysios left with him,
to rearrange the security for the quarry. The secretary Nikostratos came in to take Hieron's letters, and Archimedes went out
into the garden. He was glad of a chance to rest and compose
himself before venturing into the streets. He felt more shaken
and confused by what had happened than he would have thought
possible.

⌁ HE WAS SITTING BESIDE THE FOUNTAIN, STIRRING THE
water with his fingers, when Delia came into the garden on her
way to breakfast. She stopped short, her breath catching, and
watched him a minute in silence.

Ever since Hieron had promised his exceptional engineer
wealth and honor, something which she had dismissed as impossible had been insinuating itself to her as possible after all, and
she had not known what to do. She was wretchedly aware that
just because her brother wanted to keep Archimedes in Syracuse
did not mean that he wanted to marry his own sister to a middle-
class teacher's son. But a devious, untrustworthy part of her mind

had begun to whisper to her that even though Hieron might not actually *want* her to make such a marriage, he would probably *accept* it if he had to—if, for example, she declared that she loved Archimedes, and Archimedes threatened to go off to Alexandria if Hieron refused his permission for the match.

Like the secret meetings, it was something she should never have contemplated. She owed her brother a political advantage from her wedding. He had given her a great many things, and that was all she had to give in return. And he deserved whatever advantages he could get. Hieron had taken a city shattered by the Pyrrhic Wars, a bankrupt city which had lost its fleet and its treasury, its citizens rebellious and its army mutinous, and he had made it strong and whole and prosperous again. That in itself was extraordinary enough, but to have done it without violence or injustice—that was an achievement unparalleled in the history of Syracuse. She knew what she ought to do; she'd known all along: tell Archimedes that they must not meet again, and resign herself to her fate. But when she thought of him, she had no resignation in her at all.

But the thought of going to Hieron, of admitting what she'd been doing and what she wanted to do, of facing his anger—or, worse, his bewildered pain—appalled her.

She also had no idea whether Archimedes wanted to marry her. She felt sometimes that he loved her, sometimes that he must despise her as shameless—it *was* shameless, the way she'd thrown herself at him! Did he really want to go to Alexandria? Did she want to be the chain that kept him in Syracuse? She was afraid to see him again, afraid that if she suggested this impossible scheme he would turn it down.

In the end she'd decided to talk to his sister, to see if she couldn't discover what he thought about her. That had been a disaster. Philyra didn't appear to have heard *anything* about her, good or bad, and, what was more, had disliked her. She wasn't sure why, though she supposed she'd mishandled the interview; she often did. And Queen Philistis disapproved of the invitation, though she'd had to concede that it was perfectly proper. She had stayed in the room the whole time Philyra was there, frowning whenever Archimedes was mentioned. Philistis disapproved of Archimedes generally—a conceited young man, she thought, who was being treated with altogether more honor than he deserved, and who had had no business disturbing her husband at the end of particularly exhausting day and making accusations of deceit. Hieron thought it important to cultivate the man, so Philistis was cooperating, but she did not like it.

And now here was Archimedes himself, rumpled and tired and staring sadly into the basin of the fountain, while around him the early-morning light cast fresh shadows through the leaves of the garden.

Delia stepped forward, and he looked up. He blinked at her vaguely, without surprise, his mind still fixed on whatever he had been contemplating in the water.

"Good health!" she said, struggling to keep her voice steady. "What brings you here so early?"

At that he grimaced, scrunched up his shoulders, and got to his feet. "Nothing pleasant," he told her unhappily. "My slave Marcus helped two Roman prisoners to escape. One of their guards was killed, a man I knew, a good man."

"Oh, by the gods!" she exclaimed with concern; then added quickly, "I'm sure my brother doesn't blame you for something your slave did."

He shook his head, but remained hunched unhappily. "He's being locked up in the prisoners' place—Marcus, I mean—though Hieron has implied he'll be exchanged or released with the other Romans. I—feel ashamed."

"It's not your fault if a slave does something wicked!"

He shook his head. "Not like that at all! I never really noticed Marcus before. He was always just *there*. But he's really quite an extraordinary man. He's actually a Roman citizen, and the reason he helped those men escape was that one of them is his brother. He could have escaped as well, but he didn't because he didn't want to betray Syracuse. And I realized that that's exactly like him. He had an obligation to his brother and an obligation to Syracuse, so he fulfilled both as well as he could, and then stood there expecting to die for it. He didn't even complain about it. He's always been absolutely honest and scrupulous. I *should* have noticed. But I don't notice people, even when they're under my eyes. All I notice is mathematics." His voice had filled with disgust.

She did not know what answer to make to this. She went over to the fountain and sat down on its rim. "I suppose mathematics is rational, and people aren't," she said.

He gave a rueful snort. "You know the song of the Sirens?

" 'Halt your ship and stay to hear our song.
For sailor none in his black ship has gone
from listening to our honey-voicèd call
but goes his way delighting, knowing more . . .
For we know as many things as come to pass
upon the fertile Earth.' "

His voice lowered, and he continued:

" 'So they cried with lovely voice and clear
and I wished with all my heart to hear
and commanded my friends to set me free . . .
instead they bound me with more chains.'

"Mathematics is a siren. It's probably just as well that most of the world has its ears stuffed with wax and can't hear her. I'm saying this now as though I'm ashamed of it, but I won't change. The moment she sings to me again, I'll ignore everyone and everything else."

She was silent for a long moment, thinking about him, and about herself, and about her brother. Then she repeated slowly, "Chains. Do you know, Hieron talked about chaining you to Syracuse. Do you hate it?"

He did not answer at once. He had thought that morning that Hieron was summoning him as though he were a slave, and he'd been surprised by his own sense of outrage and betrayal. He had not realized how much he had started to believe that he would stay in Syracuse and work with the king. *With* the king; that was the point. Not *for* him. He had been more or less resigned to being under another man's command when he'd thought it unavoidable, but that resignation had been crumbling as he came to appreciate his own power. The way Hieron had tried to manipulate him had impressed him. He hadn't liked it, but it had been interesting, as elegant in its way as a geometrical proof, and it had seemed to him a clear indication that the king genuinely preferred persuasion to decree. And he had begun to like Hieron himself—the subtlety, the quick perception and efficient action, the good humor. And then there was Delia. She was worth staying in Syracuse for, if he could get her, and he had begun to wonder if he might. After all, Hieron had promised him almost anything.

But was that only another trick? The position Hieron had been inventing for him had impressed him as something more than the kind of straightforward contract he could get in Egypt, but what if it was something less? What if it was only a counterfeit meant to cheat him? Would he be a friend of the king, an adviser, on an equal footing—or would he be a hired servant?

"I am deeply in your brother's debt," he said at last, slowly, "and I suspect that's where he wants me. But there's nothing he's given me yet that I can't repay—not even Marcus' life. What I can make is worth a great deal, so I don't mind. Chains. Well." He frowned down at his own flat, big-boned wrists as though contemplating shackles. "Sirens eat people. Odysseus only heard them and lived because of those chains. Maybe I need them. Maybe I ought to be tied to a city, and to people who aren't mathematical. And there'd be chains anywhere. If King Ptolemy does offer me a job, it will be because of water-snails and catapults, not pure mathematics. So really all I can choose is whose chains, and how heavy."

"So you are *still* thinking of going to Alexandria!" she asked.

He looked up at her and groaned. "Oh, don't! *Everyone's* been quarreling with me about that."

"I don't want you to go!" she said unwarily, and then crimsoned.

He caught her hand, and her neat, strong flute player's fingers clenched upon his own. "Delia," he began urgently, then stopped, not knowing what he wanted to say. They gazed at each other for a long moment, not in any rapture of love but simply trying desperately to judge the other's will, the other's mind.

"I want to ask you this, then," he said at last. "Is there any chance you could be responsible for my staying?"

Her blush darkened. "Hieron might . . ." she whispered. "He might . . . no!" She had promised herself that she would *not* try to force Hieron's agreement; that she would *not* return all his kindness with this—this *insult*. She looked away and tried again. "I can't . . ." She became aware that she was still clutching Archimedes' hand, and stopped, tears of shame springing to her eyes. That was how much strength of mind she had: trying to give up the man, she couldn't even let go of his hand. She shook her head and cried despairingly, "I *can't!*"

"It's not up to you," came his voice beside her. "It's up to your brother. I'll talk to him."

She risked looking back at him, and saw that his face was alight with joy. He had understood enough: her mind.

"He *did* promise me anything except the Museum," he told her reasonably. "And I never expected the gods to favor me as far as this. Why not ask for more? The worst that can happen is that he says no. I'll ask him. I'll find a good time and ask him. When the three-talenter is finished. I'll ask him then."

13

Marcus was literally put in his brother's place, in the middle of the three sheds at the quarry, with Fabius' leg irons clamped about his own ankles. The other prisoners were astonished when he arrived, and suspicious of his account of himself. He did not much care, and spent most of his first day in prison asleep. The guards woke him around noon, when they chained each prisoner to the next as part of the newly increased security. The sawn-through planks of the shed wall had been replaced even before he arrived, and another two guards now took their place in each shed, at the far end, where they could keep an eye on everything the two on the door might miss. Marcus did not much care about that, either. He did not much care about anything. He supposed he ought to feel glad and excited—it seemed that he might, after all, be a free man again and still live—but he was too exhausted. The sheer effort it would take to adjust to his own people again, even if they didn't kill him, appalled him. He ate the meal the guards brought him and went back to sleep.

He woke with a sensation of being watched and sat up abruptly. Archimedes was squatting at the end of his mattress, hands hanging over knees and an anxious expression on his face. On all sides the other prisoners were watching the visitor with impassive suspicion, and a guard was hovering nervously a few paces away. In the dimly lit shed it was hard to tell, but Marcus thought that it was evening.

"I'm sorry to wake you," said Archimedes.

"I've been asleep all day," replied Marcus, embarrassed. He did not know what to say; the other seemed almost a stranger to him. Yet he knew Archimedes as intimately as he knew Gaius: he had watched him grow from childhood to manhood, and they had shared lodgings and short money in a foreign land. But though he had only rarely thought of Archimedes as his master, his own slavery had always defined the relationship between them, and now by Hieron's judgment he had never properly been a slave at all. With that tie cut, he could only flounder in a sea of shapeless emotions.

"I, uh, brought you some things," Archimedes said, as embarrassed as Marcus. He set a bundle down on the end of Marcus' mattress.

Marcus saw at once that the bundle's wrapping was his own winter cloak. He drew it over and unknotted the corners. Inside was his other, winter tunic, a terra-cotta statue of Aphrodite he'd bought in Egypt with money from the water-snails, and some other small knickknacks he'd picked up over the years. There was also a small leather bag that chinked and a long oblong case of polished pine. He stared at the case, then picked it up and opened it: it held Archimedes' tenor aulos. The hard sycamore wood was darkened about the stops, polished with use. He looked up in shock.

"I, uh, thought maybe you could teach yourself to play it while you're here," said Archimedes. "It would be something to do while you're waiting to be exchanged."

Marcus picked up the flute; the wood was water-smooth in his hands, and warm. "I couldn't, sir," he said. "It's yours."

"I can buy another. I can afford one, after all. And you have a good sense of pitch; it's a shame to waste it. I don't know why you never learned an instrument before."

"It's not a Roman thing to do," Marcus told him helplessly. "My father would have beaten me if I'd asked it."

Archimedes blinked. "Because of all the jokes about flute boys?"

"No," said Marcus, in a low voice. "No—he'd say it was unmanly to waste time studying music. He'd say that music is a luxury, and luxury corrupts the soul. He tolerated it at work, or as an amusement, but he always said that the only studies worthy of a man are farming and war."

Archimedes blinked again, trying to accommodate his mind to this bizarre idea. Greeks too believed that luxury corrupted, but Greeks didn't consider music a luxury. It was an essential: without it men were not fully human. "Do you not want it, then?" he asked, giving up.

Marcus ran one calloused thumb along the flute, then whispered, "I do want it, sir"—and his heart suddenly rose. Going back to his own people need not mean giving up everything he'd learned. Why shouldn't he play the flute? He had never agreed with his father anyway! "Thank you."

Archimedes smiled. "Good. I've put three reeds in the case. They should last you a little while. If you're here for a long time, I'll bring more—or you can get your guards to buy some. And when you're able to manage this one, you'll want a second flute. You can decide for yourself what voice it should be. There's some money." He gestured vaguely at the leather bag.

"Thank you," said Marcus again. "Sir, I'm sorry."

Archimedes shook his head quickly. "You couldn't abandon your own brother."

Marcus met his eyes. "Perhaps not. But I did abuse your trust and put you in danger. I think Fabius would have killed you if he'd realized who you were when you came in. I should never have brought him to the house, and never have given him the knife. So—I'm sorry."

Archimedes looked down, his face going red. "Marcus, my trust deserved to be abused. Do you remember when we came back to Alexandria after making the water-snails? How I told you to take all the money back to our lodgings? My friends said later that I was an idiot to trust you with so much, but it had never even occurred to me that you might steal it."

Marcus snorted. "It occurred to me!"

"Did it? Well, why not? After all, it would have been freedom and independence. But you didn't. You took it home, and then nagged me for days to make me put it in a bank. And what I meant to say was, I had no right to trust you that far. It was arrogant. I had never done anything to earn that sort of loyalty. As a master I was negligent and careless. Yet I relied on you absolutely, and never considered that you deserved any credit for not failing me. So—I'm sorry, too."

Marcus felt his own face go hot. "Sir . . ." he began.

"You don't need to call me that."

"I was in your debt for a great many things even before this morning. Music is one of them; mechanics is another. Yes, that is a debt. I don't think I've ever enjoyed any work as much as I enjoyed making the water-snails. Since this morning I owe you even more. If I'd been anybody else's slave, I would have been flogged and sent to the quarries. The king treated me leniently because you pleaded for me—you know that as well as I do. I have no way to repay what I owe. So don't burden me with your apologies as well."

Archimedes shook his head, but did not respond. After a moment he changed the subject and asked, "Do you want me to show you how to play that flute?"

There followed a short lesson on how to play the aulos: fingering, breathing, the positions of the slide. Marcus played a few wobbly scales, then sat stroking the silken wood. Its touch was a promise for the future, and gave him unexpected hope.

Archimedes cleared his throat uncomfortably. "Well," he said. "They're expecting me at home. If you need anything, send me word." Marcus opened his mouth, and Archimedes said urgently, "Don't! You've been a member of my household ever since I was a child. Of course I want to help you if I can."

Marcus realized suddenly why he had felt so numb. He was losing home and family for the second time in his life.

"Please tell them at the house," he whispered, "that I'm sorry. And tell Philyra I hope she will be very happy, with Dionysios or whoever she marries. I wish you all much joy."

Archimedes nodded and got to his feet. "I wish you joy, Marcus." He turned to go.

The sight of him turning away suddenly filled Marcus with an almost panic-stricken urgency. Something between them was unresolved, and the thought of being left with that undigested lump of emotions terrified him. He jumped to his feet with a clank of irons, and called "Medion!"—then bit his tongue, realizing that he had used the family nickname for the first time.

Archimedes didn't appear to notice the slip. He looked back at Marcus inquiringly, his expression just visible in the growing dark.

For a moment Marcus did not know what to say. Then he held out the flute. "Could you play me that tune you played last night?" he asked.

Slowly, Archimedes reached out and took the instrument. He adjusted the slide. "I really need the soprano as well," he said apologetically. "It won't be the same without it." But he set the flute to his lips and at once began the same sweet dancing tune which had filled the courtyard the night before.

Everything in the shed seemed to hold its breath. One of the guards, who had gone to fetch a lamp, came back with it and stood silent in the aisle listening. All around the eyes of prisoners gleamed in its light, drawn into the dance, and then bewildered by the inexplicable grief that crept into the tune. The melody was clearer on a single aulos, the shifts of tempo and mode more precise. There was the same sense of disintegration, and the same almost miraculous resolution. At last the same sad march faded softly into silence. Archimedes stood for a moment with his head bowed, looking at his fingers on the stops.

"And now I wish you joy," said Marcus, quietly into the quiet.

Archimedes looked up, and their eyes met. The unresolved thing between them solved itself, and the ties severed. Archimedes smiled sadly and handed the flute back to Marcus. "May you indeed find joy, Marcus Valerius," he said, stumbling a little on the alien family name.

"And you, Archimedes son of Phidias," said Marcus. "May the gods favor you."

~ ARCHIMEDES WALKED HOME FROM THE QUARRY THROUGH the dark streets slowly. He did not want to think about Marcus, so he thought about the tune he had played. A farewell to Alexandria, he'd called it. He did not like the way his mind seemed to be making up itself about Alexandria, without consulting him. Even before Delia. If Delia . . .

He lost himself for a moment in the memory of kissing Delia, then went on, more grimly. What he needed to know was whether Hieron saw him as an ally or as a valuable slave.

The test was Delia. Hieron might refuse his permission for the match for many good reasons, but if the request was viewed as an affront, he'd do better going to Egypt if he had to slip out of Syracuse in disguise.

In the house there were lamps burning in the courtyard, and the family was waiting: Arata and Sosibia spinning, little Agatha winding wool, Philyra playing the lute, Chrestos sitting in the doorway doing nothing in particular. Archimedes had not been home all day, though he had sent one of Hieron's slaves to the house to tell the family what had happened, and to tell Chrestos to pack up all of Marcus' things and bring them to him at the catapult workshop. He had not wanted to talk to his family: not about Marcus, and not about Delia—yet. Now they were all waiting to talk to him.

Arata, with her usual patience and clear sense of priorities, first asked him if he'd eaten, and when he admitted that he had not, took him into the dining room and sat him down with a plate of fish stew. But Philyra, red-eyed and sniffing, sat with her elbows on the table as she watched him eat, the slaves hovered anxiously, and even his mother was frowning with anxiety. He gave up and started telling them about Marcus after the first few mouthfuls.

"Will he be all right?" asked Philyra, biting at her fingernails—

a habit which her mother had striven to break, and which only reemerged when she was deeply unhappy.

"I hope so," was all Archimedes could say. "Hieron said he's welcome to answer anything the Roman general asks him. And his brother is there to speak up for him. I would think he'd be all right." But he was not altogether certain of it. Marcus *ought* to be all right—but he was so uncompromisingly honest. He had not prayed for the destruction of Rome for a Tarentine mercenary; he would not pray for the sacking of Syracuse for a Roman consul.

But perhaps the Roman consul would not ask it. Marcus would be returned in company with eighty other prisoners, and his brother would, presumably, be in the army to welcome and protect him. He *ought* to be all right.

"They're barbarians," said Philyra, blinking at new tears. "They might do *anything* to him! Can't he just come back to us? It wasn't his fault—you did *tell* the king that, didn't you, Medion? I mean, it was his own brother, or he wouldn't have . . ."

"The king has already been very lenient," said Arata quietly. "For your brother's sake, Philyrion. We can't ask more. After all, a man was killed because of what Marcus did."

Archimedes cleared his throat unhappily, then said, "When I saw Marcus just now he, uh, said to tell everyone that he was sorry and that he wished us all much joy. And he said he hoped you would be very happy, Philyrion, with Dionysios or whoever you marry."

Philyra pulled her torn nails out of her mouth and stared, and he realized that he hadn't told her about Dionysios.

"Dionysios only offered last night," he said defensively. "I was going to tell you this morning."

He told her about Dionysios then. There was considerable discussion of the man and his offer, and eventually it was agreed that Archimedes would invite the captain to dinner so that the rest of the family could have a look at him. But when the others went to bed, Philyra sat for a while alone in the courtyard under

the stars, playing upon the lute, and it was not Dionysios who
filled her thoughts.

"I don't want you to think ill of me," Marcus had told her,
only the night before. "Whatever happens, please believe that
I've never wanted any harm to this house."

She did believe it; she did not think ill of him. That morning
his quiet admission had redefined courage for her. She realized
that she no longer thought of him as a slave, and that when she
thought of him as a free man, it was as a man she loved. A brave
man, honorable and proud, who had—she could see it now—
loved her.

"Remember once," she sang, carefully picking the strings of
the lute,

> "Remember when,
> I told you this holy word?
> 'The hour is fair, but fleet is the hour,
> The hour outraces the swiftest bird.'
> Look! It's scattered to earth, your flower."

She suspected that for the rest of her life, when she remembered him it would be as something that went tragically wrong—
an appointment missed, a letter mislaid, a person misunderstood
with devastating and irremediable consequences. Already it was
too late to retrieve what had gone by; the flower's spent petals
were scattered to earth. She played on for a while, then put the
lute away and went to bed.

~ THAT NIGHT A ROMAN FORCE ATTACKED THE SYRACUSAN
seawall under cover of darkness. The extra guards Hieron had
posted saw the stealthy movements against the gleam of the sea,
however, and sounded the alarm. The Romans were inside catapult arc of fire when they were discovered, but so close to the
cliff that it was easy to drop catapult shot directly onto them
from the walls. A few hundredweight of stones were followed by

some catapult fire canisters, which exploded and splattered the attackers with burning pitch and oil, so that the scene was lit by the burning clothes and bodies of the men who occupied it. Many of the Romans jumped into the sea to escape the fire, and were swept off their feet by the strong currents and drowned. The remainder fled. In the morning it could be seen that they had brought ropes and ladders, which had been woefully short for the height of the cliffs, and which now littered the rubble at the cliff foot, together with the bodies of the dead—and a few more wounded prisoners for the quarry.

The following night, the Romans left. The Syracusans keeping watch from the north wall saw the camp settling itself for the night in the evening, and the campfires glowed throughout the hours of darkness, but in the morning the army was gone, and only the fires remained, with the neat rows of flattened grass where the tents had been pitched.

Hieron sent out scouts to track them. He sent out a letter to the Carthaginian commander as well, writing it in his own hand, because it was still too early in the day for his secretary to have arrived at the house. He warned General Hanno that the Romans might now be heading in his direction, and offered to attack them in the rear if the Carthaginians could engage them. He had sent a similar message when the Romans first appeared outside Syracuse, inviting the Carthaginians to a similar feat, but there had been no response.

As he sealed the letter he wondered how long it would take for the Carthaginians to realize that, faced with an enemy like Rome, they needed Syracuse whole and strong and on their side. Stupidity, he thought, pressing his favorite signet into the wax that fixed the red cord binding of the letter. The Roman campaign, too, was one of blatant stupidity—if the Carthaginians *had* appeared in their rear, they would have been in a very sorry state. And they had left Messana only lightly guarded, with most of their supplies and all the ships that had carried them from Italy: if the Carthaginians stormed *that* in their absence, the whole army would be forced to surrender. It was a stroke Hieron was much tempted to himself: load his army onto his own ships, take them up the coast, sail into the Messanan harbor with some big catapults mounted on naval vessels and some incendiaries, fire the Roman ships, and storm the city!

Yes, but to do it would weaken Syracuse while the Romans were too close to her for comfort, and who knew how the Carthaginians would react? They still wanted Messana themselves. The last thing Hieron could afford to do was drive them into open alliance with Rome.

They might well have some kind of understanding with Rome already. Perhaps the reason they were doing nothing at present was that they'd promised not to interfere in any Roman campaign against Syracuse. Still, even if such a promise had been made, Appius Claudius was an awful fool if he trusted it. Just as Hanno was a fool to let what might be his only opportunity for victory slip by. Hieron's envoy had returned from Carthage with the news that the Carthaginian senate was growing impatient with their general. It was very stupid of Hanno to think that he had time to do nothing. Stupidity; it was altogether a stupid, blind, and pointless war, and Hieron felt a sick certainty that it was far from over. He tossed the sealed letter onto his desk and clapped his hands to summon a messenger.

When the messenger came in, Agathon was with him, holding a bundle of the day's other letters. The messenger took the king's letter, vowed to deliver it to General Hanno within three days, saluted, and marched out. Agathon watched him go, then set the other letters down on Hieron's desk. Hieron picked them up and glanced through them; the doorkeeper busied himself in trimming and lighting one of the lamps on the stand beside the desk, even though it was morning. Hieron paused and looked up at his slave inquiringly.

Agathon gave his sour smile. "You said you wanted to see any letters to Archimedes that came from Alexandria," he remarked. "One came yesterday. I had the customs official divert it." He pulled a small, thin-bladed knife out of his belt and began warming the end in the lamp flame.

Hieron looked down to the bottom of the sheaf, found the relevant letter, and handed it to him. He and Agathon had been in the habit of intercepting other people's letters long before he became king, and if he'd ever had any tremors of conscience over it, they had long since faded.

Agathon carefully slid the hot knife between the parchment and the wax of the seal, then handed the letter to the king with a bow. Hieron sat back and read it. Reading aloud was the usual custom of the age, but Hieron, to his slave's disappointment, read almost silently, barely moving his lips.

> Conon son of Nikias of Samos to Archimedes son of Phidias of Syracuse sends greetings.
>
> Dearest α . . .

Hieron frowned slightly: "Dearest *Alpha*." Had the writer chosen that form of address because it was the first letter of Archimedes' name—or because it was the number one?

> Dearest Alpha, you've been gone less than a month, and I swear by Delian Apollo it seems years, and empty years, too, with nothing but wet afternoons in them. I never hear a flute but I think of you, and there's not one person who's had anything remotely intelligent to say about tangents of conic sections ever since you went away. Diodotos was blathering on about hyperbolae the other day, and I told him what you'd said about the ratio, and he swelled up like a frog and asked me to prove it. And of course, I couldn't, though I gave him a list of propositions instead. He came back later saying *he'd* proved one, but he hadn't. I'll tell you more about that later.
>
> The main thing I want to say is, I have a job at the Museum, and you can have one too! In fact, it's thanks to you that I now have my perch in the Muses' bird cage.

The king has been investing in the most enormous engineering works at Arsinoitis, and when he went up to
have a look at them, apparently the first thing he saw
was a water-snail. "What is it?" asked the king. "By Zeus,
I never saw anything like it in my life!" And shortly afterward, Kallimachos . . .

The poet? wondered Hieron. *The head of the Library of Alexandria?*

. . . Kallimachos himself came knocking at my door in a
great sweat and said, "You're a friend of Archimedes of
Syracuse—where is he? The king wants to meet him."
So I told him you'd gone back to Syracuse, and he swore
by Hades and the Lady of the Crossroads (and several
other divinities I wasn't sure about; poets can't even
swear like other people these days) and took me to meet
the king instead. Ptolemy was amazingly civil to me, and
gave me dinner, and we talked. Kallimachos was there,
too, but he just sat and picked his fingernails and made
eyes at the slave boys. The man's incapable of talking
about anything but literature and boys. The king, though,
knows quite a lot of mathematics—you know Euclid was
his tutor. He said it was quite true about Euclid saying
there was no royal road to geometry, he was there at the
time. And he was very interested when I told him about
eclipses, and asked me when the next one would be.
That's nothing to do with what I'm writing you about,
though. After we'd talked for a bit, and I'd told him some
more about you (you can believe I sang your praises,
Alpha!), he said he wished he'd known it sooner, and he
asked me to write to you and invite you to come back
and take a job at the Museum, with a big salary and
everything. Then he offered me a job too (Diodotos is
perfectly green about that) but it's you he really wants.
I think it's really engineering he's after—he kept telling

me how wonderful the water-snail is, and when I showed him my dioptra he wanted to buy it, and laughed and said he didn't blame me when I said I'd sooner sell my house and the cloak off my back. I warned him, though, that you weren't interested in doing any more water-snails, and he said that was fine. I know you like making machines if it isn't the same thing all the time and it doesn't interfere with geometry. Write to him, or to me if you prefer, and he'll send you the letters of authorization at once. Please, Alpha, come back quick! Why be poor in Syracuse when you can be rich in Alexandria? You could bring your family here if you're worried about them. It's much safer, anyway, with none of your garlic-eating barbarian armies about. As for me, I am pining away in your absence, or I would be if I didn't keep eating Dora's cakes to console myself. The Museum banquets are on a Homeric scale, too.

The proposition Diodotos says he proved is this . . .

There followed several pages of abstruse geometrical reasoning, which Hieron skipped. He read the warm farewell at the close, and the still warmer hope that the writer would see the recipient "soon, by Hera and all the immortals!" Then he refolded the letter and set it down with a sigh.

"Well?" asked Agathon.

"King Ptolemy is offering him the Museum," said the king resignedly.

Agathon picked the letter up and squinted at it. "It's not the royal seal," he observed.

"No," agreed Hieron. "The offer comes through a friend—a close friend, from the sound of it. But I don't think there's any doubt that it's genuine. Ptolemy was evidently much impressed by an irrigation device. I'll have to ask Archimedes how it works." He waved a hand at the letter. "You'd better seal that up again and return it."

"You don't want it to go missing?"

Hieron shook his head glumly. "He'd realize. I just want to see the reply." He turned back to his other letters. They were mostly business notes from within the city, but one caught his eye. He held up a hand to check Agathon just before the door-keeper left. "Note from Archimedes himself," he said; then, glancing through it, "He says the three-talenter will be ready in another three days, and he invites me to stop at his house on my way back to the city after the test-firing, either for dinner or simply for wine and cakes."

"He wants something," said Agathon flatly.

"Good!" replied Hieron. "He can have it." He tapped the invitation against his desk. "That other letter—*delay* it, until I've seen what he wants. Tell whoever was taking it to say it was mislaid or forgotten about until he came to clear the ship."

Agathon looked at his master dubiously. "Don't you think you're spending more on this man than he deserves?"

Hieron gave him an exasperated look. "Aristion," he said, "think a minute. I was toying earlier with the idea of a naval assault on Messana. If I wanted to do that, I would need to lash ships together and build artillery platforms—each stable for the weight of catapult or they'd come to bits when the shooting started. And I would need counters to the Messanan harbor defenses, which means I'd need somebody to reckon their distance and strength before we reached them. Then I'd need siege ladders—and they'd have to be the right height or we'd have a lot of men dead for nothing. I'd need battering rams that were strong enough to do the job and light enough to move in quickly. In other words, the whole success or failure of such a raid would depend upon my engineer. Now, Kallippos is good, but I wouldn't gamble my whole fleet on his getting it right. With Archimedes, it would be no gamble. Top-quality engineering can make the difference between victory and defeat. No, I do not think I am spending too much on it."

"Oh," said Agathon, abashed.

"You and Philistis," Hieron went on, smiling, "don't like Archimedes because you think he's been disrespectful to me."

"And he has been!" said Agathon warmly. "The other morning—"

"Aristion! If somebody came and arrested *you, I'd* be disrespectful!"

Agathon, who had not thought of it this way, grunted sourly.

"He has, in fact, treated me exactly as I would wish. And he
told me I was a parabola. I think that's the most unusual compliment I've ever been given. I might have it engraved upon my
tomb."

"If you say so," replied Agathon, who had no idea what a
parabola was and remained unconvinced. After a moment he
asked, in a low voice, "And the naval assault?"

Hieron shook his head, turning back to his letters. "Can't do
it without knowing where the Romans are and what the Carthaginians would do if it worked. But it's still true about top-
quality engineering. If it hadn't been for our catapults, the
Romans would still be camped by the north wall and living off
our farmers' lands."

THE THREE-TALENTER WISH YOU JOY WAS INSTALLED IN
the Hexapylon precisely on time. Archimedes was not pleased
with it. It was heavy to pivot, the loading mechanism was finicky,
and the range was, he felt, short of what it could have been.
Everyone else was delighted with the machine, however—the
biggest catapult in the world!—and at the test-firing that afternoon a great cheer arose when the first massive stone crashed
into the field where Romans had died only the week before. The
king's son, Gelon, had asked to go with his father to see the
spectacle, and his shrill cheer rose above all the others.

All the way back to the city the little boy talked excitedly to
Archimedes, leaning down from the saddle of his father's horse
to offer his own ideas for improving the defenses of Syracuse.
Archimedes, who was sidling toward the moment when he must
ask the king for his sister's hand in marriage like a dog toward a
scorpion, found the child's chatter both an irritation and a relief.
At least it was easier than talking to Hieron. Even if he hadn't

been oppressed by the awful imminence of his outrageous request, Archimedes would have found Hieron's company wearing, for the king kept trying to persuade him to borrow a horse. Archimedes regarded horses as large, dangerous, bad-tempered animals that were very likely to throw you off and trample you, and he stayed on his own feet.

The house near the Lion Fountain had been prepared for the royal visit almost out of recognition. Arata and Philyra had been horrified to learn that Archimedes had invited the king to have cakes and wine—it had been shocking enough to have such an eminent person turn up at the wake, but at least then there'd been no necessity of providing entertainment proper to the guest's station. Since Hieron could not be uninvited, however, they had set to work to uphold the family honor. The house had been swept, freshly daubed, and garlanded, and all the laundry boards and buckets removed from the courtyard, which looked quite empty and rather desolate. Sesame cakes purchased from the finest confectioner in Syracuse were oozing honey onto the best Tarentine pottery plates in the dining room, and wine from the best vintner trembled darkly in the antique red-figure mixing bowl. The slaves had been provided with new clothes, and when Hieron arrived, they stood scrubbed and uncomfortable by the door to meet him. The king, looking at them, saw that he was going to have to work at it if the visit was to be a success.

He detailed one of his attendants to take his horse down to the nearest public square and look after it, sent the rest back to the Ortygia, and came into the house accompanied merely by his son and by Dionysios, who had been invited to the afternoon gathering in lieu of a dinner party. Arata and Philyra, who were permitted to show their faces at an informal daytime occasion such as this, exchanged stilted greetings with the guests and offered them cakes and wine. There was a move to the dining room, and the slaves hurried anxiously about offering food and drink. Then Hieron said casually to Archimedes, "I've been hearing more from Alexandria about this water-snail of yours. Could you tell me how it works?"

"I have the prototype," Archimedes replied, delighted to escape the formalities. "Marcus put it somewhere. Mar—" He stopped in the middle of the summons and went crimson.

"I think it's in the storeroom," Philyra said quickly, though she too reddened.

The water-snail was fetched, and the laundry boards and buckets emerged with it to reclaim their rightful domain. Gelon, who'd been silently stuffing himself with sesame cakes, abandoned all thought of sweets and descended upon this new toy as soon as it was set up. He was invited to turn it, and after being corrected and advised to turn it *slowly*, he watched the water run out of the machine's head with unalloyed delight.

"By Apollo!" said Hieron softly. He crouched down beside his son and gazed at the machine. He had asked about the device to set Archimedes at ease, but now, at the sight of it, forgot that he'd ever needed any reason but his own delight in ingenious contrivances. "I think that's the cleverest thing I have ever seen in my life," he said, and looked up at the maker of it with his son's beaming childish pleasure.

Within minutes, all the remaining stiffness was gone. The king of Syracuse, his son, and soon the captain of the Ortygia garrison as well crouched in the courtyard and played with the water-snail. Gelon got wet—something he greatly enjoyed on a hot summer day. Dionysios also got wet, and had to be fetched rags to dry his armor quickly before it tarnished. Philyra giggled at the sight of the scarlet-cloaked captain polishing himself, and he looked up at her in embarrassment—then grinned at the look in her eyes. A plate of cakes was put down on the ground so that the guests could help themselves, and then, inevitably, stepped upon: Sosibia could be heard shortly afterward in the back of the house, scolding Chrestos, who was the culprit. "Oh, don't be hard on the boy!" Hieron called to her. "It's our own fault for sitting on the ground."

When the fascination of the water-snail began to thin, Philyra brought some of her brother's other machines out from the jumble in the storeroom: an astronomical instrument, a hoist, a set of gears that did nothing except turn each other. "That was supposed to be part of a lifting machine," Archimedes admitted shamefacedly, "but when you attach the weight to them, they jam."

"You built a machine that didn't work?" asked Dionysios, much amused. "I am shocked."

"He was only about fourteen!" protested Philyra. "I always loved them anyway." Fondly she rotated the top wheel. "See? They all turn at different speeds."

"Gelon loves them too," said Gelon's father dryly, observing the boy's expression of open-mouthed greed.

Archimedes cleared his throat. "Well," he said. "Umm—Gelon son of Hieron, would you like them?"

Gelon looked up at him with shining eyes, nodded, and grabbed the gears.

"Gelonion," said Hieron sharply. "What do you say?"

"Thank you!" said the boy, with all the requisite warmth.

Hieron smiled for a moment at his son's delight, then looked at Archimedes inquiringly. It was time, he felt, to hear Archimedes' own request.

Archimedes too felt that the ideal occasion had now presented itself. "Umm," he said, trying to quell the quaver in his gut. "Lord, may I speak with you a moment in private?"

They went back into the dining room. Through the window came the sound of Arata talking to little Gelon, and Dionysios asking Philyra about music. Hieron sat down comfortably on the couch; Archimedes perched on the edge of one of the chairs. Now that it had come to the point, all his new confidence was ebbing away. It had seemed better to ask his question in his own house, where he was master. But the house, even garlanded and at its best, remained the residence of a middle-class teacher, with walls of plaster and a floor of packed clay. When he compared it to the marble-floored mansion on the Ortygia, he was ashamed. He was not of a rank to ask for the sister of a king. But he cleared his throat and said, in a low voice so that the others in the courtyard would not overhear, "Lord, if my request is too bold, forgive me. You yourself encouraged me to ask above my expectation."

"I promised you anything you might get in Egypt, except the Museum," replied Hieron seriously. "If you have something to ask of me, I am delighted."

"What I want I could not get in Egypt," said Archimedes. He curled his big bony hands together and took a deep breath. "Lord King, you have a sister, who . . ."

Hieron looked at him in utter amazement, and all his prepared speeches went out of his head. "That is," he stumbled on, "she . . . I . . ." He again remembered kissing her, and felt his face heat. "I know I have neither wealth nor noble birth nor any other quality that makes me worthy of her. I have nothing to offer, apart from what my mind can conceive and my hands can shape. If that is enough, good. If it is not, well, I have asked you for what I wanted, and you have said no."

Hieron said nothing for a long time; he was stunned. He realized immediately that this request was something he should have foreseen, and he was shocked because he had not foreseen it. He was accustomed to thinking of Delia as a bright, adventurous child he had rescued from her grim uncle, a girl whose sharp observant mind he had delighted in for the kinship it showed with his own. He had been aware that she had reached marriageable age, but that knowledge had seemed a thing apart from Delia herself—something for the future, something beyond the war. He had been aware, too, that she was interested in Archimedes, but he had considered it a shallow interest, casual and soon forgotten. He contemplated his own failure to understand her, saddened and ashamed.

"You know," said the king at last, "that Delia is the heiress to all our father's estate."

Archimedes' face turned a deeper shade of red. "No," he croaked. "I didn't."

"In law, I am not her brother at all," said Hieron flatly. "In law, she is our father's child, and I am not. Our father was a rich man, and I have looked after his estate carefully on her behalf.

The total income from it last year was forty-four thousand drach-mae."

"It's not the estate that I want," said Archimedes, turning from red to white. "You can keep the estate."

"I could, if I broke the law and stole it from her," said Hieron coldly. "I have always assumed that I held it in trust for her future husband. I've never used the money from it, I've always rein-vested it, to build it up for her." He paused. "You've already spoken to Delia about this, haven't you?"

"I . . ." whispered Archimedes. "That is—she would never go against your wishes."

"In other words, she's been lying awake at night wondering how I would reply. I thought she looked tired and miserable. Zeus!" He found himself a wine cup, ladled in a drink from the mixing bowl, and gulped down half of it. "And if I say no, I suppose you'll take yourself off to Alexandria?"

"I haven't made up my mind about that," Archimedes said slowly. "I will do all I can for the defense of the city in any case. But. Well." He paused, then said, with quiet fervor, "I am not a hired worker."

"Well, I'm not going to say yes if you plan to take her to Egypt!" said Hieron. "If you marry my sister, you're going to stay right here and make certain that you do provide me with what your mind can conceive and your hands can shape."

"You mean . . . you might say yes?" asked Archimedes breath-lessly. Then, appalled, "You don't mean give up mathematics? I told you . . ."

"Yes, yes, you swore to your father on his deathbed and so forth! No, I didn't mean give up divine mathematics." He looked at the anxious young man opposite him, then set down his cup of wine. "Look," he said, "I'll tell you what sort of considerations are in my mind when I think about a husband for my sister. First, money *doesn't* come into it. I don't need her money. I've got plenty of my own, from various sources. And she has plenty of her own, and doesn't need to marry it. Second, politics." He flipped one hand dismissively. "It's true that there are situations where it's useful to cement some alliance with a marriage. If I hadn't married Philistis, I would probably have died in the year I became tyrant: it was Leptines who secured me the city. But on the whole, if an alliance won't hold without a wedding, it's unlikely to hold with one. And, to be honest, promising someone a half sister who isn't even related to me in law is never going to be the same as marrying somebody's daughter myself. So, politics matters, but it isn't of the first importance. What is of the first importance . . ." He stopped. Outside in the courtyard, Philyra was tuning her lute. "Dionysios has asked you for your own sister," said Hieron more quietly. "When you make up your mind about that, what will matter most to you?"

"I don't think I'm a very good judge," replied Archimedes, blinking. "I'm leaving that to Philyra and my mother. All I want is that Philyra should be happy—and that her husband should be a man I don't mind having as a kinsman."

Hieron smiled. "Precisely," he said softly. He picked up the cup again and rolled it between his palms. "You know that I am a bastard," he went on, looking down intently into the shallow bowl—the arch-manipulator fearfully exposing a fragment of his own heart. "I think that because of that I probably prize my kin more than those who can take them for granted. I like having a sister. I was always perfectly clear in my own mind that I wouldn't marry her to any foreigner, however important he was. I want to gain family by her, not lose it. And I want to *see* her happy." He took another sip of the wine, then looked back at Archimedes. "Now, it's perfectly true that you're not at all the sort of man I thought I would get as a brother-in-law. But—by all the gods!—do you really think I can raise objections about wealth and birth? You know I owe nothing to either! You would certainly be a more natural kinsman to me than someone who was merely *born* important. And on top of that, I like you. I want to go back and talk to Delia, and be sure that she knows her mind about this, but if she's happy about it, and if you promise to stay in Syracuse with her, then the answer is yes."

Archimedes looked at him for a long moment, disbelief slowly cracking into amazed delight, and then into an immense grin of pure joy.

Hieron grinned back. "You don't seem to have any doubt what she'll say," he observed, and was amused to see his prospective kinsman blush. "Humility is generally reckoned a becoming quality in a young man," he added teasingly.

Archimedes laughed. "And were you a very humble young man, O King of Syracuse?"

Hieron's grin became wicked. "When I was a young man, I was arrogant. I was quite certain that I knew how to run the city far, far better than the people who actually were running it." He paused, contemplating that time with satisfaction, then added softly, "And I was right, too."

14

Delia was waiting for her brother when he came home.

All afternoon she sat in the first courtyard, where she could hear it when people entered the house. She tried to read, and then tried to play the flute, but she could not concentrate, and in the end she simply sat, watching the movement of the leaves in the garden and listening to the small sounds of the house. A kind of despairing rage built in her as the slow hours wore away. Two men she cared for were elsewhere, deciding her fate and perhaps quarreling about it, and she merely sat helpless, a dead weight upon the earth.

At last, toward evening, the door opened on the sound of Gelon's shrill and excited voice. Delia jumped to her feet and ran across the garden—then forced herself to walk into the entrance hall.

Gelon was showing Agathon his new toy; when his aunt appeared, he at once called her to look at it as well. "Look what Archimedes gave me!" he crowed. "See, you turn this wheel and all the wheels in the box go around, only some of them go *that* way and some of them go *that* way, and look, this little one goes faster! Look!"

Delia glanced at it, then looked at her brother. She could tell from Hieron's face that Archimedes had indeed asked his question, but whatever answer Hieron might have given was masked under the usual bright pleasantness. Hieron smiled at her, as impenetrably as ever, then said to his son, "Why don't you go show that to your mother, Gelonion? I need to speak to Aunt Delia a moment."

Gelon ran off to show the gears to his mother, and Hieron gestured toward his library.

In the small quiet room, the king lit the lamps, then sat down on the couch and asked Delia to do the same. She obeyed stiffly, still rigid with angry despair at her own impotence. "Archimedes asked you if he could marry me?" she demanded, before Hieron had a chance to speak.

He nodded, taken aback by her urgency.

"He said he would," said Delia. She glanced down at her hands, which were pressed against one another tightly, and then looked up and met her brother's eyes. "I didn't ask him to," she declared proudly. "I'll marry whoever you want me to, Hieron. I'll be glad if it's useful to you. I swear it by Hera and all the immortal gods, I'd rather stay a virgin all my life than marry against your will."

His expression suddenly softened into one of profound affection. "Oh, Delion!" he exclaimed, and caught both those angry hands in his own. "Sweetest life, you've always wanted to make yourself precious to me, and never believed that you already are."

The tenderness when she had been braced for anger completely overthrew her. She began to cry, and drew her hands away to use in a vain attempt to press back the tears.

He made no attempt to retrieve them: he knew her, and knew that she was furious with herself for crying, and didn't want more sympathy. Instead he went on quietly, "What I told Archimedes was that I would talk to you and make certain that you knew your own mind on this. He seemed to think it was something you wanted too."

The tears came faster. "Not if you don't want it."

"Sister," he said with a touch of impatience, "*I* don't want to marry the man. What I am trying to find out is whether *you* want to marry him."

She gulped several times, then got out, "Yes, but not against your wishes!"

"Leave my wishes out of it for the moment! I want to be sure you understand what it is you could expect from such a husband. You like his flute-playing, but there's more to marriage than music. You know that the man's whole soul is devoted to pure mathematics, don't you? If you marry him, he will regularly get drunk on inspiration and forget everything else, including you. He will never be home on time, or remember to buy you a gift on a feast day, or pick up whatever it may be in the market that you particularly asked him to collect. He will take no interest in your everyday life at all. Asking him to manage your estate would be like expecting a dolphin to pull a cart: you would have to take charge of everything yourself. He will also never notice when you're upset about something, unless you tell him so, and then he'll be baffled by it. He will disappoint and infuriate you, many, many times, in many, many things."

She stared at him, shocked out of her tears. She could see at once that it was all quite true—indeed, Archimedes had warned her about it himself. And yet, she had seen and heard enough of him to know that it was not the whole truth—that for all his love for the honey-voiced siren, he had a warm nature and an uncomplicated devotion to his family. And the prospect of a thousand petty frustrations in no way clouded that great prospect of living in continual dance upon infinity's edge. She lifted her head and said determinedly, "He might disappoint me in small things, but never in great ones. As for the Muses, they are great and wonderful divinities, and I worship them myself. And"—her voice rose—"and I don't need him to manage my estate. I'd *like* to learn how to do that; I'd like to take charge of things myself. I'd like"—she grasped helplessly at the air—"not to have to sit and wait all the time!"

"Ah," said Hieron. "So you know what he's like and you *still* want to marry him? Listen, then. Say I was looking to buy Philistis a present. I could buy her an olive press for one of her farms, or a vat for making fish sauce, or perhaps a new vineyard—all useful, desirable things, and no doubt she'd thank me for them. But you know as well as I that if I gave her a silk cloak with tapestry borders, her eyes would light up and she'd kiss me. Now, you could have brought me a kinsman with influence, or one with connections or money, and I would have thanked you. But when Archimedes asked for you, he offered me what his mind could conceive and his hands could shape—and Philistis was never as pleased with a silk cloak as I am with that. Sister, you could not have chosen a man who would please me better."

She looked at him as Archimedes had, with disbelief that gave way to amazement, and then to joy. Then she flung her arms about him and kissed him.

THE ANNOUNCEMENT OF THE BETROTHAL, WHICH WAS made the following day, for a time eclipsed even the Romans as a topic of conversation in the city. It was generally agreed that the king had exchanged his sister for the world's biggest catapults, which the citizens of Syracuse considered very public-spirited of him—though some of the women felt that it was a bit hard on the sister. Queen Philistis was shocked, but rallied quickly, and at once set to work trying to cast a gloss of respectability over the match, and managed to win over the wives of the aristocracy and even her horrified father. Little Gelon was entirely delighted. Agathon disapproved strongly.

In the house in the Achradina, the reaction was one of stupefaction verging on panic. "But Medion!" wailed Philyra. "What are we going to do about the house? You can't bring the king's sister to live *here!*"

Archimedes glanced about the house where he had been born, then said reluctantly, "We'll move. There's a house on the Ortygia that's part of Delia's inheritance."

"I don't want to live on the Ortygia!" protested Philyra angrily.

"Dionysios has to." Archimedes said in surprise, "and I thought . . ." He stopped, puzzled, at his sister's glare. Philyra and Arata had both liked Dionysios, and had told Archimedes that he could give his consent to the match at an appropriate time.

He did not know what was inappropriate about the present, but both his mother and his sister frowned at unseemly haste.

"Now it's the house itself!" exclaimed Philyra miserably; she was nearly in tears. "Medion, why did you have to change everything so *fast?*"

"What was I supposed to do?" he demanded in exasperation. "Refuse to build catapults when the city needs them? Pretend to be stupid? *Ignore Delia?*"

"I don't know!" shouted Philyra. "I don't know, but it's all happened too fast!" And she flounced off to cry.

Arata wanted to cry, too, but refrained, and merely looked about the old house with a lingering sadness. She had been happy here, but she'd known for some time that they would have to move. That had become clear to her as soon as she understood that her son's talents were something kings would compete for. She was resigned to the move, braced to learn a new way of life. She found the prospect of a royal daughter-in-law alarming, but her son was so profoundly happy about the match that she thought the girl must be agreeable when you got to know her. She just wished, with Philyra, that all the changes had not come at once. In June her husband had been alive and she had expected her quiet middle-class existence to go on forever; now it was August, her son was to marry the king's sister, her daughter the captain of the Ortygia garrison, the family was to become unimaginably wealthy—and her husband was dead. That last brutal fact still numbed her, and rendered all the other changes almost insuperable.

"I thought she'd be happy if we were all living on the Ortygia!" Archimedes irritably protested to his mother. "I thought she'd want us to be close by!"

"Yes, darling," said Arata patiently. "I'm sure she will be. It just is a lot of changes all at once, and we're all still upset over your father."

At that her son came over and put his arms around her. "I wish he were alive to see us."

Arata leaned her head against the bones of his shoulder and

imagined Phidias watching his son's wedding. The image of his passionate delight released the tears. "He would have been so proud," she whispered, and resigned herself to going on.

∼ IN THE ATHENIAN QUARRY, MARCUS WAS INFORMED OF the announcement by the guards.

The men of the Ortygia garrison had at first treated him harshly and looked for opportunities to punish him: they knew that he had helped Straton's killers, and Straton had had many friends. However, Marcus was the only one among the prisoners who spoke really fluent Greek, and his services as an interpreter were called upon dozens of times a day. It was difficult for the guards to avoid talking to him, and, after a perfectly ordinary conversation, hard for them to maintain the same pitch of hatred. The announcement of the betrothal helped again: the garrison were as interested in it as the rest of the city, and the opportunity to question Archimedes' slave about it was too good to be missed. Marcus, once he'd got over the initial shock, willingly spoke of flutes and Alexandria, and insisted that catapults had not been the king's first concern. "Archimedes was always going to build as many of them as were needed," he said. "The king didn't need to give him the girl for that. After he built the Welcomer, the king tried to pay him two hundred drachmae more than the price agreed, and he turned it down. 'I'm Syracusan,' he said. 'I won't profit from Syracuse's need.' "

The guards were impressed with this, though one asked cynically, "And what did you think of that?"

"I was pleased about it," said Marcus levelly. "I've always believed a man ought to love his own city."

When the guards had gone back to their posts, Marcus leaned back against the shed wall and smiled over the news. He remembered Archimedes beaming when he received Delia's warning, and thought of Delia applauding madly at the demonstration of mechanics. His own sense of pride and delight was curiously shapeless: it was neither a friend's nor a servant's, and though it had a touch of elder brother in it, it was not that either. As a loyal Roman he should have wanted Archimedes out of Syracuse, but the shapeless delight held no regrets. The boy had done well, and good luck to him!

The following morning, the tours began. Thirty prisoners were shackled together in groups of ten and marched together down to the harbor, where they were shown the sea walls, the merchant ships moored along the quay, trading freely despite the war, and the naval vessels drawn up in the ship sheds. Marcus was brought along to interpret. "If there's danger of a naval assault," the file leader in charge of the party informed the prisoners, "the whole of the Great Harbor can be closed with a boom—but your people don't have the ships for it, do you?"

"Why are they showing us this?" one of the prisoners asked Marcus.

"You understand that, surely?" replied Marcus in disgust. "It's so that you can tell the consul that he can't take Syracuse by starvation."

In the afternoon, another twenty prisoners were selected and taken along the walls to the fort of the Euryalus, where they were shown the catapults. Two of the hundred-pounders were there, and the two-talenter copied from Good Health. "We'll have a three-talenter as well, in a few days," the fort captain told them with relish. "The archimechanic is working on it now."

"I thought it was going to the Hexapylon," said Marcus.

The fort captain stared in surprise, and the file leader murmured an explanation of who Marcus was. The fort captain gave him a resentful look. "The Hexapylon got the first one," he admitted. "But we've been told that *ours* will be better."

"You should have asked him to do you a two-hundred-pounder instead," said Marcus.

The fort captain hesitated, torn between the proud desire to ignore a slave's comment and the itch to have a bigger catapult than the Hexapylon. The itch won. "Could he?" he asked eagerly.

"He certainly could," said Marcus, "but if he's already halfway through a three-talenter, it's a bit late to ask him."

"Tell *them* he could do a two-hundred-pounder," commanded the file leader, waving at the other prisoners.

Marcus nodded, turned to his fellow prisoners, and flatly reported that the fort was expecting a three-talenter and asking for a two-hundred-pounder next.

"Built by your former master, the flute player?" asked one of the prisoners.

"Yes," agreed Marcus. "He can do it, believe me."

The prisoners looked at the ammunition heaped beside the fort's towers—hundred-pound shot, two-talent shot—and sagged. "Why are they showing us this?" asked one angrily.

"So that we can tell the consul," said Marcus. "So that he knows he can't take Syracuse by storm."

"And why do they want us to tell him that?"

Marcus stood silent for a minute, looking at the prisoners in their chains and the guardsmen in their armor. "So that he'll offer terms for peace," he said, and knew with a lift of the heart that it was true.

There were more tours the next day: one to the Ortygia, and one to the Hexapylon, where the three-talenter was demonstrated. Not all the prisoners were fit enough to be dragged about the city, but all of those capable of walking were shown the strength and splendor of Syracuse. They discussed it unhappily among themselves afterward, and called on Marcus for more details. When he first appeared, they had suspected him of being a planted spy, but the initial hostility of the guards and his own openness about his sympathies had convinced them that he was what he claimed to be. Like Fabius, they thought he'd gone very Greek, but they accepted that he'd been imprisoned with them because of his Roman loyalties, and believed most of what he told them.

Early the following morning, two guards he didn't know came into the shed, went down the row of prisoners until they reached Marcus, then unlocked the leg irons and told him to get up. Marcus rose slowly and stood silent, waiting for further orders, and one of the men cuffed him. "The king wants you," he said. "Come on!"

He stooped quickly and picked up the cased aulos before he obeyed—just in case he never came back.

The two men marched him down to the gate house, where they locked an iron collar about his neck and fastened shackles to his wrists; he managed to slip the flute case through his belt before they snatched it away. They attached a chain to the collar, as though he were a dog, and tested it by jerking it so hard he staggered. "I'm not going to try to escape," he told them mildly when he'd recovered his footing.

"You don't need to be rough," agreed the file leader in charge of the quarry, who was watching. "He's a philhellene."

Marcus blinked at the title: so, the guards reckoned he'd gone very Greek as well? But the strangers only glared, and one said harshly, "He helped kill Straton," at which the file leader could only shrug.

The two new Ortygians led Marcus out the gate into the street, then turned right toward the New Town. Marcus had expected them to go straight toward the Ortygia, and was nearly jerked off his feet again by the chain. "Where are we going?" he asked bemusedly, but they did not answer.

They passed the theater and climbed up onto the Epipolae plateau, here an unpeopled region of dry scrub, and he realized that they were once more walking toward the Euryalus. He glanced sideways at his guards and decided not to ask any questions. He would discover the purpose of this journey soon enough.

The Euryalus stood at the highest point of the limestone island of Epipolae, a massive castle from which the land dropped steeply on two sides. They entered the courtyard to find it full of soldiers—a full battalion of two hundred and fifty-six men. Tethered near the outer gate was a white horse Marcus recognized, its harness draped with purple and studded with gold. His guards marched him over to the gate tower, then up into a guardroom. King Hieron was indeed there, discussing something with a number of high-ranking officers, none of whom Marcus knew. His guards struck the butts of their spears on the floor and stood to attention, and the king glanced over.

"Ah," said Hieron. "Good." He crossed the room, drawing red-cloaked officers after him like a ship trailing seaweed, and stopped before Marcus. He regarded the shackles with raised eyebrows. "You've been enthusiastic with the chains, haven't you?" he remarked to the guards. "But I suppose it's for the best. Marcus Valerius, how's your voice?"

"My voice, lord?" repeated Marcus in surprise.

"I hope you haven't got a cold," said Hieron. "You *look* as though you have a fine pair of lungs. Are you usually able to make yourself heard when you need to?"

"Yes, lord," said Marcus. Images of screaming in a bronze bull darted wildly through his mind. He did not credit them, but they were there, nonetheless.

"Good. Your people have just decided to come back this way, and I want a few words with them. Since I don't speak Latin, I need an interpreter. You occurred to me as suitable. Are you willing to translate what I say, as accurately as you can?"

Marcus shifted with relief, and the chains rattled. Most educated Romans spoke Greek; the consul certainly must. That Hieron wanted an interpreter must mean that he intended to be understood by the troops as well as the officers. If the king really meant to return him with the other prisoners, to appear now as a Syracusan interpreter might cause problems. On the other hand, he was in chains, obviously a prisoner, and his people could hardly blame him for merely interpreting what his captors said. Besides, Hieron had treated him with mercy. He still felt little joy at the thought of freedom, but he could now believe that that joy would come in time, and something was owed for mercy. "I am willing, sir," he said.

Hieron smiled. He snapped his fingers and started into the courtyard. Marcus' guards escorted him after the king, and the officers trailed behind, scarlet cloaks flapping and gilded armor gleaming.

The king mounted his white charger, and with a blast of trumpets the gates of the Euryalus were thrown open. Hieron rode out first, followed by the officers in a spearhead formation, and Marcus found himself walking between his guards behind the royal horse, enclosed by the bright splendor of the mounted officers. After him came the Syracusan battalion, marching in close formation to the sweet call of the flute, the points of the long spears on their shoulders glittering in the sun, their shields a moving wall emblazoned endlessly with the sigmas that denoted their city.

Behind a horse and between two stocky guards, Marcus could not at first make out much of the scene before him, but as they descended from the heights, the road bent and gave him a clear line of sight, and he saw that the Roman army had indeed returned to Syracuse. A new camp had been laid out in the flat fertile land to the south of the plateau: a neat rectangle fortified by a ditch, bank, and palisade. A patch of crimson and gold before it caught his eye, and then a horseman only a little way down the hill. Then they rounded the bend, and the view was obscured by the sleek rump of Hieron's horse.

A few moments later the horseman he'd noticed trotted up the hill and fell in beside the king. Marcus saw that he was a herald, his status marked out by the gilded staff he was carrying across his knees, its length carved with intertwined serpents. Heralds were under the protection of the gods, and it was sacrilege to harm one. They could pass freely between hostile armies. This one must have been sent out earlier to arrange the parley.

"He was reluctant," the herald told Hieron, his voice almost drowned by the sound of the march.

"But he agreed?" asked the king.

"He could hardly refuse," replied the herald. "That's him, down at the front there. But he asks that you be brief."

"Lord," said one of the officers, driving his horse closer to the king's, "is it wise to ride right up to them?"

The king turned to him with a look of gentle reproof. "They don't break truces," he said. "That's one of their good points.

Claudius may burn to kill me on the spot, but he's well aware that if he did, his own people would punish him for disgracing the Roman name and for offending the gods. They're very superstitious. We're quite safe as long as we keep the truce ourselves." He rode on at an easy walk.

Marcus followed, now feeling distinctly frightened. Appius Claudius, consul of Rome, was reluctantly and impatiently waiting for Hieron just down the hill. Marcus had always resisted any inclination to be impressed by rank, but a consul was the embodiment of the majesty of Rome, which he had been brought up to honor above all else. Being impressed by Claudius left him ashamed of himself. He glanced down at his tunic of unbleached linen, which had not been clean even before he wore it for a continuous week in prison, at his dusty legs and worn sandals. Stubbled from prison and in chains, he was going to interpret for a king before a consul. He looked up at Hieron's purple-cloaked back again, and realized that the king had probably chosen to have him looking as he did, chosen it to humiliate Rome. *I am king of Syracuse. Here is a Roman citizen.* He should never have forgotten the king's subtlety. Still—something was owed for mercy.

They came down from the hills, and there on the road before them were the horses of the opposing party. Behind the gold and crimson of the consul's party blazed the standards of the legions, and perhaps ten maniples stood behind them, drawn up in neat squares, one behind another as far as the wall of the palisade, which itself was lined with onlookers. The herald lifted his staff and trotted ahead, and the king's party rode unhurriedly after him, drawing rein at last when they were at a normal speaking distance. Hieron gestured for Marcus' guards to bring him forward, and from the king's side Marcus looked up shamefacedly at Syracuse's enemy and his own ruler.

Claudius, like Hieron, rode upon a white charger and wore a purple cloak. His breastplate and helmet were gilded and shone in the sun. To either side of him stood the lictors appointed to carry out his every order, red-cloaked and holding the bunch of rods and axes that symbolized his power to punish or to kill, and behind him on their own mounts sat the tribunes of his legions, cloaked in Phoenician crimson and armored in gold. Marcus gazed at them with a dry mouth. They seemed to him faceless, entirely defined by their own majesty.

"Good health to you, consul of the Romans!" said Hieron. "And to you also, men of Rome. I asked to speak with you this morning concerning those of your people whom we have taken prisoner." He touched Marcus' shoulder with his foot and added softly, "Translate!"

Marcus started, then hurriedly interpreted the king's words, shouting so that they would carry as far as possible.

Claudius' face darkened, and Marcus noticed for the first time what the consul actually looked like—a large man, with a heavy-jowled, fleshy face; only the nose stood out from it, a knife edge of bone. "What's this?" demanded the consul, in Greek, glaring directly at Marcus.

"One of those prisoners," said Hieron. "He speaks fluent Greek, and I have brought him to interpret for me, so that your officers may all understand what I say as well as you do yourself, O consul of the Romans. I have noticed in the past that their grasp of our language does not often equal your own." Again his foot touched Marcus' shoulder.

Marcus began to translate, but Claudius at once bellowed, in Latin, "Halt!" Marcus stopped, and Claudius glared at him for a moment, then said to Hieron, "He is not needed."

"Do you not want your men to understand me?" asked Hieron, in a tone of mild surprise. "Surely you do not wish to keep from them news of their friends and comrades?"

Marcus glanced at the faces behind the consul, and saw there a look of uneasiness and dissatisfaction: the Roman officers might not speak Greek as well as the consul, but they understood enough, and they were not happy that Claudius wanted to keep the fate of the prisoners a secret from the common soldiers. Claudius must have realized, because he scowled, then said, "I have nothing to keep from my loyal followers. Have the man interpret, if that is what you want, Tyrant. But he is not needed."

Hieron smiled. Marcus was all at once certain that Claudius had just made a bad mistake.

Hieron began speaking quickly and clearly, pausing after every phrase to allow Marcus to shout out his translation. "When Fate delivered some of your people into my hands, O Romans, it was my intention to return them to you quickly. I waited for you to send a herald to ask me what ransom I required, but you sent none. Indeed, you left Syracuse during the night, and left your people in my hands. Do you not care for them, O Consul?"

Claudius drew himself straight and glared at Hieron. "When Romans make war, Tyrant of Syracuse," he declared in Latin, "they accept the risk of death, and meet it bravely. Those who do not are no true men, and are not worth ransoming. However, as you may have heard, we have besieged and sacked the city of Echetla, your ally, and if you wish we will exchange the women of Echetla for our own people. The men we have killed."

"What does he say?" Hieron asked Marcus. Marcus hurriedly translated, wondering about Echetla. It lay to the northwest of Syracuse, and was indeed a Syracusan dependency, though to call it a city was to exaggerate the scale of the action: it was a fortified market town, no more, and had had no chance against a large Roman army. The Romans had undoubtedly been angry when they attacked it, furious over their losses before Syracuse and in no mood either to negotiate or to show mercy. He imagined the desperate defense, and the massacre of all the men able to bear arms, and felt sick.

"I had intended to ask no ransom for your people, Consul of the Romans," said Hieron reproachfully. "Like Pyrrhus of Epirus, at whose side I once fought, I would have returned them without fee Like him, I honor the courage of the Roman people."

As Marcus translated this, for the first time a ripple of whispers spread out through the Roman ranks: men who'd heard what he said were repeating it to those who stood farther back. The mention of King Pyrrhus, Marcus thought, was well made: the Romans respected him more than any other enemy they had faced.

"Then return them, Tyrant, without so much talk!" snapped Claudius. "And we will keep the Echetlans as our slaves."

Hieron paused so that his next words would not be obscured, then replied, "As for the Echetlans, I will ransom them, O Consul, if you will name a price. But as for your own people, your answer has made me hesitate. I have treated my prisoners with all the respect due to brave enemies. They have been well fed and housed, and my own doctor has tended their wounds. Before you left here, though, I saw that you obliged their surviving comrades to pitch their tents outside your camp, and now it seems that you place little value upon the men I hold, since you reckon them equal to slaves. How have they offended you?"

"They lack courage," replied the consul harshly. "They surrendered. We Romans are not like you Greeks. When we fail, we expect to suffer the penalty."

"They lack courage?" repeated Hieron. "The wounds the men in my prison have suffered are the best testimony to their bravery, for few of them are uninjured. But the task they were set was impossible. Two maniples in loose formation without siege equipment were sent out in broad daylight against heavy artillery. They were ordered not to battle, but to execution! It astonished me that they nonetheless obeyed. What they lacked was certainly not courage, but a wise commander."

Claudius opened his mouth, but even as he did so, the spreading whispers turned into a growl, and then a full-throated roar. Behind him the legions hammered their spears against the ground and cheered fiercely for the two slaughtered maniples; the men watching from the palisade rattled entrenching tools against the wall. Claudius' face turned crimson and he whirled on the tribunes and shouted, "Silence! Make that rabble be quiet!"

Hieron's charger fidgeted uneasily at the uproar, and the king patted its neck.

"My fellow soldiers!" bellowed Claudius, when the noise began to die down at last. "My fellow soldiers, don't listen to this man! He is trying to seduce you from your discipline. You, soldier"—to Marcus—"stop repeating his lies!"

Marcus remembered Gaius' white face and agonized gasps as he was marched into the city, and was suddenly in a crimson fury of his own. He remembered that moment afterward like a witness remembering a fatal accident, mentally shrieking at himself, *No, stop, not that way, you fool!* But he could not stop. Because of this man, Gaius had suffered, and he had lost everything. Claudius could not be permitted to slough off the guilt.

"He's telling the truth!" Marcus shouted passionately. He waved with both shackles up the hill toward the Euryalus. "What did you *think* they had in there—slingshots? Don't you know the standard range of a catapult? Or did you just expect a city that the Carthaginians have besieged with armies ten times the size of this one to crack like an egg? Jupiter! You had no idea what you were doing. It's inexcusable to blame your own failure on the men who suffered from it! If you're a Roman, Consul, accept the penalty yourself!"

There was another uproar. Claudius stared at Marcus in astonishment and rage; Hieron, with uneasiness. "What did you say?" asked the king, but Marcus did not answer. He lowered his shackled hands and stood proudly, glaring back at the consul.

"I hope this man has not offended you," said Hieron, speaking directly to Claudius in a more normal voice. "His brother was badly injured in your assault, and he may have spoken passionately because of it. You must excuse him. I myself have no wish to insult you or your people."

Claudius turned the furious glare on Hieron. "And saying that I am not a wise commander is no insult?" he asked.

Hieron smiled. "You are certainly inexperienced at sieges, O Consul—at least, at sieges of Greek cities which are well equipped with artillery. Wouldn't you agree that when a wise commander lacks knowledge, he proceeds only with caution? If you wish to improve your understanding of what you face, you may come up to the wall, under my protection, and view the defenses. You have underrated us, Consul, and treated us with a contempt we in no way deserve."

Claudius spat. "Your protection is as worthless as your boasts, Tyrant! I credit neither!"

"You are right in saying that they are both of the same value," replied the king. The noise was dying down once more, and Hieron lifted his arms as he began to speak once more to the whole army; Marcus at once began his shouted translation. Claudius tried to protest, but even his own officers paid no attention to him, and the army instantly quieted to hear what Hieron had to say. While the consul fumed, the king's words rode out upon another ring of whispers.

"Men of Rome, I have heard that I am reported arrogant and cruel. Report lies, for I have ever acted with moderation, and honored the gods."

"And that's true," Marcus added, with a defiant glare at the consul. "All those stories about bronze bulls and impalings were made up by the Mamertini to get Roman help."

"There is no citizen of Syracuse who has just complaint against me," Hieron continued. "My lovely city is as united as she is strong—and her strength you have all seen. Your own people can vouch for that when I return them. If you wish to receive them with honor, I will return them to you today, without ransom as I promised. If you do not, I will keep them unharmed to give to the first Roman who asks me for their freedom."

"It is a trick!" bellowed Claudius.

"It is offered honestly and in good faith," replied Hieron. "Do you wish me to send them?"

Claudius looked as though he might burst. "You are growing desperate for a peace, Tyrant!" he shouted. "Where are the allies you abandoned at Messana?"

"And you are in a great hurry for a triumph, Consul!" replied Hieron sharply. "You're even willing to trust the Carthaginians to get it—willing to gamble the lives of all your men on that chance that they stay away. Yes, where are the Carthaginians? In your rear? At Messana, sacking it in your absence, and destroying the ships on which you intend to sail home? You've chosen to fight Syracuse instead of Carthage, and forgotten that you offered to fight both. Can you, O Romans? But you haven't answered my question, Consul. I have ninety-two of your people prisoner. Do you want them back?"

Claudius was silent for a long minute, while the whispers spread through his army, the translation almost obscured by the buzz of angry discussion. Then, in a choked voice, the consul said, "Yes. Return them."

"You will receive them with honor?"

"Since you say that they fought bravely, they will be received as brave men," grated the consul.

Hieron inclined his head graciously. "And the women of Echetla—what price do you want for them?"

"None!" a voice from among the legions shouted suddenly. Claudius spun toward it, but already a dozen other voices had joined it, "Honor to those who honor the Roman people! Return the Echetlans without ransom!" There was a thunder of spears against the ground, and then a full-throated roar: "Honor to the Roman people!"

Claudius looked back at Hieron. Marcus had never seen such a look of bleak vindictiveness. "You shall have them without ransom," he muttered.

"I will have your men brought from their prison and delivered to you here," said Hieron. "It will take perhaps four hours. I take it this truce holds until then?"

Claudius nodded, then, not trusting himself to say more, turned his horse away.

Hieron snapped his fingers, and the Syracusan aulist struck up his marching tune again. The files divided, leaving a space for the king to ride through them. Marcus followed between his two guards; behind him the Syracusan battalion turned about and marched back up the hill.

When the gates of the Euryalus had closed behind them, the king drew rein and looked down at Marcus thoughtfully. "What did you say to the consul?" he asked.

"That what you'd said was true," replied Marcus shortly.

Hieron sighed. "That was unwise."

"It was true."

"It is not usually a good idea to speak truth to kings—or to consuls. I am going to have to return you anyway. If I keep you, Claudius will say that you were really a Greek in disguise, and it will be easier for him to convince his army that he was right after all."

Marcus nodded. Hieron looked at him a moment longer, then sighed again. "You are a true Roman, aren't you? You accept the penalty for your own actions—whether it's justified or not. What's that you have in your belt?"

Marcus' face went hot. "A flute," he said. "My mas—Archimedes gave it to me. He thought I would have time in prison to learn it."

"I pray that the gods grant you a life long enough to become as skilled on it as he is himself!" Hieron snapped his fingers and said to the guards, "Take the chains off him, and put him somewhere shady to wait for the others. Give him something to eat and drink—it's a long walk over here, and interpreting is thirsty work."

The guards led Marcus to a room in one of the towers, a catapult platform with no catapult in it. They took off his chains and fetched him some bread and wine. "With goodwill," said one of the guards, offering the wine. "I should have believed Apollodoros when he said you were philhellene."

Marcus drank the watered wine thirstily, but had no appetite for the bread. He kept remembering the way Claudius had looked at Hieron. The consul would happily have cooked his enemy alive, in or out of a bronze bull. Hieron would be out of his reach behind the walls of Syracuse, but Marcus was going to have to face him again in about four hours.

He wished that he had volunteered nothing, that he had been content to translate Hieron's words and leave it at that. It was not as though Hieron had needed any help. The parley that morning now appeared to him as a wrestling match in which Claudius had been comprehensively beaten. Claudius was clearly a man who liked to find scapegoats for his own failures, and in Marcus he would find in ideal one: a disloyal Hellenizer, a coward who had escaped the penalty due to him by accepting slavery. Claudius could try to discredit the truth by disgracing and executing the man who had spoken it.

But perhaps the consul would prefer to forget about Marcus. A vindictive punishment would only confirm the reputation for callous arrogance which Hieron had just draped him in. Marcus would just have to hope that the consul was intelligent enough to realize that.

Time passed. The guards left him in the tower room, and he waited alone, watching the Roman camp through the artillery port. He could see a drab-colored mass of people assembled by the gate: the women of Echetla, no doubt. He supposed that there had been no way to save Echetla. By the time Hieron's scouts found out that the Romans had gone there, it would have been too late to send help to it. He was still sorry for Echetla.

Four hours, Hieron had said. That would be about right: a rider had to be sent to the quarry to tell the guards to take all the prisoners to the gates, and then there would be preparations—leg irons to be taken off, escorts to be assembled, stretchers found for those men still unable to walk—and then the whole party had to make the long walk up to the Euryalus. Four hours. It seemed to Marcus that four years passed before the sun dipped from the height of noon.

He took out the aulos and began to practice it, as something to do. He had practiced every day since first being given it, and could now play very simple tunes, very, very slowly. He picked his way laboriously through a Nile boat song, then, stirred by an ache for vanished safety, found himself struggling for the notes of a lullaby he remembered his mother singing by the fire at home.

"I don't know that one," said Hieron. "Is it Roman?"

Marcus set the aulos down and got to his feet. He had not heard the door open. The king was alone, and dust on his cloak proclaimed that he'd been riding hard.

"Yes," said Marcus in a low voice. "It's Roman, lord."

"Odd," remarked Hieron. "One doesn't think of your people producing anything gentle. Is there anything left in that flask?"

There was a little of the wine left. Hieron drained it, then sat down. The small tower room had no furniture, so he sat on the floor, crossing his ankles comfortably, and gestured for Marcus to do likewise. Marcus squatted facing him, watching him warily.

Hieron looked back speculatively. "I wanted to talk to you," he said. "I hoped there would be time. I have one or two things I wanted to say."

"To me?" asked Marcus in confusion.

"Why not? You think I spared you for Archimedes' sake, don't you?"

Marcus said nothing, merely looked back with an impassive slave's face.

"Archimedes had nothing to do with it. Incidentally, his friends in Alexandria called him Alpha, didn't they? Do you know why?"

"Because when anybody set a mathematical problem, he was always the first to find the answer," said Marcus, startled. Then, "How . . ."

"I thought it might be that," said Hieron. "Alpha. Not a bad nickname, and I need one for him. His proper name doesn't slip off the tongue easily enough. No, I spared you because—you must excuse me—I had a use for you. You're the only Hellenized Roman I've ever encountered."

Marcus stared.

"I know. Greek is the first language your people study, though most of them are very bad at it. Your coins, when you do coin silver, are based on ours. Your pottery, fashions, furniture, and so forth all mimic ours. You hire Greek architects to build Greek-style temples and fill them with Greek statues of the gods—often of Greek gods. You worship Apollo, don't you? But it's all shallow, like a film of water over granite. A bit of gloss on your own nature, which is hard. brutal, and profoundly suspicious of imagination. A Roman gentleman may read our poetry, listen to our music: he would consider it menial to write or play himself. Our philosophy is condemned as atheistic nonsense, our sports as immoral, and our politics—well, tyranny is bad, and democracy unspeakably worse. Am I being unfair?"

Marcus said nothing. He was stung, but suspicious. With a man like Hieron it seemed better to find out what the object of the speech was before responding.

Hieron smiled. "I'm glad you can be cautious," he remarked. "Very well, I'll put your people's side of things for you. You are also courageous, disciplined, pious, honorable, and extraordinarily tenacious. There is no hope that we can deal with you as Greeks elsewhere deal with barbarians: pay you off and persuade you to go away. You have taken the whole of Italy, and if you decide to take Sicily as well, there is nothing Syracuse can do to stop you. Carthage, too, is growing too powerful for us." He got up suddenly and went to the open door, where he stood leaning against the frame and looking across the plateau toward the city. "Before Alexander conquered the world," he said softly, "men lived in cities. Now they live in kingdoms, and cities must preserve themselves as they can. I've tried aligning Syracuse with Carthage, but there's not much hope there: the hatred is too old. That leaves Rome. But I find Romans . . . difficult."

"You managed Appius Claudius easily enough," said Marcus sourly. "Three falls and he was out."

Hieron glanced around, then turned back from the view and regarded him with a smile. "You like wrestling, do you?" he asked. "I was never any good at it."

"You obliged Appius Claudius to speak to you," said Marcus resolutely. "He couldn't refuse to parley about prisoners. You got him to accept me an interpreter—and then you pitched every speech over his head directly to the legions. He's a senator and a patrician; they're plebeians, like me. You slipped your finger into the difference and wriggled it around like a man prying a brick out of a rotten wall. You said he was arrogant and incompetent, and that he unjustly blamed them for failures that were his own. You said he risked all their lives when he ignored Carthage, and that he did it to further his own ambitions. And then you said you were an honest and decent man and that you honored the Roman *people*. He had no answer to any of it. And the Roman people in arms drank it down and cheered for you. Claudius won't get a triumph, and won't be reelected to command the Roman forces in Sicily."

Hieron drew a deep breath and let it out again slowly. "On the other hand," he commented, "the Senate and people of Rome will undoubtedly decide that they have not sent enough troops to deal with the situation in Sicily. The city of Syracuse is altogether more formidable than they first believed, and Carthage hasn't been touched yet. They will never retreat, will they? So they will send more men, under a new commander. Who? What I want, what I was working to achieve—I admit it—was to discredit the Claudian faction, and get a moderate put in charge of the war. But maybe the Roman people, in their usual indomitable style, will pick another Claudius, or an Aemilius, which I believe would be almost as bad. Would it be?"

"I don't know," said Marcus helplessly. "It's been a long time since I was in Rome. Yes, probably. The Aemilii and the Claudii were always allies, always pressing for conquests to the south."

Hieron nodded. "Even if the next general isn't an Aemilius or a Claudius, the chances are I won't know what faction he does represent, and even if I do, there'll be little enough for me to work on. I don't understand Romans. For example, I didn't expect to get the Echetlans for nothing. Greeks would have asked money for them: honor is a fine thing, but so are ransoms. With Greeks I know where I am. Romans are more difficult—and yet I must understand, if I'm to find a safe passage to peace for Syracuse. So you see"—he came away from the door and crouched to meet Marcus' stare eye to eye—"a Hellenized Roman, such as yourself, is potentially very useful to me."

"Useful as what?" asked Marcus harshly.

"Not as a spy, so put it out of your head! Agathon said you were so bad at lying it was pitiable, and he was right. No. You're different from the rest; your Hellenism isn't just a gloss. Your sympathies are genuinely divided between us and your own people. Uncomfortable for you, no doubt, but if we can get peace, or even a solid truce, invaluable to me. You could explain your own people to me, and help me make them understand us. This is what I would *like* you to do. Go back to your own people, get a feel for them again, wait till Syracuse is out of this war—and I pray to all the gods I *can* get her out soon!—and then come back here. I would give you a job as Latin interpreter, at once, at whatever salary you think is right. We are going to be dealing with your people for many years to come, and we need to understand them."

Marcus stared at him for another moment, his face hot. Then he said. "I would like that very much, lord. Only I don't know that I will be alive tomorrow."

Hieron sighed. "That, of course, is the problem. I wish you had been a bit less forthright with the consul. I wish I dared keep you here—but I worked quite hard to expose Claudius, and too much depends on it to allow him a chance to cover himself. But listen—keep what I have said in mind, and if you can, *lie*. I do not mind in the least if you say I threatened you or maltreated you to make you speak as you did. If cursing Syracuse will keep you alive, curse her. The gods laugh at forced oaths. It would not be treachery."

"I will try," whispered Marcus, "but . . ."

From the courtyard came a sound of trumpets, and then the sweet notes of an aulos and the beat of marching feet. The other prisoners were arriving, and it would soon be time to go.

Hieron sighed again, then added, in a very low voice, "Try. And if you fail—I have a gift for you."

He reached into a fold of his cloak and brought out a small, fat flask of black-glazed pottery. It was about the size of a child's fist, and it had been stoppered with a piece of wood shoved into a fragment of rag. He offered it to Marcus in silence, and Marcus took it slowly, with hands that were suddenly cold.

"It takes about half an hour to work," said the king. "A third of the contents will dull pain, if it's merely a question of flogging or beating. If it's death, drink it all."

"Lord," said Marcus, "you have twice showed me mercy, and I am grateful."

Hieron shook his head angrily. "I spared you because I wished to make use of you, and this mercy is one I pray to the gods you will not need. Do you have somewhere to hide it? Good. Then I wish you joy, Marcus Valerius, and I hope that we will meet again."

Marcus swallowed and nodded, then said, "Tell Archimedes and his household that I pray for the safety of Syracuse. And thank you."

Hieron touched his shoulder lightly, then rose resolutely and strode from the room.

Marcus set the flask carefully in the flute case, in the space normally occupied by the reeds. He was down to his last reed, and he wondered if he would need a new one. He closed the case and thrust it through his belt.

When he went down into the courtyard, he found that the guards from the quarry had brought along his little bundle of luggage. He slung it over his shoulder and took his place in the line with the other prisoners, who were laughing joyfully over their release. The gates of the Euryalus were opened, the flute struck up the march, and he descended from Syracuse to the Roman camp below.

15

The Romans did not assault Syracuse again that summer. After the exchange of prisoners, they returned to Messana, where the troops spent the winter while Appius Claudius went home to Rome.

He was not reelected. Reports of the army's many causes of dissatisfaction with him had been circulating widely throughout Rome by the time he returned, and he was received coldly, without honors and without thanks. Neither of the new consuls elected in January belonged to the Claudian faction.

The two legions in Sicily, however, were considered to be insufficient for the gravity of the situation there, and another six specially strengthened legions were enrolled. In the spring both consuls set out for Sicily with their huge armies, and when they landed at Messana, they proclaimed favorable terms for any Sicilian city that would abandon Syracuse. At this all of the dependencies of Syracuse, all her friends and allies on the island, fell away.

In early summer the forty-thousand-strong Roman army arrived at Syracuse itself and laid siege to the city, ringing it about by land with a bank, ditch, and wall of earth and timber. Greek engineers from the subject cities of Tarentum and Croton constructed siege machines—wheeled towers with ladders, grapples, and catapults mounted in them, and the thick-roofed, open-floored wheeled carts called tortoises, which protected massive

battering rams. In the middle of the summer the besiegers tried
to take Syracuse by storm.

They failed utterly. Over the previous summer, Hieron had
been calling upon Syracusan allies for supplies—grain to feed
the citizens during a siege, wood and iron and hair to shape
weapons for her defenses—and Egypt and Rhodes, Corinth and
Cyrene had responded. The new season had found the city more
impregnable than ever. Extra ditches had been dug about the
walls, inside the range of the defending catapults, so that the
attackers had to wheel their cumbersome siege machines down
steep slopes, then up, then down again, all the while suffering
the bombardment of the Syracusan catapults. And that bombardment was of a strength such as the Romans' Italiot engineers
had never imagined. Immense stones smashed the tortoises and
toppled the siege towers. Men who tried to right them fell under
a rain of bolts, and incendiaries smashed into the damaged machines and set them ablaze. The rams never got anywhere near
the walls, but were crushed like beetles on the slopes of the
Epipolae, and abandoned when the attackers fled. Hundreds of
Romans injured or trapped in the wreck of the machines were
taken prisoner by the Syracusans; hundreds more were killed.

Manius Valerius Maximus, the senior Roman consul, confer-
ring with his colleague and his senior advisers after the assault,
had one of the Syracusan catapult stones rolled into his tent for
their consideration. It weighed over two hundred pounds. The
Romans regarded it with horrified wonder.

"I'd heard," said the Tarentine chief engineer in awe, "that
Archimedes of Syracuse, King Hieron's engineer, could build
three-talenters. I thought the stories were exaggerating."

"It seems they fell short of the mark," said Valerius Maximus.
"Like our own assault."

The Tarentine had no ideas for countering Syracusan artillery,
and was, in fact, fearful that a man who could build three-
talenters might have worse things in store for any siege engine
that did succeed in getting close to the walls. The Romans considered the possibility of blockading the city and concluded that

it was pointless even to try: they had no fleet apart from the few Italiot vessels and the transports which had brought them across the straits, while the Syracusans possessed eighty decked warships to defend their shipping. The number was certain: the Syracusans had proudly displayed the fleet to their Roman prisoners the summer before.

Even more worrying, from the Roman point of view, was the news that General Hanno, the Carthaginian commander in Sicily, had been recalled to Africa, tried by the Carthaginian Senate, and sentenced to death by crucifixion for his inaction. There were rumors that Carthage was now recruiting mercenaries and intended to press the war in earnest.

"We must have peace with Hieron of Syracuse," concluded Maximus. "Carthage is the main enemy, but we cannot fight the Carthaginians with Syracuse hostile at our backs. And it seems that we can't subdue Syracuse by force. Carthage has given Syracuse no support since the war began. Perhaps Hieron will be willing to abandon his alliance."

No one had any objection to this change of policy. The rumors of Syracusan atrocities no longer found wide acceptance: the Roman prisoners released the previous year had had nothing but praise for King Hieron.

The following morning, Maximus sent a herald to Syracuse to ask King Hieron for a parley. The king at once agreed, and Roman consul and Greek monarch met on the plain below the fort of the Euryalus. Maximus was surprised to find Hieron so pleasant and reasonable a man; Appius Claudius had led him to expect a cunning and belligerent monster.

The negotiations went on for three days. Once she had entered a struggle, Rome was not in the habit of accepting anything short of her enemy's total surrender, and however generous she might otherwise be to the defeated, she always required that her new "ally" supply troops to fight for Rome. This was precisely the condition Hieron rejected most emphatically. If Syracusans were to fight and die, they would do it on behalf of their own city, not for foreigners. Syracuse would remain sovereign and independent, or she would remain at war. She could not hope to win, but, on the other hand, the Romans couldn't hope to reduce her and couldn't afford to ignore her. Rome at last, reluctantly, yielded and concluded a treaty such as she had never made before.

Rome not only recognized the independence of Syracuse but also granted the city the right to govern eastern Sicily from Tauromenium, just south of Messana, as far as Helorus on the southern point of the island—in fact, to keep all the territory she had held before the war began, including all the cities which had recently yielded to Rome. All this land was guaranteed exempt from war—which included immunity from attacks by Rome's deplorable allies, the Mamertini. Syracuse, for her part, agreed to provide the Romans with supplies for a campaign against the Carthaginians in Sicily, and to pay a war indemnity of a hundred talents of silver, the payments to be spread over twenty-five years. The latest batch of Roman prisoners were returned without ransom.

The treaty was formally concluded with an exchange of oaths and sacrifices offered to the gods. And its conclusion was celebrated on both sides, with feasting and heartfelt relief. Rome could now concentrate on Carthage, and Syracuse had steered her way through the channel to peace.

~ WHEN THE ROMANS WERE DISMANTLING THEIR SIEGE works in preparation for their return to Messana, two men of the second legion went to their tribune and asked permission to go into the city to pay a debt. Since one of them was a centurion of the legion and the other his second-in-command, permission was granted. So Quintus Fabius and Gaius Valerius walked slowly up the long road to the city they had left by night the year before.

It was an August morning, and around them the land baked in the summer sun. The open fields were loud with cicadas, the road white with dust. Fabius tapped his centurion's vine-stem stick unhappily against his thigh as he walked: he had not wanted to come, but Gaius needed an interpreter. He was obliged to Gaius, in an ill-defined, guilty sort of way. He had caused Gaius grief. Fabius' promotions had come rapidly over the past year, and he had taken advantage of them to haul Gaius up through the ranks after him, out of the same obscure sense of obligation.

They reached the Epipolae gate of the fort of the Euryalus, where the Syracusan guardsmen eyed them with suspicion. Fabius explained their errand in his clumsy Greek, and they were allowed to pass, though they were required to leave their arms at the gate. One of the guards escorted them into the city: the peace was still very new, and they were not trusted, least of all at the house to which they were bound.

They crossed the limestone scrubland of the plateau, passed the huts of the Tyche quarter, and descended from the heights into the marble grace of the New Town. They both glanced at the cliff which towered over the theater to their left, the edge of the plateau where the quarries were situated. But their escort led them through the New Town and into the citadel of the Ortygia.

The house they were looking for lay on the north side of the Ortygia, not far from from the sea wall. It was a large house, and had been repainted not long before: the front was a crisp pattern of red and white, unfaded by sun and unmarked by dust. The guardsman from the Euryalus knocked upon the pristine door.

Gaius Valerius stood on the sunny doorstep, listening to the guardsman explaining and a boy doorkeeper answering doubtfully, all in the rapid musical language which he could not understand. He had been eager for this meeting, but now that it was almost upon him, he wondered why he bothered. Because of Marcus. What good would it do Marcus? What good would it do anyone? Still, he clutched the small package he had brought with him and asked Fabius, "What's the delay?"

"The slave says his master's working, and doesn't like to be disturbed when he's working," replied Fabius. He interpolated a comment into the flow of conversation between the slave boy

and the guardsman, and both turned to look at him. The slave
blinked, then shrugged, and stood back, opening the door for all
three of them.

"What did you say?" asked Gaius, stepping into a cool marble
hall.

"That we only wanted to return his master's property," said
Fabius.

The boy walked ahead of them, along a colonnade which enclosed a garden, green and cool after the hot streets, then
through a narrow passage, past another, kitchen, garden, and into
a workroom which might have been part of another house entirely. The floor was packed clay, and the walls were stacked high
with timbers. In the center of the room stood a sinister-looking
box more than half the height of a man, formed of wood and
lined with lead; sitting on a corner of it was a basin with two
large neat holes in it, and scattered about it were oddments of
leather, wood, and bone and a blacksmith's bellows. Whatever
the device was, however, it had been abandoned, and the only
person in the room was a young man who crouched on a low
stool not far from it, gazing intently into a box of pale sand and
sucking on the hinge of a set of compasses. Gaius had never
actually seen his face before, though he had once heard him play
the flute, but he knew at once who it was. The magician who
could number the sands and make water run uphill, Syracuse's
extra army, his brother's onetime master.

"Sir," said the slave boy, with great respect. He had been purchased only the winter before, and he was in awe of his new
master.

Archimedes lifted one hand in a wait-a-minute gesture and
did not take his gaze off the pattern in the sand.

The boy looked at the visitors and shrugged helplessly.

Gaius cleared his throat, then called out, "Archimedes?"

Archimedes made an indistinct reply around the compasses—
then suddenly stiffened. His head jerked up, a smile of delight
on his face. For a moment Gaius found himself meeting a pair

of bright brown eyes that sought his own eagerly—and then the
delight faded, and the eyes became puzzled.

"Oh," said Archimedes. He got to his feet, glanced down at
his interrupted calculation, then back at the visitors, questioningly now.

"Excuse us," said Fabius stiffly. "I am Quintus Fabius, a centurion of the second legion; this is Gaius Valerius. We are come
to speak to Archimedes son of Phidias."

"You're Marcus' brother!" Archimedes exclaimed, looking at
the second man. He could see the family resemblance now, in
the wide shoulders and the stubborn line of the jaw, though
Gaius Valerius was slighter and fairer than his brother. "You are
welcome to my house, and good health to you! When you called
my name I thought for a moment it was Marcus. You sound just
like him."

Gaius just stared. Fabius turned to his companion and translated, which took Archimedes aback: he had somehow expected
Marcus' brother to know Greek.

Gaius nodded, then stepped forward and held out a long slim
box wrapped in black cloth. "I came to return this," he said quietly. "I think it was yours."

Archimedes stared at the box, recognizing the shape, and
knowing with cold sick grief that something he had hoped would
not happen had happened, and happened long before. He did
not take the box, even when the translation was finished and
Gaius took another step toward him, offering it again.

"Marcus is dead," he said flatly, looking up from the shrouded
flute case to meet the eyes of Marcus' brother.

There was no need for translation. Gaius nodded.

Archimedes took the flute case and sat down on his stool. He
pulled at the knots that secured the wrapping, then bit the cords
and broke them. He unwrapped the case, opened it, and took
out his tenor aulos. The wood was dry to the touch, and the slide,
when he moved it, squeaked stiffly. A cracked reed was still fixed
to the mouthpiece, and the tarnished clamp had left a green stain

upon its dry gray side. He unfastened the clamp and pulled the reed out, then began rubbing the mouthpiece clean on the cloth the case had been shrouded in. His hands knew what they were doing; his heart was bemused and numb.

"I don't play," said Gaius. "And I did not want it to stay silent forever."

Archimedes nodded. He spat on the mouthpiece and rubbed it again, then set the instrument down in his lap. He wiped his face with a bare arm, and realized at that that he was crying. He looked back at Gaius. "Your brother was an extraordinary man," he said. "A man of great integrity. I had hoped that he was still alive."

Gaius' face convulsed with pain. "He died last year, the day after your people returned him. Appius Claudius had him sentenced to the *fustuarium*."

Fabius hesitated over the last word, unable to translate it. "To the beating to death," he supplied eventually.

"Hieron told me that Marcus had offended the consul," said Archimedes wretchedly. "He said that he spoke to Marcus before he sent him back, and urged him to tell whatever lies would save his life. But Marcus was never any good at lying."

"He was a true Roman," agreed Gaius proudly.

The brown eyes fixed him, uncomprehending and angry. "Oh? The people who killed him called themselves true Romans. If they were, he wasn't."

"Appius Claudius isn't a man, let alone a Roman!" exclaimed Gaius hotly.

"You can't disown him that easily!" replied Archimedes. "The Roman people elected him and followed him. His successors are now obliging my city to pay for the war he and his friends started and forced upon us, the war that isn't over yet. Rome hasn't disowned him, and nor can you! Your people murdered Marcus. Gods! Barbarians!"

Gaius flinched, though Fabius, adding the last phrases to his translation, merely looked contemptuous. Behind them, the guardsman from the Euryalus, who had stood watching the two

Romans with his spear balanced on guard, grinned. Archimedes looked back down at the flute, trying to calm himself. He fingered the dry wood, and remembered Marcus stroking it. Marcus had never had time to learn it properly. Waste, waste, stupid waste!

"I loved my brother," said Gaius slowly. "And I wanted . . ."

He hesitated. He did not know how to speak to this man. He wished Archimedes had indeed been the white-bearded sage of his imaginings; he would have known then how to conduct himself. This young man, this foreigner who angrily condemned his own people, confused Gaius, muddling his reactions. He remembered the two voices in the dark courtyard of the house in the Achradina: this one, quick, drink-slurred, questioning and commanding; and the other voice, now silenced. He had been unable to tell then, and could not tell now, what connection bound them, what history of emotions they assumed. He took another step forward and squatted in front of the figure on the stool, trying to meet the eyes, silently raging against the need to pause, and wait at each phrase for Fabius to alter his words and render them comprehensible; longing for direct communication.

"I did not have much time to talk to Marcus last year," he said. "A little while when we escaped; a little while more before and after the trial. But he did talk a little about Egypt, and about you and your household, and about . . . about Greek things. Mechanics, mathematics—things I have no knowledge of. I do not know very much about what he was like, the last years of his life. I want to know. I lost him when he was sixteen, and almost half his life is missing for me. Please, tell me what you can. I ask it as a favor, as the brother of a man who was your slave, and for whom, it seems, you had some affection."

Archimedes sighed, still fingering the flute. "What can I say? He was, as you say, my slave, and for most of the time I knew him I took him entirely for granted. One does not ask a slave what he's thinking or feeling: one just expects him to get on with his work. My father bought him when I was about nine. We paid a hundred and eighty drachmae for him—it was during the Pyrrhic War, and slaves were cheap. We had a vineyard then, and we needed a worker to help get in the vintage, and a farm—the tenants mostly managed it on their own, but we usually tried to help with the harvest, as one does. So your brother did that, and he did the heavy work at the house, and occasionally helped the neighbors. Marcus hated being a slave—I think I always did know that—but I think apart from that he wasn't unhappy. He lived in the house with me and my parents and my sister and our other slaves. My father was a gentle man and a good master. Your brother didn't seem to dislike his work, and he enjoyed other things. We always played a lot of music, and when we went out to concerts and the theater we usually chose Marcus to carry things, because we knew he enjoyed music. Machines, too—yes, he did like them. I was always building them, and he was always interested in them. He'd help hammer and saw, and he'd make suggestions—tell me that what the next hoist needed was a way to fix it halfway up and so forth, and then when I'd worked out how to make it do that, he'd grin about it. So we liked each other.

"When I was nineteen, my father gave Marcus to me, and we went off to Alexandria for three years. I was not a good master. Marcus would say, 'Sir, we're out of money,' and I'd say, 'Oh well,' and forget about it, leaving him to sort out how we were to live without it. He was very resourceful and always amazingly honest. When he took money out of my purse—he had to, I never remembered to give it to him—he'd always tell me how much and for what, even though I never paid the least attention, and he always used to remind me who I owed money to. And he used to mend clothes and make sandals himself, and he'd do odd jobs for the tradesmen in exchange for this and that we needed. He never complained. But he never liked Alexandria— at least, that was the impression I had. He was always telling me we ought to go home. But the last year we were in Egypt I designed a machine to lift water, and he told me once that he'd enjoyed building that more than any other work he'd ever done."

"The water-snail," said Gaius.

Archimedes smiled at the word, which, being Greek, needed no translation. "I'm not surprised that he told you about that: he loved that machine. We didn't make them for long. I got tired of them. He was furious with me about it; he kept telling me we could make a fortune with the god-hated things. He never saw the point of geometry—not that he admitted to me, anyway."

"He seems to have . . ." Gaius hesitated: *told you what to do a lot* hovered on his lips, but he was afraid of offending, and changed it to ". . . spoken his mind to you freely."

Archimedes snorted. "He always spoke his mind freely. That's what he died for, isn't it?" He looked back at the flute, and continued, "When the war started, we came home. He was . . . *unhappy* about the war. We didn't know he was Roman—if anyone asked, he'd say he was Sabine or Marsian or Samnite or whatever—but we knew he had some loyalties to Rome. He kept swearing, though, that he would never do anything to harm the city or our house." Archimedes paused, then added, "Of course, he would have been even more unwilling to harm Rome. And you know how quickly he decided to help you. But afterward he kept saying that he was sorry he had abused my trust. And he was very sorry over the man you killed escaping—a fine man, and a friend." He raised his head and looked directly at Fabius. "If you are the Fabius who was with him that night, he said he was wrong to have given you a knife. And he said that he thought you would have killed me if you'd known who I was."

Fabius looked back a moment in silence; he did not translate the addition. "It was our duty to escape if we could," he said at last. "As for the other, yes, I would have killed you. We had heard of your catapult-making, and I thought you were likely to cost Rome dearly. As you have. Many men are dead, and the peace we achieved has gained us little, because of you and your catapults. I do not say you were wrong to defend your city, but I would have been right to defend mine."

"No one was attacking Rome," Archimedes pointed out coldly. "Your reasoning puts the bully on the same level as the victim who fights back. I find it fallacious. Nor do I understand how your consul could justify putting a brave and loyal man to death merely for speaking his mind."

Gaius had been listening to this incomprehensible exchange anxiously, and now cleared his throat nervously. Fabius resumed his translation with the complaint against the consul. Gaius Valerius looked away with an uneasy hunch of the shoulders that reminded Archimedes suddenly and painfully of his brother.

"The consul was a weak man angry," said Gaius. "As soon as he found out who Marcus was, he had him arrested and tried. He was the judge and the principal accuser. Nobody would have put Marcus to death for what happened at Asculum. Not even at the time—he was sixteen when it happened, and he'd been in the legion only three weeks! But our father had taught us to expect harsh punishments, and Marcus was always hard on himself: he'd convinced himself that he deserved to die, and he'd expected to. But even Claudius couldn't rely on Asculum after so many years. The big charge he had was that Marcus had dishonored the Roman name. Through accepting slavery, you see, and through saying that the Romans were wrong to attack Syracuse."

"And he wouldn't lie and say he thought they were right?" asked Archimedes, with resignation.

Gaius nodded wearily. "I think he meant to. But when it came to the point, he was angry, and he didn't. The consul had accused him of other things as well. Foul things."

Archimedes looked at him, frowning, and Gaius went on reluctantly, "Of prostituting himself to Greeks. To King Hieron, and to you, among others." Archimedes flushed angrily, and Gaius went on hastily, "Stupid accusations, but he had no way to refute them, except to get angry. So he got angry, and did not tell any lies, and the consul sentenced him to death."

Gaius reached over to the flute case and took something else from it: a fat black flask about the size of a child's fist, empty. "I was very glad that he had this," he went on, low-voiced. "The legions knew that Marcus was innocent—but since the beating had to take place, the fact that no one wanted to strike only meant that it would last longer. But in the morning, when they went to take him out of the tent where they were keeping him, he was already dead. He had this with him, this and the flute. Your gifts, weren't they?"

Archimedes shook his head. "Only the flute," he said soberly. "*That* was from Hieron. He told me that he'd given it to Marcus, just in case."

Gaius looked at him in surprise and doubt, then ran a finger around the top of the flask. "A gift from the king of Syracuse? I am indebted to the king. But I don't understand how King Hieron knew Marcus, or why he bothered."

"He knew your brother through me," replied Archimedes. "And he wanted Marcus to come back to Syracuse after the war and be his Latin interpreter. It would have been a good position, and Marcus would have filled it very well. Hieron told me about it. Your news will grieve him too." Archimedes got to his feet, holding the flute carefully in both hands. "It is waste, and nothing but waste. I don't know what your people will do to the world."

Gaius rose too, and bowed his head in a gesture that was neither denial nor acceptance. "Marcus was a Roman," he said. "I would ask you, sir, to remember that of us as well. But I don't want to quarrel with you. I am grateful for your kindness in speaking with me, and grateful also for your kindness to my brother while he lived. He admired you greatly."

Archimedes shook his head angrily. "I did not realize how exceptional your brother was until too late," he said. "I am much to blame. I hope it is some consolation to you to know that even as a slave he earned the respect of those around him." He hesitated, trying to think if there was anything else he should say, then realized that the visitors must have had a long walk from their camp, and asked them if they would like some wine.

They thanked him and agreed that they would, indeed, like something cold to drink. Archimedes started back toward the main part of the house; as he did, Fabius gestured at the lead-lined box in the center of the workroom and asked uneasily, "What is that machine? A new kind of catapult?"

"May all the gods and heroes forbid it!" Archimedes exclaimed vehemently.

He had never been so sick of anything in his life as he was of catapults. He'd lost track of how many he'd built: one-talenters, two-talenters, three-talenters, three-and-a-half- and four-talenters. And arrow-firing catapults, with particularly long ranges and particularly large bolts. Outworks to the walls had come as something of a relief. The nasty little surprises he and Kallippos had invented for any siege machine that did get close to the wall had seemed like the comedy tacked onto the end of a tragic cycle at the theater. There was a long list of other things that could be done, with time and supplies, if the war went on, and he was infinitely glad to have escaped them—for the time being, anyway. His relief at the peace had been as great as that of anyone in the city. "*That* is a water-aulos," he told Fabius happily. "Or it will be, when I finish it."

"A what?" asked Fabius confusedly.

Archimedes' eyes lit. "A water-aulos. See, you fill the tank with water, and you put this hemisphere in it." He hooked the holed basin off the tank's corner and held it, upside down, in the empty cistern. "And then you have one pipe coming down to this opening *here*, and another coming out from *here*, which is shut off unless you press the keys to open the valves—the valves are the cleverest part—and you pump the air in with the bellows. The water pressurizes the air, so that when you release it through the pipes, it produces a good volume of sound." He put the basin back over the corner of the tank. "I'm waiting for the pipes from the bronzesmith."

"But what is it *for?*" asked Fabius.

"It's a musical instrument!" said Archimedes in surprise. "I said it was a water-*aulos*, didn't I? My wife wants one."

"A musical instrument!" exclaimed Fabius, and shook his head wonderingly. "So peace has already reduced the greatest of engineers from the making of catapults to the making of flutes as an amusement for women!"

Archimedes stared at him in complete bewilderment for a moment, then went red. "Reduced?" he repeated furiously. "Catapults are stupid, god-hated lumps of wood which throw stones to kill people! I hope I never touch another of the filthy things in my life! *This* will sing with a voice like gold to the glory of Apollo and the Muses. *This* is as much superior to a catapult as . . . as . . ." He fumbled for a comparison, then gestured impatiently at the abacus, ". . . as *that* is to a pig!"

"But I don't know what that is, either!" said Fabius, amused.

"A calculation of the ratio between the volumes of a cylinder and an enclosed sphere," replied Archimedes with cold precision. He edged back toward it, and looked down, frowning. "Or an attempt to calculate it, anyway." The way into the problem, and the answer to it, had eluded him.

"But what use is that?" asked Fabius, coming over to look down at the drawings scratched in the sand: spheres and cylinders labeled endlessly with letters; letters repeated down the sides in inexhaustible calculations, in curves, in straight lines, in figures balanced and not balanced. So much intelligence, he thought, to be squandered upon air!

"It doesn't need a use," declared Archimedes, still looking down at his diagram. In his mind, a circle slipped up the line of the cylinder, its height the diameter, then revolved at the midpoint to form the sphere: perfect, more perfect than anything on earth. "It simply is." He studied his calculations and saw that they would get him nowhere. He picked up a flattened piece of wood and carefully smoothed the blind alley out.

"What are you saying?" asked Gaius in Latin. Fabius had translated nothing about the water-aulos: he had no idea what a "valve" was, or "pressurize," and he suspected that the words simply didn't exist in Latin.

"The box in the middle of the room is part of a musical instrument," said Fabius. "I said it was a sad descent from catapults to that, and he took offense. He said that music was nobler than war, and that this"—he gestured at the box of sand—"is nobler than anything."

As the dead end vanished into the sand, Archimedes saw suddenly the path along the spinning of the circle to the truth. Breathlessly he hooked the stool over with his foot and picked up his compasses. "Just a minute," he said to the visitors. "I've just seen something. Just go into the house and have a drink; I'll join you . . . in a minute."

The others looked at him in surprise, but he was already oblivious to them. The compass marked out its precise reckonings in the fine sand, and his face following it was rapt, intense, joyful. For the first time in his life, Fabius felt the foundations of his own certainties tremble. This mind was not bent upon air. The suddenly quiet room was filled with something that made the hair stand up along his arms, something that existed for no human use. Perspective altered dizzyingly, and he wondered what his own use was to a universe. Unaccountably afraid, he ducked his head and backed away.

~ WHEN DELIA CAME INTO THE WORKROOM A COUPLE OF hours later, she found Archimedes sitting on the ground, resting his head on the stool and gazing fondly at the abacus. "Dearest?" she said gently.

He raised his head and beamed at her. "It's three halves!" he told her.

She came over and knelt beside him, putting an arm about his shoulders. They had been married since January, and she was beginning to feel that she was going to be very good at estate management but would never understand geometry at all. "The ratio is?" she asked, trying to take an interest.

He nodded, and swept a hand toward the thicket of calculations. "It all comes out so perfectly," he wondered. "A rational number, after all that. So exact, so . . . perfect!"

He was so happy that she hardly liked to disturb him. But after a moment she said, "I heard that there were two Romans here earlier. What did they want?"

The happiness vanished. He looked around in alarm. "By the god! I said I'd join them in just a minute. Are they . . . ?"

"They left some time ago," said Delia sourly. "Melias said they talked to you, and then you sank out of sight into the abacus, so he gave them a drink, and they went. What did they want?"

He told her, sadly, and showed her the battered flute. "Though all Gaius Valerius really wanted was to hear about his brother," he finished. "I liked him. He *was* like Marcus, very straightforward and honorable. The other one, Fabius, was a true Roman. He thought it was a *reduction* to go from catapults to music!" He rubbed angrily at another spot of corrosion on the reed clamp. "Marcus told me once that the Romans don't think music a fit subject for serious study at all. He said that his father would have beaten him if he'd asked to learn the flute. He wanted to learn it anyway. But they didn't give him the chance."

She put her arm around him again, remembering the slave who had sat in the dark garden, listening to the music. She could not remember his face, but she was sorry he was dead. Sorry mostly for Archimedes' sake, but a little for the slave's sake as well. "I pray the earth is light upon him," she said.

He turned toward her, put both arms around her and kissed her, then held her, feeling the shape and warmth of her against his chest, a comfort for every grief. When he asked Hieron for her, he had not known that it was even possible to feel for a woman what he felt now. From the first day of their marriage, she had astonished him. It now seemed to him that she was best at everything he was worst at, that, like the second leg of a compass or the second flute of a pair, she completed him.

Even with war, even with siege, even with *catapults* they had been so happy.

He thought, painfully, of Marcus dead; Marcus burned, and the smoke rising from the funeral pyre high into the sky above Syracuse. Perhaps he had seen it, and not known what it was. He had noticed Marcus little enough in life.

Marcus had done his best to fulfill all his obligations honorably, and had died in their contradictions without complaint. He himself, no better a man, had everything to make himself joyful. By what calculation could those shapes be made to balance? Archimedes sighed and glanced down at the small riddle he had solved, the perfect ratio, already dwindled in his estimate.

And yet, that ratio was perfect still. Perfect, and known. It rested whole in his mind, needing no use, sufficient in its existence. Like the soul. But unlike the soul, comprehended.

HISTORICAL NOTE

Archimedes of Syracuse is generally reckoned the greatest mathematician and engineer of antiquity. There are a number of anecdotes about him, but few hard facts. The date usually given for his birth—287 B.C.—comes from a statement that he was seventy-five at the time of his death in 212. That his father was an astronomer and named Phidias we know from Archimedes himself, who refers to one of his father's calculations in his monograph *The Sand-Reckoner*—a serious work whose title I have stolen for this light one. Cicero refers to Archimedes as being of humble origins, but Plutarch says he was a relative of King Hieron. It is not known who Archimedes married, but it's perfectly possible that his wife was a relative of the king. We know he was married to *somebody* (his "household" was well treated after the Roman conquest of Syracuse), and, since the Greeks considered it rude to talk about a respectable woman by name, we could not expect the connection to be publicized.

For those who know some classical history, I must stress that this book is set in 264 B.C. during the *First* Punic War, and not in 212 during the Second, when the more famous siege of Syracuse occurred. Rome in 264 had no navy and was just beginning her expansion, though she was already recognized as a formidable power. I have not followed the standard, Roman account of the war, as given by Polybios. It is clear from Polybios himself that there was a rival Greek version. Modern historians of the period usually try to reconstruct a version of events which takes account of what both sides said, and I have followed their example.

The poems and songs quoted are all my own translations. They are: page 40—Simonides, fragment 521; pages 62–63—Thymocles, *Greek Anthology* ix.v; page 105—Sappho, fragment 1; page 151—Philemon, *Comicorum Atticorum Fragmentum v. II*, p. 486; page 157—*Carmina Popularia* 848; page 281—*The Odyssey*, XII.185–196. The obscenities, if anyone is interested, are taken from Aristophanes. Likewise Aristophanic is the reference to Cloudcuckooland, the old and established English translation of Nephelokokkygia, the fantastic airborne city of Aristophanes' *The Birds*.

I am, alas, no geometer. I have struggled through some of the works of Archimedes to research this book, but most of the time I had no idea what the man was on about. I have tried, however, to reflect the kind of calculations which engaged him. I have also tried to represent accurately the capabilities of Greek engineers of that period. All the machines referred to in this book are real. The water-aulos (or organ) gave its name to the field of hydraulics; its inventor, Ktesibios of Alexandria, also founded pneumatics. Greek artillery really was as powerful as I have depicted it—in fact, I have erred on the side of caution in describing the size of some of the large catapults. (People in all eras are prone to exaggeration.) I have also been cautious in my retelling of the story of how Archimedes moved the ship. There are three ancient versions of this. In one he uses a kind of lever, in another a machine called a *barulkos*, which involved windlasses and toothed wheels, and in the third the system of compound pulleys, which I found most credible. But in all of the stories the ship itself is larger—"the largest merchant ship in the king's fleet"—and is dragged up fully loaded. I thought this a bit unlikely—though there is very little I would put beyond Archimedes. The man invented a form of integral calculus that had no impact on the ancient world because it was *two thousand years* ahead of its time.

Some people may find King Hieron a bit too good to be true.

Ancient historians shared this feeling—I have followed the rather awed account of Polybios, who singles him out as an example of the sort of good ruler historians ought to focus on instead of telling salacious tales about tyrants. Hieron ruled Syracuse for fifty-four years, maintaining his city in unparalleled peace and prosperity. He died in 215 at the age of ninety-one; for much of that period he reigned in amicable conjunction with his son Gelon, who, however, predeceased him. Hieron's successor was his grandson Hieronymos, an excitable teenager who unfortunately decided to reverse all his grandfather's alliances and fatally committed his city to war with Rome. It was in that war that Syracuse—impossible to take by storm—was besieged and blockaded until starvation drove her citizens to open the gates. The city was comprehensively sacked. Archimedes, then seventy-five years old, was among those killed. According to the stories, he was doing calculations, oblivious to bloody events surrounding him, when a Roman soldier interrupted him. He shouted angrily for the man to "leave my circles alone!" The irritated looter killed him—much to the distress of the Roman general, Marcellus, who was an educated man and had fully intended to spare the life of a man so famous in the annals of thought.

AUTHOR'S NOTE

Over the years I have enjoyed the company of a number of distinguished theoretical physicists. This has undoubtedly influenced my portrayal of one of their number, but my characterization is derived in essence from the accounts in the ancient sources and is not based on any living person.

(Oh, all right, the habit of chewing writing implements was borrowed from someone in particular. I would not base a whole character, however, on someone I love so much. It would make for bad fiction.)